JAIRZINHO'S CURBSIDE GIANTS

WRITTEN BY

JUD WIDING

ILLUSTRATED BY

REBECCA COULSTON

ASTRID

LADYBUG

SHERIFF

DUCKY

KELSO

MEATBALL

BARMIT

BOO

MISHA

aUTHOr's NOTe

As you may have noticed on the preceding pages, this book has illustrations of cute dogs in it (by the immensely talented Rebecca Coulston; more info on her can be found at the end of the book). Most books with cute dogs in them are fun for the whole family. I really cannot overstate how much that is *not* the case with *Jairzinho's Curbside Giants*.

Having learned the hard way that brightly colored books with animals on the cover are universally (and not unreasonably) assumed to be children's books, I thought it prudent to plant this flag of warning here at the top: *Jairzinho's Curbside Giants* is, emphatically, not a book for kids. Very bad things happen in it, and sometimes to the cute dogs. Consider this the R-rating, the parental advisory sticker.

That said, if you are a child who has grabbed hold of this book: hiya, and congratulations! You're about to learn a lot of new words!

Naturally

It had been a dumb fight, naturally. They all were. What had they ever argued about that mattered? When had they ever awoken in each other's arms, after making such a point of saying goodnight from their *separate sides of the bed*, and thought 'I sure am glad I stuck to my guns last night' as they silently untangled themselves? Why did they refuse to obey their foam-crowned Queen, into which the contours of their love had been stamped so deeply that pouring themselves back in was but the natural course of the evening? How could both the ebb and the flow feel so perfectly natural?

And more to the point: who was going to apologize first?

Not Jairzinho. He had decided that pretty early on last night. About when…god, what *had* they been arguing about? It had started, as always, with a lovely dinner. Indiscriminately spiced fish, overcooked asparagus, and wine wine wine. Wonderful conversation came next, followed by impassioned debate. And somewhere in there, passions would runneth over as the Pinot never had a chance to. It would happen. The night would take

The Turn. They only ever spotted it in the rearview, but its passage was unmistakable, and doubling back, impossible. It was like watching a timelapse of an apple rotting. So nauseating, so hopeless, and always about something unspeakably pointless (not talking about apples now), like...

. . .

Well, whatever it was, Jairzinho was positive that he had been right and/or not been the one to send the conversation careening into The Turn. He remembered thinking this *in situ*. And logging the thought. Like correct people do.

He sat up on the side of his bed that was *his*, palms flat on the mattress, and stared at *his* wall. Bare, save a thumbtacked Boy Bison print and the scuffmarks that bloom on all cheap drywall. Studio apartment chic. There was a frame for that Bison print in a bag in the closet, and nails upon which to hang it in the toolbox under the bed. Jairzinho never put them all together though, because then he'd have to look at the hole in the print itself, currently full of what had created it: the thumbtack. College-aged Jairzinho had never imagined twenty-six-year-old Jairzinho buying a frame, apparently.

6:16, the clock insisted. Ok. Thinking time was over. Going time was...now.

Jairzinho had his workday routine down to a science. He ran through it in his head: Reveille at 6:15. Piss, pills, dress (big-pocketed cargo shorts and a tee, to be drenched in sweat by day's end), cereal in the bowl by 6:23. Fill thermos with shitty Keurig coffee, brew and chug an extra cup of the same, fill second bottle with water, load backpack, out the door by 6:45. In an absolute crisis scenario, 6:52. Beyond this point, he could only throw himself on the mercy of the MTA. Trade science for faith, pray the trains run on schedule. They never did. If there is a God, He meddles not in our affairs. Just sometimes makes unintelligible announcements over the intercom.

Tia wasn't getting up. Jairzinho turned towards her in time to watch her grab a handful of duvet and sweep it up towards her chin, like a vampire's cape. She settled on her side, back-to.

There were two other parts of the morning routine. Both involving her. Involving as in *requiring*.

First: Tia-talking time. Slotted between pouring cereal and making a hasty exeunt. Wherever it would fit. Hear about her dreams, tell her about his. Find out how she slept. Maybe just hold her against his chest and imagine they were back in bed, dreaming more dreams to tell each other about. She worked nights three times a week. The morning was sometimes the only part of the day they had together. It was more precious to Jairzinho than anything.

Second: she made him lunch. Every single goddamned day. No matter how much she had on the docket. She woke up and fixed him a turkey and cheese sandwich, packed a little baggie of carrots. Put it all in a perfectly-sized cold case she got from a specialty vendor. Just for this. Just to make Jairzinho lunch.

He'd told her she ought to stop. For the first week. *Oh Tia, that's way too generous; it must be so hard for you to get back to sleep; I really can't let you keep doing this.*

Into week two, he still told her to stop. Just not as often, not as loud. *Oh, come on. You're too nice. This is really something.*

His objections had long-since ceased, in the year and a quarter between then and now. For fear they would be sustained. Because he relied on Tia's lunchmaking. Regressive "sammich" optics be damned. They were convenient meals. And she didn't just stick stuff between bread slices. Hers tasted special. Jairzinho had no idea why. But they did.

13

That, and it was a part of his routine. 6:44, she gave him lunch. 6:45, he was out the door. Sometimes 6:52. It would *always* have been 6:52 without Tia.

That, and maybe in some dark pocket of his heart he felt he was entitled to her generosity. If he was expected to sacrifice his happiness for hers by living here, then he didn't see why she shouldn't return the favor. Fair was fair. So maybe unfair was unfair, too.

That, and maybe in some even deeper part of himself he *enjoyed* feeling like a lifestyle martyr. What higher moral ground was there than a cross? And what did it matter if he'd dragged it up the hill and nailed himself to it? Without anybody asking?

Twenty-six was too young to be a bitter old man. Jairzinho detested the grievances he stockpiled. Even as he nursed them.

A miracle: like Lazarus from his tomb, Tia rolled back the hard-won comforter and arose.

Jairzinho wanted her to say something. Something like "I'm sorry". Then they could have a nice morning. He could forgive her. The morning could be nice.

Instead, without saying a word, Tia rubbed her eyes and padded around the bed to the "kitchen" — which was to say, the wall with the oven sticking out of it — and Jairzinho rose to begin his routine.

His apartment called him names. The flushing toilet bellowed *chum-um-ump*. The sink hissed *asssssss*. The closing drawers snapped off *dick. Dick.*

Fuck you, furnishings. He had been right. He was not the one to apologize first. She was. It wasn't just principle. It was practice. *Precedent.* He couldn't set the precedent that she could just wait him out. Even when she was wrong.

14

He'd be teaching her the wrong things. That wasn't what made a good relationship. A good relationship was teaching the *right* things.

So: cereal poured by 6:23. Full backpack by 6:38. Tia handed him lunch at 6:39. They hugged. Jairzinho said he wanted to talk about it later. The Turn. He did. That was true.

He just expected *her* to start.

Tia pressed her head against his chest. Mumbled something. Jairzinho didn't know what. But it definitely wasn't "I'm sorry." He had nothing to say to words that weren't "I'm sorry."

So: Jairzinho kissed Tia's forehead with a frown. Out the door by 6:41. All that time saved, not talking.

He wondered what her dream was, if she remembered it. He didn't remember his.

He caught an earlier 2 train than usual. So he transferred to a much earlier 1 train. All this time to spare! Maybe there was something to be said, for not talking.

The conductor crackled onto the intercom. Gave a sermon in an alien language.

A stop later, Jairzinho realized what Tia had mumbled into his chest. Before he had wordlessly slipped out the door.

She had mumbled "I love you."

"Shit," Jairzinho mumbled to himself. Now all of a sudden *he* was the big asshole of the morning.

He looked to the seat next to him. An old lady with a toddler on her lap frowned. Jairzinho knew he should apologize. For swearing. But actually fuck them, what did they expect to hear on the workaday 1 train?

He averted his eyes from the frown.

Tia's wasn't the only important message he failed to understand that morning: the conductor's garbled descent from the piss-misted mountaintop had been to announce that this earlier 1 train was going express. As this earlier 1 train always did.

It went express. Straight past Jairzinho's stop. And four more besides.

He was late to work.

HI PUPPIeS!

- 1 -

Ok, so, that was his bad. The "I love you" thing. Not the train thing. Well, both.

First opportunity he got, Jairzinho would send Tia a text. Explain that he'd only belatedly recognized what she had said, right as he was leaving. Which, like, that was barely even fair, to expect him to stop his whole goddamned morning, just to figure out what she said, because she couldn't be bothered to speak more clearly, or…

Anyway. It was his bad. He might even apologize for his lack of response. As long as he could make the limits of the *mea culpa* clear.

But he wouldn't have a chance to send that text until about noon. Just how the schedule worked. Until then it was go go go.

Now. 8:03 in the AM of Wednesday August 7th. Jairiznho slalomed around scaffolding and slowpokes. The whole city was in his way. Standing between him and The Edbrooke. Get out of the fucking way!

Go go go.

The Edbrooke was basically an eleven-story brick with pretty windows. Hogged an entire block in Greenwich Village. It had been a warehouse for Customs agents or something. Long since gutted and reborn. As luxury apartments. A whole complex. It had a grocery store and dry cleaner on the first floor. Top umpteen floors were *four hundred and eighty* lofts. The cheapest of them ran seven figures. A phenomenal concentration of wealth. And so, the first place Jairzinho had canvassed for clients. Naturally.

He was up to *twelve* clients in the Edbrooke alone. Spatial consolidation was the holy grail of the dog-walker. More clients in a single building meant quicker pickups and drop-offs. Which meant more dogs walked throughout the day. Which meant more money. Enough to pay for his studio way down in the ass-end of Brooklyn, and then some. Not much some. But *some* some.

Jairzinho weaved around the lunatics who went grocery shopping at, Jesus, 8:06 AM. Slowed to a trot as he spotted one of the doormen at his usual post. The guy's name was…Philippe. Something like that. Philippe didn't like Jairzinho. None of the doormen did, for no good reason. This really bothered Jairzinho, for good reason. He didn't know what that reason was. But it was definitely good.

"Good morning," Jairzinho said with a thoughtful nod.

"Good morning," Philippe returned. With *that look* on his face.

It was almost perverse, this mock civility. Both Jairzinho and Philippe clearly wished very *bad* mornings on one another. And they both knew it. And they both *knew* that they both knew it.

What neither knew was that both of their wishes would be coming true, very soon.

Being his own boss meant so many wonderful things. But it also created a few unique problems. On the one hand, Jairzinho made his own schedule (wonderful thing).

On the other, he had scheduled himself very, very tightly (problem).

The day's first walk: pick up nine dogs from the Edbrooke. Hustle them twenty-odd blocks up to Chelsea. Grab another dog. Bring all ten back down here. Drop off the first nine.

That's walk one.

After that, he picks up the other three dogs he walks in the Edbrooke. Then he's off all over town for walks two through four. This corset-tight schedule wasn't ordinarily so suffocating. He'd researched the route extensively. Strategically adding dogs to walks where they wouldn't disrupt the rest of the day. It was tough but no (problem). As long as he didn't run behind.

It was very difficult for him to make up time. If he was running behind. Almost impossible, really.

And right now, he was running behind.

Ok. He'd just blast through these pickups as quick as he could. If he didn't, he'd have to go late on walk two. Cut into his noon break.

Not an option. He needed his noon break to write the text to Tia. He needed time to get the language right. So she knew what he was sorry for. And what he *wasn't*.

The elevator was waiting on L (wonderful thing). He jumped in, slapped 4, threw his backpack down and took a knee. The doors shut slowly. Like it was trying to be sensual about it. No way to make the closing *clunk* anything but clumsy. Stupid elevator.

Jairzinho tore open the zipper of his backpack. Yanked a short, tattered, sun-paled purple rope from the gaping top pocket. Slung it around his waist. Hooked the looped end onto a carabiner dangling from the other.

Ding, floor 2.

He pulled his big ring of keys from the small top pocket of his backpack. His bread and butter. They keys, not the backpack. Well, both. But whatever. With his right hand he clicked the keyring into the carabiner. The main one holding up his DIY utility belt. With his left hand he reached into the biggest pocket of the backpack. So big you couldn't really call it a pocket. What was it? It was the backpack, really. The whole backpack.

Ding, floor 3.

Whatever you called the abyss, Jairiznho summoned a Lovecraftian tangle of leashes out of it. He picked the nine he would need by feel. Each was frayed in unique ways. Like braille. He threw the nine chosen leashes around his neck. A lei of grody leads. Mele Kalikiwalka. Ugh. Cast the unneeded leashes back to the abyss. Zip, zip, zip.

Ding, floor 4.

On his feet before the doors opened. Down the hall before they'd even thought to close again.

Pounding down the corridor. Jairzinho snapped the keys off his hip. Fingered through them. These, he had to look at. No signatures of distress. The keys were all variations on the same theme. Gold and toothy. Hence why Jairzinho had bought numbered tags to slide though the ring. A number for every key. Misha's was…this one. Number 8.

He grabbed it by the fat end. Charged the door to 414.

Sniff. Sniff sniff. Sniff! SNIFF!

THE BRRRREEEEAAAAKFAST MAAAAN!

Ahem. Yes, The Breakfast Man. He smelled a little bit different today, a little saltier than usual…*sniff sniff*…and a little less of that angry-pretty stink. But it was definitely Him, though.

Misha prepared for The Ritual as she always did: by laying  down on the bathroom floor. Great view of The Door from here, and anyway and also *anyway* the smell of this room was *fascinating*. It smelled more like family in here than anywhere else…even though they tried to hide it with angry-pretty! Why did they *do* that? Humans were weird, that was why. Weeeeeiiiiird!

But they were also kind of magical, weren't they? Especially The Breakfast Man.

His Ritual proceeded thusly: every morning, The Breakfast Man broke in. He took Misha to meet her friends. Together, they all showed The Breakfast Man where the best bathrooms around town were. He never took their suggestions though. He simply witnessed. Such was His role, Misha supposed. Oh well. His loss!

Upon their return, The Breakfast Man would leave Misha's friends on the other side of The Door. What followed was a Rite for her alone: the Fetching of the Bowl, the Stations of the Bag, and *pawlelujah!* From Nothing, Breakfast.

And then The Breakfast Man would go to the other side of The Door, and take Misha's friends away.

But then He would be back! Later in the day! And sometimes He had TRREEAAAATS!

No, don't get sidetracked. Disruptions to The Ritual could prove calamitous. Sometimes, if The Breakfast Man felt insufficiently appeased, He would forgo Breakfast. It was *so important* that The Ritual went off *exactly* as He had designed it. If not…oh boy, it was too horrible to think about!

How The Ritual began, why The Breakfast Man had chosen her, whence He came, these were questions that had never occurred to Misha.

Though, to be fair, she was a golden retriever.

The Door announced a new visitor with its customary jingle-click. Misha rose and approached with a suitably reverant wag. This step in the Salutation required exquisite timing, which Misha was always refining. She had to plunge her nose into The Breakfast Man's redolent crevasse at *just* the moment it popped out from behind The Door. This was essential, so she could snuffle up His recent history, investigate His trek through the screaming underground (and so, by proxy, explore it), mentally retrace His path here by cutting the layer cake of His stank. She adored it, this tale of adventure and excitement that He lovingly transcribed for her between His legs. It was the highlight of her morning. Second to Breakfast. And treats. And friends. And walking. And bathrooms. Oh, she had so very many highlights!

But to the matter at paw: the timing. Exquisite, that was what it had to be. Thrust the nose too soon, and she would bonk the door. Too late, and He would deny her His story.

The Door opened…hold…*hold*, Misha…hold…

CHARGE!

Misha stuffed her nose into Jairzinho's crotch the second he opened the door. As always.

"Hi Misha," he whispered. As always.

He clipped the fat blue leash to her collar. Clipped the looped end into a second carabiner, which was itself clipped to the carabiner securing his rope belt.

Quiet as possible, Jairzinho tugged Misha out into the hall. He closed the door. Quiet as possible.

Misha's owners apparently had jobs that paid them Edbrooke money *and* let them sleep in on weekdays. It was enraging in an envy-pumping sort of way. But it also meant Jairzinho had to worry about waking them up. He'd done that a few times. By accident. It was usually the keys jingling. Misha's owners had assured Jairzinho that it was totally fine. Him waking them up. But they'd done it in a way that made him think it was fine because they didn't expect anything more from a poor brown kid in his twenties. They'd never explicitly said anything that even approached that sentiment. They just had a *way* about them.

This whole *building* had a *way* about it. With its disapproving doormen. With its spotless, columned lobby. With its halls wallpapered the pea green of cash. Like, *come on.*

Some things were impossible to ignore. Like how all of Jairzinho's Edbrooke clients were rich and white. Like how all of the people who worked for them were…neither. Did this bother him? Naturally.

How could it not?

- 2 -

Form sprawled upon a plinth of Earth by tread of titans shatteréd, black breadth bereft of breath save grave sepulchral inspirations as do shear the petal from the rose. How fine the line twixt morning's walk, and catafalque! O wretched respiration, o accursed insufflation! Yea, to draw you forth does solemn promise tender, though so firmly is it kept. Ah, *breath*, thou most rapacious, two-faced buddy shaped to bosoms! Lo, what pleasures lay beyond your reach? What devilment's devise did tower but upon your promise? *So I shall beget myself*, thou whisper from the storm. But has the world yet known such

dreadful condemnation? Exorcise your phantoms of repose; elysian greens by rose-red speckled, though no petal dareth tumble from untrem'bling stalks. Begone, cruel specter! Thou art exorcised! Oh, salted fangs make mince of eager lungs! To exorcise treads perilously near to exercise! To exercise lays claim the fruits of painful harvest; life reclaimed whilst still it keeps its sweetest secrets, though the tree whence stolen knowledge rots from core to timbrous skin! Ay, timorous, ay, fearful flesh doth loathe its belching engine. That it should be plagued by *hope*, that rot of mind and heart! By hope that outward breath be given, taken not by palsied paw! By hope that leash which slackens least, the leash of *life*, may give for ventures cordial in intent. For can not life be led, but that it follow savage masters? Must one's inky chest and throat be torn to pieces, as must Man's beloved slipper? Hope, thou furtive blight! Now darken not this spot of ink, so moribund upon her throne! Let inhalation now grant inspiration; so let exhalation mark an expiration. Yes, this final, rattling breath a fitting epitaph shall make! Now exhalation marks and so begets. And so, she died. Farewell to all. Exeunt fair Ladybug.

ALIVE. But what was this? That Ladybug still lived? O damn, and damn and skyfire! What infamies by her paw perpetrated must this life be making recompense? How marked by mayhem must her journey be, though not a single dastard's deed doth live in memory? Yawns there a world beyond the veil of recollection, one of dastard's deeds by darkest paw designed? Or yawns instead the gulf twixt fate and justice? O, how bleak a cosmos must that be! But no, and no, and no again! Tis *action* makes the Girl, deeds Good or Bad that fate repays in kind. Yet when had Ladybug been Bad Girl last? Perhaps that shameful day of Indoor Defecation, 'pon which she had vowed to never dwell again! And yet, she must! Was this that day 'pon which her breathless doom was sealed?

But hark, there shines a light amidst the gloom! For did beginnings not imply the end?! Dear heart beworn by ceaseless toil, this shall not your lot forever be! Rejoice, for even now annihilation lives within you, patient death indebted unto life, to that which labors long enough to earn its taking. O obliteration, lovely absence, this belonged to Ladybug, and she to it! So why two debtors make, when each should be so eager to repay the other? Yea, but take the final walk beyond the veil; the leash is longer than you think. There mark, beget, and be repaid. O sweetest sleep, be gentle. Rough (so ruff) is holding on, yet soft is all release. Farewell to all! Cruel life unclips its lead. And thus does Ladybug to rest descend.

ALIVE.

Oh damn and damn it all again! If only she could but explain her plight, to live and die with every breath, to live and die, to live and die! Her friends, alas, they did not know. They could not know. This solitary sentence nearly drove poor Ladybug to madness, made of her a prisoner inside her mind, philosopher entombed in highest tower! If o-

But soft, what light through yonder…ah, yes. The Ferryman.

Jairzinho slipped the carabiner with Misha's leash off his belt. Clipped it to the deadbolt hole. To keep Misha outside.

She sat patiently in the hall. As always. Bless her.

Jairzinho shouted "Ladybug!" No need to worry about waking anybody up here. He slipped through the door. Closed it against the deadbolt-clipped carabiner. Gently. Only because he didn't want to damage the carabiner.

He pursed his lips and exhaled. Damnit. Some days he could do a proper whistle. Most days, like today, he could only make the sound of a tumbleweed blowing through a ghost town.

Speech never failed though. "C'mere Ladybug! Whistle noise," he added for his own amusement.

She wasn't in the front hall bed. Which meant she was probably in the living room bed. Ladybug had multiple beds. Like her owners had multiple residencies. Naturally.

From very nearby: *hbbLAACH!*

"Ah." Jairzinho bent down and squinted at the darkness.

28

Ladybug the Little Pug was under the knick-knack table. Plopped across her owner's shoes. Her favorite spot. Despite all the beds.

She wheezed through a great big grin. As always.

Poor girl was a pug in a categorical sense. Her face was so scrunched that her nose was practically *behind* her eyes. Sounded like she had a hell of a time just breathing (exhibit A: *bbbL-AACH*). Even at rest. Only got worse on the walks. Oh well. She was probably used to it.

"I'm happy to see you too," Jairzinho cooed. He plucked her from the footwear and snatched her beer-and-pizza themed harness off the tabletop above her head. The harness wasn't just to be cute (though it definitely *was*). It was in lieu of a regular collar. The last thing Ladybug needed was something squeezing her airway. Even her adorable ladybug bandana was probably pushing it. Poor girl.

A thin red leash for the harness. Clip, clip.

Jairzinho led Ladybug through the door. Misha rose. The two dogs rushed towards each other. Normally Jairzinho would give them a quick second to greet one another. No time today, though. So he tugged them apart and dragged them towards the stairs.

Twas quite the lather into which the Ferryman had worked himself today! Such gruntly grousing o'er the leash-strung saddle! Yea, such ruthless haste twixt hearth and hall! What grounds had he for pique? Oh ho, what grounds? To what bipedal ends? To seek the keeper?

O, but whom save fools seek sense in Men? Far sooner would the noisebox tell its tales, than Man might his! Whence spring the lights, Man's joy. Whence cry the sounds, his fury. There and thus did end their kinship; Man alone stole bléssed moments. Ah, to wit: now passéd had the moment of departure, when ought Ladybug have chanced to bid her friend fair morn. What say you, Misha, and draw near, that we may each the o'er's perfumed caboose enjoy! But not today, there was to be no fellow-feeling felt from fragrant fannies, not on *this* day. For the Ferryman was piqued! Was not this cause for piquancy from Ladybug, this snatchéd salutation? Naturally, it was. And pique she might have raised, but for the peek she'd had beneath the veil. *Beyond* the veil. Far better to be Good than Bad, for Bad brought naught but *this*. This life. Forever.

Scant more than fleeting eye and curs'ry snuffle had she chance to grant to Misha, thus did exigency render scant to plenty; wag from Misha, met with hack from Ladybug. Then keen was Ferryman to conjure many deaths, to spirit pug to pulmonary purgatory, hoisted high on gallows heedless of the drop! Part not, you loudest door! O Ferryman, deliver us from being dashed upon this Damnéd Ziggurat!

How Ladybug did *loathe* the stepwise clamber daily due this Damnéd Ziggurat!

Misha bounded up the stairs. Every step was one step closer to brreeeaaaaa...aw, where'd Ladybug go?

Oh, *doy*. Misha turned around and watched Ladybug huffing and puffing her way up the stairs. She always huffed up the stairs. *And* puffed! Misha couldn't figure out why she didn't just climb up like a normal dog, except that Ladybug was some kind of wonderful weirdo.

The Breakfast Man seemed more annoyed by Ladybug than usual. Hm. On Next Walk, He tended to get grouchy. First Walk, though, He was usually in a better mood than He was now. Misha hoped that wouldn't dist...oh, but silly her, The Breakfast Man couldn't disrupt the Ritual!

Ladybug finally got to the top of the stairs. Misha gave her a friendly snuffle. Ladybug gasped.

It was so wonderful to have friends!

The Breakfast Man guided them through a big, angry door that always yelled at them as they stepped thr-*WHAM*, see, that was it! They walked through that, and down the hall. Misha watched as The Breakfast Man removed His Golden Devotions from His waist, thumbed through them, discovered the one He wanted, and separated it from the rest. With it, He demanded entry to Sheriff's cloister. He got it, naturally. Then He clipped a clip off of his clippy clip, and clipped it on to a clippable clip on the door. Clip!

Then The Breakfast Man disappeared, leaving Misha and Ladybug in the hallway. Ladybug laid down and gasped. Misha looked at her and wagged. A bubble appeared in Ladybug's nose, then popped.

Misha liked Ladybug.

- 3 -

"Sheriff!" Jairzinho shouted before he hardly had the door cracked. He opened it slowly. Sheriff always did his little soft-shoe routine right on the other side. *Tap tap tap* up on his hind legs.

Jairzinho had a recurring daymare of opening the door too fast. All of a sudden *tap tap* goes *crunch squish*. This wasn't a part of the morning he could rush. No matter how much of a hurry he was in.

Another inevitable timesink: talking to Olivia.

"Hey Navi!" she called from the loft.

Jairzinho nudged his way through the door, glancing at his watch as he did. 8:09. Should be 8:02. Hooo boy. He bodyblocked Misha and Ladybug from following him in. Not that they ever tried.

The troublemakers came later in the pickup.

Sheriff was up on his hind legs, raising the roof. Like always. He staggered forward. Wrapped his toasted-marshmallow paws around Jairzinho's shin. Activated his Puppy Dog Eyes. Milky and gentle. It was like Sheriff was appreciating everything you took for granted. On your behalf. "Hey buddy," Jairzinho whispered. "Heyyyy buddy." He presented Sheriff with an upturned palm. Sheriff gratefully rested his head on it. Jairzinho scratched the bottom of his chin. Smiled despite his being so goddamned late. "Hi Olivia," he called back.

When he had first started walking for Olivia, he would try to pick up Sheriff as quickly as possible. To bypass the conversation. Then he heard about how flies in spider webs get themselves more and more tangled the more they struggle.

That rang very true.

Thump thump, he heard her coming down the steps. "Pretty hot out, huh?"

"Sure is." He unslung the thin blue leash from around his neck and clipped Sheriff's collar. "Not as bad as last week, though."

"*Oof*, tell me about it! Last week was so muggy." She used the banister to swing herself in to view.

Jairzinho didn't dislike Olivia. She was just a ray of sunshine, in a very literal sense: bright, warm, relentless, blinding, fatal in cases of prolonged exposure.

"Do you want some water?" She asked him. "It's so important to stay hydrated, Navi."

Jairzinho disguised a sigh by rising to his feet. That nickname. It was a curtailment of his surname – Navias – that he had never once suggested to anybody. He was a Colombian-American with a Brazilian name. He was used to people of all walks mispronouncing it.

What he still wasn't used to was the way wealthy people went straight for the surname. Like they were going to rob a bank together. It was enraging. Especially when he'd encouraged them to use his first name. Three times. *Olivia.*

If only she weren't so nice.

"I'm all set on water, thanks." He slapped his backpack. "I loaded up!"

"Oh, right." Olivia slapped her forehead. *Far too lightly*, Jairzinho felt slightly bad about thinking. "You're always on it. I should have known."

Sand, slipping through glass. A text message unwritten.

"Well," Jairzinho said from halfway out the door, "have a good day!"

"Did you hear about the doggie day care on 23rd?"

"Nope," Jairzinho replied from three quarters of the way out the door. He unclipped the carabiner from the deadbolt. "What happened?"

"Somebody went in with a hidden camera. They filmed the employees hitting the dogs."

"That's terrible," Jairzinho declared. Seven eighths gone. "They better stop doing that."

"I think so too."

"Me too. Have a nice day!" He closed the door quickly. Before she had a chance to say anything else. Like, for instance, "Navi".

As per usual, Sheriff sprinted through the door the moment Jairzinho cracked it open. The little guy managed to parkour-kick off Ladybug's face before Jairzinho could wrangle him in and clip his leash into the carabiner belt.

He hustled the dogs down the hall towards the elevators. "I think Jairzinho is a good name," he told Sheriff. "All mutts have weird names. But mutts are *tougher* than purebreds. Aren't they?"

Sheriff wagged his frilly little cockapoo tail at that.

Sheriff wagged his tail down the hall! He wagged his tail into the loud room! And out into the Up hall! He wagged his tail because this was his favorite part of the adventure! Except for all of the other parts!

Oh, and the parts that *weren't* the adventure, they were just *terrific,* also! He wagged his tail when it rained! He wagged his tail when it snowed! If he smelled something amazing, he wagged his tail! Guess what he did when he smelled something awful? Did you guess *he wagged his tail?* No way! That's *exactly* what he did!

What a wonderful stroke of luck, Sheriff reasoned, to have a tail! If you didn't have a tail, you couldn't wag. Oh no! A sad thought! Happy thought, instead!

Wagging was the whole point! It was *brilliant!* Every moment not spent wagging one's tail was a moment wasted!

Wag wag wag! There was so very much to wag about! The world was a big beautiful place and it was just *stuffed* full of nice people who wanted to pet little old Sheriff! Family loved him to bits! And gave him food when he was hungry! Then sometimes they would take him to the grassy land and he would just run and run and run and they would throw the ball and he'd run around after *that!* Gosh, that was his *favorite!* Except for when the Babble Man came to show Sheriff his friends, that was *so much fun!*

Some of Sheriff's friends didn't wag their tails so much. Misha did most times, but not *all* the times. Ladybug never did, but then again, she never had a tail. Even if she had, though, Sheriff didn't think she would wag it. She didn't seem like she liked everything that much. Her pee always smelled…weird. Kind of…sour. She always looked kind of…Sheriff didn't know what. Like excited in reverse? It was kind of scary. It looked like how Sheriff's  heart felt when The Babble Man made his scary noises. It was like somebody was always making scary noises that only Ladybug could hear.

But it would all turn out alright! If Ladybug would just wag a little more! It had all turned out alright until now, hadn't it? So it would keep turning out alright forever!

Sheriff played his absolute *best* favorite game, which was Run Under Misha's Very Long Legs! It was *so* much fun! And it got

Misha wagging her tail a bit! That was the stuff! Sheriff couldn't help but wag at th-*urk*

"No." Jairzinho yanked on Sheriff's leash. Dragged him back out from under Misha's legs. Jairzinho loved the little guy. But he was a damn Scrambler. No doubt. Ducking under tall dogs. Jumping over small ones. Running circles around the mid-sizes. Sheriff was a non-stop scrambler of dogs and leashes alike. It was enraging. Only for a bit though. Because how could Jairzinho stay mad at that cute little face? At that wagging tail?

He couldn't. So he smiled and shook his head. "You're a damn Scrambler, you know that?"

Sheriff wagged his tail.

- 4 -

DUCKY'S WORLD had just the TWO TYPES of THING in it. There was the TYPE of THING he could HUMP all the  live long DAY, just REALLY go BUCK wild on. Then there was that OTHER type of THING that he COULDN'T hump. But NOT for LACK of TRYIN'! It was just FUCKIN' LOGISTICS. That SHIT on the HIGH SHELVES? You better BELIEVE he'd be UP there HUMPIN' every FUCKIN' ONE of those, ONCE he FIGURED OUT how to GET UP there.

THAT'S why he PRACTICED JUMPIN' as HIGH as he COULD, ALL DAY EVERY DAY BRAH. So he could GET to the TYPE of THING he COULDN'T HUMP and MAKE it a TYPE of THING that he COULD HUMP.

DUCKY could DO it, BRAH. DUDE! HE could hump ANYTHIN'. He was BASICALLY the FUCKIN' HUMP-MEISTER of ALL the DOGS who EVER LIVED. He HAD the POWER. He WASN'T AFRAID to USE IT.

OK, there was SOME shit that WOULDN'T make SENSE to HUMP. Like his DINNER. Or…actually that was BASIC-ALLY IT.

Sniff…fuckin' SNIFF, broheme.

OOOOOOOH yeah.

He SMELLED 'EM. Smelled HER.

COMIN' in HOT.

LADYBUG. Hubbah HUBBAH! aROOOOOOgah, brah! Fuckin' aROOOOOgah!

ONE of these DAYS DUCKY was gonna HUMP the SHIT out of LADYBUG.

He only HADN'T because of BAD man.

The DEAL is, every time DUCKY tries to hump LADY-BUG, BAD MAN PULLS on the STRING and ba-BOOSH, ALL of a SUDDEN Ducky's FLYIN' through the GOD-DAMN AIR. And BAD man BARKS at DUCKY, and GETS like RIGHT in his FUCKIN' FACE, and totally POINTS his FINGER. And BAD man just STAYS there and BARKS and POINTS until DUCKY sits DOWN. Then BAD man FOR-GETS he was MAD and goes and LOOKS at somethin' ELSE.

And DUCKY's THING was like, WHO gave BAD man those FUCKIN' STRINGS!? So BAD man GETS to BE some

KINDA fuckin' LOGISTICS? It's his FUCKIN' STRINGS sayin' what IS or AIN'T-IS HUMPABLE? How'd THAT happen? WHAT makes BAD man the GUY gets to SAY whose PISS can DUCKY and AIN'T-can DUCKY DRINK?

DUCKY wasn't SCARED of THIS JABRONI. EVERY DAY Ducky just got RIGHT UP on this FUCKIN' DORK, SHOWED him who was BOSS.

BAD man NEVER gave DUCKY the FUCKIN' STRINGS yet, but THAT was YET. HE WOULD!

The DOOR said JINGLE. THEN it kind of OPENED. THEN it said CLUNK.

Then BAD man came IN and DUCKY got RIGHT UP in his DORK-ASS BUSINESS.

"Ducky," Jairzinho sighed.

The stocky French bulldog was crude in both color and temperament. He clamped on to Jairzinho's leg. Thrust with all his might. A deceptive amount of might, really. Ducky was small. But he was powerful.

That wasn't an accident. He had been conceived for a single purpose: to strut. He was bred from two show dogs. He, too, was a show dog. Theoretically. He'd just never been entered in a contest.

Which wouldn't matter to Jairzinho. Except Ducky was under contract. And some subsection of that contract said that Ducky couldn't be neutered until he placed in a contest. To stay plucky and self-assured. So he'd strut.

But his owners had never entered him in the goddamned contests.

And so his balls remained. Two spunky lodestones dragging Ducky down into the dregs of animal id. Oversexed, over-confident, understimulated.

It felt weird, to hate a dog. But Jairzinho kind of hated Ducky.

Naturally, he was stuck walking the little shit twice a day.

He let Ducky pound away at his leg. Just while he got the collar off the coathook. Jairzinho didn't want to encourage the humping, but he was hopeful that allowing it now might tire the little bastard out. Maybe make him easier to handle on the walk. That had never been the case. But Jairzinho was glad to see he could still be an optimist about something.

Collar on Ducky. Thin red leash on the collar. Ducky snorting and fidgeting all the while.

Sigh. Jairzinho paused with his hand on the doorknob.

For as much of a hurry as he was in…he could take a brief pause to appreciate this blessed moment, before Ducky joined the Giants and threw everything into (even greater) chaos. The blessed moment before Jairzinho would wrap the thin red leash around his hand, make a fist and pull, before Ducky would greet his fellow Giants with a beeline for Ladybug's bee-hind, which would invariably send Sheriff into a scrambling frenzy, the moment before Misha assumed Ducky's lunge meant it was playtime, which for the vertically advantaged golden meant bopping her smaller friends on the head with her paw.

It was too early for that kind of chaos. Or, Jairzinho noted with a sigh, too late. 8:13 AM. It should be 8:08. In a perfect world. Which this wasn't. He was picking up *some* time, but not as much as he'd like. Not as much as he needed.

Ok. Appreciation time over. Back to business.

He pulled the leash taut. Opened the door.

TALK about JUICY! EVERY time Ducky SAW her, it was like the VERY first TIME all OVER again. DUCKY didn't figure LADYBUG knew WHAT made HER so fuckin' HOT. It wasn't JUST her full FIGURE, it was BECAUSE she was BASICALLY a BODY with a BUTT at BOTH ENDS.

Did ANY other DOG squirt SO much SHIT outta their FACE? Or MAKE so MANY weird SMELLS? Come at her from EITHER SIDE, she was, AY-ay-AY, she was MONDO HUMPABLE. Like, DUCKY was STILL a BUTT DOG. No DOUBT. ONCE he got BAD man out of the PICTURE, DUCKY was goin' STRAIGHT for that KEISTER. But he was ALSO SOPHISTICATED enough to APPRECIATE a BUTT-faced BITCH.

Just THINKIN' about HUMPIN' was MAKIN' him WAN-NA to HUMP. So he RAN as HARD as he COULD at LADYBUG, which was REALLY HARD because he was SO fuckin' STRONG.

But THEN he was FLYIN' through the AIR because BAD man was a FUCKIN' CHEATER and a COWARD and he'd PULLED on the STRING!

So DUCKY stared BAD man DOWN. BAD man was so SCARED of DUCKY that he LOOKED AWAY. He PRE-TENDED he was TICKLIN' the DOOR but THAT was STUPID because DOORS only OPENED for DUCKY, and they OPENED by THEMSELVES.

Like he ALWAYS did, BAD man put DUCKY on ONE side of his STUPID ugly DORK LEGS, and then he WENT and put LADYBUG on the OTHER side.

DUCKY wouldn't fuckin' DEIGN to HUMP bad MAN'S long TREE-ASS shit LEGS, except for the TIMES when he DID. But THAT was ONLY to PROVE a POINT.

Misha ALSO did NOT have good LEGS for HUMPIN'. She DANCED from ONE of her BORIN' LEGS to the OTHER and then PLOPPED a PAW on DUCKY'S NOGGIN. Then MISHA sort of fell OVER like a STUPID IDIOT. And she KIND OF LANDED on DUCKY and MADE him FALL.

Bad MAN yelled "DUCKY" at DUCKY because HE blamed DUCKY because BAD man REALLY had it IN for DUCKY.

So DUCKY just IGNORED bad MAN and LOOKED at LADYBUG the whole WAY to the LOUD rooms.

Here began the bad behavior. The troublemaking. Jairzinho yanked Ducky back into line, once, twice, over and over again. Sheriff and, to a lesser extent, Misha took a few extra yanks as well. But it was their own damn fault. They thought it was playtime. Just because Ducky was gallivanting. It wasn't fucking playtime.

Jairzinho made a point of *not* looking at his watch.

- 5 -

Kelso remembered happier times. Oh yes he did. Times when the world was just psychedelic smells, and every sniff twisted the kaleidoscope. Always greater pleasures and promises, that was all the world had ever shown him. Back then, man. Back then he could hardly look up without seeing a highly fetchable stick soaring across the sky. Family was something to shake his stubbly little tail about, and they couldn't look down at him without smiling. Kelso remembered.

He remembered the times before Barmit.

When Barmit first arrived, Kelso thought she was one of those clumps of hair his Woman was always yanking from the handbath. By scent and sight, Barmit was a dead ringer.

And then she'd turned her square head towards Kelso, and trembled. Always trembling, always glaring. Turned out her personality came in clumps too.

Nothing made sense anymore. Family loved Barmit, but Barmit hated Family. Family wanted to play, and Kelso wanted to play...but Barmit never did. So *nobody* got to play anymore. And if Kelso ever tried bowing and panting at Barmit to get a game going? Kibosh. "Leaverlone," Family would say.

And that was the last word on the situation. Family didn't play anymore. But it got worse. Oh yes. No more trips to the park because Barmit puked in the car, no more couch privileges because Barmit peed on Woman's favorite pillow. No more fun, because Barmit got biological about the mere concept of mirth.

Here came the Walker. Here he was. But that didn't matter, no it didn't. Even *he'd* been treating Kelso differently since Barmit arrived. Kelso had never been the Walker's favorite. He knew that. He wasn't an idiot. But he also used to get a *couple* seconds of petting before they were on their way. No longer. Now the Walker just swept into Home, clipped his clip onto Kelso's collar, and immediately called for Barmit.

42

Just look: sweep clip call. Always the same, man. Kelso just ducked his head and frowned. He didn't know what else to do.

"Barmit!" Jairzinho called. Goddamn that little rat. She was always hiding.

Jairzinho tried not to get frustrated with her. She'd been rescued from a Starbucks bathroom. Pretty clear she'd been abused. Fear was an understandable response. It was also just an *enraging* one when he was running late.

He glared at his watch. 8:15. *Hell.*

He double checked the door. Checked that it was closed against the deadbolt-clipped leashes. With Ducky on *this* side. So he wouldn't have a chance to ravish any of the other Giants waiting on the far side.

All set.

Jairzinho set off to survey the usual hiding places.

Not under the bookcase.

Not behind the couch.

Not under the kitchen table.

"Barmit, come on." Jairzinho looked to Kelso. A big grey puggle with the most demented snaggletooth smile he'd ever seen on a dog. It could be endearing. In a Hieronymus Bosch kind of way. "Where's she at, Kelso?"

Kelso just ducked his head a little bit more. He hadn't always been this dour. Jairzinho wondered what was causing it.

He turned back to the furniture and said "Barmit!"

...barmit trembled...her very least favorite moment of the day had arrived...the one that was currently happening...

...she rested one side of her head on the ground so she could glare at mr. comeon from underneath the couch...he had looked right at her and then sighed and clomped off towards the kitchen...yeah, there were advantages to looking like a pile of dust...

...barmit hated mr. comeon...she hated the couch...she hated the home...she hated dust...and she hated the advantages of looking like it...she hated family...she hated kelso... she hated her food...she hated her water...she hated walks.... she hated sleeping...

...she hated everything...and she hated everything equally... a fact which she hated...she hated that she couldn't even find anything to hate more than she hated anything else...

...barmit, comeon...mr. comeon shouted...hatably...

...kelso nosed his way over to the couch...oooooh, how she hated him...

...so barmit just smushed her head into the floor more...her lower lip pouted out slightly...it made her bite herself a little bit...which she hated...but she would not give kelso the satisfaction of making noise or moving...she would have hated to see his tail wagging...just as much as she hated seeing it not wag...

...mr. comeon wasn't far behind kelso...mumbling and reaching...

"How did I miss you there?" Jairzinho gently pushed on the back of Barmit's head. Leading her out from behind the couch. On went her harness. On went a thin pink leash. He pulled yet another carabiner out of his backpack and clipped it to his belt.

He was up to six dogs now. Still three more to pick up yet. Walk one was a two-carabiner walk, without a doubt.

He spotted an envelope on a sidetable. *J'S CURBSIDE GIA-NTS*, it said. *FROM KELSO AND BARMIT.* And then they'd drawn two little pawprints.

Took the time to draw pawprints. Couldn't be bothered to write Jairzinho's full name out.

"J" rolled his eyes. Grabbed the envelope and resumed the pickup.

Next stop: the other side of the Edbrooke.

- 6 -

Somebody had decided it would be a good idea to split the Edbrooke into two halves. Even-numbered apartments on one side. Odd-numbered on the other.

The only way to get from one side to the other was to go through the laundry rooms on the odd numbered floors. Or else go back down to the lobby and take a different elevator back up.

There was probably a very good reason for this. Jairzinho couldn't imagine what it was.

He was on the ninth floor now. He could cross straight through the laundry without having to go up or down a story. Hence why he'd scheduled the pick-ups like this.

He glanced at his watch.

8:18. Should be 8:12.

Goddamnit. Losing time again. Fucking Barmit.

He jockeyed his six charges down the hall. Splitting the dogs between the carabiners as he went. Ducky, Misha, and Sheriff on his left. Kelso, Barmit, and Ladybug on his right.

He herded them into the muggy-ass ninth floor laundry room.

There, as ever, was Adriana.

"How are ya, Adriana?" he shouted over the rumbling of the washers.

"Headache!" she told a polo shirt as she folded it in a single smooth motion. "Too much Jim!"

Jairzinho laughed. "On a Tuesday?"

"*Because* of it was Tuesday!"

"You want some ibuprofen?"

"Hah?"

He paused at the far door. Against his better judgment. *8:18.* But he liked Adriana. "Headache pills!"

"No no, I took already! Have a good day!"

"You too!" The door closed halfway through the last word. No way to know if she'd heard him or not.

Moving towards the elevators, Jairzinho took a moment to appreciate how long it had been since he'd done laundry. He worked all day. Tia usually had hers free. So she ended up doing most of the dull household chores. It made Jairzinho uncomfortable that she did. Being a modern man and all. So he made a point of getting all the groceries. Running as many errands as possible.

Back in California, on *his* turf, he'd been the provider. He'd taken care of *her.* That had made him feel good and strong and manly.

46

And then a year and a half ago she'd told him she wanted to move back to *her* turf. New York City. Jairzinho hated New York. But Tia loved the city, and Jairzinho loved Tia. He'd assumed the latter of those emotions would be more robust than the former.

He had assumed.

He hit the 'down' elevator call button, and the corners of his mouth responded.

Maybe someday, he'd tell her how much he hated this city. But he was scared to. He was afraid she would chose New York over him. He was afraid that would be the logical choice.

Ding!

Astrid considered the tell-a-vision. What was it? What gave it the power it wielded so indiscriminately over humankind?

It was not a window to a different room, nor was it a crate for small fires. It could not be entered. Its scent was unyielding. It took orders only from the lumpy little stick on the low table.

So what *was* it?

She reached out and pressed the lumpy stick with her paw.

The tell-a-vision blinked and showed Astrid new people.

She tilted her head to the side. Bopped the lumpy stick again.

Blink. Now there was a dog in the tell-a-vision!

Astrid almost barked, but caught herself. No. She was being foolish. The dog wasn't *in* the tell-a-vision.

Where the dog was, she didn't know. But the tell-a-vision was like the second Astrid who lived in the mirrors. Which was to say, not real. Something beyond Astrid's comprehension.

For now. She would figure it out, though. Everything yielded to logic in time.

The door jingled, hushed, and clunked. Ducky snorted and whimpered into Astrid's apartment.

Correction: *almost* everything yielded to logic.

Jairzinho brought him in, Astrid had worked out, to keep him away from the other Giants during pickup. She understood and respected this…but she didn't care for having Ducky in her home. Oh well. Nothing to be done about it.

"Astrid!" Jairzinho shouted. "What're ya watching, girl?"

She looked at him, then back to the tell-a-vision. Jairzinho laughed, because he *clearly* didn't understand.

She *was* watching.

Jairzinho clicked the thick rope leash onto her choke collar and led her towards the door. As she often did, she rushed forward a bit and then doubled back, drawing the chain around her neck taut, and then slackening it. The principle of the collar was something else Astrid had worked out by experimentation: the choker was a series of pointed links that dug into her neck as the tension on the leash increased. And, she'd learned, the opposite was also true. It wasn't at all difficult for Astrid to use Jairzin-  ho as a prop to help her slip out of the collar. And a challenged human like poor Jairzinho would think these slips were an accident.

She felt bad, taking advantage of such a slow-witted goober. He just made it so *easy*.

They all did. Humans, in Astrid's experience, were *all* goobers: erratic, emotional, dangerously unpredictable. At best. An example: "down" might mean *lay down on the ground*, or it might mean *get down off the bed*, or it might mean *stop hugging a new human friend*, or it might just mean *sit*. How was a dog to know?

It was Astrid's ambition to one day make sense of these strange creatures, to taxonomize their grunts and gurgles, to learn whether or not they had a first person experience comparable to hers. Or even to the tell-a-vision's.

She wasn't optimistic.

Jairzinho loved Astrid's big idiot grin. It was his favorite smile of the Giants'. After Sheriff's.

All the dogs – save Ducky – rushed forward to greet Astrid as she stepped into the hall. Being different heights, each got to sniff at their own, pre-determined snuffle-spots.

The Frenchie kept his distance, save a juke-around for the caboose. Jairzinho tugged him back into position. Pulled them all down the hall.

"Who's my goofy girl?" he asked Astrid once they got to the elevator.

Astrid the blue-nosed pitbull was smart enough to formulate a working definition of the word *goofy*. But she just smiled at Jairzinho and wagged her tail so hard her whole body wagged with it. She was still a dog, after all.

"YOU are!" Jairzinho clarified. In case there had been any confusion. "*You're* my goofy girl!"

The elevator *ding*ed them onto the sixth floor. The doors opened. Ducky made a hard drive towards the right.

"Nope!" Jairzinho told him. He yanked on the leash. The apple of Ducky's eye was undoubtedly Ladybug. But he was almost equally vexed by Astrid's rear end. So Astrid always landed on Jairzinho's right side. But this meant keeping an eye on Barmit. Barmit would deliberately put herself beneath the tread of a larger dog. Who the hell knew why. But it was clearly deliberate. More times than Jairzinho could count, Astrid would step on Barmit. Barmit would yelp. Which would set Sheriff to scrambling. Which would set Misha to slapping. Kelso would be fine. As long as Meatball wasn't in the pack.

If she was, well, Jairzinho would have two fights to break up.

Half his job was sorting out the social hierarchy of his breakfast club. Organizing them accordingly. It was enough to swear him off children for life.

Another thing he would mention to Tia. At some point.

- 7 -

When Meatball thought about where she was, which was in a tiny crate in a gloomy closet in a dark apartment in a loud city…it was more than she could handle. More than one little bulldog could bear, this claustrophobia, this *torture*…

Which was why, when she thought about that…she [let the Other Dog take over.]

For a long while, Meatball had merely been Meatball. Then, one long and lonely day amongst the millions, she discovered within herself [the Other Dog. The Other Dog weren't so woe-is-me, capeesh? The Other Dog's got frickin' grit. So the Other Dog gives that dog, the one calls herself *"Meatball"*, a frickin' break. That'd give *"Meatball"*, which is some kinda frickin'

50

name, but anyway that'd give *"Meatball"* a chance to get outside that dog, have a frickin' outtabody, outta that bulldog body there's got a coat all splattered with blobs of brown and white like some pup took a shit in a lava lamp, and got a tongue lollin' out off an underbite. And we're havin' fun 'bout how that dog looks now, but gettin' a little into the tragedical, that dog's been sat there like a frickin' mermaid for hours and hours and hours. Which is how come Meatball wanted out, ya see? Why'd she wanna let the Other Dog take the frickin' string. It's so *"Meatball"* ain't gotta experience none of this stuff. Lets those bad feelins be] acknowledgments, not experiences.

They *couldn't* be experiences.

Because were Meatball forced to sit in [that dog's noggin, in the crate in the closet in the apartment in the city, this *"Meatball"* dog, she woulda lost her frickin' biscuits ages ago.]

So Meatball dissociated. Left [that bum-luck bulldog's head, and let the Other Pup take over. That ain't losin' biscuits, got it? It's *misplacin'* em.]

Here were acknowledgments that Meatball could permit herself to, okay, experience: the bouquet of her buddies, the creaking of the door, the pounding of footsteps.

She turned her eyes towards the full bowl of food just outside her crate. [No, it weren't enough for that dog's tormenters gotta lock her up here in this dark-dank dungeon. They gotta leave her food on the far side of the bars, too!]

At least Meatball had The Liberator.

Jairzinho opened the door to Meatball's closet. He managed to open it about ten inches. Then it thudded against something firm.

He mumbled profanity. Quietly. He didn't know if that conspicuously placed nanny cam on the shelf recorded audio.

Jairzinho reached around the door to identify the jam. There was always some obstruction or another. A suitcase, as usual. Maybe to remind *the help* that they worked for real jetsetters. Ugh. He hoisted the suitcase up and swung the door the rest of the way open.

Poor Meatball. What a dreadful little closet her owners stuffed her into. Take the travel aisle of a department store and accordion it into a five square feet. That was roughly the shit-to-space ratio of this little hutch.

To keep a dog in a crate all day was cruel. To keep an animal as sweet as Meatball cooped up in *here* was almost…

Well, *evil* was a strong word.

"Hey Meatball," he cooed. He threw the latches of the crate. Swung the door open. Didn't unclip the other dogs from his waist. The closet was narrow enough that he didn't have to. And even inside buildings, if he could avoid unclipping…he definitely preferred to. Avoid it.

The Giants tugged him off-balance. Back into the hall. But Jairzinho was stronger. He fought them and held steady.

"C'mere," he beckoned Meatball. More firmly than usual. Given the time crunch.

Meatball hoisted herself onto all fours. Lumbered out of her cell. Tentatively. Like it was the first time. Like every time was the first time. She snorted over to her food just as slowly.

Once she got in striking distance of her breakfast, though, it was like someone flipped a switch. Meatball's essential dogginess returned. She fell to. With alacrity.

It was impossible to listen to Meatball eat without smiling. It was like a pig getting to second base with a vacuum cleaner.

Jairzinho looked at his watch.

It was impossible to look at the time and *keep* smiling.

Fortunately Meatball had more than sound in common with an Oreck. She looked from her empty bowl to Jairzinho. Gave him a *what are we waiting for?* face.

He got his smile back. Unslung Meatball's leash from around his neck. Clipped her up. Meatball barreled through the closet door. Dragged Jairzinho behind her.

Meatball blew straight past Ducky, whose daily intrusion into her space she tolerated but in no way endorsed.

She was no longer a passive observer; Meatball had returned to the captain's chair, was currently steering the ship towards Ladybug's scrunched mug. The two had a brachycephalic bond, an agonized link forged by their anvil-shaped faces.

Ladybug gasped in greeting. Meatball rumbled her jowls in reply.

From behind her, Kelso rumbled too. Not in a friendly way. Meatball gave him some side-eye. Kelso seemed to have it out for Meatball. She'd never understood why. He was *half* a scrunch-face, after all. He should at least *half* like her. Oh well.

When The Liberator was done jingling the door, Meatball instinctively shuffled over to *her side*. Except for Bathroom Times, Meatball always kept to *her side*. If she didn't, The Liberator was quick to put her back. He was a breaker of cages, but that was not to say he was without a sense of order. He had his own bonds, ropes that prevented Meatball from straying too far. It was different than the crate, but how different? Didn't the cord lashing Meatball to her Liberator make a crate of the entire world? She thought it did. Her twice-daily walks were tastes of freedom — [but tastes ain't a full frickin' meal. That dog didn't got no clue what made the Liberator so big on tradin' one restriction for another. But] Meatball returned to herself. Dissociation was a terrific coping mechanism…but it could be unwieldy.

- 8 -

Down the elevator to the second floor. To the last pickup.

Jairzinho checked his watch: 8:22. He usually liked to be out of the Edbrooke by 8:15.

Boo was a quick pick-up. Maybe 8:25 was plausible. On the *street* by 8:25. Ten minutes behind schedule wasn't terrible. He could really gun the Chelsea run. Maybe get back on track by noon. Perfect.

Less perfect was waiting for Jairiznho in Boo's apartment.

Boo was out of his crate.

Immediately, Jairzinho looked at the floor. "Boo," he said to the hardwood in a deep, hushed voice. "Come here, Boo."

In Jairzinho's peripheral vision: Boo's shaggy auburn ears clicked up. Framing his face in isosceles.

Boo was a piebald Springer Spaniel. Shaped by artificial selection into a world-class hunting buddy. A dog, in short, that should not be living in Manhattan and getting one walk a day. The lack of exercise had created a pup whose hyperactivity

54

lacked a clear outlet. Like Ducky's all-consuming love of humping. But without such a clear mission statement.

Boo was all juice, no concentrate.

He was also a submissive peer. Not peer as in associate. Peer as in *one who pees*.

Direct eye contact with Boo would mean a manhole-sized piss puddle. As would an energetic inflection in the voice. As would a sudden movement.

Basically, there were only a few ways to approach Boo without getting your shoes wet.

Boo's owner Brett (of course) usually left him in the crate. This solved the piss problem. Because if (who was kidding who, *when*) Boo peed during the pickup, it was onto the removable floor of the crate. Brett comes home, pulls it out, towels it up. All good.

Not so good: Boo standing on the white carpet (why oh why did they get a *white* carpet). Front paws splayed. Head ducked. Tail wagging.

Boo's eyes were locked on to Jairzinho.

Just *waiting* for an excuse.

8:23, said the watch. Better hurry up.

Jairzinho crouched down. Fixed his gaze on his own knee. Offered Boo an upturned palm. "C'mere Boo."

He didn't hear any jangling tags. He took a surreptitious glance up.

Boo remained rooted to the spot. On the white carpet.

Another look at the watch. Still 8:23. Not as bad as 8:24; not as good as 8:22.

Jairzinho clenched his fists. Debated the merits of just walking up to that pissbag. Of dragging him off the carpet. He'd pee all the way off and then some. Boo would. But why was that Jairzinho's fault? If Brett didn't want to get piss on his carpet, he shouldn't have left Boo out.

Patience. Patience. Jairzinho had always struggled with that. He didn't have the longest fuse in the world. Not that he'd ever phrase it that way. He just didn't suffer fools or take any shit. No sir. That was how he liked to imagine people described him. As opposed to "short-fused".

Boo was a fool. Boo had so much shit to give. And piss.

Now it was 8:24.

"Fuck it," Jairzinho said. He rose to his feet.   —

At last, movement! After being still forever now finally the Slowman was standing up slowly slowly slowly he rose to his two feet one two slow feet his knees went pop *pop* and they popped for one hundred years and ages passed and empires rose and fell and the Slowman picked one foot up moved it so it was in front of him slow slow so slow and then a few months later he put the foot down also in front of him and he was so slow it was almost like he wasn't moving at all but Boo could see it all happening he was used to everybody being so so so slow that he could see *all* of it like how the Slowman shifted his weight to the foot he'd just put down in front of him and then he rested until infinity days later and then the rear foot tore itself from the ground.

Such was Boo's existence.

He'd been left alone for so long and he had all this energy but he never got a chance to use it and then one day *pow!* all the energy he wasn't using burst and bled into the world and but then the whole world got really tired and it got so *slow*, at first Boo thought maybe he had gotten faster because he felt his belly going *bahbahbahbahbahbah* and noises got louder and then everything was noises but then instead everything reversed and his belly was going *bah…bah…bah…* and it was like this big heavy blanket fell on the world and the blanket was made of wet and then it curdled and the world lived in mud and everybody could hardly move except for so slowly and it wasn't just the people it was the not-people too like if somebody threw a ball the ball didn't soar through the sky like it was supposed to but it burrowed like those chalky Eatits Master tried to hide in peanut butter yum *yum* Boo hadn't had peanut butter in *millennia* but peanut butter wouldn't fix playtime which was actually purgatory because you can't play games over thousands of years because that's not wrestling it's just basically like sleeping on your pals its so *boring* and even pats from Family were boring because they were separated by a generational gulf *and nobody seemed to notice* they'd all gotten slow and only Boo was the right speed and how did they not notice that the whole world needed to hurry *up* but they never did notice and so the only way Boo could not just totally go *bonkers* was any

time he saw something that moved at anything like his speed he loved it like a long-lost friend so if he saw a bird jumping off a tree or a person across the street waving their hand fast or a flag blowing really fast in the wind he just couldn't believe his *luck* and he just wanted to drink it in because it was so rare to see the world running at speed but it was pretty selfish for Boo to drink and drink and drink and never give anything back to the world so if it was a leaf blowing in the park he couldn't really give anything back to that because it was a leaf and leaves just happened they weren't people but sometimes the leaves *were* people and their speed was a gift granted like here the Slowman was trying to make Boo feel better by running at him as fast as he could and Boo was just so so grateful that the Slowman was trying to move faster for Boo so but Boo didn't know how to let the Slowman *know* about all that gratitude except by pumping his bladder full of all his most satisfied scents and spreading the message far and wide and the Slowman must have gotten the message because now he moved even faster and made lots of fast noises which was so nice for Boo it was so lovely and he was so happy to have the Slowman because there were not many people who understood how slow they were and tried to fix it so anyway that was why Boo was pissing on the carpet.

Jairzinho clamped on to Boo's collar just as the spaniel settled into his squat.

Jairzinho yanked. "Get...OFF!"

Boo dismounted the carpet in a leaky crabwalk.

Jairzinho glanced at his watch. 8:25. Terrific.

A brown leather leash clipped onto the collar. Boo was ready to go.

As was Jairzinho. He'd try dabbing up the piss when he got back. Maybe. If he had time.

Right now, he didn't have any goddamned time.

He hustled his Giants down the hall. His only concern was how fast *he* could walk. He wasn't thinking about the dog's individual limitations right now.

58

Astrid, Kelso, Barmit, Ladybug, and Boo jogged along on his right without too much confusion.

On his left, Ducky, Sheriff, Meatball, and Misha were already becoming a bit more scrambled.

Jairzinho and his Curbside Giants stepped into the elevator at 8:27 AM. Down to the first floor, through the lobby, out the door.

The first walk of the day had officially begun.

walkies

- 1 -

First thing's first: all nine dogs rushed for the curb.

Jairzinho begrudgingly thanked maybe-Philippe for holding the door open. Even though the guy had worked out how to hold doors open *sarcastically*. Jairzinho still said thanks as his Giants dragged him to the curb, for the first and most dramatic bathroom stop of the day.

He did his best to steer the pups to the left. As always. There was no hope of getting them more than a few feet from the Edbrooke's door. But he could at least ensure they didn't lay a scatological obstacle course right on the welcome mat. Seemed like the decent thing to do.

Jairzinho pulled his phone out. Opened a note. Began the bathroom report. For the owners to keep tabs on their pups' regularity. For health reasons. Not just as a goof. Wouldn't have been good goof anyway. Because boy, were these dogs regular. Jairzinho updated the report as the story broke. But he could just as easily have filled it out on the morning train ride in. Probably still get it at least 85% right. It wasn't just the frequency. Like how Misha *always* peed and pooped once each per walk. It was the patterns. Like how Meatball began each day by spreading a water hazard, and then releasing what Jairzinho affectionately referred to as "the Plug". These were two or three small, hard turds, the advance party to "the Purge", which always occurred on Christopher Street. And the less said about that, the better.

It was quaint to think of how squeamish he'd been when he'd first started this job. He'd almost given up (ha) *dreams* of dogwalking. He couldn't countenance the biological parts of the gig. And now here he was, scrutinizing the process and the product. Divining the dogs' health by their output. Like a mystic over tea leaves.

Also amusing to him: he logged the movements on his phone as tersely as possible. For time's sake. And so the data from yesterday's first walk read:

Misha pee poo
Meatball pee poo pee poo poo
Kelso pee pee pee pee poo
Sheriff pee
Astrid pee pee poo
Ducky pee lee (sic) poo pee poo
Boo poo pee
Ladybug pee
Barmit (blank, for lack of input)

66

Sometimes it was the simple things.

He shook his head. Erased the old data. Updated today's log as the dogs dropped today's logs. Fished a roll of bags from his left rear pocket as he re-holstered the phone in his right front one.

He could feel maybe-Philippe's eyes on him. Drilling through the back of his head. Jairzinho used to make light of this morning shitzkrieg. An attempt to be chummy with the doorman. To say they were in it together. Which, in a way, they were. Or should have been. Millionaires and celebrities brushed past both doorman and dogwalker alike. Workers of the world, unite. Or something.

That, and the day's first bathroom extravaganza must have been unplesant for maybe-Philippe to behold.

But maybe-Phillippe never returned Jairzinho's "boy, we've all been there!" variations.

So Jairzinho had quit trying to be friendly. Now he kept his back to maybe-Philippe. That judgmental, holier-than-thou prick. He seemed to forget who was holding the door open for who. For *whom*.

Jairzinho snapped off two bags, knelt down. Cleaned up after other people's dogs.

Misha needed to piddle, but she held it. Now was not the time. The Ritual required that she make water on the brown ground under the tree that always smelled like cats that was next to the tall building that made screaming trucks. Then she would complete the transubstantiation of last night's Breakfast on that corner right over there, almost right back in front of Home.

And then?

BRRRREEEEAAAAAAKFAAAAAAAAAST!

She looked up to The Breakfast Man as He was wrapping the presents from Misha's friends and putting them in the Collection Bin. He saw her looking at Him, and He pet Misha with His eyes. He seemed a little less vengeful now.

So she had done well to keep her friends in line! The Breakfast Man recognized Misha, recognized her missionary zeal!

She would need to work extra hard to keep her friends in line. They needed to FEEEEEL HER ZEEEAL!

Her friends liked to make their offerings just wherever they wanted. Casual apostates, all of them. Aside from Meatball. She seemed to understand the precariousness of The Ritual. Her offerings had a kind of irreverence built into them (and to even *imply* structure was perhaps overselling it), but at least she was consistent.

That was what The Breakfast Man most adored. Consistency and stability.

Misha would ensure these were observed.

She wagged her tail at Him. Even if He wasn't looking at her anymore, she knew He could feel it.

The dogs actually walked pretty well after they'd done their business. He'd have to choke up on scramblin' Sheriff's leash to keep him from tangling the others. Or keep an eye on Ducky as he'd stare at Ladybug and hump the air whenever they stopped at crosswalks. Boo was always dashing ahead for— the Alpha position. So Jairzinho would have to yank hard from time to time. Ladybug's leash he held loosely in a hooked pinky. She walked obediently, but he needed her leash separate from the others. She was his canary. To know if he was walking too fast, if it was too hot out. The pug would be the first to go down. He could keep a gentle grip on the leads of the most obedient dogs. Misha, Astrid, Kelso. Barmit…he had to drag her no matter where he put her. He just held on tight to her leash and walked.

These were just the first of the million microadjustments that had to be made on the walk. Jairzinho'd had to think hard about each and every one when he'd first started. *Ducky's drifting to the right — tug gently to the left. Misha's dragging — slow down, she might want to pee. Meatball's leash just jerked a bit — check to see if she snapped up a street treat.* It had been exhausting. But by now it was second nature. He just put the leashes in his hands and walked down the street. His body did the rest. It was kind of amazing. Except it was also pretty boring. *Now* what was he supposed to think about for nine fucking hours?

Most times he thought about how he wished the rest of life could be like that. Like he could just practice being patient or nice so much that he wouldn't have to think about it anymore. He'd just *be* it.

"Hi Puppies!" someone shouted from up the block. Jairzinho ignored it, hoped they would just keep walking. Sometimes people would lunge at the dogs. Take photos. Steal pats. Fuck up the walk. Others had the decency to keep on moving. Everyone, though, shouted *Hi Puppies*. It was eerie, how universal this salutation was.

Jairzinho tried to practice patience. Tried *really fucking hard.*
"Hey Navi!"

He frowned. Then he thought about it. Then he smiled. "Hey, Esther."

Esther pounded out of the deli. Bagel in hand. Plain with cream cheese. Which Jairzinho felt described Esther pretty well. She was a fellow dogwalker. Probably mid-fifties in both years and inches. She carried herself like she was still waiting by the phone to hear from *The Sopranos'* casting director. But then she also poofed out her (often dyed, now naturally grey-brown) hair, and wore visors and shirts with cartoon characters on them. She was...yeah. Plain with cream cheese.

"All the Giants in a line, eh?" she asked. She carefully plucked her smoldering cigarette from its usual holding zone. Balanced on the edge of the Village Voice dispenser. The same dispenser that two French bulldogs were tied to. Esther's morning charges.

Jairzinho couldn't even *imagine* leaving his dogs unattended outside. In New York City? Absolutely not. So goddamned irresponsible.

"Yeahhhp," Jairzinho replied. Thinking about it. "The gang's all here." Looking at his watch. "I'm sorry Esther, I can't talk right now. I'm in a h-"

"I tell you about my ankle?" Esther took a drag from her cigarette. Blew smoke on the offending joint. And the two dogs she was walking. They sneezed. "Fuckin' hurts. I put some ice on it."

Jairzinho looked to the crosswalk. To the illuminated red hand across the street. Sigh. Back to Esther. "Did it help?"

"Sure. Hey, listen, I tell you what I call these two?" She shook the leashes. Tugged the sneezing Frenchies off balance.

"The Frenchie Connection," Jairzinho said. So she wouldn't have to.

"Oh yeah, I told you! Anyway, I let 'em play around a bit, one of 'em lands funny on his leg. Turns out," she took a step

70

towards Jairzinho. Her voice went dusky, "he *broke* his damn leg." She stepped back again. Made a *wow* face. Like she expected Jairzinho to reflect it. He didn't.

Smiling again, she sucked on her cigarette. "Six hundred dollar surgery to fix it. Can you believe it? I couldn't believe it. *My* ankle didn't run that much. Ha! Like a joke!"

Jairzinho snuck another glimpse of the crosswalk. The little white man had arrived.

"That's crazy," he said as he flicked the leashes towards the other side of the street. "I hope he's alright." He wanted to ask her if she was going to be held liable. Why neither of the Frenchies was wearing a cast. But shop talk would have to wait. The white man said Jairzinho could walk. And so he would. Wasn't that always the way? He thought about it and said "anyway, have a good one!"

"Yeah he's fine. This was years ago."

Jairzinho felt like it was fair for him to ignore her. Since she'd just ignored him.

Then she said "Anyway, have a good one Navi!"

"Uh-huh."

He tried to let the name thing slide. Esther was such a nice lady. Mostly. Well…she meant well, at least. But Jairzinho's hands did most of the thinking now. So his mind was free up to sweat the small stuff.

And that *was* always the way.

- 2 -

Jairzinho was something different to each of the dogs, but one thing he most definitely was not was In Charge of the Walk.

This wasn't his fault, though: how could he be expected to recognize that *Astrid* was in charge of the walk?

She kept everyone on the straight-and-narrow by way of embodying benign authority. Any dogs stepping out of line would be cowed with a steely gaze. If she spotted a mischievous playbow trembling the legs of approaching rivals on the sidewalk, Astrid would crank her ears back against her skull and stick out her snout, to make clear that it was well within her power to deem dogs Good or Bad.

This wasn't a responsibility she was particularly happy to have arrogated unto herself. But who else was going to do it? *Jairzinho?* Certainly not. He was too…human. He hadn't the intellectual hardware to distinguish between deference freely granted, and obedience extorted by force. Astrid's humans were actually the exception to the rule; it was by holding their conduct up against that of the rest of the world's and studying the contrast, that Astrid came to develop her appreciation for how pitiful was the average human mind.

Jairzinho was like most members of his species, who apparently thought that dogs could best be shown 'who was boss' by bodyslamming them into refrigerators and throwing them down a flight of stairs. Near as she could tell from the tell-a-vision, it was known as the Cesar Milan/People's Champion method of training. And good heavens, did most humans at the

Edbrooke adore it. It had quite clearly traumatized each of the dogs on Astrid's walk, to greater or lesser degrees. And if it wasn't their people who had inflicted this terrifying, violent brand of "training" upon them, Jairzinho was quick to fill in.

Did he believe in the whole Alpha Dog narrative? He sure seemed to. But Astrid suspected it was really just a convenient pretext to give vent to the thunderhead pressures that defined his blunt, stupid emotional life. Such as it was. How else to explain the variation of his responses from day to day? Sometimes he could endure the worst of Ducky's antics; on others, he would attempt to holler at Astrid herself (naturally, she had little reaction to this save pity for the poor man and his kind).

Uh oh. Here it came. Looked like today was going to be one of the less amiable ones.

She felt him make the decision before he was likely even aware of it. That unmistakable quaking through the leash, that thrumming of her joke of choke collar.

Astrid turned and looked to her dogs.

Ducky was pulling his usual shit. Cavorting around Jairzinho's feet, lunging for Ladybug. Asking for trouble.

Which Jairzinho was all too happy to provide.

- 3 -

The FUCK was BAD Man's PROBLEM? DUCKY was just TRYIN' to WALK and the SILLY son of a BITCH just FALLS on him? HE was just WALKIN' and yeah TRYIN' to HUMP LADYBUG! So WHAT if HE was TRYIN' to TRIP bad MAN and MAKE him FALL and DIE? THAT made DUCKY some KIND of FUCKIN' bad DOG all of a SUDDEN?

73

BAD man GROWLED like he KNEW the first THING about GROWLIN'. NOW he was FUCKIN' UP the whole WALK. ALL the DOGS gettin' TANGLED and SHIT. And DUCKY'S SUPPOSED to be the ASSHOLE? ALL of a SUDDEN?

BAD man PICKED Ducky UP, RIGHT up to his DORK-ass FACE. But his FACE didn't DESERVE to get called ASS, RIGHT? BAD man's FACE was TOTALLY FUCKIN' UNHUMPABLE. The ONLY THING on the WHOLE PLANET Ducky WOULDN'T even DREAM of HONORIN' with his-

HEY HEY HEY BRAH! BAD man got a FISTFUL of DUCKY'S back MUSCLE and HEY HEY he was SQUEEZIN' IT REALLY FUCKIN' HARD!

So DUCKY fuckin' BARKED because THAT fuckin' HURT!

BAD man just SQUEEZED Ducky's MUSCLE HARDER and LIFTED Ducky RIGHT up into his DORK-face FACE and growled "IMNCHARGEDYUNDER*STAY-AND?*"

So DUCKY fuckin' BARKED right in BAD man's MOUTH because FUCK THIS GUY.

Then ASTRID, that SLEEK silver BITCH who DUCKY had NEVER HUMPED because of LOGISTICS, she WOOFED at BAD man.

So BAD man LOOKED at her like SHE had a GOOD point, like HE had the FIRST fuckin' CLUE about WOOFIN'.

Then HE growled "GRRRR" in DUCKY'S HUMPABLE-ass FACE, you BETTER BELIEVE Ducky'd HUMP his own MUG if it WEREN'T for LOGISTICS.

Then BAD man put DUCKY DOWN. Really SOFTLY. Like he GAVE a SHIT.

DUCKY ran as FAR from BAD man as his LEASH would LET him. He COWERED from BAD man NOT because he was SCARED of HIM or some SHIT, he WASN'T a GOD-DAMNED PUPPY. He COWERED because he KNEW it was a GOOD way to make BAD man FEEL like the ASS-HOLE he WAS.

NO, NOT an ASSHOLE. Just a BAD man.

HA! It WORKED because BAD man was a GODDAMN-ED PUPPY. He just STOOD there for a SECOND like a STUPID shitty DORK boy and THEN he said "SORRY-DUCKY" which was human BARKIN' and IT meant "I AM A FUCKIN' STUPID SHITTY DORK-"

HEY BRAH HEY!

Misha raised her paw and plopped it on top of Ducky's noggin a second time. Ducky jerked back a step, head tilted far enough to reveal the pale whites of his eyes.

"HEY!" The Breakfast Man shouted. "No play!"

Misha met His gaze and wagged her tail. She couldn't have agreed more. No play.

The Rite of Breakfast was not a game. Ducky was causing too great a deviation from The Ritual. What awaited them then? Famine. Pestilence. Rumbly tummy. Astonishing, that she should be the only one who truly grasped the enormity of what was at stake.

It seemed that The Breakfast Man was especially hungry today: He was really hauling booty. Misha thought of herself as pretty quick, but even *she* was having a hard time keeping up! Where there were normally opportunities to stop and sniff around for current events, today it was all go go go.

Misha had mixed feelings. On the one paw, yes, good, more food faster. Er, ahem, see The Ritual through to a prompt conclusion. On the other paw, hers was a largely hermetic life. Save these Pilgrimages with The Breakfast Man and her friends, she spent most of her time behind The Door. Sniffing around the city's high-traffic latrines wasn't just a way to see how everybody in the neighborhood was doing – who was happy and who was sick and who had just returned from some far-off land and who had somehow gotten some No Drop It food – no, it was also a way for Misha to live vicariously through these other friends, many of whom she had never met but whom she knew rather intimately, as they must surely know her. She was usually pretty happy, and sometimes she got sick. But she never got to travel to far-off lands, and she never got to eat No Drop It food. A little inspiration through the nostrils let her, though. In a way.

Couldn't it be argued that this, too, was a part of The Rite of Breakfast? She did it every day, after all.

So...then couldn't it be argued that, by *not* stopping and letting Misha sniff around...wasn't thaaaaaat...sort of Him interfering with the Ritual? In a *way?*

Surely The Breakfast Man would understand.

So Misha hung back a second, then hooked left behind Meatball for a sharp detour towards a particularly fragrant tree-pit.

And so, she began one of those Invisible Pilgrimages carried to her by the wind.

Sniff...that smelled like Gaspode, redolent of the prickly-sweet water smell like what blew in from the river, but...*sniff*... not quite as *wow* alright. The Breakfast Man apparently *didn't* understand. He'd pulled on her leash pretty hard there.

Clearly He'd meant that for Ducky, the greatest blasphemer of the bunch. Mistakes happened, that was what being a dog was all about. She stepped *again* nope see He did it again there. Probably another accident. So she'd just *ah nope.*

She sized up The Breakfast Man's low-angle profile and had a blasphemous thought of her own:

What was this guy playing at?

His role in the drama came later. With the Stations and the Bowl.

She was the one with the job to do here. Keep her friends in line.

The Breakfast Man came to a complete stop. Oh no! He'd felt her thought! Had she irreparably corrupted the day's Ritual? NOOOOO! He must forgive her! He wasn't looking at her though. He was just staring at the honkboxes in the road. There were a lot of them, and they were all being extra honky.

Poor Breakfast Man. Must have been scared out of His wits.

And here was Misha, ungrateful Misha, transgressing in thought!

So she sought forgiveness. She stepped forward and

- 4 -

licked his hand. Nuzzled her nose into his palm.

Jairzinho patted Misha's forehead with the meat of his thumb. Poor girl must have been freaked out by all the honking. "Jesus," he mumbled. "That's a mess, isn't it?"

It was. Seventh Avenue was bumper to bumper gridlock across all three lanes. Or four lanes. Or five. The way most people in New York City drove, that number changed every few minutes.

Today, though, it was academic. There were no lanes. Nothing was moving.

The problem-solvers of the bunch laid on their horns like game-show contestants who didn't understand the buzzer system.

In hindsight, there had definitely been more cars than usual coming down Christopher. Quick-thinkers peeling off of this mess, probably. Good luck to anybody who didn't pull out of the logjam. Or couldn't.

If he remembered later, he'd try to look up what had happened on his break.

After he texted Tia. Obviously. That came first.

For now: he was still behind. No time to gawk. So he walked North. Against the Southbound not-so-flow of very-much-traffic. He kept the Giants hustling towards Chelsea.

He heard the siren on Charles, but didn't see the ambulance it was attached to until West 11th. It was stuck in traffic like all the other rubes. At least it had a good reason to be making so much noise.

The driver of the ambulance waved wildly at cars to get out of the way. Either that or he'd just realized there was a bumblebee in the cab. Hopefully the latter. It had far less disturbing implications.

Where did the ambulance driver expect the cars in front of him to go? A few tried to nose forward. There was no give. And the sidewalk was awash with with gawkers and lookie-loos. So the curb was hardly an option.

Still, the ambulance driver flailed and the siren blared. Either he didn't understand how stuck he was...or it was *so imperative* that he get where he was going that he couldn't countenance sitting still. Doing nothing.

Jairzinho shuddered. Threw a glance over his shoulder.

Nothing to see. Just a river of red taillights and the skyline of downtown Manhattan. Both punched into a cloudless, fast-maturing dawn.

Another shudder. Then a stumble.

Jairzinho tripped over something squeaky. Stumbled into the intersection. Landed hard on the hood of a Lexus. Good thing nobody was moving. That could have been bad.

Speaking of bad:

- 5 -

Sheriff positutely, absotively *loved* getting stepped on! It was one of his most *favorite* things about being so small!

Yeah, the first bit always hurt. When their foot slammed into his flank, or sometimes his head. That hurt. And then when they were dancing around sometimes they'd accidentally squash on his tail, or his paw. That made him ouchie, big time.

But then here was the trick that he discovered! As long as he yelped his loudest most *yelpiest* yelp, the human would jump up way fast and start petting poor little Sheriff! And they would say his name over and over! Sheriff Sheriff Sheriff!

Boy oh *boy* was that something to wag about or *what?!*

Sheriff did his own little dance and he went *tap tap tap* until he was sitting and making his eyes just as big as any pup's eyes had ever gone in the whole wide world, and then…nobody petted him.

The heck?

The Babble Man was done with his dance, only instead of petting poor Sheriff he was Babbling at a Person who got out of his rolybob. Person babbled at The Babble Man, which just went to show that Person had never met The Babble Man, because The Babble Man? He could babble *well* loud. Which he did.

Sheriff looked to Person, who was making his arms big up in the air.

Sheriff looked to Babble Man, and he was flapping his like a bird. Only except he had the leashes in his hand so he was kind of, of *dringling* everybody's necks with them. Sheriff looked at Ladybug and she looked confused like Sheriff's heart felt, so at least he had a friend! That was almost as good as getting petted!

Sheriff looked back at Person. Now he was spinning his arms around and around in BIG circles! Sheriff wagged his tail about that! Because it was almost like a game! The game was called Watch My Arms Spin Around And Around In Big Circles! Sheriff was winning! *Everybody* won! Those were Sheriff's favorite kinds of games!

Kelso kept trying to cross under Babble Man's legs! And Misha kept poking him in the side!

Why had Sheriff ever stopped wagging?! Everybody was still playing games! Playtime had never ended!

So Sheriff darted between The Babble Man's legs! And he wagged at Person so that Person would know how much Sheriff loved his game! Which was how big his arms had been in the air and then maybe even *more!*

Person pointed at Sheriff and started barking, very loudly. He then barked at all the other dogs. And then the Babble Man.

Sheriff hadn't seen people do that before. It was very scary. He was used to his old human friends making angry noises sometimes. But new friends never yelled at Sheriff. Especially when he was wagging at them.

Then The Babble Man made a sneezing noise, grabbed up the leashes and walked. Person made more angry barks. Then he got back in his rolybob and then *that* started barking again. It was a bad sound. The whole world was bad sounds today. They were scary. Sheriff didn't like them.

Which was something to wag about! Usually Sheriff liked everything, but today he didn't like *anything*, which was different! And different was new and new was good and good was fun and fun was wag wag wag! Right?

Right?

Sheriff darted between The Babble Man's legs again!

The Babble Man pulled on Sheriff's neck. Hard. And he barked "NO". That was not Sheriff's favorite word. Sheriff just looked at him while they walked.

Then Sheriff realized he wasn't wagging. That didn't usually happen. Usually the wagging happened or didn't happen, all by itself.

So…that was different? Worth wagging about?

Sheriff wagged his tail. And it was nice for a bit!

Then The Babble Man looked down at him and babbled again and it sounded like

- 6 -

"*...make me look* stupid. Come on, buddy." Jairzinho tried to be calm. But his pulse kept pounding. Few things keyed him up like Arguing With Strangers.

He Argued With Strangers here a lot more than he used to back in California. Maybe the dogs gave him the freedom to follow his heart into a dark alley. After all, who was going to take a swing at a guy up to his ankles in puppies?

Or maybe this was just a cute way to reframe a troubling trend.

Seventh Ave reached around the slight eastward tilt above West 11th. Still gridlock to the horizon. All the way uptown. Dozens and dozens of blocks.

Jesus. Jairzinho slowed down. He was in a hurry, yeah. But he couldn't help but gawk. What a jam. What a goddamned jam. The parking in Manhattan had never been so good.

Meatball lunged towards the street. Jairzinho yanked her back.

His phone buzzed. Like there was a flash flood or an Amber Alert. One person's misfortune intruding into everyone else's life. He ignored it. As always. He also ignored the buzzing of everybody else's phone around him. As always.

He kept walking. It took him ages to thread the dogs across West 14th. The cars were packed so tight. Why did people scoot right up to the bumper? How the hell was that supposed to help anything?

A few people jumped out of their cars and shouted "Hi puppies!" Even in this fucking mess, the *Hi Puppies* people were out. One brave soul approached and asked Jairzinho if he could pet his dogs. While Jairzinho was in the middle of trying to drag Barmit out from underneath a low-rider. That brave soul/silly son of a bitch had no concept of how near he'd come to getting popped in the nose. Jairzinho sure as hell wasn't about to be deterred from violence by his puppies.

But he just said "NO" (and ignored that brave silly son of a soul calling him a "piece of shit") and pulled Barmit out. She dug in. Her nails scraped along the macadam. Loud enough to hear over the honking, the buzzing. It couldn't have been comfortable for Barmit.

Some of the drivers were climbing out of their cars. Clambering on top and squinting southward. Other bystanders on the street asked what they saw. Nothing valuable to report. Just shrugging and head-scratching.

Meatball bolted for the curb again. Jairzinho snapped her leash and dragged her back into line. "The fuck is your problem?" he shouted at her.

No one on the curb so much as looked at Jairzinho. Usually when he yelled at the dogs, he got a few sideways glances. Not today. Everyone was looking at the street. At their phone. At each other.

People laid off their horns. Like there was some city-wide signal. For a moment Jairzinho could hear horns crying out way uptown. Echoing through the canyon of Seventh. Then they died out. All that was left was idling engines. And screaming phones.

Manhattan was something resembling quiet. Far from silent. Certainly more hushed than it had been since the eighteenth century though. Like the island had just been told an off-color joke at a party, but didn't know the teller well enough to say anything.

Meatball lunged for the street.

"FUCKING CHRIST," Jairzinho shouted as he

- 7 -

hauled her back. "NO," The Liberator thundered. Meatball gave him [that dog's best frickin' stink eye.]

[That dog'd gotta poop for half the walk. Yeah, she'd already pooped once. So what? That dog *always* pooped *twice*. How's that gonna be a No all of a sudden? Frankly, The Liberator was bein' the frickin' No. What did he have against poop all of a sudden, huh? Seemed like he could hardly get enough of it just a few minutes ago.]

[That dog's guttyworks were near to frickin' *bustin'*. Felt like she'd gobbled down a chipmunk while it was still kickin'. Which, damn, she knew what the feel was like since that dog was] Meatball. Meatball felt that way.

Gah! Dissociation wasn't cutting it. Meatball really *really* needed to go. But The Liberator wasn't letting her excuse her-self to the curb, which was where she was *supposed* to go. Where she *always* went. What was [that dog gonna do, pinch one off in the middle of the frickin' sidewalk? She wasn't a frickin' *animal!*]

This was typical of The Liberator. Grant the illusion of freedom, only to impose his own strictures. What governed the times when Mea...when [that dog could and ain't-so-could drop horse apples? Huh? What was the big idea? Weren't logic. It was The Liberator and his frickin' whims!]

[That d...] *Meatball* respected The Liberator. He did so much for her. Showed her so much. Gave her food to boot.

That said: she also really had to poop. And since The Liberator gave Meatball food, and poop was food that wanted its own freedom, Meatball's having to poop was basically The Liberator's fault, wasn't it? Which meant The Liberator and his whims could go visit the farm upstate, didn't it?

[That dog] tried again for the curb. *ACK!* Foiled, with a vengeance! This time The Liberator

- 8 -

pulled back on Meatball's leash hard enough to lift her front paws off the ground.

But Jairzinho was as surprised as Meatball herself must have been that he didn't scream at her. Didn't get in her face. It wasn't just his hands that operated without thinking, after all.

Which was why his surprise was only dimly appreciable, even to him. Because he wasn't looking at Meatball. Hadn't been thinking about her.

He was looking directly at the center of the intersection between Seventh and West 15th. The lively, dead center.

It was impossible to say for certain, what with all the cars and pedestrians. But it looked a little bit like the pavement was...expanding? Engorging?

Breathing?

The phones buzzed. Same as they had for the past several minutes. But that noise somehow seemed to grow more shrill as the street itself found Pranayama.

Only not quite. There was no exhale. The pavement only drew breath. In in in. Or so it appeared. Because Jairzinho was losing his mind. Clearly. Streets didn't breathe. That was dumb.

The people standing between the cars in the intersection mumbled and stepped off towards the street corners.

So Jairzinho wasn't going crazy.

That was much, much scarier.

He tightened up on the leashes. Instinctively pulling the dogs backwards. So they'd be behind him.

They didn't get it. They bumped and bungled into each other. But didn't actually go anywhere.

Right. They were terrible with abstract direction. Unless Jairzinho led, they never knew what he was trying to tell them.

So he stepped backwards. They got the idea.

He took another step backwards. Bumped into somebody. They didn't move. He didn't ask them to.

Through panting diesel: reports from downtown. From the Financial District. Muted, playful. Unmistakably sinister. *Krakrakra*. Like somebody trying to open a bag of funyuns at a funeral.

Nobody spoke up here on West 15th. Still. Maybe nobody knew what to say. Jairzinho sure didn't. Mostly because he knew what the only thing to say was. It was a question nobody wanted to ask. Because everybody knew the answer.

Jairzinho watched the people around him shifting their weight from foot to foot. Folding their arms. Conferring quietly with close friends.

A loud, guttural *wwhhhOOOOM* swept through the intersection.

Everybody flinched together.

A physical shockwave ripped through in its echo.

It shoved Jairzinho. Gentle but firm. He shifted his feet to keep his balance.

"Okay," Jairzinho whispered. He felt the dogs…well, he felt the *leashes* doing something. But he couldn't be sure what. He was inexplicably transfixed by a young girl on the opposite corner. Because of her sunny yellow dress. It was billowing.

There was no wind today. That was so unusual. Seventh was a veritable wind tunnel. But today was perfectly still.

And the girl's dress was billowing.

The dogs at Jairzinho's feet jostled. Astrid whimpered. Ducky snorted. Ladybug was…trying to howl? Hard to tell. She sounded like a harmonica full of macaroni and cheese.

"Easy everybody," Jairzinho told himself. "Eeeeaaaaaasssss-yyyy."

And then the intersection exploded.

- 9 -

Wheeeeeeeee! Finally, for the first time in millennia, Boo found something that moved at his pace.

For a while everything had been boring and so so *so* slow and they were walking down the street and nothing was exciting and everything was boring Meatball would run for the drop-off to the Forbidden Zone and that was basically the closest thing that happened to exciting and when the Slowman tripped over Sheriff that was kind of interesting but mostly it was boring and then they were walking and the only thing that was different from usual was this was a really *loud* slow and then the Forbidden Zone started growing. Really fast.

Wheeeeeeeee!

The car in the center of the Forbidden Zone launched straight upward, like a startled cat! Yippee! The cars near the drop-offs tucked and rolled any which way got them to the side quickest! Ass over end or the other way around. Whichever way was *quickest!* Boo watched as the faces of those trapped inside the cars morphed way way way too slowly into scolding grimaces or like they were screaming really loud only there was no way anybody could hear anything over the excitement and why would they want to it was all so exciting and *fast!* One guy who had climbed onto his car had gotten launched through the air by the ground as it was growing bigger bigger bigger. His trajectory was clear enough – he was going to hit one of those light-suspending bars, neck first. Probably gonna hurt, that was. Boo didn't like seeing hurt. So he looked elsewhere. Which he probably would have done anyway. There was so very much to see!

The asphalt kept expanding, like it had eaten a great big meal and was *still* eating. Still! It really did look like it was liable to burst at any second. Boo had never known the Forbidden Zone was so flexible. He'd only known it as a rock-solid searer of paws. Just goes to show, huh?

One of the cars spinning through the air connected with a person. Ouch! The person gave it a crooked hug and then rolled with it. They did not look delighted by this development.

The big big belly stopped growing. Finally full? Maybe not. It didn't burst but it did do the opposite: it collapsed with a satisfied sigh. But where had th-

Boo swung his head around. Back the way they had come there was all kinds of excitement sort of like what was happening in front of him, only more.

Back there the entire *street* was already collapsed. That was where the collapse in front of Boo had come from. Come on *really* quick. Neat!

So gradually as to be almost unnoticeable and therefore *boring*, Boo felt his collar tightening.

Back at this bit of the Forbidden Zone that had gone up up and was now going down down, cars were bonking back on to the ground. The street seemed like it had been pretty pleased about not having any cars on it though, so it collapsed even *faster.* Then the ground around *that* ground thought it liked the look of that, so then *that* collapsed. So the hole widened, and swallowed up a bunch more cars and people.

Oooh, what was *that?* At the bottom of the hole there was a little winking light. It danced really fast. Hello, light! Boo wagged his tail as the light yawned and stretched, then reached its paws up up up through rock and people to as high as Boo was on the street!

Then the paws disappeared. That was too bad, but it had been a *very* interesting light while it was there.

More cars and people were falling to the ground. Still fast, still interesting, but Boo had to admit he was getting kind of b-

WOAH! The light was back! Like, *really* back! It was growing and growing and *growing!* Really fast! It was hot, too!

Too hot.

And then Boo's collar finished tightening and he was flying, all four paws pointed to the sky.

He felt his tongue flapping and flopping in the air. The air was *really* hot! Not a nice hot!

Craning his neck, he checked on his friends. They were all flying, even the Slowman, who had never struck Boo as the flying type.

Everyone around them was flying too. Except for that one guy who had hit against the pole with his neck.

Okay, so maybe the air hurt. It was hot and sharp and itchy. Not ideal, sure. But how often did the world run at Boo's pace? Not often!

This was cause for celebration, and for gratitude!

Boo released a streamer of urine. It glittered in a sharply descending arc. His greatest work yet! It made him think, though — he was *also* flying on a trajectory that was gonna end up being *down*. He only hoped that they landed on something

- 10 -

CRUNCH.

Jairzinho gasped. Realized that hadn't been *his* body crunching. It had been the body of the person he'd landed on. Or maybe one of the three *other* people between Jairzinho and the rack of CitiBikes.

He looked at his Giants. Sprawled all around him. They'd landed almost exclusively in wince-inducing positions. Except Barmit. She'd somehow landed on her feet.

Feeling cross-eyed, Jairzinho tried to look back towards the intersection. Nothing to see. Just a slash of smoke running from 15th down to…maybe 12th, but definitely 13th.

A bomb in the 14th street stop. It must have been.

Car alarms bleating. People screaming. A fire Jairzinho could hear and smell but not see. Where there was smoke though. Haha.

Dogs barking whining howling. *His* dogs. His Giants.

And the ringing ringing ringing of his ears.

It had been so quiet here just a second ago. Relatively speaking. He'd just thought how quiet it had been. Just a second ago.

There was no way that could be true.

Jairzinho felt hands trying to lift him. Hands from below. They were rough. Not helpful.

"Relax!" he shouted.

"GETOFFME!" the hands shouted back.

"I've got dogs here!" Jairzinho looked down at his hands. Yes. He *did* have dogs. Somehow he'd kept hold of the leashes through the blast.

He dropped them. The carabiner system would keep them attached to him. That was why he kitted himself out with the damn thing every day. Hands-free, if the need arose. Obviously this wasn't the need he'd imagined arising. But arose it had.

So he let go. It felt wrong. But he did it.

He tried to climb off the human dogpile without hurting whoever was groaning beneath him. The bikes shifted. So did everybody atop them. The groaning redoubled.

The guy under him shoved Jairzinho the rest of the way to his feet. So a little bit helpful after all.

Jairzinho stumbled on the landing. The leashes strained against his belt. He nearly stumbled backwards again.

Regaining balance came at a cost. His left trap spasmed. His neck muscles clenched. One of his ribs tickled him from the inside. Dabs of moisture spread on his low back.

He wheeled around to really let the guy under him have it. The guy who'd pushed him.

The guy had to have been about eighty years old.

The guy Jairzinho had crunched.

"Holy shit," Jairzinho said. "Oh my god. I'm so sorry."

The old guy wasn't listening though. He was shaking the younger woman next to him. Younger being relative. The woman *also* being a relative, probably. His granddaughter? Someone he loved, it seemed. He was shouting for her to wake up. She wasn't listening.

What if he had landed on…

"Oh Jesus…" Jairzinho put his hands to his mouth. "Oh Jesus Christ. I'm s-"

Jairzinho stumbled. Was pulled.

Astrid had taken her leash in her mouth and was using it to pull Jairzinho away from the demolished intersection.

"Uh," was all Jairzinho could say. "Uh. Uh." He felt wet on the tops of his fingers. The fingers still plastered across his mouth. He shook his head.

Astrid pulled.

"Uh."

He looked back to the guy on the pile.

The guy was hugging the younger woman. He was just whispering now. She still wasn't listening.

The people underneath them were screaming. Clawing their way out from under with desperate, crooked fingers.

Jairzinho took his hands off of his face. They were covered in soot. Except for a few clean streaks.

And the blood. His blood? Who knew?

Astrid pulled.

Jairzinho took the leashes in his hands.

His hands took over.

Jairzinho's hands pulled the dazed and dusty Giants away from Seventh Ave, along 15th. He walked about five or six yards. In that distance he saw: a kid who had been blown clean

93

in half. A man missing a third of his jaw, trying to calm down his wailing son. Barmit lapping up blood from a spre-

"HEY," his hands snapped. They reeled Barmit in. She looked like a clot. None of the viscera seemed to be hers. And thus: it was not a problem. Not right now.

Sheriff scrambled. He didn't look like he was doing it to be cute this time.

Kelso and Ducky tugged. They didn't take the leashes in their mouths like Astrid had. They were just choking themselves. Trying to run.

Ladybug screamed. Not barked. Not howled. *Screamed.*

Misha bopped the heads of everybody she could reach. One by one. Sheriff – bop. Ducky – bop. Meatball – bop. She staggered backwards as Meatball snapped at her.

Misha turned and looked at Jairzinho.

As if to say…one at a time. Take things one at a time.

Okay. Uh. Okay. Jairzinho, not his hands but *him,* he told the Giants to "sit". Calm as he could. Meatball already had been. Sitting. Astrid immediately dropped her leash and sat. Boo, Kelso, Sheriff, and Misha joined them. Barmit was always halfway between sitting and standing, so that was fine. That left the screaming Ladybug and the snorting Ducky.

Jairzinho grabbed their leashes and *tugged.* They sat.

The world was fury but one at a time.

Jairzinho took a knee and checked the dogs, one at a time. Soot rode beads of sweat into his eyes. He wiped it away.

His hands trembled as he lifted their paws, one at a time. Someone running past had a purse that smacked Jairzinho in the head. He blinked and ignored it.

Once or twice a phlegmy sob escaped him, often as he rose to a half-crouch to inspect the back halves of the dogs' bodies,

94

one at a time. A secondary explosion from the cratered inter-section shattered the windshield of a car. Jairzinho flinched and let it go.

Astonishingly, they all seemed to have escaped with fairly minimal injury. Misha's right paw curled in the air – something lodged in the pad. She wasn't whimpering though. Which made it all the more amazing that she'd gone around and bopped her buddies the way she had.

Some of the Giants were panting, cute little tongues hanging from big dumb smiles. That was a byproduct of artificial selec-tion, Jairzinho knew. Dog smiles didn't signify the same things as human smiles. But it was impossible not to see them that way.

Sheriff, god love him, was wagging his tail.

Ladybug had the right idea. The screaming had subsided, but she kept on with a baleful keening. More guttural than anything Jairzinho had ever heard from her.

Scenes from Jairzinho's peripheral vision: an old woman lay-ing flat on her back in a blasted-out sidewalk divot, a Nissan Sentra pinning her to the ground. "I love him," she kept saying, completely dispassionate. "I love him."

A young girl sitting between two corpses, an eye dangling from its socket by a pink stalk. She cradled it in her palm. Blood-cut tears poured from the hollow. Onto her yellow dress.

A couple, dusted but unharmed. Trying to start a daisy chain to rescue those trapped in the crater.

And here sat Jairzinho Navias. With nine smiling dogs strap-ped to his waist. Except they weren't actually smiling. They just looked that way. Because that was how they'd been selected.

95

"I love him," the old woman repeated. More and more quietly each time. "I love him."

Tap tap tap. Somebody checking a hot mic, hooked up to a weak PA system. *Tap tap tap.*

Tap tap tap tap tap.

Tatatatatatap.

Jairzinho didn't recognize the sound. And then people started screaming. Then he recognized it. From the movies.

Embarrassing, that it took the screaming. But in his defense, he'd never heard real live gunfire before.

runnies

- 1 -

Jairzinho realized it was gunfire at the same moment as the man across the street. He and Jairzinho looked at each other. Made eye contact.

The man's head burst like an overcooked Hot Pocket. Pink mist hung where his face had been. Even as the body fell.

Jairzinho just stared. Stared at the spectral head. Floating in the air. The spirit of stray bullets. And bad luck.

Astrid pulled on her leash.

Someone bumped into Jairzinho. Knocked him down. They were running. Running away from Seventh.

Where the gunfire was coming from.

They were coming in to pick off the survivors.

They? They *who?*

What the fuck was going on?

A guy tripped over Sheriff. Not watching where he was going. Sheriff yelped. The guy got up and kept running.

Someone from a window overlooking the street was scream-ing words. Jairzinho couldn't understand what they were. Oth-er than words.

A young woman barreling past the Giants paused long enough to wheeze "Hi Puppies!"

Jairzinho didn't see who knocked him flat on his ass. It could have been anybody. There were so many people.

Tatatatatatap.

He heaved himself to his feet. Gripped the leashes. Spun his dogs in a giant 180.

Tried to, anyway. The dogs just jostled and bonked into each other. They didn't get it. Just like backing up without being shown how.

"TURN," Jairzinho explained, "GODDAMN YOU!"

Some ambitious dickhead tried to jump over the dogs as he ran from Seventh. Got himself tangled in the web of leashes. Crashed to the ground. Pulled Jairzinho off-balance. Terrified the dogs.

"Dickhead!" Jairzinho screamed at him. He helped untangle the guy. Considered punching him in the head. Managed to not do that. "Goddamnit!"

The dickhead untangled himself and kept running.

Enough standing. Jairzinho needed to move. He forced the dogs to about-face. Joined the panicked Westward charge. He was in the very back now. Vulnerable. So he ran.

Tried to, anyway.

Here was something he hadn't thought about in a while. Jair-zinho covered about fifteen miles per day walking dogs. He'd convinced himself that this constituted exercise. That it was good enough to justify his staying as far away from treadmills as possible.

Which meant it had been…quite some time since he'd moved much faster than a brisk trot. About a year and a half, come to think of it.

He very much *had* to think of it now that his brain was telling his legs to pump as fast and hard as they could. They followed those orders spectacularly. Unfortunately they pumped with little regard to forward locomotion. If only speed were correlated to knee height. He'd be in Brooklyn in no time.

Had he forgotten how to run?

Boo and Sheriff sprinted out ahead of Jairzinho, pulling and wagging. Ducky ran, but tried to juke towards Ladybug, even now. Astrid made an oddly poignant attempt to match pace with Jairzinho. Misha, limping with one paw held high, still ran better than the man holding her leash.

But Barmit, Ladybug, Kelso, and Meatball were all even less prepared for physical exertion than their walker. They anchored themselves in place, gasping and panting. Preemptively exhausted. Even if Jairzinho had been able to run, they would have held him back.

So actually it was *their* fault that Jairzinho couldn't run.

"Come on," he called to his Giants in a trembling voice. He slowed the speed-demons in the group to a walking pace. Led them towards Eighth Avenue, as orderly as possible.

The *tatatatatap* behind him turned plosive.

PAPAPAPA.

Bullets screamed past. Near enough to Jairzinho's head to heat his cheeks.

"AAAAH!" Jairzinho's lizard brain screamed.

Gunfire ripped up the street. Little geysers of dust, drawing a straight line towards a man running for his life. Not realizing how little running he had left to do.

Jairzinho shouted at him, a single meaningless syllable. He wanted to tell him to juke hard to either side. But his admonition was no match for ammunition.

The man's back unzipped from the bottom. He thrashed a few times and fell.

Jairzinho wanted to scream. But he didn't have any noises left to make. They'd already proven useless.

He swung his head around towards Seventh.

Two gunmen. One had pried open the door of an overturned car, and was...helping the people trapped inside?

The other was drawing a bead on Jairzinho. That made more sense.

Jairzinho followed his own advice and juked hard to the left. Choking up on the leashes, he curled behind a parked car and pulled the dogs in as close as he could. Not a moment too soon. Another lead conga shimmied through the space he'd just been filling.

A kid slowed just a hair to take in Jairzinho cowering with his Giants. "RUN!" Jairzinho screamed at him. But the kid just wanted to take in the dogs. Which he did, along with five high-caliber rounds that sent him crashing into a recycling bin.

Sheriff was still wagging his fucking tail.

This was a dead end, sitting behind a car like this. Jairzinho had slid himself into a trap. Behind a Westmore Electric.

Was a battery-powered car more or less likely to explode when shot?

Time to move.

He assessed his options: rejoin the human flow and keep running towards Eighth Ave, or duck into that Laundromat a third of the way up the block and hope there was a back door. Then h-

Something above Jairiznho shattered. Glass tinkled onto the sidewalk right in front of him.

He looked up. Saw the long barrel of a rifle sliding out of a third story window.

How many of these people were there?

CRACK. The shot from the long barrel was confident enough to stand alone. Jairzinho tried to pull the Giants in tighter. He felt Ducky fidgeting as he drew closer to Ladybug. Heard Kelso grumbling as he entered Meatball's orbit.

RAKAKAKA. The gunman on the other side of the sreet stopped firing and pointed to the window above Jairznho. "There!" he cried.

So…a citizen up there had a gun of their own, and was firing on the gunmen. Fighting back! This was a welcome diversion. It was also the most terrifying thing to have happened thus far.

Was this how things finally fall apart?

Misha barked right in Jairzinho's face.

Jairzinho flinched. Misha didn't usually bark.

One at a time.

"Good point," he said to her. "Let's go!"

He pushed himself up. Grabbed the leashes tight. Stopped dead in his tracks.

Everybody who had just run *that-a-way* was now charging back *this-a-way*. Jairzinho had exactly three seconds to wonder why before he found out.

A long green snout rounded the corner off Eighth. The rest of the behemoth was close behind.

A tank rolled off the battlefield at Kursk and onto West 15th Street. Except somebody had spraypainted "AMERCA FIRST" on it. Too bad they hadn't left enough room to slip the "I" back into "AMERICA". It hovered just above the rest of the word.

Jairzinho stood hypnotized by that beautiful button of idiocy.

Then the tank rode up and over the cars parked in the narrow shoulders. Crushing and crunching vehicles just like the one Jairzinho had been hidden behind.

He laughed. He couldn't help it. Where the fuck had these dipshits been hiding a tank? Was it just a matter of time before the Jaegers showed up?

Laughter later: now, the turret atop the tank grew a trigger-man, who did what his title implied.

A hail of bullets sliced down the back of the human stampede. Which had, until very recently, been the front. They must have imagined themselves to be home free, those people now getting pulped by light artillery.

More cartoon zips and whistles.

Time to go.

Where?

The Laundromat. Where the fuck…

It was behind him. He'd run past it. Either that or geography was broken. So that was how they got the tank in. Ha, ha.

How *they* got it in? All together now…they *who?*

One at a time.

Jairzinho turned his dogs again. Choking up on the leashes and leading with his hips. He leaned forward at an Everest-climbing angle. Drove his feet into the ground. One and the other and the other. Some of the dogs trotted with him. Others dragged. He could guess which were which. But he didn't want to turn around.

Bullets flew in every direction. Order had collapsed. All was *CRACK* and *RAKAKAKA* and *PAPAPAPA* and screaming and crying and stomping.

Jairzinho felt like he'd been running for one hundred years. He hadn't gotten one yard from his hiding spot behind the car.

The carabiner belt crushed his crotch. Somebody was digging in! Who the fuck was

taking a stand. Was she scared? Of course she was. But this carnival of, of...*contempt* being shown to Breakfast, to the Ritual...it was innnnntolllllerable!

Which meant Misha had a decision to make. She could sit (er, run) idly by while the Big Box put the final clip on the kibble hutch for today's Breakfast...or she could take a stand. Because what if this was a test? What if the Breakfast Man was challenging her commitment to the Ritual? To Him?

To her friends?

It was that final thought which gave Misha the courage to take her stand. To be fair, Breakfast probably would have been a strong enough motivator on its own. It just might have taken another second or two of courage-screwing.

Misha braced for her neck to hurt, then planted her paws and dropped her front legs.

The Breakfast Man stumbled.

Misha pulled as hard as she could, choking herself in the process. But she would do what was necessary. To preserve the Ritual. To see the Rites through to completion. To testify to her belief in Breakfast.

To help her friends.

She turned herself fully around, dropped into a defensive crouch and *bark bark bark barked* at the Big Box. The little man at the top was scared of Misha. The Big Box kept coming but the little man hid behind a toy! Misha *bark bark bark barked* as the Big Box got closer and closer, which was scary but it was for Breakfast! It was getting *really* close now, and the little guy was pointing his toy at Misha, and then he *baaaaarked* back and

"GODDAMNIT!" Jairzinho screamed. "COME ON!"

He turned to see who was about to get a personalized curse.

Misha dragged herself forward with a single functioning paw.

Along the street.

And she was bleeding. A lot.

She must have been shot at least three times.

None of the other Giants had been hit. And the piece of shit in the turret had turned his attention back to the people running east.

Jairzinho fell to his knees. Swung the backpack off his back. He wanted to say something to Misha. Tell her there was a doggy first aid kit in here. Buried under all this *shit*. Tell her she would be okay.

But he couldn't speak. He could only wring husky sobs from his clenched, dry throat.

He reached into the backpack full of stupid *bullshit*. Pulled out the Marenghi novel he'd been meaning to start for about a year now (and never would) and threw it to the side. Tossed his thermos full of shitty K-cup coffee onto the pavement. He... carefully removed the lunch Tia had made him, and transferred it immediately back into a smaller pocket.

He dug and rummaged and searched and Jesus Christ where the fuck *was* it?!

The tank on one side, the people on the other. And no god-damned...first aid...fucking...*KIT!*

He dug and dug and so failed to notice

- 2 -

that this was all Barmit's fault. Probably. Kelso wasn't totally sure about that, but this wasn't the sort of thing that had ever happened before Barmit showed up. These packs of slathering humans, the scary ones with the snapping sticks, had Kelso ever seen them before? Of course not. And now Misha was leaking, and The Walker was all out of sorts about it. What, was he dumb all of a sudden? Dogs leaked every day. The Walker helped them *get* to the places they were allowed to leak. The only difference now was that Misha was leaking out of new holes.

Kelso glanced over at Barmit. She was covered in wet from the wrong hole.

Oh no!

Instinctively, he licked her. To make sure she was okay.

She *was*, because it wasn't her wet that she was covered in.

Barmit stared at Kelso, matted with blood save a tongue-sized streak across her face. She blinked.

Kelso blinked back. He dropped his head and turned away. He didn't even *care* about was Barmit okay or not. That was so weird that he'd done that. Who cared? He didn't. Nobody cared. Didn't even matter now!

Preoccupied with how much he *didn't* care about Barmit, who was *definitely* at fault for all of the noises that were happening anyway, Kelso locked eyes with Ladybug.

She must have seen him in peripheral. She rolled her soggy little peepers towards him.

He didn't like what he saw in them. Not that he knew what it was – he just knew he really, *really* didn't like it.

Ladybug turned towards the rest of the dogs, and Kelso followed her gaze. Everybody seemed pretty antsy. Probably natural, since The Walker wasn't paying attention to them.

Woah hey now, The Walker wasn't paying attention! They could do whatever they wanted!

So what did Kelso want to do? Kelso wanted to...

Bite Meatball. Why? Because the Walker wasn't paying attention!

But why bite Meatball?

Because why *not?*

Kelso spun his whole body around, crouched down and got *WHAPPED* on the head.

He barely had time to wonder what that was when he saw Astrid turning away from him, to put herself between Ladybug and an armycrawling Ducky.

Kelso glared at Astrid. So she imagined she was the new Walker, did she? She got to make the rules? What

- 3 -

the hell did he think he was gonna do with a first-aid kit once he found it? Misha had been *shot!* The most Jairzinho had ever done with this fucking kit was bandage a chipped toenail on Ducky. And that had been when there *wasn't* a goddamned *tank* barreling down on him, from the *one* side, and on the *other* a whole horde of…

Misha glanced up at him. Her heavy head trembling.

One at a time.

Okay. Good girl.

So what did he have? There was gauze. Non-adhesive wrapping. A little pair of scissors. That looked like a place to start.

There was a tube of antiseptic spooge, but that could wait until there wasn't a goddamned tank. One thing at a time.

Astrid barked. Slapped Jairzinho on the ear.

"HEY!" he snapped. He planted an open palm on her soft chest. Shoved her away as hard as he could.

Three gauze pads, would that be enough? One for each… wound? He pressed one into a quarter-sized bullet hole on Misha's left hip. Blood and pus oozed as he applied pressure.

Misha barked and tried to stand. Jairzinho looped his arm under her neck, half consolation and half restraint. "Easy baby, easy." Even over the bedlam around him, he heard his voice crack.

The pad was already soaked through. Useless. He only had ten pads total, and

Slap.

"ASTRID, NO."

Bark.

Jairzinho shook his head at Misha. Looked at the tank-driven stampede coming from the west. Looked at the gunmen to his right, still distracted by the guerilla fighter with the rifle. The one directly above Jairzinho.

And the Laundromat just ten yards away.

He slid his hands back towards Misha's head, seeding a thick stroke of red through her coat. "You gotta walk," he gasped. Her head was so heavy in his hands. So heavy. "Please, Misha. Please. We can't stay here."

She smiled her doggy smile at him. Her tongue rolled out the side of her mouth. It broke Jairzinho's heart. But even now, he couldn't help but smile back at it. "Come on!" he whispered. He rose to his feet.

Vrrrrrrrrr.

To his left, the turret of the tank swung towards his side of the street.

Misha rested her head back down on the curb. She stared up at Jairzinho the way she did when he was picking her up for her second walk on a scorcher of a day. *Don't make me go* eyes.

"Goddamnit." He stepped towards Misha. Tripped over Sheriff. The poor little guy yelped. "Goddamnit!" That wasn't what Sheriff yelped.

As Jairzinho was regaining his balance, Ducky made a lunge for Ladybug. The pug screamed and backed up into the street full of people running for their lives.

"No!" Jairzinho shouted.

Astrid leapt into the street first. Used her meaty head like a plow. Pushed Ladybug back onto the curb.

Even running for their lives, people avoided running in to Astrid. Gentle though she was, she could look mean. When she wanted to.

Jairzinho got a hold of Ducky's leash and pulled him back.

Meatball broke for the curb with all of her considerable bull-dog muscle. She dragged Jairzinho hip-first behind her.

Kelso lunged for Meatball. The latter snarled at the advance.

"STOP, GODDAMNIT!" Jairzinho bent down to separate the two.

Ducky charged Ladybug once again.

A pair of human legs leapt over Misha. A sneaker that looked like it was brand new kicked Jairzinho in the shoulder, knocking him onto his back.

He pushed himself up. That muscle in his neck seized again. The ache spreading like a rumor. "FUCK!"

Kukukukukuku.

The barrel of the tank clicked up up up, towards the concealed gunman in the apartment.

Directly above Jairzinho's head.

"MISHA! COME ON!" he screamed. He quit wrestling with the other dogs and focused on the golden retriever. One at a time.

One of the gunmen on the East side of the street opened fire on the returning flow of would-be survivors.

One shot popped a five-year-old's head open. His parents, each holding an arm as they ran, didn't notice.

Ducky humped Ladybug.

The door to the apartment behind Jairzinho swung open. Terrified tenants poured out as the tank's cannon clicked ever higher.

Meatball pooped, even as she snarled at Kelso.

Six men charged one of the gunmen, likely assuming that he couldn't get *all* of them. They were mistaken.

Barmit lapped up blood directly from Misha's wounds.

Jairzinho bent down. Wrapped his arms around and under Misha. Commanded himself to rise.

Someone shot him in the back.

He screamed. Misha fell from his arms.

He swung his hands over his head. Tried to, anyway. He looked at his chest.

No exit wound.

He felt his back as best he could.

No entry.

It was a muscle spasm. Not a gunshot. Just a muscle spasm.

Just looking at Misha's sixty pounds of almost-dead weight sent Jairzinho's shoulders and neck into further paroxysms.

So he wrapped the leash around his hand and pulled toward the Laundromat. Same result all the way around.

The tank stopped clicking.

Meatball stopped pooping.

Someone shouted from the open window above him.

Ducky wailed, thrusted.

Kelso snarled.

Jairzinho shoved them each away from the objects of their attention, and knelt down in front of Misha.

He stroked her face, his hands steadier than his vision. "I'm so sorry baby," he whispered as he unclipped the leash from her collar.

"You're a good girl," he told her. "You're such a good girl."

She smiled her doggy smile at him, and wagged as best she could because

- 4 -

she'd done it. She'd passed the test. That's what this had been. A test.

The Breakfast Man was trying to tell her that the Ritual could change. Misha had been too wrapped up in the specific

Rites — she'd lost sight of what mattered. What mattered wasn't peeing on the same corner, or walking in the right order.

It was about being Good. Being a Good Girl. That was the lesson that He wanted to teach her. Good Girls were the ones that got the Breakfast.

So if the street exploded, what was that to her? If angry people with noisy sticks were causing a ruckus, how did that touch her essential Goodness? And so, her mealtimes?

Yes, the toy on the Big Box had hurt her. A whole heck of a lot. But the pain was fleeting. Breakfast was eeeeeterrrrrrnnnn-aaaaaal!

The Breakfast Man stroked her face and told her she was Good, so Misha wagged her tail. Wagged at judgment passed down just before a full bowl. Here was an odd place for Breakfast, but The Breakfast Man worked in mysterious ways. Whence the yum-yums? Presumably from wherever The Breakfast Man was going now, as He stood and charged up the street. Dragging Misha's friends behind Him, like so many sacks of kibble. Mmmmm-MM!

She wondered why she couldn't go with her friends to get the Breakfast. Maybe for the same reason she couldn't stand up.

That was okay, though. The Breakfast Man pounded on a door because He needed to get Misha her Breakfast. Because she was a Good Girl.

She never once doubted this, even as He vanished through the door. Ladybug hung back just a moment, looking terribly upset. Then she got yanked through.

Then the door closed. That was okay too. Breakfast was a secret. There were still formalities to observe, stations Misha was unworthy to witness.

The thunderclap of the tank rattled her bones and burned her wounds, and still she did not doubt. The apartment above her sprang to life, roaring, belching fire and smoke, doing all the things a Good Girl would never do, and still she did not doubt. Four and a half stories' worth of brick and iron rained down on her. And still.

She could be patient, was her final thought. She was a Good Girl.

- 5 -

The WHAM *of the tank's* cannon rattled the building. The destruction of the apartment next door sucked the air out. Then caked the windows in dust.

Jairzinho was on the floor. Cold, sticky tile. He didn't remember sitting down. Couldn't remember which wall he had his back against. All he knew was that his hands were trembling. His dogs were doing dog stuff. He didn't know. He couldn't see them. He couldn't see anything.

He wiped his eyes. His hands shook so much he ended up bopping himself on the nose.

"You're alright," whispered the woman who'd opened the Laundromat door for him. Who'd saved his life. She patted him on the shoulder. It hurt. He didn't say so. "You're alright."

Jairzinho shook his head. Tried to make words with his language. Oops. No luck. Just honking, wheezing, gasping.

"Do you want some water?"

"I…" Jairzinho finally managed, "I lost one."

The woman stopped patting. "A dog?"

"Yeah. Misha. I lost Misha."

"Well…" the woman paused. Labored over the most tactful way to articulate an impossible thought. Settled on: "…eight to go!" Somebody else in the Laundromat whispered something to her. "In a good way," she added.

Well, yikes. But the thought had perspective buried in it.

One at a time. For Misha. One at a time.

Jairzinho used the wall to push himself back to his feet. It was one of the hardest things he'd ever done. He tilted his head clockwise – CRACK – and counterclockwise – cr-POP. He sighed without meaning to.

One at a time. Okay. What came first? He needed to get these dogs back down to the Edbrooke. Back to their homes. They were too much for him to handle right now. That was first. Get them home. So he could get home.

To Tia.

Jairzinho fished his phone out of his pocket. Pressed the buttons that weren't even buttons, they were just passing spots imagined onto an ever-changing screen…he pressed the made-up spaces to call her. When was the last time he'd called somebody on this thing? Not a business but a person?

Irrelevant. Focus on the new first thing.

"Hey buddy," said a guy in an unseasonable sweater. "You ain't gonna get who you wanna get."

Jairzinho was about to ask what the hell that meant. Then his phone hollered "-PEAT!" into his ear. Jairzinho started and dropped the device.

Ducky ran over to it. Snatched it up into his maw. Meatball charged him for it. Kelso leapt in.

Astrid bopped them all. There was a new Misha in town.

Jairzinho trembled. The way her head had felt in his hand, the terrible weight of it…a thin groan escaped him.

116

He focused on the phone. It was loud enough to hear through the roughhousing. Good. Jairzinho didn't have the strength to break them up again.

"STAY INSIDE AND YOU WILL BE SAFE!" a deep, nervous voice assured them from Ducky's mouth. Jairzinho stared down into the Frenchie's eyes. They looked...*mocking*.

Then Meatball snagged a corner of the phone. A tug-of-war began.

"Tell that to *those* poor schmucks," somebody murmured. They cocked their thumb towards the Laundromat wall nearest the tank-blasted apartment. Other people sheltering in the Laundromat said 'mm' and 'mhm'.

Ducky tilted his head. Turned back up to face Jairzinho again. "WE HAVE NO INTEREST IN ACTS OF AN AGGRESSIVE OR INQUISITIVE NATURE!" The pup's eyes grew wider. "SO JUST STAY OUT OF OUR WAY! IT'LL BE SAFEST FOR EVERYBODY!"

"Inquisitive?" someone asked.

Jairzinho bent down and snatched his phone from Ducky's mouth. "I'm pretty sure he means *a*cquisitive," he corrected the phone. Then he killed the call. "Probably bullshit." Astrid sat. Jairzinho smiled at her.

A kid with a 'Sarcastic Comment Loading' T-shirt planted his hands on his hips. "How do you know?"

Jairzinho didn't have the energy to respond. He didn't know. He didn't care. Who was doing this? Why were they doing it? None of that mattered to Jairzinho. Those weren't the One thing.

He missed Misha. Already. Was that weird? Probably. Too bad.

"So," asked a woman wearing her laundry-day sweatpants, "what do we do about it?"

Jairzinho looked around the Laundromat, at a group of people who were now inexplicably looking to *him* to answer that question. Like they were his Giants too. Like they were his responsibility.

Fuck that.

Jairzinho drew his eight charges towards the guy standing behind the counter. "Is there a back way out of here?"

"Aaah," replied the Laundromat employee, "yeah, but it's where we put our garbage."

Jairzinho blinked. "That's fine. How do I g-"

The employee pointed over his shoulder. "Just through here. Your phone said to stay inside though."

Jairzinho shook his leashes. "I gotta get rid of these guys, man."

"You wanna throw 'em in the garbage?"

"…"

The employee shifted his weight from the outer edge of one foot to the other. "…ha ha, that was a j-"

Jairzinho pointed towards the back. "I need a key to get through that door?"

"Ah, nope," he replied without pause. "Can I pet your dogs?"

Without another word, Jairzinho hauled his Giants through the, as it was labeled, *"Employee's Only"* door.

Throw them in the garbage, the guy had said. Ha. No. It was too soon for jokes. Or too late.

- 6 -

The door led to a hall led to another door. That door dump-
ed the Giants into a narrow rectangular alley. Four squat buildings sharing a patch of concrete. Big enough for *maybe* two cars
parked nose to nose. The lone, rusted folding chair bespoke
pretentions of courtyardhood.

The door behind them closed.

Jairzinho's Curbside Giants looked up at their leader, and he
down at them.

On the right: Astrid, Kelso, Barmit, Ladybug, Boo.

On the left: Ducky, Meatball, Sheriff.

Imbalanced.

He considered who to move over. Who he *could* move over,
without upsetting the temperamental teeter-totter.

He settled on Barmit. Because she was barely a dog to begin
with. More of a wind-up nightmare doll that only stared straight at the ground and walked. Or, apparently, drank blood.

Once he dropped these fucking dogs back at the Edbrooke,
he never wanted to see any of them ever again. He hated this
job. It was the most stressful, enraging, lonely, awful occupation imaginable. To be surrounded by people and have to think
of them all as obstacles. Because every human interaction
threatened to completely derail any order or momentum he'd
generated with the dogs. These fucking dogs. If he'd just quit
this bullshit job months ago, things would be so much better
with Tia. He'd have way less stress in his life. So things would
be much better with Tia. And he wouldn't be here. In a fucking
garbage alley. With other people's fucking *DOGS!*

Jairzinho caught himself wanting to kick each and every one of them in the face.

It would have been so easy.

Because they were all looking up at him. Sitting obediently and looking at him…*to* him.

Jairzinho threw his head back. Allowed himself a wail. One quality wail. It turned into a bit of a roar at the end. Couldn't be helped.

Distant gunshots crept their way into the alley. Or maybe they were just the echoes of gunshots.

Set into the western wall: a bright red mesh door. Just beyond it lay Eighth Avenue.

Here was the one thing. The one thing at a time.

He would take that South. Hope like hell that part of West 14th hadn't been hit too hard. Keep following Eighth until it hooked left and became Hudson. That would get him back down to Christopher. Back to the Edbrooke.

About eleven blocks.

Easy.

He walked up to the red door. So easy. He turned the knob. Just the easiest thing in the world. He hesitated. Easy peasy. What was *peasy*, anyway?

And then, he kept hesitating.

Wow. The easiest.

This was stupid. He needed to go. The longer he stood here, the emptier the streets would get. The emptier the streets were, the more he'd stand out to whoever had the guns. Even more than he was going to, with the dogs.

The guys with the guns clearly weren't shy about shooting at a fella ankle-deep in puppies.

Still, Jairzinho hesitated.

He turned back to the dogs. "We're all going to *walk*, right?"

Three cocked heads, six tongues, one wagging tail.

"Right? *Ladybug?* No dragging?"

Ladybug made no promises.

From above, the sky boomed and cracked. Or maybe that was all coming in from the sides. Or below. Or from inside the dogs. Who the fuck knew. Who cared.

Jairzinho sighed. He supposed he'd have to care. At least for a while. Until he got these idiots back to their people. So *they* could do the caring.

He didn't care for that at all. But there it was.

"Oh, shit." Jairzinho pulled out his phone. Still crack-free, despite the battle and the fall and the tugging. Good thing he'd splashed out for the pricey case.

Swipe that thought aside.

He opened up the bathroom report. Added W 15th between 7th and 8th, just after 9AM next to Misha's name. Cackling quietly and blinking at a painful clip, he added a poo for Meatball.

"Ok." He locked the phone. Put it in his pocket. "Ok."

The dogs looked up at him. He did not return their gaze.

So they looked to the door.

Jairzinho opened it.

THE EDBROOKE

- 1 -

How dreadful is the riddle posed by absence! O, but sweet and kindly Misha, dearest friend possessed of fairest fanny, far too soon has your perfume been snufféd out! Twas true that Ladybug was far from bloodhound; also true, one needn't be, to know a trail gone cold.

So how in Misha's name did they persist, or persevere? To trot like naught was known? Incredibly, though none among the pups evinced awareness as to Misha's fate...the Ferryman displayed despair consistent with some grasp of tragic incident, however feebly gripped. Unlikely though this seemed – for Ladybug knew well that Man was dull and unreflective, milky as an eye that time saw fit to blind – the Ferryman, he stank of salt and blood in ways surpassing simple fright. And how he rushed them home, so hasty Ladybug could hardly touch her paws to pavement!

Another bolt of lightning, this one red: the Ferryman had given Ladybug no chance to sniff her friend this morn. So how had Misha passed the day and night that none could know would be her last? Had she been blessed by pleasure, or at least by suff'ring spared? There was no way to know.

So where had Misha gone? It was a place t'which none could follow, nor whence souls so gone return.

Then how had Misha made the jaunt? By car? Ba *ha!* No likelier than paw was this.

But think not now of paws, nor pause! The Ferryman pulled ever onwards, heedless of the lives he held on leash. It was the work of wheezes worth a week's exertion just to stay from being dragged – but nothing shielded her from Boo, who in his endless frenzy failed to notice when the ground beneath his feet was fellow canine *being* ground to kibbles, yea, to bits!

Return to riddles, then, for fellow fleabags follow fancies free from fucking *ouch* Boo, watch where you tread!

Ahem…consider please, a simple stick, now thrown to chase. Of course twas not for Ladybug to fetch, for fetching sleep from midnight's talons poséd challenge t'which she seldom rose. Consider this for Misha, though, this fictive stick now thrown. Keep eyes aloft, admire as it spirals through the air; now witness Misha dashing after, keeping pace! The stick, she flies and flies, as Misha runs and runs. Forever onwards, never touching ground, the stick does soar. And so must Misha run and run, place paw and paw and paw, eternally towards the heavens must her gaze remain, forever flapping through the stillness will her tongue hang free. And free will Misha be, for what she chases, none have caught. For what she chases, none are *meant* to catch.

Consider please, a simple stick, not thrown to fetch but simply thrown. An image such as this did hey *hey WATCH IT!*

bbbLARGPH! spake Ladybug.

This reprimand she offered not to Boo, who 'pon her head did tread, but to the Ferryman, for roughly did he shunt her and her friends into a doorway set into an edifice that Ladybug had never seen! Now what on Earth were – but *soft*, you brutish lout! A second shunt! What options left did Ladybug possess, but gasping at the boorishness of Man (and also for air to breathe, but leave that to one side!).

Around the corner of the doorway, slow and redolent of fear, the Ferryman did peep and peer.

He sucked in air through tight-clenched teeth, and sharply snappéd back the leashes. And what choice had they, as dogs, but that of following the lead?

But Ladybug was well-equipped for small rebellions; what, one wonders, was a breath through scrunchéd nostrils drawn, if not rebellion 'gainst biology?

And thus the pug did peep and peer around the corner of the doorway; lo, by more than men could such a gesture be effected!

Look: there scooted by a car too big to be a car, and full of folks with sticks.

These sticks were not the sort one threw to fetch, nor threw at all. These sticks were not the sort that Misha chased into the endless night.

These sticks were just the sort by which poor Misha had *been* chased into that dark.

So this was why the Ferryman was so distraught! Of course. The barking sticks had chased poor Misha, poked her full of pouring holes. The Ferryman was being rough, but only that he might the rest of Ladybug's dear friends protect, from chasing sticks which into darkness led!

Good Man! Perhaps he credibly could be mistaken for a credit to his kind!

Assuming that his capabilities to his intentions could arise. O, how deeply did she hope that this the case could be. For Misha and her long-leg'd ilk, in chasing sticks unto eternity might entertainment yet be found. For gasping, wheezing, living, dying Ladybug?

T'would be Hell.

- 2 -

...ugh...they were running now...barmit hated it...

...they'd been standing for a while and she'd hated that... but now they were running...

...she hated that she was on the wrong side of mr. comeon...she hated being in misha's spot because she hated misha...just like she hated that misha wasn't here anymore...

...she hated that they weren't on their usual route...which she hated...she hated how loud everything had gotten...she hated how her feet had been hurting...but had since stopped hurting...she hated how hungry she was...she hated how thirsty she had been...until she drank the bodywater...

...about that.

...

...no bones about it...barmit hated the bodywater...it smelled and tasted like the jingly-janglies on mr. comeon's crotch strap...she'd only drunk it because it was there...and she'd been thirsty...

...it had sloshed down her throat like normal stupid boring awful water...but once it settled in her gut...

...it wasn't...

...well who cared what it wasn't...it was hardly settling now that they were sprinting down the streets...more loud stuff was happening and mr. comeon was screaming his own name again...like he thought life was anything other than complete shit...this was so pointless...a loud thing rolled down the road next to them...mr. comeon just screamed a lot...ugh, what a moron...

...ducky plowed into barmit as they took a turn...barmit hated ducky so much...like running...barmit hated ducky and running...and now both were happening...

...barmit was done with this...so she straightened her legs and dropped her weight...that usually ground things to a halt...

...she bounced along the pavement like...something stupid that she hated...and she remembered today wasn't a usual day...

...but bouncing got the bodywater churning...which barmit hated...but down in there it was still warm...still...laughing.

the bodywater laughed in her tummy, it giggled and gargled and goofed. barmit wasn't used to things that goofed. especially not inside of her. it was unlike anything she'd ever experienced. it wasn't the worst.

...er, no, she hated it...just not in quite her usual way... today wasn't a usual day after all...

129

- 3 -

Kelso thought his nose was playing tricks on him. He most certainly did. But then they had all crashed to a halt. So just before they leapt down a new street, because the one behind them was going *thkthk-thkthk*, he took three good whiffs. Just to be sure.

No trick. No trick at all, man. No way.

Barmit smelled different. Less…or more…well, she smelled a bit less like scolding and more like petting. Did that make sense? Yes it did. It did to Kelso.

Except it wasn't quite that big a leap. Not like from one opposite to the other. It was more of a *hint*. Like somebody put a dab of peanut butter in a bathtub full of awful soap smell. But when you're talking about Barmit, when Barmit's the one getting that little hint? That Barmit was suddenly anything other than as perfectly unhappy as she made everyone else? Hoo, boy. You're on a whole new world, just about.

Kelso broke into a full run to keep up with the Walker. Which was absurd, wasn't that absurd? The Walker was *running*. But it was also fun to run again. Even if whatever was happening on the walk today was pretty high stress, too high stress for Misha, which was probably why she'd peeled off back there… this was still a bit like playtime, wasn't it? How long had it been since Kelso had *played?* Since he'd really pumped his legs like this, let his ears flap in the breeze?

Ugh, right. Since Barmit.

He looked over and saw Barmit bouncing, stiff-legged, behind the running Walker. She looked like, what did she look like?

Like when Kelso's Family had their special party and then they tied loud cans to the back of their car. She looked like one of the cans.

So here was the thing. The thing was, since when was *bouncing down the street while the world screamed* the optimal state for Barmit? To make her even a teeny bit happier?

Like…since when had Barmit ever thrived in adversity? Barmit *was* adversity.

Was it because…Barmit wasn't on Kelso's side of the Walker anymore?

Oh, probably not. Almost definitely not. Not that Kelso would even *care* if that was it, he didn't even *like* Barmit, not at all. So if she was happier being *away* from him, all the way over *there*, who cared, right? Who cared?

…it didn't have something to do with Meatball, did it? Because Meatball was over there, and…

Ooooh, Kelso *seethed* at the mere possibility. He *hated* Meatball. Always had. Maybe it was her face. Or the way she walked. Who could say? But also who cared? It wasn't like you needed a good reason to trust your gut when you looked at a dog and thought *if I get the chance, I should bite her in the eyeballs.*

So if it was Meatball that had made a little green bud pop up through Barmit's cesspool soul…

Because it wasn't like the view on the Far Side of the Walker could be that different, right? So it must have been something about Meatball, that loathsome gristle-faced swine. Mustn't it have been? It must have been.

The Walker muscled them all into a narrow street. They had to really squeeze to get over these big slabs of concrete that *woah* were *really* hot to touch. Then they walked under a tree with slow fire in its canopy, and the Walker looked up.

Stopped paying attention.

So Kelso stuck his lower teeth out and charged at Meatball's eyes.

Meatball saw him coming and *lunged*. Like she'd been waiting for him.

Next thing Kelso knew, he was on his back. Looking up at the tree. He wriggled his way back onto his feet. Where was Meatball?

Underneath the Walker. He had her on her back. He was leaning on her with his palm. She was thrashing *hard*, but he wasn't letting her up. Ha! Served her right!

Kelso readied himself for another charge and *bop*.

He glared at Astrid.

She kept her paw halfway up, ready to *bop* again.

Kelso looked to Barmit. Just so *she* knew, that *he* knew that *she* was…uh, Meatball was making her happy or something?

Barmit wasn't looking back. She wasn't paying attention. She was, in fact, laying on her stomach, legs splayed in every direction, her face flat on the ground.

A terrible thought occurred to Kelso: what if, just hypothetically, not at all serious, not at all, but what if…it was something about not being near *him* that made Barmit happy? Well, not happy, but happ*ier*. As in, he'd always assumed Barmit had been making *him* miserable, but what if it was exactly the other way around?

No.

He remembered the happy times again. There had been happy times, when Kelso had had Family all to himself. Those times had ended when Barmit came. Therefore, Barmit had ended the happy times.

That settled it.

They were running again. Meatball was back on her feet, shooting glassy, cross-eyed glares Kelso's way. Whatever. Let her stare.

He had his eye on her too. His really sleek, powerful, aesthetically pleasing eye.

Kelso turned to look at Barmit and walked into a big blue mailbox.

- 4 -

DEAD ASS, BRAH, all this RUNNIN' was GASSIN' Ducky UP. Every TIME he JUMPED it SENT his BOYS, you know, his fuckin' JUNK, his big old NUTS, he JUMPED and they went WHAM right INTO his BELLY. Then they SNAPPED back DOWN real TAUT, OOOOOOH. WHAM and SNAP and WHAM and SNAP.

Shit was LIT. So LIT shit was goin' RED at the EDGES. HE could barely SEE because the whole WORLD was just like, NO WAY. WOAH. All RED.

SURE some BAD shit was GOIN' down. Besides DUCKY'S FETCHABLES, GET IT, his NARDS. WHAM and SNAP. ANYWAY, this BAD shit was ALL the LOUD cars and PEOPLE who were SCREAMIN'. Not SCREAMIN' like OH LOOK at the CUTE dog which was WHAT people USUALLY SCREAMED around DUCKY. These PEOPLE were SCREAMIN' like OH man I'm HAVIN' a BAD time. Which put DUCKY in a REFLECTIVE MOOD. Made him THINK about WHAT in LIFE really MATTERED.

Which was FUCKING. HARD G, BRAH. FUCKING-*GUH.*

FUCKING-*GUH* was like HUMPIN' except it was BET-
TER. DUCKY didn't REALIZE there WAS such a THING,
but THEN he SAW the WHOLE world gettin' FUCKED by
INVISIBLE stuff. IT was like MISHA. FIRST she was a
DOG, THEN she had HOLES in her BODY. And SOME-
THIN' about THAT really SPOKE to DUCKY. And IT said
YO BRAH YOU HEARD ABOUT FUCKING-*GUH* YET?

And so THEN while BAD man was PUTTIN' his FING-
ERS in MISHA'S new HOLES, DUCKY climbed UP on
LADYBUG JUST because it SEEMED like the THING to
DO. And YEAH he HUMPED. He HUMPED and HUMP-
ED. And NOW all of a SUDDEN there's THIS, this FUCK-
IN' ROOF for GOOD FEELINS and he was HITTIN' it.
And HE was just like WHEN the FUCK did THAT get
THERE?

THEN they were RUNNIN' AWAY but even STILL
DUCKY could HEAR Misha's BODY sayin' YO REMEM-
BER WHAT I SAID ABOUT FUCKING-*GUH*?

WHAM and SNAP and WHAM and SNAP.

DUCKY looked OVER at LADYBUG. He SAW her
PANTIN' and her DROOL was flyin' BACK while they RAN,
WOWZA, like ACTUALLY LITERALLY WOWZA.

But then ASTRID fell BACK a bit so SHE was RUNNIN'
right in FRONT of LADYBUG. Like RIGHT in FRONT of
FROM how SHE was STANDIN' between DUCKY and
LADYBUG. ASTRID was just like STARIN' really HARD at
DUCKY and HE was SUPPOSED to CARE? HE'D fuck-*guh*
her TOO, he JUST needed SOMETHIN' to STAND on.
MAYBE he could FUCK-*GUH* LADYBUG and then
STAND on her and USE her to FUCK-*GUH* ASTRID?

EASY. Except for BAD man who would TRY to STOP Ducky. HE didn't even WANT to fuck-*guh* BAD man, unless it was like to like FUCK him in terms of like FUCK him, instead of FUCK-*GUH* him. Because FUCK him. BUT don't FUCK-*GUH* him.

DUCKY said YARP at ASTRID so SHE knew what SHE had COMIN'. BAD man YANKED hard on DUCKY'S LEASH and honestly THAT wasn't as UNPLEASANT as it USED to be. EXCEPT still FUCK that DORK because

- 5 -

Jairzinho deserved pity. Even by human standards, Astrid was regularly and repeatedly driven to distraction by his obliviousness. How could he fail to notice that the day's mayhem was fraying the metaphorical leashes that bound the hounds? That there were several intercanine disputes threatening to spill over into something truly catastrophic? The only ally Astrid had had in preserving a semblance of order had been Misha. And now she was gone. Gone to where? Perhaps the same neverland where things in the...*on* the tell-a-vision lived.

Was all of this running and ducking and peeking Jairzinho's attempt to distract his wards from their squabbles and strife? Granted, there was evident danger through which he was attempting to shepherd them. For that, Astrid was grateful. But he was going about it as a showdog might. What strange, hominid pleasures did he derive from all of this running and screaming?

Ducky *yarped* at Astrid again. Jairzinho gave his leash another yank. So occupied, he tripped on a curb and nearly took a header into a garbage can.

So perhaps that explained it. Why he'd failed to appreciate the tenuous equilibrium upon which his dogs teetered, even after Astrid had *warned* him! And what had he done? Shoved her away! Like she wasn't doing *all of the hard work* in *keeping this walk in...*

Astrid shook her head. Felt the chains of her collar tightening and loosening, tightening and loosening. It had a calming, centering effect. Reminded her who was in charge. She could slip her collar any time she wished. Jairzinho was not in charge. She was. And what she chose to do with this power was to feel...pity.

And what did Good Dogs do with pity? They helped the objects of the emotion. Simpleton leash-slinger though he was, Jairzinho was trying to keep them safe. Even if he did have a tendency to...see, like here, he was screaming "GO GO GO" as they ran across a completely deserted street. Was that necessary? No, and it was just these unnecessary engagements of his *profoundly* limited attention that rendered him so oblivious.

Astrid's collar loosened again. Yes, she could go her own way any time she wanted...but she cared for her friends. She cared for Jairzinho. And it was clear enough he couldn't care for himself.

So she would protect him from his own imbecility. It was the right thing to do. How did she know that? Well, because she was a Good Dog. Didn't all Good Dogs know the difference between right and wrong? Could there *be* a greater authority?

What puzzled Astrid was: what, if anything, did humans know about these things?

- 6 -

Sheriff couldn't believe his luck! They were almost home! It had been a really stinky and weird walk. And Misha had quit. And then they turned around and came Home early by going a new way.

A fun change of pace! But Sheriff was also so super *duper* happy to be going Home!

The Babble Man was playing his new game which was just *brilliant!* It was called Run Up To The Corner And Then Peek Around And Just Stand Still For A While And Look And Then Scream And Shout And Run Across The Street! It was a game Sheriff had never played before! It was his new favorite!

Yay! They turned the corner! And they were *Home!*

Except it was weird because there was a big old pile of junk-aroonie-roo in the way. So Sheriff couldn't see Home, because of the junkaroonie-roo in the way.

The Babble Man made them all go so slow that they stopped. He made them stop in the street, which Sheriff had always thought it was such a big no-no to stop in the street. But here they were.

Sheriff looked from The Babble Man back towards the junk-aroonie-roo, because he was just looking at it and making his mouth go open and close and open and close. No Babble. Uh oh.

The junkaroonie-roo was sort of the same color as home, and it was *well* big like home. Kind of almost the same size, but only the sides were tall, instead of the whole thing was tall. The middle part where the Home-bits were was just a big pile with a lot of fire and smoke coming out. But…Home was not a big pile with a lot of fire and smoke coming out.

This was really confusing.

Sheriff looked at Ladybug. She sounded like she was screaming even though her mouth was closed.

He looked at Boo. Usually Boo was fun to look at because he was kind of always playing. But even he looked kind of like, uh oh. Like he was definitely not having as fun of a time as usually.

And actually *everybody* looked kind of sad. Everybody except Misha, who was not here.

This was all scary and confusing. So Sheriff tried to wag his tail. Because then everything would be better! And normal! And happy!

He had to really think about it. Work really really *really* hard to make it wag.

Something in the way-far-away place of Sheriff's thinky-bits barked.

He looked at the junkaroonie-roo. Then he looked at the Babble Man. Then at his friends. Then at the pile that was where Home used to be.

Now even though he was thinking really hard about wagging his tail, he couldn't make it go. It just blew in the wind and then the wind went away like Misha. And Sheriff's tail just hung, because it was the heaviest thing in the whole wide world.

CHIMPISH

- 1 -

It was like some ghastly work of art. *The Edbrooke Sacked.*

The main entrance had been punched out. Littering the street with its interior decoration. Yet the rest of the building seemed to have imploded. Chunks of the exterior towered, straight and powerful as always. Like someone had been playing Jenga with the Edbrooke. And now the game was over.

This was the risk of concentrated wealth, Jairzinho supposed. Made for a good target.

He heard the musical *clinks* of bricks settling.

A sobering reminder: this had likely happened in the last thirty minutes or so. Maybe less.

His first thoughts were of himself. He couldn't help it. Even as he acknowledged how deranged that was. He thought: *whatever device had obliterated the Edbrooke was probably in the building at the same time I was.* He thought: *if whoever was doing this decided that 'go time' should have been just a little bit earlier, I'd be dead.* He thought: now *what do I do?*

He thought: *now what* I *do?*

143

After all that. After his mad dash from West 15th. Breaking his back (not literally, but it felt like it) lugging these dumbass dogs through gunfire, and *actual* fire. Running to get them back home so he could be done with them. So he could get himself home, somehow.

After all of that: *the Edbrooke Sacked.*

There was no way anybody in there was left alive. Or if they were…they wouldn't be for long. Jairzinho could see the rising heathaze from here.

And if that had been *his* home?

God. What an asshole he was. He knew it. He shows up to a graveyard and thinks about himself. Woe is me. Asshole.

Jairzinho plopped himself on the curb. Put his head in his hands. Didn't even tell the dogs to sit. The dogs could do whatever the fuck they wanted.

He had blood on his shoes. Probably Misha's. How terrifying, that he could get no more specific than *probably.*

Booms and bangs echoed from nearby streets. But this particular corner was still, silent.

Except for the Edbrooke. With its tinkling bricks. Their settling sounded a bit like human voices crying for help. But if you kept telling yourself they were just settling bricks…

Crunch echoed in his head.

Bricks. Just settling bricks.

Then he couldn't really hear the bricks over his own gasping. So that was alright.

Meatball scaled Jairzinho's thigh. Licked his chin.

Then Kelso lunged for Meatball. Boo pulled hard towards the river. Ducky made a play at Ladybug.

Jairzinho could just unclip the carabiner belt. It'd fall to the ground and make a little *clink*. Just settling bricks. He could walk away. He'd wanted to get the dogs home, and he had. All of their owners were probably dead. Olivia, Sheriff's talkative, sweet-as-pie keeper? Bricks. Poor Adriana, she of the laundry room hangover? Bricks.

There was no way to contact any surviving owners until the phones got unblocked. Safest thing for the dogs would be to leave them here. Hook them to a pole. Or just unclip the leashes. Wish them luck. *Clink*. Bricks.

He returned from his reverie.

The dogs were calm. Separated. Sitting.

Astrid whimpered quietly and licked Jairzinho's face.

Ladybug gasped and buzzed at the ruins. As though she understood.

Blood-caked Barmit looked Jairzinho square in the eyes. Squatted and shat.

Wow. Barmit never made eye contact. Barmit never pooped. Not for Jairzinho, at least.

Out came the phone. Up came the bathroom report. Jairzinho added a **poo** after Barmit's name. Fetched a bag from the back pocket. Scooped, stood, slung it into the trash.

Ok. Stop crying. It was a simple question.

Was he the guy who left eight dogs to die? Or was he the guy who tried to keep them alive?

In truth, he was somewhere in between. So phrase it this way: which guy did he *want* to be?

Which guy did he want to take home to Tia? All the way in Brooklyn?

He looked at the dogs.

At his Giants.

They looked back up at him. Patient. Behaved.

He needed to get back to Brooklyn. He didn't know if this was only happening in this neighborhood, or on the island of Manhattan. But if it was happening in Brooklyn too, and Tia should be there...all alone...without even dogs to keep her company...

Ladybug burped quietly. Boo stuck his nose right in her face. Recoiled sharply.

Jairzinho betrayed the dead with a smile. He shook his head. "Goddamnit." He took up the leashes. With hand and heart alike.

He closed his eyes. Took a deep breath.

Opened his eyes and asked his Giants, "have any of you ever even *been* to Brooklyn?"

"You wanna go to Brooklyn?" Esther asked from *right next to him Jesus*

"CHRIST!" Jairzinho fell back down. Shook his head. Tugged hard on Boo's leash. To try (and fail) to calm him. "Don't sneak up on people when there's a...war-thing happening!" he whisper-shouted.

"Hell of a mornin'," Esther proceeded. Like Jairzinho had given her a goddamned hug, instead of yelling at her. "Eh?"

Jairzinho gave her a goddamned hug. Wept into her shoulder. He didn't know whether she was crying or not. He did feel her torso hitch a few times though.

And he couldn't help but notice, she didn't have those two little Frenchies with her anymore.

- 2 -

Esther took a deep pull of her cigarette. Jairzinho wasn't a smoker. Couldn't stand the smell. Esther intuited this, though. Once she realized Jairzinho was sitting downwind of her, she got up and sat on his other side.

Jairzinho had never pegged her for such a conscientious person.

"Did you get her tags?" she asked, after Jairzinho explained Misha's fate.

He shook his head. Snapped Ducky's leash to make him sit. "No. I didn't think to. I should have."

Drag, blow. "Ah, you did good. Grace under pressure."

"Thanks," he replied, less-than-endeared by Esther's vaguely condescending tone. "Did you...lose your two?"

"Mhm. The Frenchie Connection!" She laughed. Took another drag. Exhaled thoughtfully. "They got hit. I didn't. But they did. I can't figure out how that..." Leftover smoke steamed out of her nose. "I kept runnin' em," she told the ground through a hollow smile. "I didn't notice right away. So I kept runnin' em. I'm yellin' 'come on, come on!'" Her smile filled out, with something that didn't belong there. "I figured they were gettin' lighter because of adrenaline or somethin'." Her upper lip twitched. She ashed her cigarette on the street. "Dog that small gets hit...they're all exit wound."

Jairzinho shivered. Glanced at Sheriff. Poor little Sheriff, trembling eyes looking to Jairzinho. As though for explanation. *They're all exit wound.* He couldn't even ima-

No. No no no.

147

He wiped his eyes. What he was doing probably didn't count as crying. Or else, it was crying in extreme slow motion.

Ladybug trembled and whimpered. Jairzinho picked her up and put her on his lap. "I don't know what to do," he said to the pug as much as Esther.

Esther laughed. A great, big, booming laugh. *HA HA HA HA HA.* It rolled and echoed. People three blocks away probably thought another bomb had gone off.

Ducky leapt up to get onto Jairzinho's lap. Jairzinho made to push the little shit off. Astrid beat him to the punch: she bopped Ducky with her paw.

Then she fixed Jairzinho with a look of such chillingly human comprehension…

He blinked that away and reared on Esther. Belatedly. "Why are you laughing?! I'm trying to be fucking…vulnerable!"

"What, you read that word on the back of a book your girlfriend got ya or what?"

"No! It's…a thing Real Men do now!"

Esther pointed her two cigarette-holding fingers. "Lemme give you a tip from a lady's perspective, pal: vulnerability ain't a fuckin' steamroller."

"What's that supposed to mean, a *steamroller?*"

"You steamrolled."

"I did not *steamroll.*"

"You steamrolled. I told you about some real traumatic shit I just went through, and you go straight to…" she pouted out her bottom lip and switched to a stupid voice, "…*oh, what am I gonna do, I don't know, me me me.*" She took a triumphant drag of her cigarette.

"Well," Jairzinho's mouth snapped while his brain repeatedly hit a big red button, "that's because my traumatic shit is still happening. Yours is *done*."

Esther cackled her smoke out. "You're some kinda fuckin' terror, huh? Right for the throat! Your poor girlfriend."

"STOP TALKING ABOUT MY GIRLFRIEND!" he howled. The red button in his brain must not have been connected to anything. Or else, it didn't do what he thought it did. "YOU DON'T KNOW THE FIRST FUCKING THING ABOUT MY GIRLFRIEND!"

"How long you been together?"

"Ahp...I don't know, two years?"

"Then I know she's a goddamned saint." Esther dropped her smoke. Ground it into the sidewalk with her heel. "Wouldn't wanna start a fire," she giggled through a deep frown. Then she rose and clapped her hands. "Right! So you wanna sit here talkin' shit, or are we goin' to Brooklyn, or what?"

Jairzinho shook his head. "W...I don't...you were...just being mean to me!"

"Oh, so poor baby's gonna turn down a pal because he got his widdle feewings huwt? We're just talkin' shit. Only difference is I'm doin' it from the friendly part of my heart. You're doin' it from the fuckin' spleen."

All eight Giants stared at Esther. In unison, they turned their heads. Looked at Jairzinho. Not *to* him this time. *At* him.

"Ah" was as much of a response as Jairzinho was willing to give. Or able. "Ahem."

"Come on, gimme one of them clips you got on you. I can help ya."

Jairzinho regained moral firmament. "Absolutely not. I'm sorry," he added as Esther wilted slightly, "but it's like…a professional scruple. I never let my dogs out o-"

"HE-EH-EYYY!" Esther cried to a point in space over Jairzinho's shoulder. "Well, *look* who it is!"

"Oh, what?" Jairzinho pointed at Esther. "Steamroll!"

Esther waved his finger away. Extended her arms towards a silhouette approaching from the far side of the ruins. "What do we got here, but it's an actual *friend!*"

Jairzinho's shoulders fell. He looked to the Giants.

They were all looking at the ground. Real intently. Like they wished they had hands to stuff in pockets and tuneless songs to whistle.

It was only today he'd started to feel judged by his dogs. Was this a new development? Or had they always done this? And he'd just never noticed?

Bricks, his brain thought. Which wasn't helpful.

- 3 -

"I am standing by the river," Esther's friend, an annoyingly handsome man with a swell of black hair and the fashion sense of a tech bro, explained once they'd drawn near enough to each other to speak, "and I hear they have begun their explosions again. But I think to myself th-"

"That it sounded like Esther's laugh?" Jairzinho chuckled.

"This is just it!" the man, maybe five or six years older than Jairzinho, had an unplaceable accent. Middle Eastern? "I hear these booms and I think to myself, why, these booms, they sound like my dear friend Esther! Also," he added to Jairzinho, "you are a bit of a steamroller, no?"

Jairzinho frowned. "Oh, so steamrolling is interrupting now, too?"

The man turned to Esther. Tilted his head towards Jairzinho. "Your friend, he is, eh, a little aggressive?"

"I'm not agg…"

"He ain't bad," Esther smiled at Jairzinho. *Talking about* Jairzinho. "Just ain't got a leash for himself like he's got for the dogs."

"Yes!" the man exclaimed. "What kindly dogs you have!" He knelt down to pet the dogs. "Esther has told you what is my job?"

Jairzinho pulled the dogs back. "I don't even know your name, guy."

"Ooh!" The man turned to Esther. Still kneeling. "He is like the toy." He lifted a hand. Pinched thumb and forefinger. Lilted it through the air. "You pull the string, and he says something that is not so nice!" He leapt to his feet. Extended his hand. "I am Vatche. I board!"

Jairzinho nearly fired back with something along the lines of *what, you want me to entertain you?* Then he realized he'd misheard. And that what he'd nearly said was…not so nice.

Jesus. Was he a *pull the string* guy now?

Jairzinho pinched his lips tight. Extended his own hand. Took Vatche's. "Jairzinho. I sorry."

"…my friend, do you mock the way I sp-"

"Not on purpose. I'm just…" Jairzinho blinked. "Today's just been a *day*, you know?"

Vatche nodded. "Yes. Today is a day."

Esther wrapped Vatche in a hug. "It's good to see ya, buddy."

"You as well." He pulled back from the hug. "It is good that you laugh when you do! My car is stuck *so* far uptown, I have been walking for quite a long while. Normally I turn in sooner, for going back to my home. Cutting east. Today, though, I say to myself, I will walk further. On the West Street. I did not know it was to hear you laugh, but ah! God is good!"

"Uh..." Jairzinho pointed to the ruins of the Edbrooke. Which they stood closer to now. Close enough for Jairzinho to feel the heat radiating off the bricks. Like a kiln. He imagined how it must be baking the survivors alive. *Clink. Clink. Clink.*

Vatche shrugged. "It is a sliding scale, yes?"

Jairzinho frowned and looked to the kiln. So he didn't have to look at that stupid shrug anymore.

He spotted maybe-Philippe. Most of him. He lay clumsily against bricks. From the sneer down, anyway. The top of his skull was missing. The tear seemed clean. Right at the jaw. Jairzinho could see his tongue and bottom teeth in the cradle of his skull. The bed of clay beneath him roasted his back. It smelled *good*.

Jairzinho's stomach grumbled. He very nearly gagged.

"Say," Esther cut in, "you happen to get wind of is this happening just here, or is i-"

"Only Manhattan," Vatche interrupted.

"For f..." Jairzinho welcomed childish frustration. Encouraged it. Infinitely preferable to existential terror. "That was a steamroll!"

Esther and Vatche both waved him off. "I ask," Esther continued, "because *we're* goin' to Brooklyn." She shot a glance to Jairzinho. Daring him to say otherwise.

But he didn't. She was right. He needed all the help he could get.

"You go to *Brooklyn?*" Vatche marveled. "Why?"

Esther cocked a thumb at Jairzinho. "He's a shitty boyfriend, we gotta get him back before his girl thinks he's dead."

"It would break her heart to find out she is wrong?"

Esther laughed her artillery laugh.

Jairzinho just shook his head. And, alright, laughed a bit too.

Then he imagined maybe-Philippe's half-head rattling with laughter. He imagined the tongue sloshing around the basin of his skull. Like a riderless skateboard on a halfpipe.

Jairzinho wretched slightly.

Vatche must have seen. He planted a hand on Jairzinho's shoulder. Then took it off when Jairzinho flinched again. "How," Vatche wondered, not unkindly, "will you get to Brooklyn? It is on the other side of the island, yes? And then *off* the island?"

Jairzinho pointed West. To the Hudson, just two blocks away. In the opposite direction of Brooklyn. "Cross the Hudson. Go into Jersey. Get a Zyp or something, to take us all the way around." He sighed. "You wanna come?"

"You will cross the Hudson? On what, you have a large dinghy for so many dogs?"

"A…what? No. We'll cross the bridge, dude."

"Dude! I am a *dude!*" Vatche's shoulders bounced as he laughed. "Well, I am afraid I must also be the bearer of the bad news, *dude.* The bridges? Kaboom. Not Esther's laugh."

Esther's jaw dropped. Like she couldn't believe there could *be* a more destructive kaboom. "They blew the fuckin' bridge?"

"Which bridge?" Jairzinho demanded. The dogs at his ankles jostled. Feeling his anger. His terror.

Vatche shook his head. "No. Not which bridge. *The bridges.* All of them."

- 4 -

"What are you doing?" Vatche demanded.

Jairzinho froze just as he finished crossing West Street. He stumbled forward a bit. The Giants weren't so good at freezing. "Um...I'm...following you? To look at the bridge?"

"With one hundred dogs?"

"..." Jairzinho looked to Esther for explanation. She just shrugged.

Vatche pointed to a hill. It rose gently between West Street and the Hudson River Walk. "You understand what is on the other side of this, yes?"

Sigh. "A view of the bridge."

"Men! With guns! We must be secret to see the bridge, and they do not see us! Crawling, yes? Secret. Your dogs can be secret?"

Boo caught a glimpse of his own tail. Set to chasing it. As he spun, he knocked into Kelso. Kelso barked.

"I can't just tell them to *stay*," Jairzinho protested. "They're not that well behaved."

Esther tapped Jairzinho's beltline. "You got the clippers! Just clip em to something!"

"Ah..."

"Oh, right," Esther rolled her eyes. "The kid's got a *professional scripture.*"

"Scruple."

She elbowed Vatche. "See what I'm sayin'?"

154

Vatche narrowed his eyes at Jairzinho. Squeezed out all of their humor in the process. "You do not have respect for your dogs?"

Jairzinho tapped his palms together. Time out. "Nuh-uh, no. That's not how this works. They're not *my* dogs. I didn't train them. It has nothing to do with how much they respect me. Which, by the way, is actually a lot."

Vatche smiled. "My friend, this is not what I asked you." He turned around before Jairzinho could respond. Walked to a thick-stalked bush. Reached in. Shook the boughs. "Very sturdy, these arms."

Jairzinho looked down at his Giants. Respect for *them?* That didn't make any sense. You don't...you *love* dogs. You *appreciate* them. But *respect?* That was absurd. Respect had to be earned. By doing...stuff. Human stuff. Like being funny, or smart. Or something. What kind of a dumb question was that, did he *respect* his *dogs...*

"Hey," Esther snapped, her face inches from Jairzinho's ear. "Clip 'em already. I wanna see the fucked up bridge."

Aaaahh...well...Jairzinho could just wait here. Keep the Giants clipped to his waist. Wait for Esther and Vatche to go see the fucked up bridge. There was no reason Jairzinho had to go up the hill. Just to see the fucked up bridge.

But...that said...he *really* wanted to see the fucked up bridge too.

So Jairzinho walked his Giants to the bush. He placed his hands on the clips of the carabiners that connected to the larger clip of his rope belt. He...kept his hands there for a while.

It felt how he'd always imagined bungee jumping must feel. When you scoot up to the edge and look down. You know it'll be safe. Only your *body* doesn't know it.

155

Jairzinho took a deep breath. Unclipped the carabiners. His hands fought him. He won.

He reached the unclipped carabiners, *unclipped*, he had his dogs outside and they *weren't clipped*…ahem. He reached the carabiners into the bush. Felt for sturdy boughs. Clipped. Clipped.

He shook the branches. All of a sudden, they didn't feel so sturdy.

So he wrapped the carabiners around the boughs. Around each other. Clipped the two carabiners into the other's hook.

There.

The Curbside Giants now belonged to a shrubbery.

Jairzinho loomed over the dogs. Tried to look as Alpha as he could. Raised his hand above his head and snapped. "Hey." Snap. "Right here."

All eyes on Jairzinho. Except Barmit and Boo. Close enough.

"Sit," he ordered.

Astrid, Sheriff, Ladybug, and Kelso sat.

Meatball *melted*. Her tongue unrolled like a sun-bleached red carpet.

Oh, shit. Water. He'd been running them in high heat. They needed water.

One at a time. One thing at a time.

Jairzinho snapped again. Mostly at Ducky. Barmit and Boo were always and never sitting, respectively. And thus, to Ducky: "*Sit.*"

Ducky glared at him.

"SIDDOWN!" Esther screamed from over Jairzinho's shoulder.

Vatche shushed her.

Ducky sat.

Jairzinho frowned. Extended a flat palm. *"Stay."* He spun around.

Turned his back on his Giants.

Without their being connected to him.

This wasn't scooting up to the edge. This was swan-diving off without double-checking your bungee. And realizing, maybe you'd only clipped it to itself.

"Ok," he grumbled to Esther and Vatche. "Quick look. Let's go."

[It was a cruel joke bein' played on that dog. That bulldog there, who was too frickin' tired to lift her big old melon up off the ground. First The Liberator runs 'em all over the shop, and everythin's goin' whizzpop all around. Then what does he do but go and walk away! Leaves his strings behind!]

[Now was that dog's chance! Make a break for it! Blow this pupsicle stand!]

[Except they done all that runnin', that dog and her pals. So she was some kinda beat. Then her big shot comes, and she can't hardly lift her damn head. She's just pantin' and pantin', lickin' the frickin' grass.]

[That dog looked around at her friends. Weren't none of 'em makin' many breaks. They was just standin' around lookin' confused. Scram, friends! Now's your shot! But didn't none of 'em move. They just watched The Liberator walk up a hill, then crawl around with his pals.]

[So then Sheriff turned and bopped that dog on the head, and the Other Dog went and tried to bite the little guy! Which]

157

Meatball didn't much appreciate. So she shouldered her way back into herself and tried to make a contrite noise.

Sheriff looked at her like he just found out squeaky toys had teamed up and decided they weren't gonna take it anymore. He whimpered a bit.

Meatball noticed the little guy's tail wasn't wagging. That was pretty unusual. Not having much of a tail herself made Meatball rather perceptive about them on others. Sheriff was always wagging his. Now though…poor fella looked more than a bit put out about something.

It made Meatball feel…not great. So she marshaled her energy, lifted her paw a few inches off the ground, then let gravity do the work of bringing it back down.

He might not have gotten back to wagging, but Sheriff did a little dance and started slapping at Meatball's head again. Her big heavy head that was [keepin' that dog from sayin' sayonara to this walkin' talkin' hoosegow that was the so-called *Liberator*, and] Meatball wanted so badly to let herself go, to let the Other Dog wrestle with this colossally frustrating situation. But if she did, the Other Dog might snap at Sheriff again.

And even if the little guy wasn't wagging now, he was dancing and slapping. He was trying. So Meatball could too. Because she didn't have much of a tail to wag, on her own.

"I have a saying," Vatche said yet again as they stared across the Hudson. Three soldiers fanned out across the section of the Hudson River Walk below the hill. All armed with assault rifles. Piles of quotidian shit were sprinkled along the bank, just in front of the railing. Backpacks, purses, boots, hats. Non-essential cargo jettisoned by people who'd hoped to swim across

the river. But the swim to Jersey was the least of their worries. Vatche claimed that the soldiers encouraged people into the river, by blandishment or threat. Then riddled them with bullets when they'd barely pushed off. From this angle, Jairzinho didn't see any bodies. But he believed it. He'd seen enough to believe just about anything. "Chimpish."

Jairzinho flinched in slow-motion. "What?"

"Chimpish," Vatche repeated. "This is my saying."

"This one's my favorite," Esther whispered.

Vatche nodded. "Yes. It is good. Chimpish is being more like a chimp instead of a human. Good, yes?"

Jairzinho sighed. He'd hardly known Vatche for ten minutes. Yet he already knew a handful and a half of his 'sayings'. Turned out "steamroller" was one of his. So was Chimpish. Whatever the fuck that meant.

How this guy could be spouting 'sayings' right now, Jairzinho couldn't imagine. Not while faced with the sheer scale of the carnage they were witnessing. And Jairzinho wasn't even thinking about the bleak, distinctly more human-sized implications of those piled belongings on the bank just below them. Was making quite a point of *not* doing so, in fact.

No, now he was looking further to the South.

To those three powerful columns of concrete plunging into the riverbed. That cruciform steel that stood as tall as ever.

The rest of the bridge...the bits that *made* it a bridge...had been reduced to a triptych of hard angles. Steampunk beaver dams in a soft, oblivious river.

From this distance, it was impossible to appreciate the scale of the destruction. The Babcock Bridge, nearly a mile long. Obliterated.

How many people had been on it when it blew? Jairzinho thought he could make out cars in the wreckage. If he squinted. So he didn't squint.

Instead he turned back towards West Street. Towards his dogs. Sheriff was trying to play with Meatball. But his heart wasn't in it. Boo was looking for whatever invisible things he always looked for. Barmit and Kelso pouted on either end of the pack. Everything seemed under control. They were…okay. Without him.

Could he hear the android laughter of steel suspension cables dancing in a high breeze? Could he hear anything *but* that?

Jairzinho tried not to think about it. Couldn't stop thinking about it.

"Like you," Vatche explained, "you are Chimpish, you see! You do not think your dogs can play nice without you shaking their leash. Speaking to the dog, that is human. Sit, stay, roll over. Human. But when you grab the leash, you shake it around, you bare your teeth. As you do. This is Chimpish. As if a Chimp were holding the leash. Instead of a human."

"I get it," Jairzinho said.

"You know how a dog can be Chimpish? Wolfish. Are they dog or are they wolf? Think about this."

Jairzinho couldn't think about it. He could still hear the bridge. If he closed his eyes, he could see it. Even more clearly than when they were open. His eyes.

See the bodies washing downstream. See the corpses of people shot swimming to Jersey, being swept into river-kissed debris. He couldn't think about anything else.

He couldn't think.

"Give the kid a minute," Esther suggested quietly.

Jairzinho would have to remember to thank her for that. When he remembered how to talk. Like a human. For now, he just stared at the sky.

Everything was so boring and lame again and for a while things had all been really like *yaahhoooooooo!* when all the loud stuff was going on and Boo was flying around the world with his friends and then they were run-a-run-a-running and everything got *fast* like it was supposed to be but now it was back to boring ho-hum sitting next to this dumb hill and then the Slowman and *his* new friends all walked away and laid down on the hill and died and Meatball laid down and died and Sheriff was trying to raise Meatball from the dead but basically Kelso and Barmit were dead too they were just sitting there even though their eyes were open and once every thousand years their eyes closed and then they opened again really slowly so they were alive but could you even call this *living* this this this *syrup world* they lived in where nothing happened except for so so so *slow* and Astrid looked too focused to be dead but ALIVE she moved she saw something in the bush that scared her and she ran over to it and sat on it and then she looked okay again so that was interesting it was interesting when dogs moved fast and that was something to keep in mind but until then there were definitely interesting things happening around the city because so not because *but* Boo knew they were happening because he could smell them and hear them and where most things sounded like thiiiiiiiiiiiiiiiiiiiiiiiiiiiiiiiiiiiiiiiiiiiiiiiiiiiiiiiiiiis these things sounded like *this! this! this!* and that was definitely really exciting and Boo wanted to go see those things but nobody else wanted to and how were they even going to get to them because the Slowman had been dead for infinity trillion years just laying there rotting and meanwhile all of the exciting stuff was happening like way out over *there* and *not here* and so Boo just wanted to go to those places but not be *here* but if that wasn't an option maybe there was a way to bring the interesting things to him because interesting things had to be caused right like they couldn't just happen by themselves so maybe Boo could cause an interesting thing like how Astrid saw something in the bush that scared her and she jumped to it maybe Boo could be a thing in a bush that scared somebody or something anyway it was an idea that Boo had and had to think about for the rest of time because they were going to be here on the hill forever and they would never escape and ooh what was *that* something *so cool* was happening *that way!*

And somebody was making it happen!

"Racists."

Jairzinho rubbed his eyes. Lifted his head. "What?"

"This is a, what is the word." Vatche pinched his thumbs to the second knuckle of his first finger. Waved his hands wildly. Like Obama doing an air drum solo.

"Can't wait to hear what this word is!" Esther chortled.

"Ts'eghaspanut'yun!"

Jairzinho waited patiently for the translation he knew was coming. Esther was a late-middle-aged white person though. And she'd just heard a long, foreign word. Which made her socially, if not legally, obligated to say "guh*bless*you!"

Vatche showed her that he'd bothered to learn about *her* culture with his middle finger. He turned to Jairzinho. *"Ts'eghaspanut'yun*, this is Armenian. You know history? This was done to my people. Also to the Jews. You have done this to your Natives, yes? When one group k-"

Jairzinho pushed himself up onto his elbows. "Genocide?"

"Yes!" Vatche brightened in a way that seemed an inappropriate reponse to the word *genocide*. "I have watched these men, as I am walking down the river. They shoot only at the people looking like you and me. They do not shoot the Esthers."

"Wow," Jairzinho ventured sarcastically, "they *must* be racist!"

Esther laughed and poked Jairzinho on the chest. On the heart.

Jairzinho shrugged. Gave a small smile.

"Hello?" Vatche waved his hands. "May we not giggle for the racist genociders?"

"Ah," Esther nudged him, "lighten up."

Jairzinho pushed himself all the way up to sitting. "I don't think it's a race thing. They blew up the Edbrooke. That's almost entirely white people."

"In the work hours?" Vatche asked.

Jairzinho thought about that.

Then Jairzinho thought about what he'd seen on Seventh. When the bomb first blew. When he saw one of the gunmen pausing to try and help somebody out of an overturned car. Had those people he was helping...had they been...

He thought of Misha.

He looked to his Giants. To the puddle formerly known as Meatball.

"One at a time," he mumbled.

"What?"

Jairzinho faced Vatche straight-on. "I need to get my dogs some water. Before anything else. They need a rest."

Vatche nodded. "My home, it is not far."

"How far?"

"Four, five blocks. It is very safe. We have the bowls and the food and the crates. I board, as I have said. As you misunderstood in a way which was, quite problematic. But you are Chimpish sometimes. I see this. And so I forgive you."

I didn't ask for your fucking forgiveness was Jairzinho's first thought. It was, sure, fair play, a Chimpish thing to think. Pure pride.

Pointless.

So Jairzinho swallowed it. Thought and pride alike. "Hey Vatche."

"Mhm?"

"Chimpish is good."

"Huh?"

"It's a good saying. Chimpish. It works."

Vatche smiled. First at Jairzinho, then at Esther, then at the dogs, and finally back at Jairzinho. "Oh, how happy that makes me! Chimpish of me too, to feel so big for so little. But Chimpish is not all bad, you know?" He practically somersaulted off the hill. "Nothing is all bad!"

Jairzinho wondered if he'd lost any dogs yet. Or people.

Seldom had Jairzinho known relief such as he felt upon returning to his Giants. He reached into the bush to grab the carabiners.

They weren't there.

But...what?

The Giants were here. Their leashes were all attached.

He followed the leads with his eye. They all converged on...

Astrid stood up. Took a step back. Sat down again.

She'd been sitting on the carabiners. They were still clipped together. But they'd been pulled off the bush at some point.

And Astrid had...spotted this? And understood what it meant? And...

That wasn't possible.

Dogs weren't that smart.

Yet Astrid glared at him in such a human way. In a way that implied folded arms and tapping toes.

Jairzinho thought of a show from when he was a kid. *100 Good Deeds for Eddie McDowd.* It was about some little bully who got turned into a dog. He had to do one hundred good deeds if he wanted to get turned back into a human. The show had gotten cancelled before he'd finished the deeds. Before the writers had a chance to make an ending. So as far as prepubescent Jairzinho had known, the show had been cancelled because Eddie had failed in his quest. Which left him doomed to lived out his life as a dog, and then die at age eleven. It had, come to think of it, been Jairzinho's first collision with the concept of mortality.

Astrid had just done him a good deed.

He shivered. Knelt down. Took up the carabiners. Detached them from each other.

Clipped them back into his carabiner belt.

Clip. Clip.

He looked Astrid in the eye. Studied her. Had the awful sense that she was studying him right back.

"You," he told her, "are a *very* good girl."

Her face exploded into the softest, silliest smile Jairzinho had ever seen. She stood up. Wagged her tail. Licked Jairzinho's face.

He laughed. Scratched behind her ears. Then stood up and turned around.

Astrid stopped wagging. It was nice to get some appreciation from that poor putz Jairzinho. Left to his own devices, he'd have gotten them all killed six times over by now.

She followed him, but only because she allowed him to lead.

crates

- 1 -

Vatche's house was four or five blocks away. As promised. The journey there was fairly uneventful. Unnervingly so. That the initial convulsion of violence could be over so quickly implied surgical precision. In planning and execution alike.

Or maybe it was simply that the violence was less convulsion than wave. Distant booms and claps rumbled the silence. From way uptown. Perhaps the tide was still rolling.

Vatche and Esther clearly appreciated the lingering danger. They proceeded quickly, cautiously. Silently. Jairzinho did his best to guide the dogs around broken glass, slicks of blood, charred lumps of flesh gnarled into unrecognizable shapes.

He didn't realize he was holding his breath until he got dizzy.

At one corner, a window on the third floor of an apartment squeaked open. Jairzinho looked for somewhere he could hide. The street was single-lane, no shoulder. Too small. Nowhere to hide.

"Around the corner to your left," a voice from the window stage-whispered. "Five guys with guns. Be careful." The window groaned shut again.

Vatche turned them around. They cut south a block and resumed heading east.

Cars smoldered in the road. On the sidewalk. One had plowed into a bodega. Jairzinho saw a man's body sprawled across the crumpled hood. He was wearing denim overalls. For some reason, it was noticing the man's garb that most disturbed Jairzinho. It was such a specific fashion choice. He'd looked in the mirror this morning and decided what he was going to wear. Maybe he'd picked it out last night. Just when the driver of the car might have been thinking about what they'd have for lunch tomorrow. Maybe they'd buy it from the neighborhood bodega. They'd had no idea. Nobody had.

Actually: *they* had. Whoever *they* were.

Jairzinho turned away quickly. The bleating of the store's alarm followed him for two blocks.

More drawn faces peered down through windows above them. Some pointed. Most bore mute witness. The only other person who opened their window did so to hiss "GET OFF THE STREET YOU IDIOTS". In unison, Vatche, Esther, and Jairzinho flipped him off. That felt good. They heard the guy in the window laugh. This would be his anecdote. Everybody who survived this would have their anecdotes. Their own unique angle on the same history. Jairzinho would tell tales of gaunt, hopeless faces snared by webs of cracked glass. They would remember the idiots creeping down bombed-out streets with eight dogs in tow.

A block away from Vatche's, a kid on a motorized skateboard swung out from behind a four-door Toyota. He hopped onto the sidewalk and whizzed towards Jairzinho and co. They cleared a path. The boy couldn't have been much older than twelve. He had a T-shirt balled up and pressed to his forehead. The bright green cotton was soaked through with blood. It dripped crimson ellipses behind him. But the boy was fully clothed. So the shirt had likely begun the day as someone else's. To judge by the boy's face, it had been someone he had known.

And then they were at Vatche's. Fairly uneventful.

- 2 -

Unless, of course, one took the journey from just a foot or two above ground level.

Twas from such vantage, Ladybug did find herself by howling phantoms haunted! Hale though be the lead which lashes homesick hound to heartless hope, what bond may bear the butchery of bricks that bury, burn, and bake? O spirits, out from 'neath the mountain! Towering shoes of titan's tread so tailored for a pug's repose, you bed so poorly matched to purpose (lest perhaps the pointless purchase *be* the purpose), and of course you toys so pleasing to the eye and so the heart, but to the heart the bane if motions made there be towards mouth! All gone, all gone, all gone as Misha was! For just as dogs could perish, couldst not perish shoes and beds and toys? Did Ladybug her kibble kill, upon each morn's repast? (And to the question very nearly poséd; horrible, her hunger was!) Was this a world which tended always towards extinction? Did this life a purpose pose? What purchase could a life devoid of purpose offer scrabbling paws, if purpose be the purchase sought? Although, mayhaps her thoughts betrayed naught more than hunger's aptitude as midwife to edacious anger. Lo, near-fixed in fact it was, that

DUCKY was gonna GET all UP in that ASS. YEAH there were THINGS in the WAY but ALL that MEANT was that DUCKY just HAD to get RID of the THINGS. THEN the only THING in his WAY would be NO thing. Only BEFORE he'd been THINKIN' about USIN' his INCREDIBLE STRENGTH to get RID of the THINGS, but NOW he saw KELSO and MEATBALL were TRYIN' to BITE the SHIT outta each OTHER. And ASTRID was TRYIN' to STOP 'em. So WHAT if DUCKY could DISTRACT ASTRID by MESSIN' with

[that dog's frickin' pot which was frickin' whistlin', ya hear that? *So close*, that dog got *so frickin' close* to gettin' free, and then what? Her fat ass got sleepy. A frickin' embarrassment, she was. And what'd that leave that dog with, huh? Just] as Sheriff drifted nearer, Meatball dropped herself back in. Yes, her home had been destroyed. It was in passing by the ruins a second time, paired with the rather alarming scents emerging from Ladybug, that Meatball came to realize this. But The Liberator and his new friends clearly had a plan. He would [probably dig a big hole and throw 'em in! He ain't got no more claim to that dog now than any old schmo off the street. That dark dungeon what that dog loved him for breakin' her outta, that don't exist no more. So now the so-called Liberator ain't liberatin' nobody from nothin'. Now he ain't nothin' more than a dungeon on legs. So who cares if] he knew where he was going, all Meatball had to do was keep it together and trust in The Liberator, trust that

Meatball had turned Barmit against him. That was all that mattered, man. Barmit had been a homewrecker, yes she had, so Kelso didn't really care if Meatball was wrecking the home-wrecker. That didn't even matter, because who cared? Kelso didn't care. It just wasn't fair because, uh…because! Because if anybody was going to wreck the homewrecker it'd be the wreckee? Sure! That sort of made sense! So it wasn't like Kelso was thinking about saving Barmit *from* Meatball, then, no it wasn't, but *really*, it was more like he was trying to save her *for*

bodywater…but every time she tried to drink some…mr. comeon pulled on her leash…which she hated…but since she hated the bodywater less than most things…and mr. comeon wasn't letting her have the thing she hated less than most things…she hated that he was pulling on her leash…*more* than most things…and a few other things were falling into that spectrum…of being more or less hatable…like more hatable was how boo kept

stepping on Barmit like maybe she would go speeding out from under and that'd be an exciting thing but that didn't work and Boo was starting to worry maybe he'd never see an exciting thing again for the whole history of the universe because it had already been like one hundred infinities since he'd seen the last cool or interesting thing and if he didn't see something soon he was basically gonna go fizzy-bibble *bonkers* or something bec-ause this was so boring it was

nothing to wag about. Sheriff kept trying and trying just as hard as he'd ever tried to do anything in this whole wide world, but nothing worked. He tried playing with Meatball in the park but she'd just growled the first time. Then now she kind of tried to walk in a way that was almost playing if Sheriff got close. But when he was walking further away from her it kind of felt like she was actually angry at Sheriff. Which made him so not happy. So…sad? What was he sad about? There had to be a good reason for not being happy, right? Because happy was why you wagged…right? So what had he wagged about before? Maybe thinking about that would help him turn sad back into wag? So he thought about…about…gosh, what *had* he ever wanted to wag about so much? It was really scary but he couldn't

believe Jairzinho couldn't smell this. The Giants were falling apart, positively *reeked* of discontent. It was like that baffling semi-regular tradition whereby humans decided to buy small explosives and fire them into the sky. Before those dreadful sprinkle-winkers bloomed in the air, even before they went screaming heavenward, there was the tense stench of fire and powder in kissing distance of each other. It was a unique, tight-jaw smell you only got under the hiss of spark and fuse. And maybe it was her imagination, but Astrid thought she could hear that hiss. Oh, if only she could be in charge, she knew she could bury that smell, that sound, so nothing had to whistle and fly and explode. But Jairzinho…he reeked of *smug*. Like he'd figured it all out. Like under his rule, the Giants were somehow magically

"not safe," Jairzinho hissed.

Esther turned to him. "You scared?"

"Of course I'm fucking scared!" What had rattled him most was Astrid sitting on the leashes. Staring at him. He'd never been made to feel like such a fucking idiot in his entire life.

And so for the first time in his life, he considered that he might truly be one. A fucking idiot.

He just didn't know what to do with that. Except paralyze himself with self-doubt. Which, you know. Now wasn't really the time or the place.

So he split the difference. Let himself be scared. *Fucking* scared, to be precise.

Esther read his face. Then turned to Vatche. "We almost there, buddy?"

"Not almost..." Vatche said in a way that made it clear the next word was going to be "here!" He fished in his pockets and said "fairly uneventful, this journey, yes?"

Esther put her arm around Jairzinho and shook him gently. It hurt his back. He didn't say so.

At his feet, the dogs jostled.

- 3 -

Vatche Hamasyan and his family lived in an old four-story colonial. Like, 19th century old. Except the bottom floor was a sports bar. But it used to be stables. And owned by Aaron Burr. Vatche had been a veritable font of unprompted trivia in the last block. Ordinarily that would have annoyed Jairzinho, seeing as they'd been moving through a warzone. But Vatche was scared. Clearly. Jairzinho was scared too. And he figured fear manifested differently for everyone. Including lashing out at "scumhead *Hamilton* tourists."

The colonial, though. The Hamasyans owned the top three floors above the sports bar. All four stories had sandy brick façades, art deco diadems on muntined windows. Jairzinho might have called it gorgeous. If he'd been the sort of person who used words like that. Out loud.

175

Vatche looked up at the almost-perfectly undamaged property and sighed. Relief. The door to the sports bar was dented, but still firmly shut. The apartments above were pristine.

On the outside, at least. But that was another thing Jairzinho didn't say. Out loud.

Vatche fiddled with his charmingly anemic keyring. It was only then that Jairzinho realized he'd had his own, far less charming keyring on his belt this entire time. After all that sneaking he'd been doing. He'd somehow failed to notice the jingle-jangling. Like his crotch was celebrating his subtlety with every step. He shook his head and chuckled curses and praises into his chest. Because the alternative was screaming until he passed out. He unclipped the keys. Tugged his backpack around. Zipped the keys into the big pocket.

CLUNK

Jairzinho jumped. Not the hammer of a handgun falling. Just Vatche twisting the key in the lock of the modest door next to the sports bar's more resplendent entrance.

Vatche paused. Hand still on the key. He turned back to Jairzinho and Esther. "Are you huggers or kissers?"

"Not lately," Esther announced.

"Um…" Jairzinho tried to read Vatche's face. "Like…?"

Vatche rolled his eyes. "When you meet a new person. Do you hug them, or you do you kiss on each cheek, *mwah, mwah*?" He mimed pecking a stranger on each cheek.

"Oh, no. I mean," Jairzinho added, glancing down the street. "Neither."

Esther leaned back from Jairzinho. "You don't do neither?"

"Could we maybe have this conversation inside?"

Esther turned back to Vatche. Wrapped her arms around the same poor phantasm Vatche had just gotten to first base with with. "I hug 'em sometimes!"

"Great," Jairzinho concluded. "So tell us whatever Armenian greeting we need to know and let's please go insi-"

"NO!" Vatche roared. As though Lin-Manuel himself had joined the conversation. "I ask because, these are things you should not do when you are first meeting someone. You will hug and kiss a stranger? Is this not a MeToo Moment? You shake hands, like a regular person!" With that, he shouldered the door open. Led the way inside.

"You first," Esther offered with a wave of the hand.

So she'd never taken a posse of dogs up a flight of stairs, then. "That's alright," Jairzinho demurred. "It'll be easier if I go last."

"I thought you wanted to get off the street real fa-"

"*I do.*"

"Oh. Jeez. Alright." She preceded him through the door.

Jairzinho followed. Stopped at the foot of the stairs. They had castle-tower dimensions. Two and a half feet of clearance from one wall to the other. If that.

He looked down at his eight Giants. They seemed more Giant than usual. They, too, stared at the stairs. Silently negotiating who among them would take the ceremonial fall. Because even on wide, modern staircases, if there were more than four dogs on the walk, somebody always had to fall. It was practically tradition. Jairzinho suspected it would be Sheriff. As always. Sheriff treated staircase tumbles as both passion and calling.

"Alright guys, nice and easy." He walked them up to the first step. Guided the right half of his brood up first. Threaded himself in behind them. He turned and tugged the left-handers up to close out the procession.

"Eaaassyyy." Stairs provided enough of a challenge to smooth out the interpersonal issues. Ducky never tried for Ladybug on stairs. Nor did Jairzinho expect Kelso to rear on Meatball. The challenge was largely down to the different speeds at which they all ascended.

And wonder of wonders, it went smoothly. About time something went smoothly.

Sheriff only fell once. A good omen if ever there was one.

- 4 -

Turned out the whole Hamasyan family was in the house. The second story was his maternal grandmother's. The third belonged to his mother and stepfather. The fourth had been surrendered to his two younger half-siblings. Vatche was starting to say something else, maybe about where *he* slept, when he, Esther, Jairzinho, and the Giants reached the first landing.

Vatche cut himself off the moment his foot touched down. Mid-word, amazingly. Like someone pressing *next track* on an audiobook.

"Hello Mother! I am home in one whole piece!" he called up the stairs to the third floor.

A response rolled back down in Armenian. It sounded almost indifferent.

"Wasn't she worried about you?" Jairzinho asked.

Vatche laughed. "Yes, but she pretends like no."

He led them around a second, equally imposing set of steps. This one, though, was threatening less for its limits than its expanse. It was a surprisingly wide staircase. In keeping with the unexpected, TARDIS-style dimensions of the Hamasyan apartment. Jairzinho couldn't figure how they'd fit all of this high-ceilinged-atrium in the space above the sports bar. Opted not to dwell on it. Lingered instead on the gratitude of not being made to ascend the aforementioned second stairs.

Instead Vatche guided them down an irritable little hallway. "My bedroom! Here you will find the crates. I have one small and two large, I hope this will be enough." He pushed open a door likely cut from the same timber as the creaking floorboards under their feet.

Jairzinho looked down. At the floorboards…at the red on the…oh shit.

He looked behind him. At the bloody pawprints stamped into the dust. The blood looked a bit too fresh to have been entirely *tracked* in. "Shit," Jairzinho observed. He made a quick study of his pups. None held a paw aloft, or otherwise signaled a wound. He'd have to check them. One at a time.

He swung his backpack off. Unzipped the b-

"Leave it!" Vatche called from down the hall.

Jairzinho froze. Left it.

Jesus. So that's what *that* felt like.

Vatche's head sprouted from behind the doorframe. "I will clean it! What kind of host says to the guest, 'you must tidy your own blood puddles'? A rotten host, which I am not! Enter!" He pointed Jairzinho into a room. While he himself vanished back down the hall.

Jairzinho heeded the spirit of this second command without a second thought. His own pliancy annoyed him.

Vatche's room was modest. That was a very nice way to phrase it.

An invitingly pert twin bed claimed the corner to the left. It was crisply made and covered in throw pillows that could *only* have been the work of a doting grandmother. The far wall had a tiny desk. Big enough for maybe three magazines. Below it, an exquisite corpse of repurposed drawers. A DIY plywood shelf ran around the upper perimeter of the room near the ceiling. The shelf was covered in books, stacked on their sides. Those titles written in English belonged to the classics of literature and philosophy that Jairzinho had always insisted were "on his list."

Then there was the wall above the little desk. A graphic wall. Nearly a dozen framed photos of various sizes. All of musicians playing on streetcorners. Very stylish.

Jairzinho thought back to his single print thumbtacked onto his wall. To the frame sitting in a bag in the closet. To the toolkit under the bed.

Just one more reason to make it through this alive.

"Have you been to New Orleans?" Vatche asked Jairzinho as he appeared with two bowls of water. "Beautiful city. The most beautiful." Vatche put the bowls down. The Giants fell to, tugging Jairzinho by the belt as they did. He stepped nearer the bowls.

"I love this city of New York," Vatche continued, "but I am sorry to say. New Orleans? Much better. And as of this day, no longer more likely to be wiped into sudden nothing, yes?" He politely body-blocked Jairzinho's view of the pictures. Directed his attention to the crates. "Here we have crates! And…oh!"

Oh indeed. There were two large crates and one small crate. As promised. But inside one of the former sat a big, drooling boxer. The solitary small crate was occupied by a longhaired dachshund.

Vatche took a deep breath. Recovered quickly. "So much excitement, I have forgotten my houseguests!" He stepped up to the large crate. Dropped a hand to the boxer. The boxer didn't tilt his head to look at Vatche. Just rolled his eyes back. And drooled. So much drool. "The big boy is Topher, and that yappy little weenie," he pointed to the dachshund, "is Vegan. This is her name, not her dietary restriction. I do not name these dogs," he clarified, pre-emptively defensive.

Jairzinho looked down at his own temperamental brood. "Are your dogs…"

"Not my dogs. You know this."

"Are *these* dogs well-behaved?"

Vatche sat with that one for just a little too long. "Topher has the heart of gold. But he loves to play. If he has the chance. So I would say, you put the dogs who will not try to play with him, in with him. Vegan can be quarrelsome. You see this bark collar on her? This is in everyone's best interest."

As if on command, Vegan flapped her mouth open. Made a choked sound. Flinched.

"Shit," Esther marveled from Vatche's bed. Which she'd sat herself on. Vatche didn't seem to mind. "That thing chokin' her or what?"

"No choking. Simply, she barks, her neck vibrates, and *pssht!* The collar will spray some mist that is not so pleasant into her face."

"Hey Navi! I bet you wish you had one of them for me!"

181

Vatche raised an eyebrow at Jairzinho. "Oh, hello stranger. Your name is now Navi?"

Jairzinho sighed. Shook his head. Slowly, slowly. "No, um… I prefer Jairzinho, but…I answer to Navi too. Sometimes."

"What?" Esther didn't rise from the bed. She did sit a little straighter, though. "You don't like gettin' called Navi?"

He scratched his neck. "Not really."

"Why didn't you say so?"

"I fu…I *did*."

"If you did, I wouldn'ta kept callin' you Navi!" Esther slumped down slightly. "Well shit Jairzinho, I'm sorry. I thought it was like a…an endearment."

Jairzinho just stared. The apology was sort of like a thought stuck on the tip of the tongue. Just in reverse. He couldn't process it. Its simplicity. Its earnestness. Its…

"I shall leave you two to rename each other, hm?" Vatche headed towards the door. "If this is not enough crates, you can release your nicest dogs out to run around this room. We will close the door. But, please, not one who will make the mess, or destroy my pillows. My Mum Mum made these, very precious to me."

In his heart, Jairzinho pumped a fist. Called it!

"Huh?" came a voice from the other side of the thin, crate-flush wall.

Vatche turned to yell at the wall. "I have said your name, Mum Mum!" As an aside to his audience: "her ear, it is uncanny."

"Yes?" Mum Mum shouted.

"Do you wish to meet our new friends?" Vatche called to her.

"Yes!"

"We will be in shortly!"

"Ok!"

Vatche smiled and clapped his hands. "You will meet my Mum Mum. She is very precious to me as well. Not as much as the pillows though. Ha!"

"Like a joke!" Esther recognized.

"Yes!"

FLUNF. Esther let herself collapse backward onto the bed. "Hey J, you mind if I call you J?"

Jairzinho laughed. Rolled his eyes. "Sure."

"It's just that Jairzinho, that's too fuckin' long."

"Okay."

"Hey J, I'm gonna take a nap with the pups here. Don't mind me."

"Yes," Vatche nodded, "please, sleep if you are so inclined! Or declined, this is a wordplay?"

"*Re*clined," Jairzinho corrected.

"De-, re-, you understand my meaning. And now! I will go collect Mum Mum and say hello to Mother upstairs, dry the tears she is crying on the inside." Vatche slapped Jairzinho happily on the shoulders. Jairzinho suppressed a wince. "You make yourself at home like Ms. Tubcut! Sleep anywhere that is to your liking. For as long as you would like to stay, this is a new home for you."

Jairzinho didn't know what to say. So he said "thank you. Seriously. Thank you."

Vatche waved the sentiment away. Bent down. Scooped up the now-empty water bowls. "You will get these dogs comfortable. Then you come say hello. Or sleep like Ms. Tubcut. But you must say hello eventually, of course! For then we shall eat and drink, and perhaps be not scared that we will be killed for a moment! This is my one condition!" He pounded Jairzinho once more. The wet bowls in his hand splashed slobber-water onto Jairzinho's shoulder.

Jairzinho consciously stopped himself from grumbling.

Vatche skipped out of the room to fetch a blood rag.

Jairzinho was nearly overcome with…something. Something warm. Something lovely. Something that would have to wait until he solved the Riddle of the Crates: who could go where?

- 5 -

Four minutes later, Jairzinho made his choices. Topher may have been gentle, but he was a giant nonetheless. Not a Giant, though. But anyway. Two small dogs would fit in with him. As long as they weren't likely to cause a ruckus. So in went Lady-bug and Barmit. The two pups closest to taxidermy.

Boo went into the other large crate. Given his penchant for pissing on a whim, leaving him out on a stranger…a new frie-nd's carpet was a non-starter. Not to mention, Boo was sleeker than Topher. So two slightly bigger dogs could fit in Boo's crate with him. Jairzinho's decision was largely made for him there. Based less on which two would work in the crate than on which three would be acceptable running free in the room (be-cause *nobody* could fit in that little crate with the yappy Vegan).

Sheriff and Astrid could absolutely be trusted outside the crate. Both were clean and responsible dogs. A bit scrambly and slappy, respectively. But nothing out of control. His third choice to stay out was Kelso. Far from ideal, given the puggle's recent, unpredictable lapses into aggression. But he had always gotten along with Astrid and Sheriff. And he didn't drool or drag his butt around. So: winner.

Which meant Ducky and Meatball went into the crate with Boo. This seemed something approaching safe. Horndog though he was, Ducky had never tried it on with Meatball. Maybe he, like most humans, was under the impression that all bulldogs were boys. Jairzinho could only hope that getting stuffed into cages wasn't what got Ducky all hot and bothered.

Everybody trotted happily into their designated crate. Except for Meatball.

She fought *hard*.

"Come on, cut the shit!" Jairzinho growled.

Meatball whirled around on Jairzinho. As though to bite his hand. "HEY!" He shoved her head hard to the left. Got two palms on her bulldog booty. "Why...are you being...so fucking *difficult*?!" He thrust her into the crate. Slammed the door behind her.

Boo wagged at his new crate mate. Ducky sized her up, hopefully thinking about anything *but* mating.

"Everybody fucking *relax*," Jairzinho growled. He threw the little plastic bolt on the crate door. Glanced towards Esther. Sleeping on the bed. He lowered his voice. "We're safe. We're with nice people doing nice things. Fucking relax."

Meatball rushed to the front of the crate. Barking. Snarling. If she'd had hands, she'd be grabbing hold of the bars and shouting *do you really think this prison can hold me forever?!* She'd also need a human tongue and vocal chords for that, actually.

"STOP," Jairzinho scolded her.

Meatball barked.

"Stop it."

Bark.

185

"Everybody is chill except for you."

Growl.

Jairzinho sighed. Boy, could Meatball *pout*. Her face was 80% jowls, 15% underbite, and 5% miscellaneous. Watching her emote was like watching a wax bust review flamethrowers. Her eyes got so dull and flat, her "HEY!"

Meatball wasn't a sculpture anymore. She was one of those figureheads Vikings strapped to the fronts of their ships.

All because Jairzinho had stuck his fingers through the webbing of the crate. "To *pet* you," he whined. "So you'd *relax!*" And what had she done? She'd tried to bite him. Nip his fucking fingers off.

He had nothing more to say to Meatball. So he turned to Astrid. "You're in charge."

The pitbull cocked her head at him, then smiled and wagged her tail. A born leader.

Jairzinho rose and turned to Esther. Fast asleep. He was glad he'd managed to avoid waking her with his…outbursts. He was embarrassed about them already. And more than a little unnerved. He'd really been in such a good mood. Amazed at how easily he was letting go of stuff that ordinarily got under his skin. He'd felt so happy. So warm. So safe.

That his temper could rip that all away in a second…for something so small…and that he should have such a hard time getting it back…

Short-fused. Did that describe him, after all? He certainly wasn't a guy who *didn't take any shit*. He was a guy who took shit and *couldn't let it go*.

Suddenly exhausted, he dropped his backpack. And his carabiner belt. Headed out the door. Hoped he could shake this stupid funk before he met the other Hamasyans.

He closed the door behind him.

Esther counted to thirty and then opened her eyes. Slowly, in case Jairzinho was still in the room for some reason.

He wasn't.

So she rose to seated.

Sheriff had cuddled up against her, resting his head on her thigh. He looked so sad.

"It's alright buddy," she cooed as she stroked his head.

J was having a tough day. So was Esther, frankly, but the kid'd had a point. The worst had already happened for her. Which was sort of freeing, in a way. She had nothing left to lose.

Which meant she could make the hard choices. Do the tough stuff that needed to be done. She could help the kid out.

And she'd had herself a eureka. She knew exactly how to do all that noble, heroic bullshit.

She bit her upper lip to make it stop trembling. Rose from the bed. Took a leash from Jairzinho's belt.

If she suggested this to him, he'd say no. He'd tell her it was too dangerous. And then where would they go? They needed a way off the island. There had to be one.

Esther knew how to find it. Or find out *about* it. *Only* she could find out about it. She was white, after all. And like Vatche said, this was a *Ts'egh*…a *Ts'uguh*…a race thing.

All she needed was a cover story.

And so: she clipped the leash to Sheriff's collar.

Hesitated with her thumb still on the latch of the clip.

…

Hesitating was for suckers. This was the thing to do.

She released her thumb from the latch. It *thcked* shut.

"Let's go, buddy!" she cooed at Sheriff. "Who's my little cover story? Let's go! We're goin'!"

Astrid trotted to Esther's side. Barked at her.

"Shhh." Esther forced a smile. "It's gonna be okay," she reassured the blue-nosed wonder.

She mumbled that thought for the benefit of Sheriff, and herself as well, over and over. Out the bedroom door ("it's"), down the stairs ("gonna"), out the front door ("be"), and onto the street ("okay").

- 6 -

Vatche's family got along with each other so well, Jairzinho couldn't believe they were related. No Navias family reunion ever looked like this. With the laughing and the…not shouting. Maybe that had something to do with the Hamasyans being a mixed-pedigree home. As in genetics, so in relationships: mongrels were a more robust lot.

If only we could rid the world of pure-breds, Jairzinho thought. He laughed his own demented intersectional eugenics. Laughed louder than he'd intended to. The *ha ha* bounced around the surprisingly spacious third floor Hamasyan kitchen.

Vatche's mother Arpine was *futzing* around the expansive, cream-tiled kitchen. Yes, futzing. There was no other word for it. She rushed to the stove, hummed at a boiling pot, then leapt for a wooden salad bowl on the counter that she picked up and put down, only to cartwheel to a crock-pot that she banged like a bongo. Lots of activity, none of it seeming to accomplish anything. I.e. *futzing*.

And yet. It all smelled *amazing*. Food was being made, by *futzing* or some other means. That was more than enough for Jairzinho.

"Why do you laugh?" Arpine asked over her shoulder.

"Ah…" Jairzinho tried to think of a good lie. He couldn't. But he was still smiling. So he tried to think of something sad.

So he thought about how many people had died today. He thought about how it was only 11:34 AM. And so, how it had barely been two and a half hours since everything had fallen apart. His life, and for all he knew the lives of everyone around the world. Irrevocably changed. Or ended. In less time than it took to watch anything about Hobbits. And so he thought about how tasteless it seemed, that he should be sitting at a table in a safe, sturdy building. Awaiting a tastelessly tasty feast.

Well, shit. That was an overcorrection.

"Nothing," he finally said. "It's just been a weird day."

Across from Jairzinho sat Vatche's two Baggins-sized half-siblings. A half-brother named Bruce and a half-sister named Eva. Both looked young enough to not realize adults were just overripe versions of them. "It's been a *weird* day," Eva agreed.

Bruce leaned forward on his elbows. "But they cancelled *school* about it!"

At the other head of the table to Jairzinho's right, the matriarch of the family ruled from a beautifully carved antique wooden chair. She wasn't quite tall enough to rule from just the chair, though. So she ruled from her perch atop a stack of not-so-antique *New Yorker* magazines as well. That got her head over the lip of the table. Hasmik was her name, and coughing on crossword puzzles was her game.

"You cheer for school is cancelled?" Hasmik tapped the eraser of her pencil on the table. "Why must you make me to be the old woman of usual, hm? Now I must tell you of my walk to the schoolhouse! Not four minutes as for you, no, but four *hours!*"

"Uphill in both directions?" Eva asked.

Bruce frowned. "That's *impossible!*"

Hasmik waved her pencil at Eva and laughed. Or she was having herself a death rattle. Hard to tell. It was a phlegmy hack clawing its way out of a smile, at any rate.

Jairzinho imagined Hasmik and Ladybug would have a lot to talk about. They both occupied similar spaces. *Vis-a-vis* the relative proportion of feet to graves. Plus, they were fluent in the same expectorant language.

What a nasty thing to think about his host.

Rounding out the domestic idyll was Hamazasp, the Russian father-in-law. His contribution was to trail his wife around the kitchen, quietly repeating one question in Russian, over and over.

Jairzinho watched him. Asked Vatche, "what's he saying?"

"He's asking if he can help," Eva explained on Vatche's behalf. She bounced when she spoke. As if one demanded the other. "Mom used to let him help, but then Bruce got food poisoning and she said, that was that!"

"I barfed FAR," Bruce marveled, as though he were witnessing it anew.

Jairzinho allowed himself a flash of inadequacy: these two children were already bi-, probably *tri*lingual.

Hasmik hiccupped, burped and sucked saliva from the corners of her mouth. "Bruce! No barf for dinner."

"It's *history*," he wheedled.

Hasmik's skeleton finger creaked from side to side. Like a NO TRESPASSING sign outside of an abandoned mannequin factory. "Not everything is history, just because it happened!"

"Bruce tries to get in good with Mum Mum Hamasyan," Vatche explained from the seat next to Hasmik. His eyes darted between Jairzinho and Hasmik's crossword. "She loves history. Don't you, Mum Mum?"

"I *am* history." She was overcome by a violent coughing fit that, in a different dimension, might have been mirth.

"I'd say we're all living history right now," Jairzinho noted.

"Oh!" Vatche shouted. He pointed to the crossword. "Fifteen across, th-"

Hasmik slapped his hand. "You leave me alone!"

"You will not get it!"

"You leave my puzzles alone!"

Jairzinho frowned at his lap. *We're all living history right now.* He thought that had been pretty deep.

Alas: steamrolled.

[*That son of a* **mother** stuck that dog in a cage!! That dog shoulda frickin' *known* not to trust him! She'd had her shot to make trails and no, she was too frickin' sleepy or what? So she could frickin'] endure this. So Meatball had thought, anyway. She'd tried focusing on Sheriff. He'd become a kind of…he calmed her down.

Then [that frickin' bulldog-lookin' lady, she goes and takes Sheriff to who the heck knows where? Some Timbarktu place ain't nowhere that dog can frickin' smell him. So] Meatball tried her hardest to [stick around and smell the frickin' hydrant, only all them hydrants got *got*, capeesh? Ain't nothin's left's gonna keep] Meatball in her head, being [locked up] was sub-optimal to be sure, but [bein' locked up with some other frickin' mutts, that don't] seem particularly safe. For anyone.

But especially not for them.

So [that dog gave it a real frickin' go at] staying in her head. Meatball did her best to calm down...to just relax. She wouldn't be here forever. The Liberator would come and get her out. Any second now. He [was gonna keep that dog here forever and] *be back shortly.*

Meatball ducked her head. Did her best to ignore Ducky and Boo's roughhousing right behind her.

And, of course, to ignore the Other Dog.

In the next crate over, Topher watched and drooled.

Hasmik nodded, or else fell asleep and woke up several times in rapid succession. She coughed. It sounded like she was regurgitating a toad. "What is your name?"

Vatche patted his Mum Mum on the shoulder. He didn't pat too hard. So as not to run his hand through, maybe. "That's Jairzinho, Mum Mum. Remember?"

"Ah. Jairzinho, yes. Do you know of the Armenian genocide?"

"I told him, Mum Mum."

"Mum Mum *loves* the genocide," Eva bounced.

Bruce laughed. Hasmik darkened.

"She doesn't *love it*," Vatche parried. Much more softly than Hasmik would probably have liked. "She just loves *talking* about it."

"Harrumph," Hasmik said. She added, "blech" and "kaw."

"Let's talk about something a little less dreadful," Arpine suggested from the kitchen, "hm?"

"You want to bury your head in sand?" Hasmik brushed invisible crumbs off her crossword. "You please. Go on. Me, I wish to know."

Vatche leaned in and smiled. "Unless it is fifteen across."

"You leave my puzzles *alone!*"

Jairzinho turned towards the two children. "So…uh…what do you want to be when you grow up?"

Eva's answer was clear enough from the way she blasted out of her seat. "ASTRONAUT!"

Bruce folded his arms and lifted his chin. "All I know is *I'm* not going away to college. I want to live with my Mommy for-*ever.*"

Arpine and Hamazasp both laughed into the soon-to-be lunch.

"I want to go to *space!*" Eva enthused. "I wanna be a *Guardian of the Galaxy!*"

"You can't be a *Guardian of the Galaxy*," Bruce snapped, "unless they snatch you up in their spaceship and fly you away!"

"Okay!"

Bruce grimaced. "You can't just *wait* for them to snatch you up!"

"Okay!"

Bruce planted his elbow on the table. Leaned towards Jairzinho like a soliticous neighborhood bartender. "Can you tell her about joining the *Guardians of the Galaxy?*"

Jairzinho stared back at Bruce. The way the neighborhood lush stares his Jack and Coke, on the night before he joins AA.

Topher the drooling boxer looked over to his new friends. He was always excited to have new friends in his home! Or, one of his homes! First home was with Family, but now they were always going away. To quite exotic places, from the smell of it. They came back with such unusual profusions of odor! And when they were off getting those, they brought Topher here to second home.

But the more they went away, the longer Topher stayed at second home. Then for the last year or so, Topher had spent more time at second home than first home. Loads and loads of days and nights at a time, here at second home. So it wasn't really second home anymore, was it? It was just home.

He'd been here about twenty-five days and nights this time. Quite a while. So he knew the ropes. He would definitely show his pals about them once playtime came. Which was supposed to have come by now, but it sounded loud outside. And Topher didn't like loud outside. So he was happy to wait and just look at his new friends.

He looked and he drooled.

Jairzinho recounted everything he could remember about Star-Lord's backstory, expounding well beyond the limits of Eva's interest. "He's not my favorite one," was her last word on the matter.

Bruce, meanwhile, apparently found Jairzinho's performance satisfactory. "What about you?" he asked.

Vatche laughed.

Jairzinho looked to each of the half-brothers. "What about me what?"

Vatche laughed harder.

"What," Bruce explained, "do you wanna be when you grow up?"

Jairzinho frowned. "I *am* grown up."

"…when you were a kid, you wanted to walk stranger's *dogs* around all day?"

Now Hasmik was laughing. Again: maybe.

Jairzinho couldn't help but join them this time. "No, as a matter of fact, I didn't. I…don't even want to now. Anymore."

"So why do you?"

Jairzinho sighed. "Growing up is…harder than you think."

Bruce frowned, then flung a reckless pointer finger at Jairzinho. *"You* don't know what I think!"

Jairzinho laughed. "True enough."

"So," Hasmik asked, "what is your ambition? What do you look in the mirror and you say, *this* is what I want?"

Jairzinho laughed. Ran his right palm back along his face. So his right fingers pointed towards his right ear. He twisted his neck to rest his head wholly in his palm.

It was a bizarre pose he'd never once struck before.

He blinked his eyes clear.

"I don't know. To get out of this goddamned city. Sorry," he added to Eva and Bruce. "To…have Tia love me." He rubbed at his face. He felt his cheeks flush from the outside before the heat reached inside. He sure was being candid today, huh? "Because I don't know if she does anymore."

"Tia," Hasmik asked, "this is your sexual partner?"

Jairzinho glanced towards the children. Back to Hasmik. "Uh…yes?"

Hasmik tilted her head. "You do not know?"

"I mean…there are kids here."

"And how must you imagine they *got* there?"

195

Vatche patted Hasmik's arm. "He is basically American, Mum Mum. He is verklempt about genitals."

"I'm not..." Jairzinho didn't know which charge to dispute first. "I'm not *basically American.*"

Everyone, even the children, said "eeeeeh."

"Verklempt?" Hasmik squinted at her grandson. Looked at her crossword. "Vatche!" she gasped, followed by some probably not-particularly-nice stuff in Armenian. "You have told me fifteen across!" She smacked at him. Gently.

Vatche laughed. "It was collecting so much dust!"

"As do I, you would run me from town?!"

Vatche laughed even harder, and poked at the air in front of Hasmik.

"Hey," Jairzinho said quietly. "I kind of...feel like I'm getting steamrolled here. A little bit."

Hasmik stopped laughing. So did Vatche. They both nodded solemnly.

"You are right," Vatche granted. "My apologies."

Jairzinho nodded. Waited for someone to brusquely change the subject. So he could get mad at them.

They didn't. They were all just looking at him. Apologetically.

Jairzinho marveled. Less at the apology this time, and more at what prompted it.

At how clear the air could get. If you just decided to speak, instead of stew.

...not all bodywater was equal...the stuff that barmit didn't completely hate, that was dark and thick and coppery...the

stuff dripping on her head now was thin and clear and slob-
bery...

...she looked up at the big drooling dog...he was drooling
on her...which barmit hated...and he was drooling on ladybug
too...which barmit hated...which was weird that she would
hate on somebody else's behalf...and she hated that that was
weird...

...ladybug shook herself...

...sprayed the boring bodywater everywhere...

...everybody in the other crate hated that too...especially
meatball...a big glob of slobber plopped onto meatball's
face...not as big as was on barmit's head though...

[Ka-blooey! That dog got a goober facial from that big frickin' mutt over yonder. Pretty funny. Except] Meatball noticed
that the slobber smelled like...this place. Like nowhere *except*
this place.

As though the one from whom the slobber came had been here…[trapped in this frickin' pigsty for almost a frickin' month!]

[This was where The Liberator's leavin' that dog off? In this frickin' pigsty?! For a FRICKIN' MONTH?!]

No, Meatball knew. The Liberator wouldn't do th-

[Wouldn't he? *Ain't* he? Where'd he get to then?]

Meatball [was bein' a frickin' dink, and that dog] felt herself trembling, so [that dog started smackin' her frickin' jaw 'cause it was time for somethin' to go down, ain't that right?]

No.

[Ain't it time to quit sittin' on that dog's freakin' keister and do somethin'?]

No!

[Ain't it?]

"No!" Arpine tutted at her husband, who was dangerously close to 'helping'.

Hamazasp withdrew his hand from the stove dial.

Arpine lifted her knife from the chopping block. Gestured *away* with the point.

Hamazasp complied.

Arpine returned to chopping.

Jairzinho watched them and smiled.

"You want to talk?" Hasmik asked.

Vatche leaned forward. Hands clasped. "You feel we have steamrollered."

Jairzinho felt his tongue dart over his lower lip. Another weird tic. He shrugged. "It's all good." He settled in his seat. Maybe for the first time. "Do you guys like living here?"

Hasmik narrowed her eyes.

"I mean, in the city. Not this house. The house is, uh…" Jairzinho released the word as it caught in his throat. "…gorgeous."

"Does it matter?" Vatche asked. "You do not. You expect we will change your mind, by saying yes that we do?"

"I don't know," Jairzinho shrugged. "I don't know."

"Yes!" Hasmik wheezed. "You worry about happiness, about love. You try to bully for both. Muscle them, yes?" Hasmik flexed her arms. From the sound of it, every bone in her torso exploded. "Grr, love, you shall do as I say! Happiness, you are mine! But you cannot bully for either. So you ask me, what do I do?"

After a few seconds, Jairzinho realized the silence was for him to ask. "Uh…sure."

"Life is simple. Listen!" And then she spoke in Armenian for a solid minute and a half, and everybody around the table nodded in agreement.

Jairzinho looked a question to Eva.

Her bouncing was restrained, grave. "Mum Mum Hamasyan is very wise."

"What did she say?" Jairzinho asked.

"Just, like, regular Mum Mum stuff."

"Alright!" Arpine shouted. "Lunch is ready!"

Jairzinho thought about pressing the question. About what she'd said. But…he didn't really have to. He had a feeling he knew what she'd *meant*.

Besides. He was hungry.

"Should I take some to Ms. Tubcut and the doggies?" Eva asked.

Jairzinho smiled. "In a bit. They're resting."

- 7 -

Oh yes, Meatball was getting quite upset, wasn't she? Oooh *yes*, now that she had been stuck in a *separate crate* from Barmit, and she couldn't poison Kelso's homewrecker against him! More than…she already was! Poisoned!

Kelso, roaming free outside the crates, walked right up to Barmit's crate and peered in. The homewrecker's head was basically on the floor, covered in this big droolyboy's spit.

He gazed up into the droolyboy's eyes. Droolyboy was staring vacantly at Kelso's crated walkmates.

Slowly, Droolyboy turned to look at Kelso through the bars of the crate.

Kelso was mad at him for drooling on his homewrecker. Like, in a way it served Barmit right, didn't it? Yes it did, and thus: ha ha, neener-neener. In a way.

But also: it annoyed Kelso. And that wasn't the experience he wanted to have right now, was it? No it wasn't. He wanted to gloat, man.

He walked over to Meatball's crate. Ooooh, she was so upset! So *furious* that she couldn't keep wrecking Kelso's *life*, perhaps?

Astrid woofed at Kelso. Padded over. She wanted Kelso to step away from the crate.

Kelso didn't want to do that. And he'd had it up to his beautiful, perfectly-sculpted eyeballs with Astrid's high-paw. He wanted to *gloat,* pitbull superiority complexes be damned.

So Kelso flattened his ears to the back of his head. A warning.

Astrid hesitated. Cocked her head slightly. Looked to Meat-ball. Back to Kelso.

In the crate: Ducky jumped on Meatball's back.

Meatball swung around and snapped.

Ducky fell backwards. Tumbled into Boo.

Boo wagged, juked, jittered.

The mute little weenie-dog in the small crate said *Hfff.*

Droolyboy drooled.

Outside: Kelso pressed his nose into the crate.

Meatball snapped at it.

Kelso pulled back and pressed again. Ha! Gloat! Gloat gloat gloat!

Ducky lunged forward to the front of the crate.

Astrid slapped at Kelso. Her paw connected with Kelso's right ear.

The weenie-dog said *hffff.*

Ladybug *hllARPH*ed at Astrid.

Astrid looked to Ladybug. Followed Ladybug's gaze.

To the weenie-dog in the small crate. *Hffff.* The terror in her eyes. *Hffff.* The cry catching in her throat. *Hffff.*

Even Kelso stopped to look. The weenie was trying to voca-lize. But she couldn't. There was that thing on her neck, that thing that blasted her with some truly noxious cloud every time she tried to bark.

And yet...she kept trying to bark.

Hffff.

Kelso could smell that miasmic spray from here. So if the weenie-dog was subjecting herself to that awful whateveritwas, over and over...she must have felt she had a pretty darn good reason for barking, mustn't she? She must have.

So Kelso followed her gaze. To Boo.

Boo, shaking and humming and pissing. Right behind a highly agitated Meatball.

Next to Kelso, Astrid *woof*ed. Not at him this time. She was looking at Boo too.

hhhBLAFK! Ladybug shouted. By which she clearly meant

Unthinking cad! Thou doltish spot of ink that sealést pacts of slav'rous blood! What hast thou done?

At once she glimpsed the causal chain, which bound the crated Lot to fates befitting wives. Assault, the pillar bearing burdens weighted as a dog bled dry, o edifice most hideous, thine walls of flesh do tip the scales t'wards *guilt!* For had she simply borne the salted slobber as did Barmit, shunting not her cross with shakes and shimmies selfish past compare...

But soft. Twas done. Reflections vain and toothless serve to savage naught but she whom they reflect. The

[spit told her everything she'd gotta know, see? That dog over *there'd* been *here* for basically *since the frickin' world started,* and so that dog *here* what was] Meatball tried to [keep a lid on it, why don'tcha! Fact is, there ain't no way nobody's bustin' outta here anytime soon, because the Liberator, ha, what a frickin' *laugh,* that guy left that dog high and frickin' dry...only that ain't totally true since now that dog's sittin' in somethin' kinda wet and]

Yo OH my FUCKIN' GOD brah LOOK at BOO, this LONG-nosed FREAK here just PISSED himself HA ha WHAT the FUCK DUDE? DUCKY jumped UP onto MEATBALL to TRY to get OUT of the PISS but he FELL off AGAIN so INSTEAD he just BOUNCED from his FRONT legs to his BACK legs like SPLISH SPLASH SPLISH SPLASH. HE didn't KNOW why the FUCK he was DOIN' that, ONLY that it was FUNNY and FUN and ALSO it MADE THE WORLD TURN RED at the EDGES again which was NICE in a FUCKED-up way just LIKE it WAS the LAST TIME and SO he kept DOIN' it ALL like SPLISH SPLASH SPLISH

Sssssssppppppppplllllllllaaaaaaaaaassssssssshhhhhhhhh

It wasn't fast enough it was still too *slow* it looked like Ducky was splishing and splashing as fast as he could but the world was still an underwater nightmare but it didn't *have* to be Boo *knew* this and there had to be a way to really kick things back off like when everything was all loud and cars were jumping and even when Astrid was jumping on leashes and he was really trying Boo was he needed to get back to that good life he'd gotten a taste of it he didn't want the taste he wanted the meal the whole meal gobble gobble yum at *normal speed* where was that world it was close Boo could tell Meatball was really on the edge and Kelso was close too really there was just so much in this room that was just dying to happen but it wasn't happening so Boo felt like he was dying so slowly for eternity which was why it was so annoying that the other dogs were trying so hard to *keep* things from happening if they would happen at a normal speed they wanted everything to be the slowest in the universe which made them villains which wasn't nice to think they were still Boo's friends but also they were villains kind of in a way but there was hope because as Boo's pee started to hit Meatball's feet which obviously pee isn't that big of a deal by itself but Boo tried to put all of his frustration into this pee so everyone would smell it and know like wow Boo is so frustrated and now the pee was sliding right under Meatball and she started doing her side-to-side happy dance which was still so *so* so slow and even though she really didn't seem too happy but that was okay because she was a villain even though she was a friend and anyway but it was movement the dancing was and more importantly it meant Meatball might start doing more than just the dance if she got nudged but now everybody was barking at Boo and Boo knew they were barking at him it was Astrid and the little-long one over in the corner they were barking well the little-long one was going *hffffffffff* but Astrid was *woooooooooof*ing and Ladybug was saying *hhhLLLLPHHH-HCKFFFFF* and it really felt like the way things had felt before the street sneezed and the cars jumped and everything moved the way it was supposed to and the world was normal and not torture so Boo shot his head forward and bopped Meatball on the back of the head with his nose and then Meatball spun around and lunged at Boo, teeth first. She came on fast. Too fast for Boo to fully appreciate it.

But still. The speed of the strike was beautiful, in its way. And Boo was nothing if not a lover of all things zippy. So he showed his appreciation the only way he knew how: he rolled back with Meatball's lunge and peed his gratitude all over her.

Oh dear. Meatball *really* didn't like that.

- 8 -

Jairzinho didn't even know what he was eating. He didn't care. He hadn't realized how hungry he'd been until the opportunity to eat arose. He'd have eaten dogfood if Arpine had put it in front of him. But she most definitely hadn't. This was… well, stew, that was the first thing. Which was funny. Given what he'd just been thinking. About not stewing. Not all bad, then. Ha, ha.

He wasn't the only hungry one, apparently. Lunch halted conversation. They ate in ravenous silence.

Which Jairzinho shattered by saying "mm." Followed by "Mrs. Hamasyan, this is all-"

Interrupted by ferocious snarling and screaming from downstairs.

"SHIT," Jairzinho bellowed. He slapped the table for no apparent reason. Sprang up from his seat. That made more sense. "Sorry for the bad language!" He bounded down the stairs. Vatche followed close behind.

Hasmik shrugged at her crossword. "English is not such a bad language," she reassured it.

Jairzinho hesitated at the door to Vatche's room. It sounded like some spook-a-blast horror movie in there. Demons shrieking. Dressers sliding. A lack of plausible human characters.

He couldn't hear Esther. Jesus. Had the dogs…?

Jairzinho cranked the knob and swung the door open.

Over his shoulder, Vatche said something.

Jairzinho couldn't hear him. Vatche could have yodeled through a megaphone and Jairzinho wouldn't have heard him. Not over this pandemonium.

Every single dog was barking at the center crate.

The crate unfurling an abstract masterpiece of blood and piss all over the floor.

205

"JESUS CHRIST!" Jairzinho screamed. He knew Vatche wouldn't hear him. That was blasphemy purely for his own benefit.

Ducky was smushed up against the door of the crate. Humping the corner to save his life. Eyes locked on Ladybug, naturally.

In the middle of the crate: Boo fought vainly against Meatball. The bulldog was snapping at Boo's neck. Not clamping. Striking. Like the fattest rattler the world had ever seen.

Boo's milky fur was matted with carmine. A chunk on his right flank had been torn open.

No fight, no flight. Jairzinho froze.

All he could think to do in that moment was turn to Astrid and scream "DIDN'T YOU LISTEN?!"

Astrid stopped barking. Lowered her head.

Charged at Jairzinho.

"Hey! Astrid! Sit!"

Astrid headbutted him in the thigh. Not hard enough to hurt. She'd pulled back at the last second.

She looked up and glared.

Ok. Message received.

Jairzinho raced around Astrid. Fell to his knees in front of the crate. Right into the blood and piss. He didn't care.

Up and over went the latch on the door.

As if on command: Ducky abandoned the corner. Hopped over the mauling in progress. Rocketed into the crate door.

Jairzinho let him batter it open with his head.

Free from the crate, Ducky wasted no time in barreling straight towards Astrid's ass.

"Get him!" Jairzinho ordered Vatche.

"I shall!" He turned around. Saw Ducky trying to hump Astrid from the flank. "Ha!" Off Vatche went to undo this different kind of latch.

Jairzinho watched the power with which Meatball snap snap snapped at Boo. He hesitated. Just a moment too long.

Kelso shot into him from behind. Tried to weasel under Jairzinho's arm. Trying to get into the crate.

Cognizant enough to feel bad about it, Jairzinho grabbed Kelso by the collar. Trusted adrenaline to help him out here.

He frisbeed Kelso across the room towards the bed. "Get him too!"

"I shall!" Vatche replied. He shifted the squirming Ducky to his left arm.

Stop thinking. Trust. Jairzinho plunged his hands into the cage fight. Grabbed two fistfuls of Meatball's backfat. Held tight.

He didn't bother trying to pull with his arms. He simply kept hold and tumbled backwards. Like he was trying to do a reverse somersault. As if he could.

He couldn't. Meatball was too heavy. And…*really chompy*. "FUCK! OUCH! STOP IT!"

Jairzinho was trapped. Flat on his back. Meatball thrashing and snapping on his chest. Meatball was still on *her* back, at least. If she flipped over…got a good angle on Jairzinho's face…

"Get him!" Jairzinho screamed from supine as Meatball kicked her legs and twisted from side to side. It was like trying to keep hold of a pudgy jackhammer.

Vatche paused in his crouch. Right hand holding Kelso in a sit. Left holding a squirming Ducky aloft, like a mechanic presenting a piece of engine and saying 'well *there's* your problem'.

"GET HIM!" Jairzinho screamed again.

Vatche looked from Kelso to Ducky and back. "Ah...?"

Stop thinking. *Trust*. "Clip Ducky to a leash off my belt and thr-"

"Where is the belt?"

"On the floor!" Jairzinho jerked his head away from Meatball's flailing paw. "Clip him and toss the leash over to Astrid!"

Vatche did so. Scramble, reach, clip, toss. Except Ducky's leash was still clipped to the rest of the carabiner belt. So the whole contraption flew across the air after Ducky.

Astrid dodged the flying Frenchie. Opened her mouth. Caught the belt in mid-air.

Jairzinho trusted her to know what to do. He had no goddamned idea why he trusted her to know. But clearly, she did. So *he* did.

Vatche scooped Kelso under his left arm. Knelt down next to Jairzinho. Reached for Meatball with his right hand. Grunted as Kelso bucked and snarled in his grasp.

"NOT HER!"

Vatche froze. "What?"

"HIM!!!" Meatball had wriggled onto her side. Jairzinho nodded to the crates. "BOO!!!"

"You are...not so scary."

"IN THE FUCKING CRATE!"

Vatche looked at Boo. Slumped in a puddle of her own blood. "Oh!"

Jairzinho was aware of Vatche sliding past. But nothing more. He just had to trust.

Meatball commanded his full attention. She had one paw planted flat on Jairzinho's chest*taaah* "FUCK!" he screamed as she scratched through his shirt. Drawing blood.

He could see her jowls flapping with each snap. Revealing and concealing her fangs.

Then he took a closer look at how he was holding her.

If she'd really wanted to…she could have ripped a chunk out of his arm already. But she hadn't. Perhaps that was a testament to how much she

Yoops! Spoke too soon.

"GAAAAH you *fucker!*"

The chomp was quick. More cobra than corn on the cob. Cold comfort.

Hot blood pumped from a grisly semicolon in Jairzinho's arm. He couldn't help but think of all the complications that could come with a dog bite.

No. Relax. He didn't walk any dogs without up-to-date papers.

No! Don't relax! Meatball took a few more snaps at his arm. None connected. Lucky.

Jairzinho glanced towards and past his feet.

Empty save effluvia. Vatche had gotten Boo out of the crate. Ok adrenaline. Let's do this.

Screaming himself through the pain, Jairzinho did his first sit-up in years. He pulled his hands back into his breastbone, then thrust them forward as hard as he could. Like he was chest-passing the world's meatiest basketball into the netting of the crate. Swish.

His back had the decency to hold the pain off until the thrust was done. But as he rose to shut the door, his muscles spasmed and locked.

"AAAH!" he rolled backwards. "THE DOOR!"

"I am on it!" Vatche cried. Which he was. He hadn't needed to be told.

Jairzinho struggled up onto his left elbow.

Vatche had dropped Kelso in his rush for the crate door. Kelso fought to get into the crate with Meatball.

Jairzinho flopped forward. Grabbed Kelso by the rear legs. Dragged him backwards.

Kelso whipped around. Snarled at Jairzinho.

Vatche shut the door of the crate. Locked it.

Jairzinho let Kelso go. Looked back to the crate.

What he expected was for Meatball to throw herself at the door as before. Roaring and bellowing. That would have felt like the proper dramatic conclusion.

Instead, Meatball just slumped down where she'd landed.

It was only then that Jairzinho noticed a constellation of shallow incisions all across her body. So Boo had gotten a few good licks in, too.

More on that later. For now, one at a time. Jairzinho dragged himself over to Boo.

"Good girl," he added to Astrid as he heaved himself towards the wounded Springer Spaniel. "Sorry I shouted."

Astrid wagged her tail. She didn't drop the leash from her mouth, though. Ducky choked himself, trying to tug his way towards Boo. Astrid held fast.

"You shouted at me too," Vatche pointed out.

Jairzinho sighed. "Sorry."

Vatche collapsed onto his bed, panting. "My goodness. My, my goodness."

Regaining his strength, Jairzinho crawled over to his backpack. Snatched it up. Reached for the first aid…

Oh shit.

He hadn't put the kit back after tending to Misha with it. None of it was here. The water, the coffee, the book, the kit. He'd left it all on West 15th.

Yet he'd had the presence of mind to keep the pack-lunch Tia had made. He'd moved it to the small pocket.

Why the fuck hadn't he thought to do that with the kit? Why...

The kit wasn't the only thing that was missing.

Jairzinho looked to Vatche.

Vatche seemed to have the same thought at the same time. He shot up to seated on the bed.

The empty bed.

"Where is Esther?" he asked.

Jairzinho learned about his own priorities: "Where the fuck is Sheriff?"

esther's eureka

- 1 -

Sheriff was very very sad. The magic had gone away. Bye bye, magic. What was the magic? He didn't know. If he did, he would definitely go running after it so he could fetch it.

Fetch had been fun once upon a time. It had been something Sheriff would have been just so super excited to do, was go fetch something that somebody he loved had thrown for him to fetch. That'd have been something to wag about.

But Sheriff's whole big world kept getting smaller and smaller. First one of his friends went away. Then Home turned into a mountain. Now this Babble Woman had taken him from Babble Man, and from the rest of his friends. And he didn't understand why. But it didn't really matter a huge lot. It wasn't like he'd been wag wag wagging back with his friends and now he wasn't. Maybe he even actually felt a little better being away from them, because that way he didn't feel bad about feeling sad. Now it made sense that he felt sad. Because he was alone.

Except for The Babble Woman.

She babbled even more than the Babble Man. Sheriff didn't even think that was possible like in terms of the Rules, like how you can only jump as high as you're allowed to jump by your legs. He thought nobody could out-babble the Babble Man. But he'd been wrong. Was it good to feel sad about being wrong? It seemed like a good reason. Sheriff definitely rathered being sad for a reason instead of for no reason.

Having a reason seemed like something to wag about though. Like a good thing. So he tried giving his tail the old heave-ho. Nope. Diddly-dink, that was what his tail gave Sheriff. For a while back there it almost felt like there was…something still there? But not anymore. Now it was nothin' but diddly-dink.

"Thisfrshoawazzngunawoikthoutthah *cutest* pupeesgotnthab-ahnchnaydohnseenobadydyoo?" The Babble Woman babbled. Sometimes Sheriff thought he knew what she was talking about, but then he realized he didn't. He wasn't even sure if she was talking to him, or just to the sky. The sky was very quiet today, and the Babble Woman was talking to it instead of Sheriff. He felt really really lonely. He missed his friends.

"Boyoodonseemsobraytlaykyooszooalyoomayhtwanagitsum pepnyurstep, yoogawtabe *walk* nreelpeppysowefyndemgaisdey-wanna *play with you.*"

Sheriff paused and tried *really really* hard to wag. Because playtime had always been just his tip-top *favorite.*

Still nothing though. And The Babble Woman kept walking anyway. She didn't turn around and try to have a playtime with Sheriff. So he'd just heard her wrong like a dummy anyway. Dumb Sheriff.

He missed his friends so much.

The Babble Woman walked Sheriff around a corner.

There were three boys with loud sticks across the street. They looked like they were playing a game with each other.

Sheriff did not like the sounds of the loud sticks. The loud sticks had scared Misha away. *But*, Sheriff liked playing games very very much. His especially most favorite was fetch. Which you played with sticks!

Wowee! The tail! It…come on…*hhhnnnng*…

Nope.

But The Babble Woman was walking towards the boys with loud sticks. So maybe they were new friends? Maybe Sheriff could play games with them?

He felt very sad, but maybe if these were new friends, and he could play a game with them, that might be better than sad? Wagging was better than sad but it was also harder. Sheriff had never really known about how it was harder, but he'd never been very very sad before. He didn't think so.

He looked up at the boys who he hoped would be his new friends, and play games with him. They were mainly interested in saying loud things at The Babble Woman though. Sheriff didn't like loud things that people said unless they were play-time things. But still, he missed having people say things to him instead of the sky. Even if they were loud, people saying things to you was what scared away lonely.

Sheriff didn't like lonely. He wanted it to go away. But if it did, what would he have left? What if lonely was his only friend?

He looked up at the loud boys with the loud sticks and hoped they would be loud at him. Maybe it'd get him wagging again, if they'd just look down at him and say

- 2 -

"*WHAT THE FUCK* IS WRONG WITH YOU?!"
  "DON'T YOU HAVE A FUCKING PHONE?!"
  "YOU SHOULD BE INSIDE!"
  "PUT YOUR HANDS UP!"
  "FREEZE!"
  "GET DOWN ON THE FUCKING GROUND!"

Esther put her hands up, but only high enough to seem like she was making fun of them. "Woah fellas, take it easy!"

For a moment they did, as Esther knew they would. How do you *not* take it easy, when you meet someone strolling through a warzone who addresses the occupying force as 'fellas'?

"You're supposed to be inside," grumbled the gunman on the left.

"For your own safety," Righty concurred.

The Middle, who surely imagined himself to be the smartest or the toughest or some other superlative of the group, needed a few extra seconds of grimacing before he felt comfortable concurring. "It's not safe out here," he clarified.

Esther shook her head and looked down at Sheriff. The sweet (if unusually morose) little fella craned his neck to meet her eye. "See Sheriff, I *told* you."

Sheriff didn't smile or wag his tail like usual. He just stood there. Hm. Esther had taken him to capitalize on his adorable giddiness. If she'd known he was gonna be in such a funk, she'd have gone for a different dog. Ladybug, maybe.

Oh well. He was still pretty cute, even when he was miserable. Which was what Esther usually looked for in a partner.

Esther gestured to Sheriff and chuckled, like he'd just told her a great joke. "He don't listen," she explained to the three gunmen.

The Middle was not amused. But a cheeky little grin flashed across Righty's face, and Lefty's took on an encouraging, doughy openness. A foot in the door, that was. All according to plan! Esther was basically like that British guy when it came to wrapping people around her finger. The one who convinced people to push actors off of buildings. What was he called?

"Hey fellas, you ever see the thing where the British guy bamboozles some British doofs into pushing British actors off a British roof? What's his name?"

"Brexit?" Righty offered.

Lefty laughed.

Righty scratched his neck. "Hey, I don't know. Brexit's the only British thing I know."

"HEY!" The Middle snapped. He waggled the gun at his hip. "Stop laughing! It's not menacing!"

Esther made a *pfffft* noise. "Anyway," she continued, "here's the only problem with this little cutey-patooty, is he loves his afternoon walk. Don't ya, Sheriff?"

Sheriff shone his deep-puddle puppy-eyes to Esther, then the gunmen, then back. His heavy tail lilted in a ghostly breeze.

Oh well. Esther plowed ahead as though Sheriff had done a double backflip and landed flexing like a bodybuilder. "GOOD BOY! YES YOU DO, GOOD BOY!"

She snuck a glance. Lefty and Righty were both hooked. Hook line and *sinker*, actually. Which worked twice over because that sounded like *stinker*, which was what The Middle was. Gloomy bastard. But the gloom was congealing! Which made

Esther think the stinker was sustaining that gloom purely by effort.

To think she'd been kinda scared about her eureka! She'd figured it might be kinda dangerous, but it was turning out to be a cinch!

J was gonna flip when he found out what Esther'd done. In a good way! He'd forgive her for all the times she'd called him Navi (totally her bad), for a start. Maybe let her split his dog-walking route with him? Who knew how grateful he'd be for her finding a way off the island?

- 3 -

"I swear to God, I'm gonna fucking kill her."

"Do not say such things," Vatche snapped. "There is an explanation."

Jairzinho stopped pacing. "What explanation? What could possibly justify her taking one of my dogs *without fucking telling me?"*

Hamazasp said something in Russian.

"He says," Arpine and Vatche translated at the same time, "you have to calm down."

Jairzinho sighed. Leaned his back against the wall. Slid down to sitting. He couldn't do anything but watch Hamazasp tend to Boo. The Hamasyan Pater (or whatever the Armenian word for that was) had some topical anesthetics on hand, and was somehow skilled with suturing. "From his youth," was all Vatche would say by way of explanation for both. Jairzinho didn't ask for clarification.

220

JAIRZINHO'S CURBSIDE GIANTS

Boo's chest rose and fell, rose and fell. It might have been soothing. If it weren't for the mountains of bloodstained gauze. Call it reassuring, then. The breathing.

That, and the fact that the gauze hadn't needed to be changed in a few minutes. The last three mounds of white had soaked through in seconds. That was good, right? The bleeding was slowing down…or maybe there was just less blood left.

Hamazasp's elbow pistoned in and out, in and out. Jairzinho watched the elbow. Instead of the needle piercing Boo's skin. In and out. In and out.

Another reassurance: knowing that someone could be wholly useless in one arena and essential in another. Hamazasp in the kitchen was cheap slapstick. Hamazasp with a needle and thread was art.

The artist mumbled in Russian.

Arpine said something back.

He lifted the thread.

She fetched a pair of small scissors.

Vatche sat down next to Jairzinho. "You want he does you next?"

Jairzinho kept his eyes on the elbow. "Hm?"

"Your arm."

"Oh." Right. Where Meatball had chomped him. Jairzinho looked down at his impromptu bandage. Considered the needle. "I'm good. I don't think it's that bad. Thanks though." He shook his head. "Where the fuck did she go?"

Vatche patted Jairzinho's knee, softly. "She will be back."

"What if she isn't?"

"I know this woman. She is a good woman. If she can come back, she will."

Jairzinho turned to look at Vatche. "Okay, but what if she can't? What do we do about it?"

"What do you want that I should say? Let me fetch…"

(The Giants stirred, in and out of their crates.)

"…my many large guns from the closet, we shall scour the streets? I love Ms. Tubcut, she is a dear friend, but she could go anywhere. She is her own monster."

"You mean master?"

Vatche smiled.

Jairzinho forced a smile in return, kneading his hands together. "This sounds super shitty, but…what if something happened to her, and Sheriff is out there all alone?"

Vatche scratched at his stubble. "You are a bowl-putter-downer."

Oh boy. Another little saying. "I don't know what that means."

Vatche chopped the air with his hands. "Let us say that you have a lovely bowl that has been belonging to your family for many generations. You are one day eating fruit from this beloved bowl. You are holding it in your hand and walking through the house to check on your dear Mum Mum. You walk into her room and you say 'hello, my dear Mum Mum!' Only she does not reply to your hello. Then you step in and you see, good heavens, she lies on the floor, with her face on the floor!

"In such a moment as this, there is…there *are* only two kinds of people. There is the bowl-droppers, who…" he held out an invisible bowl, then released it, "…drop this beloved bowl so they can fall onto their knees and tend to dear Mum Mum as quickly as they can. Then there is the bowl-putter-downers. These are people who will have the two thoughts at once. They think, 'I must tend to my dear Mum Mum, *but* I also must not shatter this beloved bowl, for it once was hers!' And these people, they find a place to put down this beloved bowl. *Then* they go tend to their dear Mum Mum. Do you understand that I am saying you are the bowl-putter-downer?"

Jairzinho racked his eyes towards the ceiling. "Is that a bad thing?"

"It is not good or bad. It is a thing."

"So why am I a bowl-putter-downer?"

"When we wrestle with the dogs, we must think of how I may pull Boo from the crate when I have already hands full of dogs. I am a bowl-dropper. I am thinking, I will throw this little black sexgoblin out the door. Put him on the high shelf and hope he does not jump. I am thinking of simple things, because I am not thinking with my thinking brain. But you? You think of the leash and the throwing to the responsible pitbull. This means that you must have Meatball on your tummy for longer, like Mum Mum must be face down for longer."

"*HAH?*" called Hasmik from upstairs.

"Her ears! So sharp!" Vatche leaned his head out the door. "*This is not your business, Mum Mum!*"

"*WHY AM I FACE DOWN?*"

"*Would you like I shall tell Jairzinho what is* twenty-three *down?*"

"*Blech a-hackh!*"

Vatche waved his Mum Mum away. "I say these things because you are a bowl-putter-downer. You think of what to do and you do the thing you think of. I feel you have thought of something to do about your Esther distress. You must not wait for I will work it out and tell you, yes, this is a good idea. I will not think it is a good idea. But I am home. I am with the people I love. And we are all together. You understand? I will help you as I can. But I will not expect that I will like your idea."

Across the room, Hamazasp leaned back on his shins. Laid his hand gently on Boo's chest. Spoke in Russian.

Arpine spoke back.

Hamazasp stood and said something else.

Arpine sighed and rose. "She will be alright."

"Uh…he," Jairzinho corrected. This wasn't the moment for pedantry. But he *was* a bit wary of a prognosis from a guy who couldn't tell boy dogs from girls.

Arpine glared at Jairzinho. "The dog will live. But we must let *him* rest."

Vatche shot to his feet. Offered Jairzinho a hand up. His left hand.

Jairzinho looked at his own left arm. At the bloody bandage.

Laughing, Vatche switched to the right hand. "Come, you can tell me of your bad idea upstairs."

Jairzinho grasped Vatche's hand. Winced as the latter pulled him to his feet. He shot a glance towards Meatball as he left.

She was sitting in her typical mermaid's pose. Flat on her ass, rear legs sprawled to one side, forelimbs locked. But she looked even more miserable than usual. Like someone had finally learned to speak dog, and that someone was Ben Shapiro.

Meatball had all but *told* him that she didn't want to go in the crate. Jairzinho. Not Ben. She'd fought him. Hard. And yet he'd ignored that obvious warning.

He looked deeply into Meatball's splotchy eyeballs.

In them, Jairzinho glimpsed his own blind spot.

He'd always been enraged when his dogs failed to understand him. But that failure to understand was mutual.

He'd never imagined they could have internal lives. Not really. It was hard to articulate. It wasn't that he didn't believe them conscious. It was…that he didn't believe they did anything with it. He hadn't believed that dogs could have stresses and hopes, however limited. That they could have good moods and bad moods, good days and bad days. And be just as oblivious to where these moods came from as Jairzinho was of his own.

Meatball wasn't fighting to be difficult. She was fighting because she hated crates. And who could blame her? Given the oubliette life she'd been forced to live in that damned closet? Oh, or what about earlier? When she'd been jerking for the curb and Jairzinho had kept reeling her back in? She'd had to shit. Simple as that. And he even *knew* that, yet he kept demanding that she hold it. Why? Because it didn't matter to *him* in that moment?

Well, there had been a tank, to be fair. But still!

The obvious truth, spotted in hindsight: just because he held the leashes didn't make him the center of the canine universe.

He'd triggered some alarm system in Meatball. And Boo had paid the price.

Jairzinho doubled back into the room. Knelt down in front of the crate.

"I'm so sorry, girl. You told me. I should have listened."

He had to try hard not to imagine Meatball had sculpted her face into an expression of forgiveness. That would have made him feel better. But Meatball didn't forgive him. Because she hadn't understood him. She never would.

He'd have to make it up to her another way.

"You're a good girl," he told her.

Before he left the room, he went to check on Boo. To apologize. But Boo was asleep. His eyes and lips were quivering.

Jairzinho let him dream.

225

What made it a nightmare was that there *was* no monster. No Bad Dog. No Other.

It was her. All her. Only her. When Meatball stepped back to make room for the Other Dog, all that she was actually removing was a sense of authorship over her actions. A sense of responsibility.

"You're a Good Girl," the Liberator said. And then he went to fawn over Boo.

Boo, whom Meatball had torn to pieces with her underbite. All because she'd allowed herself to [imagine that somethin' else was in charge of that dog]...

But it had been her. She knew because she had watched it all happen. So it had seemed, at least. As though she'd been watching from above.

Yet she could remember it from the *inside*. From behind her own eyes.

A Good Girl? What a sick joke. Meatball wasn't a Good Girl. She was the Baddest Girl of all.

Why had she *done* that to Boo? What had Boo ever done to her? Being on opposite sides of The Liberator during walks as they were, Meatball and Boo scarcely ever crossed paths. Never ever *ever* had it entered her mind to hurt Boo, let alone *maul* him. So why had she done it? That was the only thing she couldn't remember. Perhaps that was the answer.

The Good Girl in Meatball had left her post at a critical juncture, leaving the Bad Girl in charge. And now, Boo suffered for it.

Meatball looked to Ladybug in the next crate. Her eyes preached mortified stoicism.

The bulldog understood the pug as she never had before.

226

- 4 -

"You wanna walk your dog," The Middle rumbled, "then walk him around your fucking apartment. We got a siege-type event on."

Esther slapped her forehead. "Oh, right, great idea. I shoulda just let him piss and shit on my rug that's only been in my family for *eight generations. That's* what I shoulda done."

The three gunmen attempted to cow Esther with stony silence. They clearly didn't know who they were dealing with.

The flanks broke first, stifling reedy giggles.

"You guys gotta stop laughing!" The Middle shouted.

"She kinda got you," Lefty mumbled.

"No she didn't *get* me," The Middle snapped. "Like that was some clever comeback? She didn't *get* me."

"You gotta admit," Righty chimed in.

"No I *don't* gotta admit." The Middle stomped his foot like a petulant child. Given that he didn't seem to be much out of his teen years, the effect was compelling. "How was I supposed to know about the rug? Stop *laughing.*" The child in The Middle slapped at Lefty. Lefty juked backwards, his pursed lips threatening to break into a crooked little grin.

And then they were off, the three of them slapping at each other and chuckling, lost in their own little world. Friends, Esther quickly deduced. Young friends who'd joined a militia for fun. She'd have gambled all fifty-three dollars of her savings that none of them could legally buy a drink. And yet here they were, armed to the teeth in the middle of Manhattan.

She tutted internally. When she'd been in school, the worst thing she and her buddies had ever done was call one of those stripper businesses and sent a working lady, ambitiously named "Thighssac Screwton" (so it'd be an educational experience!), to their principal's office. That was about it. Well, that and the time she lit Reina's car on fire, but that had been personal. And *earned*.

Would she and her buddies have ever joined a white nationalist militia and started shooting people up in the middle of Manhattan? No way. But these ones had.

There was some sort of profound conclusion to be drawn from that, but Esther couldn't find her way to it. Instead she said "so you guys are shootin' up the city, huh?"

Righty looked down at his rifle, like he had to check. "Yeah. You sleep through the exciting stuff?"

The playfight stopped, as though broken up by an unseen chaperone. "Yeah," The Middle grinned, sensing his opportunity, "were you, were you *taking a nap*, you…*old person?!*"

Lefty and Righty waited for Esther's response.

Shit-talkin'! She was shit-talkin' with the youth! Right in her element, this was! "Sure I was takin' a nap. You're gonna learn they're somethin' sweet, once your mommy stops makin' you take 'em."

"My mommy d…my *mom* doesn't…" The Middle sputtered for a moment. "My…at least my mom is still alive! Yours probably isn't!"

"Why do you gotta take it there?" Righty asked.

The Middle slumped his shoulders. "What?"

Lefty shook his head. "That's fucked up, dude."

Esther frowned. Her mom *was* dead. Had been for long enough that Esther could very easily have laughed about it. But she frowned.

After all, these kids feeling bad about what The Middle had said to Esther might make them that much more likely to help her out. She knew the impulse well.

"Forget my mom," Esther huffed, "you guys notice how cute my fuckin' dog is?"

Righty flinched at Sheriff, as though he was only just noticing him. "Is he friendly?"

"Friendlier than me. You wanna say hi?"

"Can I?" Righty asked more plaintively than somebody with an assault rifle had ever asked for anything.

Esther smiled like her life depended on it. "Sure!"

The Three Stooges mistook that for an open invitation. They all three converged on Sheriff, like toy tanks pushed across a tiny map by generals.

Betrayed by The Babble Woman! At her signal, all three of the loudstick boys descended! Their horrible toys clinked and clanked against their belts!

Instinct took over! Sheriff didn't have *time* to have a little old think about what he should do! He just did what came most naturally to him, because it had always been his favorite: he scrambled!

The Loudstick Boys with Horrible Toys were scary, but running away from the scary thing was scooping something up from the bottom of the imaginary kibble bowl! It wasn't like just a *wag*, but it was a little trick that might be worth fetching!

229

JUD WIDING

Because sometimes when Sheriff used to do it *all* the time, it was something he really liked…anyway!

He ducked straight under one pair of legs and went left *really really* fast, like *veeeer* and then *vrrooow!*

Sheriff's leash caught and snapped, torqueing his head down and to the side.

Success!

He'd snared a human leg! But just one. That was okay though! That wasn't the trick!

The trick was the other leg zooming in, like *bbbrrrooooa!* Then it plowed *well* hard into Sheriff's little ribs, *pow.*

Ow.

That was the ticket! But to what? Sheriff had forgotten.

The person attached to the legs fell over! Onto Sheriff!

Sheriff's tail swished back and forth, back and forth. He turned around to try to look at it. Hey there!

The tail swished.

HEY!

Sheriff couldn't see his tail, but there was something *really* long on his butt that was the same color as him.

He was gonna chase it!

So he tried spinning in a circle but his butt ran away and so did the thing he was trying to chase. So Sheriff tried going fast, like *way* faster than any dog had basically *ever* spun in a circle basically *ever.*

He was gonna catch the guy hanging onto his butt but then he felt a bunch of hands on his back.

Wow! Have you ever spun around really really fast and then stopped really really, uh, stoppy? It was like the whole world was going *wooooaaaaaahhh!* Sheriff wobbled a bit but there were all these hands to hold him up and pet him and love him.

One of the loudsticks bopped Sheriff on the head, but that was alright! That just meant the boys started petting Sheriff on his head!

This was it! Getting tripped over! *Swish swish, swish swish.*

His tail! He felt it! Wagging!

Ow. They were scratching him kind of hard.

And when they pet him they didn't do it really soft like most people. They did it like they were one of the toys at the guh-roomers, with the sinks and the baths and all the other horrible things. The guh-roomers was basically like a dungeon for dirty dogs.

Sheriff didn't feel good, to be pet like he was just a dirty dog.

The three boys were petting him so hard he was having a hard time standing up now. Like they were all trying to pet him the *most*.

Sheriff stumbled a bit. The sharp bits on the tips of one of the hands scratched his side. It hurt. Sheriff yelped and looked up at The Babble Woman for help. But she was just looking down at the boys and babbling at them.

So he was even more alone than he'd thought.

A hand pet Sheriff on the chin so hard it made his teeth bite onto his tongue. He yelped again, but right when he did The Babble Woman made a loud flashstorm noise like AH AH AH AH AH. So nobody heard poor Sheriff.

- 5 -

What was really helpful was how the Hamasyans kept telling Jairzinho how bad his plan was.

Granted, Vatche was just living up to his word. Re: thinking Jairzinho's idea was a bad one. But the rest of the family dog-piling on was…superfluous. And a pun. Nice.

"This does not even count as idea," Hasmik roasted him from her throne at the table. "This is like if you would ask me, Hasmik, how do you plan on living longer? And then I would say to you, my idea is I will die later. You see?"

Jairzinho chuckled at the sink. Filling the last of the bottles that Vatche had donated to the bad idea with tap water. "I get it. I get it."

Vatche strode to his side. He leaned on the counter. "You know you can come back. Any time, you feel you are unsafe, you come back here."

"Thanks." The bottle overflowed. Jairzinho shut off the tap. Bent down. Loaded the last two water bottles into his back-pack.

"How come you don't leave the dogs?" Eva asked.

Jairzinho paused, crouched over his backpack. That was a good question. *The* question, really. He could leave the dogs. Go find Esther and Sheriff. Bring them back here. Wait this thing out. Whatever it was. That'd be safest for everyone.

Except he couldn't stay here. He couldn't wait. He needed to get home. To Tia. He needed to tell her. Tell her what? Everything. He just needed to tell her.

But…he couldn't leave the dogs. They were his responsibility. His Giants. And he'd already failed them twice. He already had one dog dead, and another abandoned.

Alright, maybe that was too dramatic. Jairzinho wasn't *abandoning* Boo by leaving him with the Hamasyans. The poor guy was stable. Not enough to walk, though. Certainly not to run.

They would take good care of him until all of this was over. Jairzinho had no doubt about that.

But then why not leave all of the dogs? Wasn't it irresponsible to put them back in danger?

Of course it was. That was the crux of the dilemma. The only way Jairzinho could justify it to himself was by positing that to remain on Manhattan was to remain in the greatest danger of all. So, by that logic, in trying to find a way off the island with the dogs, he was protecting them. It was a responsible and noble decision. Rather than a prideful and self-serving one.

But just one little poke at that and its logical consistency crumbled into dust. Like Jairzinho worried Hasmik would, if someone hugged her. If he was taking the dogs with him because he believed Manhattan was dangerous, why would he make no effort to help the Hamasyans (and Boo) out of the city? Was it because he respected the value of being in one's own space? Or was it because he knew they would slow him down?

This was all putting aside the most obvious concern: he had no idea how he was going to find Esther. Let alone how he was going to get off Manhattan.

He sighed. Zipped up the backpack. Rose to his feet.

Eva wasn't the only one waiting for an answer. The whole Hamasyan clan stared at him. Waiting for a good answer. Because they all saw it too. They all saw that there *was* no good answer.

So Jairzinho stopped trying to overthink it. Stopped trying to justify or equivocate. Let his heart speak.

It told him that the most perverse thing about this temptation to stay was that he wanted to succumb. His life would be so much easier.

And that was how he knew it was the wrong decision. Because it was easy.

"I wish I could," he told Eva. "But I have to know that they're safe."

Eva's brow dribbled over her eyes. "They will be."

"But I won't *know*."

"You could stay."

Jairzinho sucked his upper lip into his mouth. Bit on it. "I can't. I've got…people."

"But won't the dogs make it harder to get to them?"

Vatche with the save, thank goodness: "We do not know where is safe and where is not. What matters is the togetherness." He looked at Jairzinho. "Yes?"

Jairzinho didn't even need to nod. But he did.

The Hamasyans didn't need to say they understood. But they did.

Boo dreamt at speed. He was running running running, to where or from what, who could tell. It didn't even matter. What mattered was the supple Earth yielding beneath his feet, springing up to give each paw just the slightest extra boost, hurrying him ever onwards. He felt the wind in his face, snapping his ears like flags, cheering him on. "Boo," it said. He changed course, or maybe he'd always been moving towards it. Or he was moving away from it. The direction wasn't particularly important. Ever onwards, that was his destination. The excitement was in the going, not the getting.

"Boo," the voice repeated, and Boo could hardly recognize it. Because it was so quick. He tried to imagine it saying "Bbbbbbbooooooooooooo," and suddenly the whole identikit was right there. The Slowman. Moving much quicker, Boo noted. *Much quicker*. Or else *Boo* was moving slower.

Either way. The result was the same. Boo and the world had taken a step towards resynchronization. Pretty rad.

Boo cracked an eyelid. The Slowman was crouched nearly nose-to-nose with him. It was a perspective The Slowman had never before taken with Boo. Had Boo grown taller, or The Slowman smaller? So many changes, all exciting! Not *big* exciting, like a car jumping into the air. These were *small* exciting. But no less stimulating for their modesty.

Boo *thump thump thumped* his tail against the mattress. He stretched his nose towards The Slowman and took a sip of his human perfume.

He smelled nice. Boo had never really taken the time to smell him before, but…he smelled nice.

The Slowman stroked Boo's head as his eyes drifted shut. Goodnight, Slowman. Tomorrow you'll have a new name.

And then Boo was running again, ever onwards.

Meatball watched all of her friends become liberated, and forced herself to sit in the sad. Not [that dog] – *herself.* Meatball. The *real* Bad Girl.

Dissociation was a tempting escape, but Meatball knew it led nowhere other than a very red place. It wasn't sustainable. Sadness, unfortunately enough, was. And so it would be her punishment. The Liberator would leave her here, festering in filth like the big slobbering hamhock next door. She would stay here forever. It was what she deser-

The Liberator swung open the door to the crate. He leaned in, and said "Meatball, cayubee Good?"

235

Casting aside that nonsense in the middle, Meatball brought the bookends to touch. Meatball, Good. Good girl? He was still thumping on with that?

Except…this was different than the last time he'd said it. Last time was the way people always said "Good Girl". The voice started high and then went down.

This time The Liberator's cadence was more like "yuwanna-gofera *Walk?*" or "hoowanza *Treat?*"

A solicitation.

The Liberator wanted something of her, and it involved Goodness. He was neither demanding, nor informing, nor scolding.

He was imploring.

Was he wondering if Meatball could be Good Girl? That was…that didn't make any sense. A dog was Good Girl or Bad Girl because humans told them they were. Sometimes Meatball had figured out that a certain behavior was reliably one or the other, but she'd also received more than enough mixed signals in her life to blur the boundaries. Most times jumping up on the bed was Good Girl. Then sometimes it was BAD GIRL! You couldn't just…what, *be* a Good Girl ahead of time? As far as…ah…

The idea that one might pre-emptively be Good Girl was nearly impossible to grasp. But did that say more about the idea, or the mind trying to hold it?

Meatball huffed, licked her nose, and teetered forward out of her mermaid's pose. She lumbered tentatively towards the open door of the crate.

The Liberator smiled, rubbed her head, and clipped her up.

A familiar ichor pulsed through her body. But she made herself feel it. She stayed in her own head, giving the sensation no space to fill.

The fury left, as quickly as it came. Meatball remained. Like a ball bouncing through a room. In one door, out the other. The room was merely the space in which the ball bounced.

Meatball looked up at The Liberator and saw him as she'd never seen him before. She saw sunlight sculpting a block of ice into something beautiful.

And then it was just The Liberator's dumb face again.

Meatball blinked several times. Yep. Just the face. The vision had bounced out of the room just like the ball of anger.

She stepped outside of the crate, feeling like she had turned a corner. From what to what, she did not know. But she felt good about it, and she let herself feel that too.

The Liberator gathered the dogs around Boo on the bed. Alive, but asleep. No chance for Meatball to lick her contrition into the fur she had so savaged.

This, too, made her feel. This, too, Meatball felt.

"Stay safe," Vatche commanded. "Take your time. It is hardly past noon. You have hours of daylight. You know the turtle and the rabbit?"

Jairzinho laughed. "You wanna tell me you came up with the tortoise and the hare?"

"I did not, but they are quite good. Slow and steady. You are two short of running the Iditarod now, yes?"

Jairzinho looked down at his Giants and sighed. Six to go, as the lady in the Laundromat might have said.

No. Seven. He was going to get Sheriff back.

"Mhm," Vatche grunted. Maybe realizing it was too soon for those sorts of jokes.

They exchanged a glance. Thus was the comment wordlessly struck from the record.

They let laughter and a hearty embrace be their farewell.

a way home

- 1 -

They were like fuckin' kids again. Well, these wannabe soldier kids *were* kids. But Esther had gotten in their heads so good, and was messin' with 'em so bad, it was like she'd reversed them back to the other side of puberty. Hey British Guy, you got people to push an actor off a building? Big fuckin' deal! Esther pushed some kids off *time itself!*

But that wasn't something most people could hope to do. Esther was just uncommonly skilled at relating to the youth. She was all of her nieces' and nephews' favorite auntie. She knew because every time she asked them who their favorite auntie was, they always said "you are, Aunt Esther."

So it was basically nothing for her, to relate her way into these kids' minds and chip away at their defenses. Like a…like a secret agent of the brain or something. Agent Tubcut! It had a nice ring to it. Agent Tubcut had these *hostile enemies* (nice, that was a really solid Clancy-esque touch) right where she wanted them. Distracted by the cute puppy, fawning over sweet little Sheriff. Also known as: right at Esther's feet. Literally. Like she was a Queen and they were asking permission for something.

And now, like a Queen Cobra Secret Brain Agent: Esther struck.

"Yo," she related, "let's vibe on *level*. I'm not who you're tryin' to keep here, am I?"

Lefty looked up from Sheriff mid-*who'sagoodboy*. "Keep… here?" He glanced around the intersection.

"Nah, I mean on the island. On Manhattan. Yeet!"

"Uh…" Righty drawled. "I don't think we're trying to keep anybody here, are we?"

"Well," Lefty corrected him, "in the short term we are."

The Middle dutifully recited "it is not for us to dictate policy." He added "*who's* a good boy," but not to Esther.

"…" Esther retorted. "What I meant is, I'm not who you're all mad at. Not *really*."

"Um," The Middle replied after one second too many.

"We're not *mad*," Lefty insisted. "How could we be mad looking at a *wittle face wike dis!*"

Esther had not anticipated that this would be the hardest part of the plan to execute. "We're all on the same side, is what I'm sayin'. Fuckin'…culturally."

The Middle held fast to his "um."

"Because I'm white," Esther clarified, very cleverly.

Lefty sighed. "Why does everybody think this is a race thing?"

"Isn't it?" Righty pressed.

Lefty drooped. "Is it?" He glanced to Esther, as though for confirmation.

"How *isn't* it?"

"I figure it is," Esther volunteered.

"Uh…" Lefty shifted from one foot to the other. "I thought it was like a socialist uprising thing."

"Right," Righty nodded. "A race thing."

Lefty darkened slightly. "Socialism isn't racism."

"National Socialism?" Righty scoffed. "You kidding me? That's the Nazis!"

"I mean *real* socialism. The proletariat, and, um, handouts, and MoviePass, and all that."

"Do you even know what socialism is?"

"It's sharing, but also, it's bad. For some reason."

"Aren't the proletariat," The Middle wondered, "basically all Mexicans here?"

"Ha!" Righty cackled. "Race stuff!"

Lefty leaned back. "I just wanna clarify," he told Esther, "that this isn't a race thing for *me.*" He resumed petting Sheriff

Righty made a rude hand gesture. "It's for sure a race thing."

"Weeeell, not for me." Lefty pet Sheriff harder.

"*Weeeelllll*, it is for everybody." Righty pet Sheriff even harder.

"*Wwwwweeeeeeeeelllllll*, clearly not because it's not for me. I'm not a racist."

Sheriff yelped.

"*Wwwwwwwwwwwewwweeeeeeeeeeeeeeeeeeeeeeelllllllllllllllll*, you took up arms in a race thing, so, you know, the teapot. And the kettle."

"*WWWWWWWWW-*"

Esther cleared her throat. "Hey fellas?"

Righty and Lefty laid off Sheriff and looked up.

"What I'm sayin' is, I'm a white lady with a dog who's tryin' to get off this fuckin' island. I don't care why you're blowin' up bridges and shit. I just wanna know, is there one ya *didn't* blow."

"We'll tell you if you let us have Sheriff here!" Lefty cracked. Righty cackled.

The fear that it hadn't been a joke made Esther force a laugh that, for once, didn't come naturally. She'd have been the first to admit she pushed it a bit too hard.

HA HA HA HA HA, she thundered.

The three gunmen flinched, reflexively clutching their guns.

Jairzinho froze.

HA HA HA HA HA echoed through the empty streets.

That foghorn laugh. Esther. Jesus, what was she doing laughing in war-ravaged streets? That was some supervillain shit.

Okay. This was good. Laughing meant she was okay.

Sheriff was okay.

Jairzinho had planned on just running circuits. Increasing the search radius by a block each time. So having some direction, by *HA HA* or otherwise, was good.

He looked left and right. Never letting his gaze track up or down. He was getting quite good at that. For all the human remains littering the ground, or the blasted architecture above…eye-level was surprisingly untouched. Save the odd blood splatter.

So he kept his eyes there. Avoiding shop windows that might reflect those eyes back at him. He imagined there was quite a bit of damage there that he didn't want to see.

So where had the laugh come from? The left, or the right?

The jingling of collars distracted him. He tugged on the leashes. "Sit."

The Giants sat.

"Good dogs." Jairzinho listened.

The city hummed. It was deep, unhappy. Unsatisfied.

A distant rumble.

Paper rustling in a breeze.

HA HA HA HA HA…

Jairzinho and his Giants turned to the right.

"I don't see what's so funny about that," The Middle scowled.

Esther finished laughing by wiping her eye. "You're dreamin', kid."

The Middle crossed his arms and scowled. He was done petting Sheriff. Esther had struck a nerve. "I'm *not*. I'm telling you what he said. He said to Wade, that their last showdown could only have been at the STAPLES Center…*or* the Garden! Madison Square!"

Esther shook her head. "He's signed to the Lakers through 2021!"

"But then why would he say that, huh?"

"You'll have to ask him next time the Lakers come through!"

The Middle flapped the back of his hand towards Esther. "The fuck do you know?"

"Wait a second," Lefty protested, raising his hand. "If this is a race thing, why do we like LeBron?"

Righty didn't miss a beat: "He's an all-time great, stupid."

The Middle wrinkled his nose, like he'd just caught a whiff of his own personality. "How did we even get on this?"

Lefty scratched indiscriminately at Sheriff. "You made the basketball analogy."

"*I* made the analogy," Righty corrected.

Lefty rolled his eyes. "*Someone* made the analogy."

The Middle frowned. "Why, though?"

Righty pointed to Esther. "Because she wanted to know about the Williamsburg Bridge, and I was th-"

"OH," The Middle threw his arms up, "GREAT WORK."

Lefty faked an Esther-sized laugh. "Ya blew it, *stupid!*"

"Ah," Righty moped, "shit. Well, you made me!"

Esther planted her hands on her hips and called that a victory. "So you got the Williamsburg Bridge open, huh?"

The leash in her hand rattled. Sheriff must have felt Esther's excitement: he was starting to scramble and wag his tail again.

"Yeah," Lefty explained. "They got, like, a border thing set up. Since it's the only bridge left, they wanna keep it tight. In terms of, like, not that many people using it."

"So," The Middle further explained with a thumb pointed towards Righty, "like the opposite of his *MOM!*"

"Dude."

"What?"

"Mom jokes are really insensitive," Lefty instructed him.

Righty nodded.

"They're funny though," The Middle insisted.

"No they're not," Lefty, Righty, and Esther replied in unison.

The Middle smacked his lips. "Fuck you guys."

"Anyway," Lefty continued to Esther, "you just go up to the border thing and you tell them you wanna go across. It's like a bunch of trucks and stuff, there'll be a guy there."

"I mean," Righty amended on Lefty's behalf, "there *should* be a guy there. That was what they said yesterday."

Lefty just shrugged.

Esther looked down at Sheriff. He was tugging back towards the far side of Sixth. Pulling hard enough to lift his front paws off the ground.

It was like he was trying to get back to Vatche's place.

How long, she wondered, had she been gone for? Hopefully not long enough for them to notice her absence.

Sheriff's friends were close! He smelled them! He'd really sort of forgotten how great it was and how important it was to have friends that you just love so much, because then you don't have to be *lonely!* So he pulled at his leash and he danced up on his two best back feet and it was his best dance ever and he was just so *excited* and *happy!* His *friends!*

He made one of his happiest sounds! It came out of his ears, was what it felt like! Humans never seemed to hear it though! But that was okay because he knew his *friends* would hear it! With *their* ears! Most times if you made a noise it went out of your mouth and into the ear, but this sound came out of the *ear!* That was pretty much *brilliant,* as far as did Sheriff think it was brilliant or not!

All of the Giants' ears pricked up at the exact same time. Ordinarily Jairzinho might have ignored something like that.

He was done ignoring his Giants. Trust was so much better. "What is that?" he asked in his most excited voice. "What do you hear?"

Meatball looked back at Jairzinho. She smiled. There was still blood on her teeth.

Jairzinho frowned. Somewhat spoiled the moment, that blood. But oh well. There would be more moments. He hoped.

"What do you hear?"

Meatball, Astrid, and Ladybug all pulled together. Ducky pulled, just not in the right direction. Kelso and Barmit dragged, but that was what leashes were for.

"So this guy at the border," Esther clarified, "he's just gonna let me waltz right across the fuckin' bridge? Just like that?"

Righty smiled at Lefty, even as he spoke to Esther. "He will. And you know why? Because she's white, and this is *definitely a race thing.*"

Esther waved her hands. "I don't wanna get back into is this a race thing. I got my question answered. Thanks. You boys been real helpful. White power and all that shit, best of luck with your fuckin' racism." So she could get across the bridge, no problem. How would Jairzinho make it? Whiteface? Whiteface. There. Problem solved!

Esther stifled another laugh as she tugged on Sheriff's leash and turned him towards Sixth Ave. At which point, she saw what he'd been tugging so hard about.

Jairzinho and the rest of the Giants, crossing the street. Heading right for the racists with guns.

"HEY!" he called, waving his definitely-not-white hand. In a definitely-not-friendly way. "WHERE THE FUCK HAVE YOU…" he paused.

Esther looked back to her three new not-so-friends.

They glared at Jairzinho. Choked up on their weapons.

Thinker Brainy Fancy Clancy Agent Esther Tubcut thought on her feet. She had mere fractions of a second to get this right.

Since she couldn't figure *that* out, she decided to get it very very wrong, just in a useful way.

"Hey look," she said to the three kids, "my servant's brought the rest of my dogs over!" She turned to Jairzinho. "Come on over, Navi!" She could practically hear the gears turning in his head as he traversed the intersection. Either turning or grinding. She hoped the former. "Ah...he ain't so great at English." She raised her voice and waved. "VENTI! VENTI!"

The Middle raised an eyebrow.

Righty gripped his gun a bit nearer the trigger. "Venti is *twenty*. In Italian."

Esther froze. "I...never said he spoke Spanish. Ya fuckin' problemat."

"I never *said* you said that." Righty melted a bit. "*I* was just saying about venti. I'm not problematic, also."

The Middle socked his assault rifle against his hip.

Esther glanced over to a furiously flummoxed Jairzinho and his...where was Boo?

"Your, uh, assistant shouldn't be out here," Lefty cautioned, more than a little belatedly.

Sheriff tugged and struggled against his collar, against the leash, against Esther.

Righty took a step *towards* Esther. "Anyway, you never said anything ab-"

Alright, so long Sneaky Reacher Ryan Spy etc. This was a job for New York's own Esther Tubcut.

She whirled on the kids. "Alright, quit bustin' my fuckin' balls. You wanna pet my dogs, you better shut the fuck up about my hired help."

The three guns tracked towards the ground.

"You wanna pet the rest of my fuckin' puppies or what?"

The Middle let his gun hang on its shoulder strap and folded his arms. "Well of *course* we wanna pet 'em!"

- 2 -

"Sorry," Righty mumbled. He'd mumbled "sorry" because the barrel of his assault rifle had bonked Astrid on the head. He shrugged the strap further up his shoulder.

Sorry sorry sorry. The word buzzed around Jairzinho's head. Flashing its stinger.

Sorry for bonking a dog on the head. With a weapon that had almost certainly taken human lives today.

Not sorry about the killing.

Just the bonk.

There was no sense to be made of it. Jairzinho had tried to find some as he crossed the river Sixth. Tried to make some up. Sense. But no dice. He couldn't make sense of Esther palling around with murderers. He couldn't make sense of her calling him "Navi". Or pulling him close and saying "how's it going, paid servant Navi? Oh that's right, *you don't speak English too good.*"

Least of all, he couldn't make sense of how the Giants strained to reach the grinning gunmen. If only they knew what these kids had done to the city. To their home. To Misha.

Jairzinho wondered if the Giants even remembered Misha. If their little doggy brains had kept hold of her.

"Hi puppies!" The Middle cooed.

Hi puppies puppies puppies. How many times had he heard people shriek that on the street as he passed? Hearing it from the

251

mouth of a killer made about as much sense as hearing it from one of the dogs.

Lefty gave Meatball a vigorous headrub. "How old is he?"

"Ah…" Jairzinho was certain he could feel his parched throat peeling. He glared at Esther. Sighed. Cursed his own lazy, hopelessly American SoCal dialect.

He thought of Adriana. She of the Edbrooke laundry room. And her ambiguously South American accent. Which, he hated to admit…suited the situation much more.

It felt like exhumation, desecration. But it was a matter of life and death. So he channeled Adriana, bade her rest in peace, and asked "how you say…?"

Esther shot him a look like she was about to laugh. Jairzinho wanted to dropkick her. "Oh yeah!" She turned to Lefty. Nodded at Meatball. "He's a she."

"Ah, *cripes,*" The Middle growled. "It's a damn transsexual dog?! The *libtards* even g-"

Esther looked ready to smack him upside the head. "The fuck are you talkin' about? Your pal just read the ladydog wrong, since he's a fuckin' idiot."

"A *girl!*" Lefty gasped, oblivious to the dig. "Who's a Good Girl? *Who's* a Good Girl?"

Meatball looked plaintively up to Jairzinho. Like he was her Phone A Friend.

And the FAQ continued: "Are these all yours?" Righty inquired as he scratched behind Astrid's ear.

Jairzinho had to bite the inside of his lower lip. To his amazement, the answer he nearly gave was "yes."

"Nah," Esther cackled. "I do this doggy day care thing. Navi here, he helps me out with the shitty parts of the job. HA! Get it? He picks up shit!"

Lefty smiled at Jairzinho. "Rough day to get caught on the job."

Sigh. "…yes," Jairzinho agreed. Pronouncing it *yee-ss*.

Rough fucking day.

Jairzinho looked to Esther. She loomed over the boys – *boys* – with her arms folded. A crescent smile darkening her face. She didn't look *happy*. But she also didn't seem nearly as disturbed by this as Jairzinho was.

Disturbed for a few reasons. Most obviously: here was *them*. The *them* who had orchestrated this. Who'd destroyed the bridges. Who'd bombed out the subway system. Who'd snuck a fucking tank into the middle of Manhattan. Who'd jammed TV and internet and radio. Who'd commandeered phone services. Who were gunning down civilians in the street. Who were maybe doing much worse. The shadowy, inscrutable, omnipotent, inexhaustible *them*. Here they were.

"Who's a cutie pie," the Middle smooched at Ducky. "Who's a little cutie patootie?" Ducky replied by way of clambering onto The Middle's leg and getting down to business. "Hey!" The Middle cried. "Look at this little guy!"

"He's humping your leg!" Lefty reported.

They all pointed at Ducky and laughed. Righty took out his phone. Started taking video. They all did. They laughed and laughed and laughed.

Them. They were just regular kids who wanted regular kid things. Like to film a silly video and pet some puppies. These were certainly not the orchestrators of this catastrophe. But this was almost worse – they were its executors.

"Why…?" Jairzinho's voice sounded like a crumpled parking ticket slowly stretching back out.

"Ah," Esther snapped. Side-eyed him *hard*.

Jairzinho grimaced right back at her. Turned to the gunmen. "Why…" *MAXIMUM SIGH.* "Why you do *dee-ss?*"

"Because they're SO ka-YOOT!" Lefty screamed, still filming and petting.

Jairzinho didn't have it in him to ask again. Besides, nothing they said would make any goddamned sense. Best to reflect on the other reason for feeling so disturbed: Esther.

What the fuck had she been thinking? To take Sheriff without asking? And walk him up to boys with guns, boys who had *killed people?* Or were, at the *very* least, aligned with people who had? And now to humiliate him like this? To cast him as some mute manservant? Saddled with his loathed nickname, no less? One of these kids even made a reference to the obnoxious bug buddy from the old N64 Zelda games. How the fuck were they old enough to know about Navi the bullshit bug buddy? *Hey! Listen! Hey!* Jairzinho *hey*ted it. He *hey*ted Esther. He *hey*ted that she wouldn't give him Sheriff's leash back. He *hey*ted today. He *hey*ted everything.

But all the same…no he didn't. And he knew that. These things passed. As surely as his despair over Misha had been shouldered aside by fear. As surely as his fear could be tempered by the happiness of good company, a warm meal.

As surely as Meatball's temper had evaporated.

These things passed. And what was under them?

Jairzinho forced himself to suck in a deep breath. He'd managed to imagine what the bulldog's internal life might be like. What excuse did he have to not do the same for a member of his own goddamned species?

Esther must have had a reason for doing what she'd done. She was a bit of an oaf, yeah. But she wasn't evil. There was no

JaIrZINHO'S CURBSIDE GIaNTS

sense to what the boys with the guns were doing…but there could still be some behind Esther's actions.

Once he put aside his fury and hurt, they were easy to spot.

She'd humiliated Jairzinho with this manservant shit to protect him. To save him.

She hadn't told Jairzinho she was going out because she knew he'd have physically prevented her from doing so. If it came to that. Whether or not that was a confrontation he could have won, Jairzinho wasn't so sure. Which made that a double-mercy.

So Esther had surely felt whatever she'd needed Sheriff for was important enough to deceive Jairzinho about. She wouldn't have tried to pull the rug out from under him otherwise. She'd waited for him at the Edbrooke. She'd (unintentionally) connected him with Vatche.

And by coming out here with Sheriff, she was risking her own life as well. Which she knew. Jairzinho could tell. Now that he was looking for it, he saw her knees shaking. Sweat glazing her palms. An unusual jitteriness in the eyes.

She was terrified.

Yep. There it was. The unsustainability of anger. Jairzinho was still pretty pissed, no doubt. If Esther skimped on the explanations or apologies, he reserved himself the right to go nuclear again.

But even if she skimped…he didn't think he would.

This was a good-faith fuck-up. How many of the mistakes Jairzinho had made could be described that way? No, Jairzinho was the king of the fuck-up. It was people like Tia who brought the good-faith into his life.

He felt like crying. So he did, just a little bit. But that was okay. Nobody looked twice at the help.

Sheriff looked up at The Babble Man and wagged his tail! The Babble Man was so excited to see Sheriff that he was peeing with his face! Oh, how happy it made Sheriff to see him again too! And all of his most bestly friends in the whole wide world!

So Sheriff wagged and wagged and fought against the neck hug until The Babble Woman handed Sheriff's long string back to The Babble Man!

Back to his friends! His long string got *snicked* back in with the rest and he was with his friends again!

Sheriff wagged and wagged at all of his friends! One was missing. Boo was gone. Drats! That was too bad! But he was probably off playing with Misha though! So that was nice!

Meatball definitely *smelled* like Boo. But Meatball *wasn't* Boo. That was weird.

Also! Everybody seemed sad. That was not fun.

Why wasn't anybody wagging?

Oh well! Sheriff would just have to wag for them!

Nobody paid attention to little old Sheriff. But that was okay! Why was it okay? Because! Um! Oh!

He didn't just wag for himself! He thought he did but he didn't! Otherwise he would have kept wagging even when he was all alone! And actually that was probably why he'd *stopped* wagging way way back ago! Because he'd felt so super duper lonely even when he was with all of his friendliest pals!

But he wasn't alone! And neither were they! He had himself and they had him and they all had each other and the world was a wonderful place again! And actually it had never stopped being a wonderful place! They were getting pet by boys with scary sticks but petting was petting and friending was friending!

Sheriff wagged! Even though nobody paid attention to him, he wagged and wagged!

- 3 -

"So I looked him in the eye," Esther enthused as she and Jairzinho turned the metaphorical corner on the three little Sixth-Ave shits, "and I said to him, 'listen here kid, you better tell me how the *fuck* to get off this island, or I'm gonna make you wish your mom finished the miscarriage she clearly started with ya!'"

Esther was terrifically pleased with this. In a way Jairzinho couldn't hope to match. So he didn't try.

Several seconds of expectant silence ticked by as they walked East. Whatever Esther's gambit was, it had worked. The gunmen had let them pass. They'd apparently even told Esther about a way off Manhattan. A way home.

Apparently. Allegedly. But Esther fancied herself a raconteur. So they were blocks away from Sixth and no closer to the punchline.

"I said right to his face," Esther reiterated, "I said 'listen h-'"

"And what did *he* say?" Jairzinho barked. That whole 'anger was unsustainable' thing? Yeah. Control of Jairzinho's heart was being dictated by attrition. Anger may have been unsustainable, but so was its unsustainability. Did that make sense? It didn't have to. Sense had the day off.

Esther hadn't apologized to him. That was one of his goddamned conditions he'd made to himself. He'd accept her apology when it came. But she'd still have to offer it. Instead, she was blathering on with this whole dumb story. One that started

257

with her pretending to take a nap. Ended...no, not ended, *continued* with her claiming to have said something she almost certainly didn't say. She was a *liar*, after all.

Esther screwed her mouth into a tight knot. "Well, jeez bucko, alright. You're in a fuckin' mood for a guy who's got a way off the island like he'd been cryin' about not havin'. So we had a little back and forth, the kid I said the thing about him bein' a miscarriage to, 'cause *he* thought it was pretty snarky, and they all were just fallin' all over themselves. Laughin', you know. But I bet I should just skip right past that for t-"

"YES," Jairzinho roared.

"Tough crowd, yowza. The Williamsburg Bridge. That's where we're headed. Only bridge that's still open. Also not blown up. I guess all the bridges are open if ya think about it, only you ain't gonna wanna go across any Bridge ain't the Williamsburg! But right, anyway, it's like their big port of how they're bartering with the government or whoever. Send people over in return for food or something. Hell if I know. Oh, only thing is, it's a white-folks-only type operation. We'll figure somethin' out though. Where's Boo?"

"Whoa whoa whoa." Jairzinho tugged his dogs to a halt. "What does that mean, *white-folks-only operation?*"

"Seems pretty straightforward to me. White folks only. Means only folks allowed on it're gonna be white folks."

"So...how am I su-"

Esther pumped her palms forward. "Don't worry. I thought about this. You know blackface?"

"..."

"You ain't heard about blackface? Woah, listen to this, back in the d-"

"So," Jairzinho interrupted, "not only do you turn me into your fucking manservant, not only do you *humiliate* me after *lying* to me and *stealing Sheriff*, now you want me to wear *whiteface?*"

"...so you heard about blackface?"

Jairzinho grunted his response.

"Uh, listen," Esther sighed. "I'm real sorry about that stuff I done. But I had to do it! And I got us a way out, didn't I? We ain't but a mile and a half from the Bridge!"

Jairzinho was still angry. But...Esther had apologized. It hadn't been the falling-on-her-knees *mea culpa* he'd expected... but she'd apologized. And she was right. Her good-faith fuck-up had proven to be not such a fuck-up after all.

He closed his eyes. Begone, anger. Ha. If only it were that easy.

He tried to find something positive to think about. Some kind of gratitude catalyst.

How about this: be grateful that Esther had started her interminable story with "so I swing outta the bed," and not "so I popped outta my Ma."

Jairzinho released the leashes. Pressed his fingers into his forehead. Fuck. *Fuck*. Ooooh, even when you knew anger was stupid...it was so hard to get rid of it.

He lowered his hands. Took up the leashes again. Panic flooded his system. He was missing leashes! He...oh. Right.

Esther put a hand on Jairzinho's shoulder. Ouch. "You okay, buddy? I'm just bein' a crusty old broad."

"It's okay," he replied. And it was true. The only reason it wouldn't be okay would be because he refused to let it be. Okay. "So what am I whitefacing with?" Jairzinho laughed at the words even as he said them.

"Huh?"

Jairzinho mushed the dogs forward. They didn't get it. *Two short of running the Iditarod now, yes?* The joke was on Vatche: Sheriff was back. Now Jairzinho was only *one* short.

But these dogs didn't mush. So Jairzinho walked them forward. "My whiteface," he explained to Esther. "What am I going to use?"

"As the white?"

"No, as the face. Obviously as the white."

"Ha! Fuck if I know. I done the hard part, figurin' it out about doin' it. You got any bright ideas?"

"No. So we're on the same page there." Jairzinho took another deep breath. Made the conscious decision to be delighted by Esther's churlishness. "You know where you're going?"

"Course I fuckin' know. I lived here basically my whole life, 'course I know where the damn Williamsburg Bridge is. Don't you?"

No, was the answer. Jairzinho had never even seen it. He couldn't afford to hang out in Williamsburg. And he had no reason to putz around southeast Manhattan.

His first instinct was to lie.

His second was to wonder…what the fuck, first instinct?

"No," he answered.

Esther laughed. "*HA HA HA HA HA.* Well shit, yeah, you better let me take the lead, huh?"

Jairzinho slowed the Giants. Esther stepped on ahead.

"Hey," she called over her shoulder, "you gonna tell me what happened to Boo, or do I gotta guess?"

"You know what? Guess. That'll be fun for me."

HA HA HA HA HA. Maybe unwise, to make Esther laugh. Definitely a risk as far as being anything approaching sneaky in the dead-silent streets. But Esther's laugh had thus far only brought good things. Vatche, and a reunion.

Besides, Jairzinho was coming to appreciate it. Much the same way sailors in high mist surely appreciated the flatulent din of the foghorn.

Esther guessed. Jairzinho told her to guess again. They both laughed their way Eastwards. Tried hard not to look at what their laughter was echoing off of.

Guess. Guess again.

PISHCHIM

-1-

UUUUGGGH the WAY this shit was GOIN' Ducky WAS-N'T gonna be FUCKING-*GUH ANYBOOTY!* He REALLY thought he'd HAD a CHANCE with the STICKS those THR-EE chumps HAD. Since the STICKS had these SWEET little HOLES on the ENDS. DUCKY was all OOOOOMAMA! But NO of COURSE that was RUINED by BAD man. But THERE was ALWAYS LADYBUG. BESIDES and ANY-WAY LADYBUG should REALLY be his FIRST. He OWED it TO her. And REALLY it was ACTUALLY that SHE owed IT to HIM. The WAY she ALWAYS LED HIM ON? By LOOKIN' AT HIM with her EYES and PANTIN'? Or SOMETIMES playin' COY by not LOOKIN' AT HIM? TALK about a FUCKIN' TEASE!

So ALRIGHT. FUCKING-*GUH* LADYBUG WASN'T just gonna HAPPEN. It was TIME for DUCKY to start US-IN' his NOODLE. NO, the OTHER ONE.

BAD man had SEEMED really SCARED of the THREE chumps. Which made SENSE because BAD man was a fuckin'

265

PUPPY about loud NOISES. Just ALL like OH what was THAT and OH boo HOO I'M so SCARED. HAhaHA, ID-IOT!

THIS was IMPORTANT because DUCKY could CONTROL the CHUMPS.

IT was a POWER he DIDN'T know he HAD. But it TURNED OUT he was SO GOOD at HUMPIN' that he could BASICALLY MIND-control PEOPLE. JUST like he'd DONE to the CHUMPS. He'd HUMPED one CHUMP'S dumb STUMP and WHAT do you KNOW? They're all crouchin' DOWN and GIVIN' Ducky their COLORFUL RECTANGLES, which HUMANS usually ONLY showed to THEMSELVES.

So then DUCKY had THOUGHT at THEM, he thought MAKE the HAHA noise and BRING your RECTANGLE CLOSER.

And they DID!

So DUCKY was BASICALLY the most POWERFUL DOG who had ever LIVED. And WHEN the TIME was RIGHT he would USE his HUMPIN' POWERS to MIND control some more CHUMPS into MAKIN' their HOLE-STICKS go BA-BA-BA-BARK at BAD man's HEAD. Then BAD man would BE like MISHA and DUCKY would just CRAWL over HIM and FINALLY FUCK-*GUH* LADYBUG.

He LOOKED over at LADYBUG. OOOOOH, TEASE ME! She was REALLY WORKIN' her TREATMAKER. And SHE was just FEETS AWAY! TWO feets, actually. BAD man's FEETS. They went UP and DOWN and UP and DOWN, because THAT was how WALKIN' WORKED. ACTUALLY it was MORE like FRONT and BACK and FRONT and BACK. But DUCKY was THINKIN' about UP and DOWN because THAT was what HIS bouncy BOYS down BELOW were up TO. SNAP and WHAM and SNAP and WHAM. And ALSO now THROB throb THROB. Like when THIS one TIME Ducky's HUMAN filled UP a BALLOON with WATER and Ducky SAT on it and it POPPED.

DUCKY just NEEDED to POP and he'd FEEL a lot BETTER. Like, SOON.

BAD man's LEGS went FRONT and BACK and FRONT and BACK. Every TIME he gave DUCKY a little GLIMPSE of LADYBUG, the HOLE-Y GRAIL.

The TIME for bidin' TIME was almost OVER. DUCKY had BEEN the most PATIENT DOG and WHAT did he HAVE to SHOW for it? So ACTUALLY you KNOW WHAT? FUCK this GUY. DUCKY didn't NEED any MIND controlled CHUMPS to SHOW bad MAN who was the FUCKIN' BOSS. DUCKY was the BOSS! YEAH! BOSS! Let's DO this! Beast MODE!

DUCKY really GOT so CLOSE to BAD man's LEG before BAD man PULLED on his STRING, which was FUCKIN' CHEATIN'. And ANYWAY FLYIN' through the air was LIKE NOTHIN' BRAH, it was a MINOR fuckin' SETBACK. And ACTUALLY the JOKE wasn't EVEN on DUCKY because HE ended up LANDIN' on

barmit was chugging along like always…looking at the ground…minding her own business…and then ducky came slamming into her like a basketball…he cracked her right on the ear…and the puddle of boring bodywater from that big drooling dog in the crate…just when barmit had hatefully accepted it as a permanent feature of the divot behind her neck…

267

it sloshed out…matted the tangle of fur atop her head…dribbled slowly into her eyes…

…she hated it, of course…in the way she had only recently learned she could…in that deeper way…the way that didn't stop at the outsides of your insides…the way that went all the way into your insides' insides…where some dogs had their bodywater. not the boring stuff…the good stuff. real bodywater.

sweet, sweet bodywater.

it was so…not hateworthy. barmit had smelled it before sometimes…on humans…under fleshy little patches of fake skin they put on their real skin…sometimes on the street even…but she'd never known what it was…it had just been one of those smells you smell…and makes you wonder what it is…but you never find out…

…until today…barmit had learned what it was today…she'd learned that when you found it, and you drank it…it was… something not totally awful. but she still hadn't understood what it was…really…

but then meatball taught her how to get it.

it wasn't just the people with their firesticks that could make bodywater. anybody could make bodywater. in terms of bringing it out of creatures who had it, anyway…barmit didn't know how to figure out which dogs or people did or didn't have bodywater…but meatball definitely had a method…oh yes.

at first when meatball had bitten boo a bunch of times, barmit was very confused about why…then the bodywater came out. lots and lots of bodywater. and it dripped onto the floor and turned into the river. and it came over towards barmit's box, so she got to drink some. it was so goo…it was swee…it was something she hadn't really known was a thing.

…somehow meatball had figured out that boo wasn't really a dog…he was actually a wagging sack of bodywater…except the weird part was that meatball didn't even try to drink any of the bodywater…none of the other dogs did…barmit didn't hate that because it meant more for her. but it was definitely confusing…why would they pass up the chance…

…she'd been trying to work out what meatball's system was…how she'd figured out that boo was full of really goo… really…not hatable bodywater…and also how to get it without making mr. comeon say his own name really loud…meatball had sent mr. comeon into a *mood*…which barmit hated…but then mr. comeon got over it…so maybe once he realized what meatball was doing, he calmed down…and so when ducky came careening into barmit…just as she was thinking about all of this…she decided that maybe if mr. comeon had learned his lesson with meatball…he would let barmit alone when she tried to act on the lessons she'd learned…about bodywater…and how to get it…

…so as soon as ducky hit barmit…she reared her head back…and bared her little teeth…and plunged them into ducky's thro-

BINGO!

ah…ahem…yeah, bingo…bodywater. barmit licked sweet, sweet bodywater from her tiny, crooked chompers. had time to think that it was…not as not-hatable as some of the finer bodywaters she'd tasted. and then she was flying through the air too…which made her

Happy? How could Barmit be *happy?* Kelso must have had that wrong, right? Right. It didn't make a lick of sense that he should smell anything other than wallowing and misery coming from that little homewrecker, did it? No way, man. No way.

And yet, she was flying through the air and spraying a *happy* smell every which way. Kelso didn't have that confused with Ducky's smell. That was an impossible mix-up to make. Like the difference between trying to pick up a ball and a crab (which, in the fun pre-Barmit days when trips to the beach were more than memories, was a mistake Kelso had had the opportunity to make). Ducky's was a stink that pinched.

Not Barmit's, though. That was…ecstatic?

Ecstatic just as she was soaring away from Meatball. Who was in a fouler mood than Kelso had ever smelled her.

Kelso just turned his head and watched Barmit fly. Turned and turned until he tripped over

Little old Sheriff, and it was *playtime* again! He had gotten his wag back in a *big time* way! Ducky started flying and Sheriff wagged about that! Barmit zoomed and Sheriff wagged! Then Kelso walked on him and The Babble Man decided Kelso should fly too! Yahoooooo!

How amazing to have friends! He had taken them for granted, but he'd never do *that* again! A lot of things might be gone but he had his favorite friends in the whole wide world with him and so he could wag! Because that was what you had when you told loneliness to *git!* You had friends!

And sometimes all of your friends were flying! It was basically all of them anyway! So Sheriff jumped up and The Babble Man pulled the string and gave his neck a really hard little hug with hurt in it.

That was how you flew with friends though! Sometimes there was a little part that kind of hurt a little bit. Just a bitty bit though. Then you were flying! That was Sheriff's absolute *favorite*, flying with his friends! Flying

As did the Valkyries and vultures, born aloft on wings of flesh and tendon forged. Of flesh? Off leash? Leave off! Think not that shadows scouring blasted Earth be that which casts them, blotters of the sun, you Valkyrie, you vulture! Trust not such a supple, yielding dark, that shapes itself to tautly draw o'er concrete crags and broken bodies!

O, but Ladybug did waste her time, to lose herself in visions such as this. Her friends still failed, for reasons Ladybug could grasp but softly twixt her brit'lest teeth, to comprehend that blood and death and endless sleep were each and all together bound by leashes, ancient and unbreakable! What portraitures of suffering, what smellscapes pungent with rapine and butchery must yet unfurl themselves?

And then: dark Ducky, all this time a sleeper creature on the side of Valkyries and vultures, now awoken! No, twas not in darkest fold nor deepest flab that Ladybug did feel the smallest portion of commiseration with the lech'rous horndog. Yet that Barmit bit the bastard, did bespeak the dogs' collective failures. Lest, of course, she'd known precisely what it was she did…

So weary was the gaze that Ladybug did slip between The Ferryman's two pumping legs, now stumbl'ng o'er a Sheriff repossessed of spirits at the same time bright and dim. To wag in such a place as this…

The Man did shriek and scream, but Ladybug did tune it out. What else was new, she might have thought, had not there *been* a brand-new something snatching her attention.

How…vexing.

To see the face of Meatball and reflect upon resemblances betwixt her febrile physiognomy and peanut butter scooped into a spoon was something like the norm. To gaze into those bovine eyes, those bitter pills so poorly hidden in the buttered peanut, and be met with depth and breadth, with fear surpassing even Ladybug's transcendent standard…

'gain and yet again did Kelso seek his satisfaction 'gainst the bulldog, havoc cried o'er sleights unknown to all save him. Not once did Meatball flinch beneath these sorties by the Ferryman aborted.

Understood, the bulldog did! The boffing given Boo by Meatball's paw had in a state of ignorance been done, a state she'd shared amongst her cohort. So the blood did flow from body, bringing Meatball what it took from Boo. This was not fair, but it was how a mind was changed.

And changed this mind so clearly was. O phantom congress, only known to those who numbered 'mongst the no-nosed, strug'ling not to suffocate! Through this could Meatball speak to Ladybug, in tongues made sharp despite their ceaseless labors in pursuit of perspiration.

Yes, if one should wish to cast aside the musings of two mutts, the simpler fact remained: no no-nosed dog so short of face could e'er sustain a face so long as Meatball's was, without a reason most compelling.

But one bark from Ladybug to Meatball, made as wise and freighted as her soggy quacks could be.

A boof from Meatball back to Ladybug, made rife with juicy overtones, and underside infernal of which Ladybug knew all to well.

An ally, visiting in Ladybug's high tower! Quacked again in utter joy, the black pug did, then felt a tightness in the torso that, for once, was not a consequence of scrunch-faced nightmares!

O, that damnéd Ferryman, for reasons all his own, did pull on Ladybug's red leash, and took her towards the blue. She marveled at the shadow cast beneath her, *by* her. *Twas* her, yet, twas not. Incredible! She turned herself to face the Ferryman, at just the instant he proclaimed

- 2 -

"The FUCK, guys?!" Jairzinho shouted as he flung dogs every which way.

"They're all screwed up," Esther observed.

They'd hardly walked a goddamned block before said screwification. Jumping at each other, barking and bumping and yarping. Like balls in a lottery tumbler. But without any winners.

"Oh, well, shit, that's why." Esther pointed at Jairzinho. "Look at your arms."

Jairzinho looked at his arms. At the bandage covering the chomp he'd gotten from Meatball. "Oh. No, that's from when M-"

"No, I'm not talkin' about that." Esther locked her elbows at her waist. Extended her forearms out at ninety degrees. "Look at how you're holdin' em!"

"I'm not holding them like that!"

273

"Well not since I told you to look. But you were. You're way too edgy, they can smell that on ya. Or something."

"I am *not* edgy," Jairzinho snapped. "Frankly, I'm making a conscious effort to *not* be edgy."

"Oh, yeah, my bad. That's exactly what most not-edgy people do, is make a conscious effort."

He felt it. The rising bile. He envisioned himself planting a flag firmly upon this hill. Arguing against his being edgy unto the death. He might have, too. If he hadn't *felt* it rising. Recognized it for what it was.

For as magnanimous and empathetic as his brain was learning to be…his more Chimpish self had trained and deputized the hands to do their own thing. All those microcorrections. All those unconscious adjustments. His brain wanted to calm down. Be less personally affronted by dogs and people who weren't as obsessed with Jairzinho as he himself was. His Chimp-ass hands, meanwhile, just wanted him to shake the leashes and send for a scream.

So which part of him was getting pissed off at his hands? Was that his brain, or his hands trying to backdoor their own aggression?

Had he ever sounded like such a lunatic in his life?

"You done makin' your conscious efforts now?" Esther asked. "You wanna get to walkin' again?"

"What?" Jairzinho blinked. Ah. He resumed walking, not having realized he'd stopped. "Sorry."

He softened his arms. Loosened his grip on the leashes a bit.

The dogs calmed down. Amazing.

As they trekked east on West 4th, Jairzinho kept an eye out for a makeup shop. Somewhere they could buy him some fucking clown powder. He wasn't looking forward to that. But it was a way off the island. A way back home.

No make-up shops. And who was gonna be open, anyway? Well, there was a McDonald's over there. Wouldn't have been a shocker if they were slinging Whoppers, even now. Did Mc-Donald's sell Whoppers? Or was that the other one? It suddenly seemed important.

They had a pale Ronald cutout waving through a shattered window. Laughing. As though to say *see you on the other side of the brid- oh, that's right, nevermind.*

The roads looked like they had been abandoned for years. Cars sat empty, gathering blasted-building dust. Most had collided with one another as drivers made desperate bids to motor up onto the curb. Or maybe just plow directly through the car in front of them. Even on the sidewalks. It took the Giants and their Virgil five minutes to navigate a single block. All the while, Jairzinho couldn't stop imagining what horrors had stopped the traffic, at the far end of the street.

The good news was that the horrors were elsewhere. Nobody was watching. There were no more people peering out of windows. They'd lost interest. Now they were just waiting. Like the Hamasyans.

Lost interest. That felt like a poor way to phrase it…but it also felt right.

Distant pops and rumbles still patrolled the cavernous avenue. Just far more sporadically than before. It was now two or three minutes between each report. Rather than seconds. Or less. They sounded like the last pebbles settling after a village-burying landslide.

Or bricks.

In the two blocks they'd now walked since taking their leave of the soldier kids, Jairzinho and Esther had seen the following: one collapsed storefront, one lonely shoe, one abandoned scarf, one severed leg with an Ugg on the foot, one stray cat, eight broken windows, three dead bodies. Two of those bodies were sprawled on the street, clear victims of gunshots. A third body hung from a third story window. By her neck.

Jairzinho wondered if he had been stuffing his face with homecooked Armenian cuisine when that had happened. Maybe it was one of those three kids who'd done it. The ones who had fawned all over his dogs.

Ladybug yarped periodically. Sometimes looking straight into Jairzinho's eyes. Which took a hell of a lot of body-contorting for her to pull off. He couldn't tell if those looks were defiance or frustration. Either way, his hands wanted to yank her back into line. "Chimpish," he chanted quietly to himself. Ladybug was still walking. So he let her look at whatever she wanted to look at.

Esther turned her head slightly as Jairzinho uttered his mantra. Then faced front and kept leading. She got what he was doing. Good. He'd have felt like an idiot if he'd had to explain.

Ducky jerked towards Ladybug. Jairzinho *really* wanted to crank Ducky's leash, hard. Little sh… "Chimpish." Of course, it wasn't Chimpish to want to rein Ducky in. He was distruptive. It was the *bile* that made it Chimpish. So Jairzinho tugged Ducky back and to the side. Gentle but firm. He noticed blood spattered on the Frenchie's neck. Undoubtedly some of Boo's. They'd been in the same crate, after all.

A Frenchie kiss. Jairzinho let it go.

Meatball barked back at Ladybug. Loud enough to attract attention. "Chimpish," Jairzinho whispered. Not wrong to correct, just watch the bile. He tugged the leash gently. Meatball *boofed* and settled down.

"Hey," Esther said, turning as she threaded between two blasted-out cars. "I was thinkin', wh-*ow*," she pulled a balancing hand off the hood of a dented Ford Focus. "That's hot, watch it. Anyways, I was thinkin', well, two things. First, last time I'll ask, you sure you don't want me takin' some of those do-"

"You've gotta be fucking kidding me."

"Okay, yeesh. Fine. Second thing, though, is, and this is like…it's *kind of* a joke idea. But like, what if we both got tattoos that say 'Chimpish'? After all this shit," she waved her arms broadly, "gets done with?"

Jairzinho pretended to be completely focused on guiding his dogs between the cars.

"Like…I was thinkin'," she plowed on, "it's got eight letters, so you could get it tattooed on your fingers. Like Love n' Hate, like in *Night of th-*"

"Like in *Do The Right Thing,*" Jairzinho nodded.

Esther slowed. "Like what?"

Jairzinho slowed. His dogs tugged him a half-step forward. "Like *Do The Right Thing.*"

"Like…no, that movie ripped it off *Night of the Hunter.*"

"No it didn't."

"Yeah, it did."

Jairzinho, despite not knowing what *Night of the Hunter* was, felt himself digging in. "No, it *didn't.*"

"You even *seen Night of the Hunter?*"

"Pffft," was Jairzinho's retort.

"Love and Hate. *Night of the Hunter,*" Esther growled. "Like so when you're stressed, you could put your fists together and look at what it says. To remind you."

"I think I'm happy just saying it to myself."

"But this way you can *read* it."

"Ah…I mean, not really? Bec-"

Esther darkened. "What do you mean?"

"Well, because the finger tattoos on the fists are for you to put them together and show to other people. There's not really an easy way to get a good angle on your own fingers."

"You think I'm sayin' *we* tattoo it? It's gonna be a profess-ional does it!"

"I'm saying to read them." Jairzinho released the leashes. Put his fists together. "Just try. Pretend you have the tattoos on your fingers. Try to read them."

Esther put her fists together, connecting on the thumb-side. Tried to roll them back so she could read them. "Hm." She bent her head down. "*Hm.* Oh!" She crossed her arms and lifted her fists towards her face. They connected on the thumb-side again, but this time with her palms facing towards her. She had to lean back to see her fingers. "There!"

"But then it would say *Pishchim.*"

"You bein' thick or somethin'? You'd just get 'em tattooed the other way round."

"But then it would say *Pishchim* if you tried to show them to someone else."

"We wouldn't be *showin'* em to anyone else."

"I'm n-"

"And actually, you could do it like this…" She uncrossed her arms and positioned them as before. Facing out, palms down, connected at the thumb. Then she partially extended her fin-gers, so only the top joints were curled into the palm. "…you could get PISH on your right hand and CHIM on your left, and *upside-down,* so everybody knows it's just for you to read, and

278

then it'd also be easier to read because you could read it like this."

"I'm not getting a tattoo."

She shrugged. "Ain't kids supposed to make bad choices?"

Jairzinho just smiled and shook his head. "Where did this come from? Do you have tattoos?"

"No. I just thought it'd be nice to have somethin' to remember the day by."

"...are you worried you're not going to remember?"

"Well, no, b-"

"Is this a day you *want* to remember?"

"No, not in terms of everybody dyin' and shit. I just meant like..." Esther gestured between herself and Jairzinho. Ducked her head. The closest to embarrassment Jairzinho could imagine her coming.

It was touching...surprisingly so, considering just a few minutes ago he'd felt like he was ready to strangle her. Not literally. But *maybe* literally.

Still. He wasn't getting a goddamned tattoo.

"How about this," he suggested, "we'll..." And then he stopped.

Esther, now walking backwards, asked him "what? You thinkin' commemorative rings?"

Jairzinho couldn't respond. He just stared. Mouth agape. He hadn't thought he was a mouth agape kind of guy. But he also hadn't realized he was a bowl-putter-downer. Or a steamroller. Or chimpish. So many surprises today.

It looked like the most grotesque surprise yet was just over there. Through the trees. In the park.

Esther studied his face. Set her jaw. Closed her eyes for a moment. Turned around to follow his gaze.

There wasn't a great view of Washington Square Park from here at the Southwest corner. And for that, Jairzinho was unspeakably grateful. For a few reasons.

The first was the smell. It was the smell of maybe-Philippe being baked by the ruins of the Edbrooke. That slightly sweet stench. But thousands of times stronger.

The second was a massive smear of Ducky-black smoke billowing up from the center of the Park. Concealed from view by trees. Thank fuck.

Jairzinho and Esther stood and stared.

"I think," Esther finally managed, "I might know where all the people who ain't on the streets got to."

Jairzinho wanted to say something snide about *still want that tattoo?* He probably wouldn't have even if somebody *hadn't* shouted "HEY!" But that was just a guess.

Because somebody *did* shout "HEY!"

- 3 -

They didn't see anybody attached to the "HEY!" They couldn't see into the park beyond that first little corner grove with all the chessboards. Nobody was playing chess.

"Were they talkin' to us?" Esther wondered.

"I...don't know."

"I feel like we should be runnin' somewhere."

"Me too."

They stood still. They didn't have to explain why. Whichever direction they ran would probably be the same direction as the "HEY!" had come from.

Standing here meant hearing the Park though. Because it wasn't just the smell. Or the smoke. Once the shock of those wore off, Jairzinho's ears turned back on.

He could hear the screaming, the crying. Some of which was abruptly interrupted by gunshots. They sounded like they were a hundred miles away. On the other side of a shoddy phone line.

Even softer than the voices were the flames. The soft, edgeless *whoosh* of a well-fed fire. At first, he assumed the crackling and crunching was coming from that fire. Then he thought about the tank on West 15th. About some massive object grinding over a thousand little, brittle ones.

"That sounds like…" Esther began.

"…yeah," Jairzinho finished. And that was enough.

He felt the leashes in his hands trembling. Yeah. Sure. That was what was happening. The *leashes* were trembling.

How many of the people in the park, pulling triggers and piling bodies onto the fire, were just kids? Like those three idiots back on Sixth? Maybe none. Maybe the reason those three were hiding out just a few blocks away from the action was that they wanted no part in it.

Or maybe that was a convenient way to redemonize *them*. It was somehow less scary to imagine *them* as something other than human. And those kids on Sixth – they'd been human. Painfully so.

Of course, maybe there was no massacre in Washington Square Park. Maybe Jairzinho's imagination was just running wild with a few errant gunshots and screams.

A few errant gunshots and screams?

"I think…uh, I think we should probably m-" was what Jairzinho said before the HEY! that had been bounding around his memory once again became a "HEY!" in his ears.

The brick wall of the building behind them said *zing!*

"Pretty sure that was a bullet," Esther observed.

Zing!

Jairzinho nodded. "I think you're r-" *Zing!*

ZOW!

Jairzinho turned south off West 4th, choked up high on the leashes, and carried his Giants like groceries.

SELF-DEFENSE

- 1 -

"We're goin' the wrong way!" Esther shouted as they reached West 3rd.

"We're getting shot at!" Jairzinho panted. "There *is* no wrong way!" He tripped over Sheriff.

Zing! Little whistles, eruptions of dust. *Zing!* They were so whimsical when the gunshot itself was silenced.

And when they didn't hit you, of course.

Zing!

"Go left!" Esther gasped.

Jairzinho saw no reason not to. He spun left onto West 3rd.

ZOW!

The bullets followed them around the corner.

"Aw, bullshit!" Jairzinho called. Whoever was shooting didn't agree. *ZOW!*

Astrid barked a throaty bark. It had hard consonants on either end.

Jairzinho followed the pitbull's gaze. Up up up to a silhouette on oh fuck. "On the roof, Esther!"

"Wha?"

Jairzinho pointed to the top of the building they were standing next to. Then bunched all of his leashes into his right hand. Grabbed Esther's wrist with his left. Pulled her towards the building. The one with the sniper on top of it. He hoped that was a smart thing to do. Didn't really have time to second guess it.

Some of the dogs who didn't do well with speed were anchoring in. Ladybug and Barmit had had enough running.

Bunched leashes meant bunched dogs. Ducky tried it on with Ladybug. Astrid bopped him; Barmit *bit* him!

Jairzinho unbunched the leashes. Gave it a real go, anyway. They'd gotten so tangled.

He pressed his back flat against the wall of the building. Tried to pull the dogs in. "Come on guys," he implored them all. Quiet. Persuasive. He hoped.

They didn't agree.

"Which building is the guy on?" Esther gasped.

Jairzinho fought to untangle leashes and dogs alike. Struggled to pull Kelso back to his side. "This one!"

Esther leaned back. Narrowed her eyes. "The fuck are we doin' right where the gun guy is?"

"Because it's gonna be harder for him to hit us straight down!" Jairzinho made a fist and pounded on the building's black wooden doubledoors.

"Not if he just leans the gun over the side of the building! Could use the damn thing like a, like an aiming thing. What are you doin'?"

Jairzinho stopped pounding. "I'm trying to get us off the street!" He threw his bum-luck shoulder against the big black doors. "GAH!"

ZOW!

Jairzinho, Esther, and all of the Giants looked up. Straight up the barrel of a rifle.

"Shit," Esther marveled. She cupped her hands around her mouth. Shouted "You sick the day they taught marksmanship at the incel olympics?"

"FUCK YOU!" the rifleman screamed back down. "THEY DON'T TEACH NOTHIN' AT OLYMPICS ANYWAY! OLYMPICS IS FOR COMPETITIONS!"

"Try the knob," she suggested quietly to Jairzinho.

He did. The knob looked like brass but probably wasn't. It was cool to the touch. In this weather. On this day. Amazing.

Jairzinho cranked his wrist. The knob turned easily.

Nodding to Esther, he guided the dogs on his left side through.

Esther smiled and returned the nod. Cupped her hands again. Leaned back and yelled "OH MY BAD, I F-"

ZOW!

"Fuckin', shit!" Esther all but leapt over Jairzinho's rightside dogs. "I think I made my fuckin' point."

She closed the door behind them, gently.

Jairzinho bent over, hands planted on his knees. He looked up at Esther. He wondered what she was like by herself. All this bluster, this expansive brashness…and yet it was she who thought to try knobs. Knobs on doors she closed so considerately. Like she was trying to not wake someone up.

Misha's owners flashed in Jairzinho's mind. The ones who were rich enough to sleep in on weekdays. So Jairzinho had had to keep quiet when he picked up their dog. Who was dead. As they almost certainly were too.

He couldn't remember their names. Only Misha's.

"Okay." Esther scratched her left eyebrow with the nail of her right thumb. "Now we're stuck in the fuckin' buildin' with him. So what do we do?"

Sheriff jumped up. Put his little paws on Jairzinho's knee.

Jairzinho smiled and stroked his head. Sighed. "I…thank you, Esther." He only lifted his eyes to Esther after he said this.

Esther just stared back. "What'd I do?"

"You…" he gestured to his Giants.

"Oh. Yeah." She waved his gratitude away. So she was as bad at receiving as he was at giving. What a perfect team they made. "Sure." She looked down the hall they were in. "We still gotta figure out what're we gonna do about the guy with the gun."

Jairzinho set his jaw. "I think I have a pl-"

Esther pointed to Jairzinho. "You gotta take a shit?"

"Uh…I don't know. What?"

Esther cocked a thumb at herself. "I gotta take a shit."

Jairzinho laughed. "And you thought we'd hold hands and take 'em together?"

Esther threw her head back. *HA HA HA HA HA.* It echoed down the long, wrecked hall. It rustled the loose sheets of paper scattered across the floor. It rattled a heavy door hanging askew on only its top hinge. It stirred a congealing puddle of blood at the far side of the atrium down the hall.

They waited silently. Waiting for the laughter to melt. Maybe listening for unfamiliar laughter to come bouncing back at them…

"I'll be quick," Esther mumbled.

"Take your time. I'll water the dogs."

"If this place weren't so fuckin' creepy, I'd ask you if that's what the kids are callin' it these days."

288

"That's a stretch."

"I didn't ask you how you do it."

Jairzinho pinched his lips together. "Go take your shit, Esther."

- 2 -

A helpful directory let Jairzinho know precisely where they were: the NYU School of Law. First story. Obviously. The building went as high as four stories though. Ziggurating down to two on the East side. *Here* was the Library, *there* were the classrooms, *there* was a lecture hall. So many places for people to hide.

Jairzinho tried to ignore the man-sized crimson brushstroke that swept out and down the hall. It still looked fresh.

Barmit trotted towards the smear. Jairzinho gently reeled her back in.

It felt so strange to be in here with dogs. Jairzinho never took his dogs into buildings. Unless it was a building one of the dogs lived in. Obviously. It was a weird little thrill, to have his charges in a building that probably didn't even allow them. Sorry, NYU School of Law. *Sue me.*

He glanced over to the restrooms. "You guys want some water?" He asked his Giants without conviction. Received no response.

Come to think of it. He could stand to take…to avail himself of the facilities. It felt insane to use the restroom in the middle of a crisis. When they were trapped in a building with at least one man with a gun who wanted to kill them. Maybe more. Maybe a hundred guys with guns, all hiding in lockers. They probably didn't have lockers at NYU School of Law. Jairzinho didn't know.

What he did know was that sometimes Chimpish snuck up on you. You can't Human your necessary functions out of being. They catch up eventually.

He turned his back on the bloodstain. Forced a smile. It was worth remembering that even if humans weren't chimps…they weren't that far off.

The poor human was losing his mind. He was looking at pools of blood and laughing. Just when Astrid had been starting to think he wasn't as dumb as she'd long suspected.

He chuckled the whole way into the toilet room. It was the most colossal toilet room Astrid had ever seen. It was as though the toilet room in her…the room that *had* been in her home had been duplicated five times over.

She wondered if humans understood how ridiculous it was. How uncivilized. To make your waste in your living space? They knew enough to teach their dogs not to, yet failed to heed their own lessons?

That was okay, though. This would work in Astrid's favor.

There had been a trail of blood in that larger room back there. It was not old. Yet Jairzinho had been more interested in rushing to his *precious* toilet room than investigating.

Well. Astrid could not sit idly by, clipped to a shiny pipe under the hand toilet, waiting for whatever had shed that blood to find the Giants. She was not a creature that was so reticent about conducting her business, whatever that business may be.

Jairzinho checked the clips, hooked to pipes beneath the sink, and glanced at Astrid. Not wanting to make it necessary for Astrid to save his bacon yet again (she'd been wondering if he had the brainspace, to remember how she'd sat on the clips back by the bridge). She wagged at that. He could be taught!

And fortunately for her, he was often slow to learn.

She *woofed* quietly and bopped Ducky on the head.

Jairzinho laughed and said "good point". He unclipped Ducky, then tied his leash to a separate pipe two hand-toilets away. Far from Ladybug.

Good Jairzinho. Astrid wasn't going to be here to keep Ducky in line.

Once Jairzinho was safely tucked away in his toilet cubical, Astrid studied the clips and the pipe.

The pipe had a little lip on one edge. It must have served some function. Astrid was only speculating, but it looked like the pipe connected to something? Hmmm…maybe that was where the water from the hand toilet came from, or went. Interesting. Clever humans.

Sometimes.

Astrid ducked her head and caught the chain of her collar on the lip of the pipe. *Yanked* back as hard as she could.

Yowch! The chain dug into her neck. Astrid stifled a yelp and composed herself. Okay. Second attempt. She wedged the collar against the lip of the pipe. Considered what hadn't worked on the last go. How she might go about fixing it.

Jairzinho was laughing in the toilet closet. Yep. Absolutely lost his mind, poor little fella.

Astrid jutted her head forward and *yanked* it back.

The collar slipped up and over her head.

She stumbled backwards a few steps, allowing herself to be hypnotized by the collar, dangling from its leash.

The other Giants boggled at Astrid. Meatball *boofed*.

"I'm right here guys," Jairzinho said from the toilet closet. The dogs paid him no mind.

Astrid stared down Meatball. Then Kelso. Meatball. Kelso. Both settled into their respective spaces on the tile.

Then, quietly as she could, Astrid nosed open the door (quite light, thank goodness) and slipped out of the bathroom.

She knew she didn't have long. Humans didn't tend to spend long periods of time in the toilet room. Unless sometimes when they went in pairs, then they could be there for quite a while. Jairzinho was there by himself, though. Just him and his thoughts.

He clearly *did* have thoughts, sometimes. Deep ones, with any luck. Hopefully they'd keep him busy.

He'd never admit it, but sometimes Jairzinho felt vicarious relief when he watched a dog take a really big dump. Nothing beat doing the deed oneself, of course. But it was a bizarre kind of cross-species connection that he'd not anticipated before he started this job. It was gross, sure. But maybe kind of beautiful too? It was connection. Common experience. Most things were probably miles apart for dogs and people. As far as experience went. Sight, smell, taste, hearing. All different for pups and peeps. Emotions especially. Didn't people say love in dogs was really just them getting excited about the person who gives them food? That was depressing. But probably true. Maybe that was true about people, too. Maybe love was just you getting excited about the person who gives you sex. Jairzinho didn't think so. But he didn't know.

That was beside the point though. The point was, humans and dogs had at least one clear common experience: the relief after a really big dump. Probably. Jairzinho didn't actually know.

Now he couldn't stop thinking about dogs taking dumps. Great. Great work, brain.

- 3 -

Astrid rounded a corner and spotted a man with a gun. He was reading a book. Books were one of those human artifacts that Astrid had never been able to make sense of. Dirty pieces of paper stuck together. That was it. But humans could stare at these things for *hours!* It was really unbelievable.

This must have been a particularly fascinating example of a book, because the guy with the gun didn't notice Astrid until she was within biting distance.

He jumped and plopped his book down on his lap. "Ah…" he stared at Astrid. "Hey boy. Hey…" he ducked his head slightly, then brought it back up. "Girl. Sorry. I mean. I don't have to apologize to you. You're a dog. Dogs don't know what people are saying. So I don't know why I'm talking to you."

Astrid merely watched him. Time for a charm offensive.

She panted and wagged her tail. People loved that.

This guy loved it. He laughed. It was a nice laugh. But Astrid couldn't help noticing he had blood on his clothes, on his hands. It smelled like the same blood as was smeared down this hallway, around the next corner. "Do you even know what the fuck is going on?" he asked.

Astrid wagged harder and hopped, planting her front paws in the guy's lap. So he had to put his gun down to pet her.

So her jaws were inches from his throat.

293

She sniffed at his vest. She needed to be sure.

Blood. Burnt flesh. Despair. None of them his.

Astrid turned her head to the side and lunged so hard she felt the guy's Adam's apple knock against the roof of her mouth.

Jairzinho washed his hands. That was something else that separated him from chimps and dogs. Hygiene administered by something other than the tongue.

He took out his phone. Could hardly quit giggling as he added himself to the bathroom report. Right at the bott...right at the top. They were *his* Giants, after all.

He considered adding Esther, as long as he was running this fun little goof. His imagination provided him with an image. The smile fell from his face instantly.

Banishing the image, he stared at his brood.

At Astrid's empty collar on the floor.

He stared at that collar for a solid ten seconds. And then he made a decision.

He was not going to panic. There was no need. Astrid had more than demonstrated her competence. Jairzinho would give the remaining dogs some water. He would take his time. And if Astrid wasn't back by the time he was ready to go...he would *entertain* indulging in panic.

Slowly and deliberately, he knelt on the cool tile. Unzipped his backpack and rummaged. Down near the bottom, he felt what he was after: a small plastic waterbowl with a drawstring fabric top. He wiggled a finger through the hole and tugged it open. Placed it on the floor. Considered filling it with the water

Vatche had given him…but why waste it? Manhattan tap water was potable. And dogs weren't picky, anyway.

He rose up and ran the faucet.

The water was warm. He let it run for a few seconds, until it got cool. Then filled the bowl with it. Offered it to the Giants. At no point in this process did he panic. He had decided that he would not panic. And so he did not.

The dogs lapped up the water. Those who could reach the bowl, anyway. Meatball looked like she was going to choke herself out, straining against her collar.

Maybe…it wouldn't be crazy to let them off-leash here. Give them a break.

Jairzinho looked to the door. Astrid had apparently been able to open it with just a push…but Astrid was Astrid. She was stronger than the other dogs. Still…

It would be nice to let them run around a bit. Get some distance from each other. And, he could just stand in front of the door, if it came to that. They wouldn't get out. It'd be fine. It'd be *fine*.

Fine.

One by one, he unclipped the Giants' leashes from their collars. One by…one. He only paused at every single one of them. But, on the other hand, the pauses got progressively shorter. Except for the ones that were longer.

He was unclipping his Giants in public. Completely unclipping. Okay. It was fine. This was all okay and *fine*.

Meatball tumbled over to the water bowl. Kelso didn't lunge for Meatball. That was promising.

Barmit stayed put. Sheriff zoomed around the bathroom, wagging up a storm. Ladybug gasped and boggled.

Ducky…would stay clipped. Those Igor wheezes didn't inspire confidence. In terms of good behavior. Or anything else.

Jairzinho removed one of the bottles he'd filled at the Hamasyans from his pack and drank. It occurred to him that these bottles were *also* Manhattan tap water. The only difference was that the taps were a few blocks away from each other.

He smiled. Shook his head at his own stupidity. Did not panic.

The Giants seemed to acclimate themselves to their relative freedom quickly. Meatball had her fill of water and galumphed around the bathroom. Like she was chasing a butterfly, but the signals to her limbs were all scrambled.

Kelso gave Meatball a wide berth and came in for some water. He lapped at the bowl. Pointed his dripping snout at Barmit. Lapped some more.

Sheriff was fascinated by the stall Jairzinho had been in. This embarrassed Jairzinho for some reason. Like letting Sheriff sniff around there was akin to exposing himself to the little guy.

Astrid, Jairzinho couldn't help but recall, had seen his penis. During pick-up, he'd once dashed into Astrid's apartment for a quick piss. It was at the height of a heat wave; he'd been slamming water. Couldn't be helped. What could have been helped was his leaving the bathroom door slightly ajar. Astrid chundered right in. Got an eyeful. Then locked eyes with Jairzinho. That had been weird. Shouldn't have been. Still was.

Jairzinho felt his nose curl. "Sheriff! C'mere, buddy!"

Sheriff turned and wagged. He dashed back to Jairzinho. Got a running start and leapt onto Ladybug's face. Ladybug said *hgglBLECH* and fell over.

Ducky grunted and whined. Somehow even his whining sounded predatory.

Sheriff and Ladybug played. In as much as the latter was capable. This was surely Ladybug's favorite method of play: lay on the ground and let the other dog come to you.

Kelso started to stalk Meatball. Head down, cautious steps. "Easy, Kelso." The puggle gave Jairzinho a *who, me?* face, then drifted over to the stalls. Ah, well. If they wanted to sniff around over there, the joke was gonna be on them.

Ladybug hacked her way over to the water bowl. Sheriff orbited her like a pilot fish.

Jairzinho pet Ladybug's weird little spherical head as she drank…from the empty bowl. "Sorry, girl. Asleep at the switch." He alternated refilling the dogs' bowl and his bottle, their bowl, his bottle.

Here was another shared experience. Thirst. The need for water. He'd underestimated the number of shared experiences, it seemed.

"Look at that," he said to Ladybug. It was hard to tell if she was drinking or just gasping at her own reflection in the bowl. "So much in common. Ladybug. Ladybug. Hey Ladybug."

Finally, she lifted her head and said *ghlECH*.

"Who's my favorite little dummy?" Jairzinho asked.

Ladybug didn't know.

"*You* are," Jairzinho revealed. "You are!"

Ladybug sneezed, sneezed again, and said "goddamnit."

…

That probably wasn't Ladybug.

- 4 -

Sniffing that first guy's vest had been instructive. It had helped Astrid find the others.

She hadn't planned on tooling through the whole building. But then she'd found the staircase door propped open. And she'd smelled more people upstairs. People who smelled like they probably had guns.

They were basically inviting her up. So she accepted the invitation. It'd have been rude not to.

"Who's in here?" Jairzinho called. He accidentally said it as though he were still asking Ladybug who his favorite little dummy was. He cleared his throat. Cobbled together a halfway decent impression of authority. "Who is in here?"

No response.

"I'm not talking to my dogs anymore."

No response.

"You just said 'goddamnit'. I know you're in here."

Sneeze. Sneeze.

"Person who's sneezing right now."

Sneeze. Sneeze.

"Gesundheit."

Sneeze. Sigh. "Oh, alright," came a voice from one of the stalls.

Beneath the bottom of the sandy stall wall, Jairzinho saw two feet, shod in what he had to imagine were rather expensive black flats, climb down from atop the toilet bowl. It was the stall directly next to the one Jairzinho had been in.

298

He hoped he hadn't farted. He couldn't remember.

The stall door swung open.

A narrow, middle-aged woman with an assault rifle roared out. "GET DOWN ON THE GROUND!"

Jairzinho didn't know much about guns. But even *he* knew she was holding the gun upside-down. She had blood on her blouse. And smeared on her glasses. And she was holding an assault rifle upside-down.

Jairzinho raised his hands. "Are you one of the professors here?" he asked.

Her eyes darted to each of the dogs. She moved like a Whippet. Had the button eyes to match. "Why do you have so many dogs?" she demanded.

"I'm a dogwalker. It's been a long day." He lowered his hands slightly. "Please stop pointing the gun at me."

She drooped. Lowered the gun.

"You know this is the men's restroom," Jairzinho couldn't stop himself from saying.

The probable-Professor shifted her feet. "I'm aware." She straightened up to a more distinguished stature. "I don't believe you're one of my students."

"I don't go here."

She slumped down again. "Of course not. Otherwise you'd be…in the Park."

"Sit," Jairzinho ordered an antsy Sheriff. He returned to the Professor: "What are they doing out there?"

After several pained seconds, she finally managed: "Can't you tell?"

He grimaced and nodded. "So how did you get that gun?"

"You can't have it."

"I didn't ask if I can have it. I asked where you got it."

"Where's your friend?"

Jairzinho narrowed his eyes. "What friend?"

"I heard her laugh," the Professor explained.

"…ah." Jairzinho forced himself to calm down. This lady was probably in shock. "She's just over in the women's r-"

"NO!" The Professor screamed, breaking towards the door.

"WAIT! Watch the door!"

The Professor didn't wait. She shouldered past Jairzinho.

He raised a melodramatic hand. *So people actually do this*, he marveled. Even as he shouted "just slip out, don't open it w-"

The Professor plowed straight through the door. Swinging it wide open.

The second she did, Meatball rumbled after her.

Jairzinho dove in front of Meatball like a goalie. The impact with the ground sent a bolt up his spine. Meatball plowed into his chest.

The door patted him gently on the back. Congratulations.

"Ok, ok…" he pushed himself to his feet. Something was going on in the women's room. Esther might be in danger. Or, more likely, the Professor was about to be in danger.

But he didn't want to leave the dogs in here by themselves. Unclipped. Where any of them could just headbutt their way out the door. But he didn't have time to round them all back up!

"Ahhh…" He juked between the dogs and the door a few times. The dogs. The door. The dogs. The door. "Um… aaaah…" He held both palms out to the dogs. Nothing to it but to trust. "Stay!" He carefully slipped out the door.

He felt the hands on his lapel before he saw the face they were attached to. Then he was flying backwards. Back into the bathroom.

Astrid was fairly certain she'd gotten all of them but one. The one who'd tried to shoot them from the roof. She had smelled his gun. The sharp, powdery smell it made. No one whose throat she'd ripped out had smelled quite like that gun.

The door to the roof! Propped open! It was all too easy.

She stepped out carefully. Trotted a full circuit.

There was nobody up here.

Which meant…

Uh oh.

Astrid took off back through the door. Down the stairs. As quick as she could.

- 5 -

Jairzinho had time to think *Oh dear. I'm having a fight.* Then his head hit the tile floor. He stopped thinking for a bit. The world was colors and shapes. None of them meant anything. Oh, sounds too. Colors and shapes and sounds. New shapes and colors sounding through the shape. Colors.

Sounds: "You that fella I seen with the dogs?"

Jairzinho squinted. Trying to think. He was, wasn't he?

He looked around the bathroom. There were a bunch of dogs. Jairzinho was a fella. All checked out so far.

So where had this guy seen Jairzinho?

Where…ah…oh. Right. The very long rifle slung across his back was a hint.

"You got down fast," Jairzinho slurred.

Which he had. The guy. Must have really booked it. And this wasn't the scrawny little dweeb Jairzinho had imagined would get sniper duty. This was a refrigerator in olive and pea camo fatigues. Just in case there were any greenhouses to storm today. He looked like he could have stepped off the front of a Wheaties box this morning. Or else he *was* the box.

And speaking of shapey shapey colors: Jairzinho's face was right in front of Wheaties' heavy-duty black combat flats. Er, boots. And Wheaties wanted to have a fight with Jairzinho.

Jairzinho had never had a fight before. He'd have been happy to maintain the record unto death.

Which he still might. If he didn't get his head away from that boot.

Sheriff leapt up on the guy's pant leg.

Wheaties shunted Sheriff off. Just a shunt. Not a push or a kick. Nothing excessively violent. Which was too bad. Some righteous ire would have been really energizing just then.

Jairzinho rolled onto his stomach. Wriggled his hands beneath his shoulders. Started to push.

Something hot and hard pressed against the back of his neck.

He heard his flesh sizzle. Then he smelled it. A now-familiar smell.

It still smelled sweet.

"Ah-ah-aaaaaah!" He lowered himself down. Wheaties just pushed harder. Branded Jairzinho with the barrel of his gun.

Ladybug's boiling, bubbling *yarps* weren't helping.

Jairzinho wondered if the barrel was still so hot from the shooting up on the roof. Or if it had fired more recently. At Esther. Or Astrid.

"Your friend," Wheaties snarled.

Jairzinho tried to nod. "Ever'body wantsa meet my friend," he heard himself mumble.

Wheaties just laughed. "Yeah? She had a real mouth on her."

Past tense. Where was Esther, anyway? That'd have been a great moment for her to appear in the door. Fire off a one-liner. Then maybe a gun. A come-from-behind rescue. Unless she was dead. Then the Professor could do it. Anybody, really. Any time now.

Unless she was dead too. Or maybe Jairzinho had made her up. In the instant his head hit the ground.

"Please…" Jairzinho said. That was all. He didn't know what he was asking for.

"These her dogs, or yer dogs?"

"Please."

Wheaties stepped on Jairzinho's head. Ground his left cheek into the floor. Blood and dirt clumped from the boot sole onto his right cheek.

Jairzinho didn't think he could have his neck cranked this far for much longer. It felt like there was a buzzsaw in his back. The muscle he'd pulled in the initial explosion. Might not have been a pull.

"Please!" Jairzinho screamed.

"Please ain't an answer!"

"My back, I hurt my back, I-"

"Boy, I was shootin' atchu not ten fuckin' minutes ago! I ain't gonna give you a fuckin' backrub! Now I'm gonna ask you again, is these dogs *yers,* or is they *hers?*"

Jairzinho's world went grey. Blindness!

No. Barmit.

Barmit had waddled up to Jairzinho.

She started licking the blood from his face.

"Daaaawww," Wheaties said. Unironically.

303

Jairzinho looked past Barmit. Towards Ducky. The little shit was up on his rear legs. His front paws flailed in the air as he tugged against his leash. Against the pipe. He was…

Oh Jesus. He was humping the air between himself and Ladybug. Like they were connected via Chinese finger trap. And…the red rocket was putting in an appearance.

Okay. Not righteous indignation. But that was sickening enough to focus Jairiznho.

One at a time. He needed the boot off of his face. He couldn't worry about anything else until that happened.

"You'll hurt your ears," he sniffed from beneath Wheaties' tread.

Thank fuck: Wheaties eased off a touch. "Whatchusayin'?"

Jairzinho winced. Tried to turn his eyes to make contact with Wheaties'. Contact. Connection. That was what he needed. To get this fucking boot off. "You'll hurt your ears. If you shoot your gun in here. It'll be really loud."

Wheaties blinked. "Uh…okay? Then I just ain't gonna shoot my gun."

He put all of his weight into the boot.

Something in Jairzinho's back *SNAPPED*. Like a rubber band stretched past the breaking point. Black and red bloomed in his vision.

He screamed.

Wheaties laughed. "That din't sound good, huh? Betchu wish you ain't immergrated here *now*, eh Pablo?"

Jairzinho wanted to clap back. Land a really good zinger. But he couldn't think. He couldn't speak. All he could do was suffer. It was over. Even if he survived this, his right arm had gone numb. He wouldn't be able to walk the dogs to the bridge. All for nothing. This was all for nothing.

Wheaties leaned down. "Awww, is the little anchor baby cryin' his fuckin' snowflake tears?"

Jairzinho sniffed. He was. He was crying. He hated himself for it. But he was. See, Tia? He *could* cry. All you'd had to do was rip one of his back muscles to shreds.

He saw her face in the black and the red. She was smiling. He wished he'd given her more reasons to, towards the end.

Yeah. That's right. It was over. The end.

He squeezed his eyes shut. Tears washed the blood from his cheeks.

And unbeknownst to him, saved his life.

- 6 -

...mr. comeon was being less hatable than usual...he'd put a bunch of bodywater on his face...and laid down on the ground...so barmit could get to it...and it was not so bad...then this new guy, mr. whosedogs, he walked on mr. comeon...and something went snap really loud...and then mr. comeon started washing the bodywater off of his face...

...he was making boring bodywater with his eyes and that was ruining the *good* bodywater...

...at first barmit hated mr. comeon because he was taking away her bodywater...but then she realized it was actually mr. whosedogs who had poisoned the bodywater with boring... because he'd walked on mr. comeon...and mr. comeon had been trying to help barmit...

...which mean mr. whosedogs...he...was so hatable...

...barmit hated him...so...*much*.

she hated him more than anything she'd ever hated before

because he didn't just take her bodywater

he also walked on mr. comeon

that bothered barmit

she didn't know why

but it didn't matter

what mattered was that she hated this mr. whosedogs moth-erfucker, and now she was going to floss with his brainstem.

Blck, *Barmit said.* Jairzinho thought she was choking. Turn-ed out, she was just remembering how to bark.

She didn't remember all the way.

BARF BARF BARF, she screeched at Wheaties.

He laughed at her.

Barmit *leapt.* Like one of those horrible sub-tropic spiders that could do slam dunks.

She splatted herself onto Wheaties' camo fatigues. And app-arently dug in. Because she stayed rooted to his knee. And Wheaties shouted "Hey – OW!"

Barmit started to *climb.*

"THE FUCK!"

Kelso was frozen at first. He couldn't believe what he was seeing. Barmit was…acting like a living thing, wasn't she? Like she could play when she wanted to.

Only she wasn't playing right now. She was climbing up that guy's leg. Now biting through his pants. *Hard.*

Kelso barked.

Barmit swung her head his way. Her tiny little jaws covered in blood and fabric, her tiny little eyes pointing in different dir-ections.

The guy smacked her off of him. *Baff*, a brisk backhand.

Barmit fell. *Cracked* on the tile.

Nope.

Fuck no.

Kelso didn't like other dogs wrecking his homewrecker, so he *certainly* wouldn't abide a human *smacking* his homewrecker. *His* homewrecker.

So he charged.

It was such BULLSHIT that EVERYBODY got to DO what they WANTED and run AROUND all FREE and SHIT while DUCKY was still FUCKIN' LEASHED. But THAT was FINE because HE could MIND control this CHUMP with the GUN. He JUST fuckin' HUMPED and PUMPED and THOUGHT at him KILL bad MAN kill BAD man KILL kill KILL! And the CHUMP sorta DID only THIS chump was a PUPPY so he DIDN'T kill BAD man ALL the way.

And NOW the other DOGS were GOIN' BUCK wild on DUCKY'S CHUMP? First BARMIT and now KELSO? BULLSHIT. They were ALL goin' DOWN. EVERYBODY but LADYBUG. Or MAYBE her TOO. No REASON you couldn't FUCK-*GUH* a PUP just BECAUSE she was DEAD.

Ducky HUMPED the air FASTER and FASTER and THOUGHT in his BRAIN to KILL them ALL kill THEM all KILL THEM ALL, but the CHUMP wasn't PAYIN' ATTEN-TION since HE was a stupid DORK and he was FOCUSED on KELSO. Just BECAUSE Kelso was JUMPIN' and BITIN' the CHUMP'S fingers OFF.

KILL EM ALL KILL EM ALL KILL EM KILL EM KILL

Then ALL of a SUDDEN Ducky FELL on his FUCKIN' DICK.

He could RUN! SO he fuckin' ZOOMED at the CHUMP'S legs because MIND control was way STRONGER if you got right UP in that SHIT!

So DUCKY got right UP in that SHIT and HUMPED and HUMPED and thought KILL EM KILL EM MURDER EM KILL

"GET THE FUCK OFF!" Wheaties screamed. Kelso was busy giving him hell above the belt. Barmit crawled back up his right leg. Ducky humped up a storm on the other.

Water flooded across Jairzinho's face. The side on the floor. Not tears this time.

He tried to push himself up. "HRRRRNG!" He couldn't even get his arms under him. He splashed back onto the floor. Glanced towards the sink he'd clipped Ducky to.

Ducky had pulled the pipe clean out of the sink. It sprayed water all over the floor. The pipe. Jesus.

Wheaties tried to backpedal. Sheriff had scrambled his way behind the guy. Wheaties went down hard.

Sheriff jumped up on his chest and ran in little circles.

Jairzinho rolled over his "good" shoulder. Onto his back.

Ladybug *yelped*. She'd laid down right next to him. Like the sweetest little grim reaper.

"Sorry girl," Jairzinho mumbled as he groaned up onto his elbow.

Ladybug snuffled. Nuzzled Jairzinho's flank as he rose.

Now Sheriff yelped. Only it wasn't a yelp. It was a *SCREAM.*

Jairzinho looked up in time to see Wheaties fastball Sheriff against the far wall of the bathroom. The poor pup made a heart-stopping cry as he *thwacked* into the wall. A mix between a squeak and a howl.

That got Jairzinho moving. He forgot about his back and crawled over to Sheriff.

As he did, Meatball thundered in the opposite direction.

She wasn't going to get involved. Much as she hated seeing her friends, and, yes, even Kelso getting pummeled, Meatball wasn't about to be responsible for any more bloodshed today. She had decided to commit herself to pacifism. No more violence. No more dissociation. Even when it was hard.

Then that asshole threw Sheriff. Sheriff, who'd only wanted to play. Sweet, gentle Sheriff.

He'd fucking thrown Sheriff.

[Lemme at him. Oooh, lemme at him!]

The Other Dog – who wasn't really an Other – rattled the cage.

Meatball didn't have to think twice. She simply compromised with her Other…half. We will do this, together.

[Whatever ya say, boss.]

All together with herself, the entirety of Meatball collided with that asshole's right ear. Teeth-first, naturally.

Sheriff was okay. Shaken, probably a bit achy. But he sprang right up before Jairzinho had even managed to get to him.

Ladybug trotted over to Sheriff. Licked his nose. Sheriff flinched. Wagged his tail.

Jairzinho rolled back around to the maelstrom of snarling and screaming.

Wheaties, still on the ground, had Meatball by the neck. For most people, "Meatball by the neck" wasn't much more reassuring than "wrecking ball by the chain".

But most people couldn't be described as *industrial size*.

Meatball struggled and snapped. Blood poured from Wheaties' savaged fingers into Meatball's jowls. Her thrashing repainted the walls red.

Ducky had graduated to humping the guy's beltline.

Barmit was…Jesus, Barmit was just eating him. She'd laid down on his right thigh, drilled a hole through his pants and appeared to be snacking. Wheaties tried to kick her off, but he couldn't get enough momentum that high up the thigh.

Kelso was biting the guy's left forearm. Trying to free Meatball.

Jairzinho heard a very loud bark. A bark that none of the dogs here could have…

ASTRID!

He looked to the door.

The push door.

Which was a pull door from the other side.

She couldn't get in.

If she could…bye bye Wheaties.

The door was a solid twenty feet away.

Jairzinho tried to rise to his feet. "HRRRRRRRRGH!" He collapsed. Looked to Ladybug. "Get the door!" he screamed. Pointed. Ladybug followed his finger. Then looked back at him. "Let Astrid in!"

The door rattled in its frame. Astrid, trying her best. She barked.

A bubble of mucus bloomed and popped on Ladybug's nose.

Okay. The last resort. Jairzinho hated using it. But sometimes…there was no other option.

He reached his hand down to his pocket. Lifted it back up. Fingers curled around an imaginary ball. "See this?"

Ladybug's little ears flopped over the front of her face. Sheriff jumped up and planted his front paws on Jairzinho's thigh.

"*Gogitit!*" He threw the lie towards the door. Sheriff and Ladybug both skittered after it. Sheriff wouldn't get the idea. But Ladybug might. He just had to trust that she might.

He tried once more to lift himself to his feet. Got as far as his left foot flat on the ground, leaning on his right shin. Then he went down again.

What folly was pursuit of myst'ries ancient, blazing paths 'cross mire deep and black and ever hungry! Must thou lead a loyal dog astray, o wisps o will and nothing more, when there be bodies heavenly that, thus consigned by tiny gods, shall tarry not amongst the constellations dreamt betwixt indiff'rent stars, nor make no home where there be not a bed the worth of which lays not in how one lays upon its flaccid form, but rather in the whom it was doth laid it down?

But gild the lily not, for twas a simple riddle often posed but ne'er solved: where went that fucking ball?

Though Sheriff aided in the search, the pug knew well that most balls thrown do fall to Earth in timely fashion. Yet some thrown may never fall. Perhaps these balls are those which lead good girls, as Misha was, to places whence no dogs return.

On this day, though, the riddle vexed her not as might it have on others. Reason being: hark! A door. A door through which the ever-clever Astrid lately nosed herself. So hark and bark, the latter slipping sharply 'neath the door! Twas Astrid, eager but unable to effect reentry!

Hark, this twas the door t'wards which The Ferryman did point and pout just prior to the tossing of the damnéd ball!

And so twixt Hark and Bark, a full investigation of the door commenced, that Ladybug might come to know its

hhhhBLEGPH. *Ladybug was just standing* in front of the door. Staring at it. Like she almost got it. Like she was *so close.*

"Come on…" Jairzinho whined as he dragged himself towards the door. "Use your head! Literally!"

Ladybug tilted said head from side to side. Sheriff gave her a playslap. She ignored him.

Jairzinho could practically hear the pegs slotting into place. It wasn't like the shapes hadn't been pretty fucking well lined up.

He looked at the rest of his dogs.

Wheaties had fought his way onto his knees. Kelso's face was flat on the floor. Under the guy's left hand. The way Kelso thrashed made clear that Wheaties had almost all of his weight on that hand.

With his right hand, he was punching Meatball in the nose. With Barmit.

Barmit looked limp in his fist.

"STOP!" Jairzinho screamed.

For a split second, Wheaties stopped.

He and Jairzinho looked at each other. Anybody's guess who looked more surprised.

Ducky kept on humping. He'd never stopped. Just moved around to Wheaties' back.

Barmit made a horrible gurgling sound. She was alive. Barely.

Wheaties resumed beating Meatball.

Astrid's bark got a lot louder.

Jairzinho turned towards the door. Ladybug had dropped her head. She was pushing against it with all her might. The door.

Slowly, slowly, slowly. The door opened.

Astrid's snout poked through. Covered in blood.

She nosed herself the rest of the way in. Her eyes were revving engines. Jairzinho had never imagined a dog could look so livid.

He didn't think. He didn't have to.

Jairzinho was used to shouting orders.

Judging by his reaction to Jairzinho's *STOP*, Wheaties was used to following them.

Jairzinho rolled onto his back. Sucked in as much air as he could. In his deepest, loudest, most authoritative voice (the one he usually reserved for saying *Ducky leave it*), he belted out "*ON YOUR FEET, SOLDIER!*"

Wheaties dropped Barmit and shot straight to his feet. He couldn't have looked more perplexed if the dogs mauling him had turned into fish and leapt into the toilets.

That stupid gawp was the last thing he ever did with his face.

Astrid got a running start. Hit him right in the solar plexus.

He went down hard.

Jairzinho had to look away when Astrid turned her head to the side and spat out half of Wheaties' nose. As he turned, he saw Barmit between the guy's legs, chewing through to the Mini Wheats.

On the bright side, there was really no better place to get sick than a restroom.

Astrid felt awful. She could have stopped this guy much earlier if she'd stayed.

Instead her friends had gotten hurt. Because she'd believed she was protecting them. She'd assumed Jairzinho was clueless.

And he'd been hurt worst of all. Trying to save the others.

She went to him and licked his face. Her affection painted Jairzinho's drawn features with the blood of, what had it been, four or five guys around the building? He didn't seem to enjoy that. But he hugged her.

"You're a good girl," he told her. Which was nice of him to say.

The hug turned into a lean. Which was okay. Astrid was strong enough to hold him up.

After a few minutes, Astrid *woofed.*

Jairzinho sighed. Reached one hand out to the urinal next to him. Careful not to stick his fingers too far in. It was the one he'd just filled with authentic Armenian cuisine.

He didn't want to put the other hand on Astrid. Didn't want to use her to push himself up.

But she stepped closer to him.

Together, they got Jairzinho to his feet.

His right arm hung limp at his side. But he could still wriggle his fingers. If he grit his teeth, he could lift the arm. So it wasn't paralyzed. Just hurt a whole hell of a lot.

He looked at the Giants. They were all varying degrees of fucked up. Astrid looked like she'd been turned inside out. Had done even before she'd pulled Wheaties there apart. Jairzinho didn't want to know how she'd gotten all that blood on her.

Barmit was still eating Wheaties.

Ducky was still humping his chest.

Jairzinho shook his head and laughed. It was either that or start gibbering and pulling his hair out.

He looked in the mirror. At a goddamned zombie. One that'd been dead long enough to start rotting. He made a mental note to take a shower before he hugged Tia.

Jairzinho looked to Astrid. Gestured to the Giants. Mainly Ducky. "Watch 'em."

Astrid wagged, but did not smile.

- 7 -

The first thing Jairzinho saw in the women's room was a body without a head. The gun that had vaporized unsaid head was resting in the Professor's lap, butt to the ground.

Either she'd killed herself, or she'd *really* never figured out how to use that gun.

Jairzinho dry-heaved. Forced himself to keep walking.

Esther was sitting against the wall opposite the stalls. Eyes open. Not visibly injured.

But not moving.

316

"Oh shit," Jairzinho mumbled as he fell to his knees in front of her. "Esther?"

She blinked. Her eyes were bloodshot. More red than white.

Jairzinho put his left hand on her shoulder and doubled over. "Oh fuck. Oh fuck. Esther. What the fuck happened?"

Esther blinked again. Her eyes were flat. *Dusty* was the word that popped into Jairzinho's head.

He snapped his fingers an inch from her nose. "Esther. Wake up. It's okay. We're okay."

Another blink.

"Talk to me. Tell me what happened."

Esther's jaw shuddered and popped. Moving in every direction at once. It was inhuman. Like it was glitching. "I seen the kid in the stalls."

One glance towards the stalls answered Jairzinho's question. Legs, blood, bone.

"So I was just lookin' at him. Then I was about to come over and tell you, get a load of this shit. Only that lady comes screamin' in. Sayin' it wasn't her fault and she ain't sorry. I tried talkin' to her. She just plops down and shoots herself. Just like that. Easy as nothin'."

Jairzinho didn't know what to say to Esther, except to speak in a language she might understand. So he returned his left hand to her shoulder and said "she can't be the first person who reacted that way to you trying to talk to them."

Esther turned her head towards Jairzinho. Faced him dead-on. It was like all of the muscles above the nose were slack, and the ones beneath were clenching tight.

His heart frowned. He'd assumed some shit-talk would help revive her. Apparently he'd

Hahahahaha. Esther's laugh was subdued, but sincere. It tapered gently into a cry. She pulled Jairzinho in for a tight hug.

He woke up sitting next to her against the wall. His head spinning. Back screaming. "The fuck?"

"I hugged you and you passed out. Sorry. Your back feels fucked up."

"Yeah."

"Some shit happen in the men's room too?"

Jairzinho nodded. Opted to let the pun slide.

They each studied the floor. Failed to find what they were looking for.

"I can't do it, buddy," Esther croaked.

He sighed, resigned. "Do what?" He knew the answer.

"I can't keep goin'. I'm real sorry. I thought I could. But I…" Esther's voice quivered and caught. "I ain't cut out for this shit."

Jairzinho stared at the ground. He needed Esther. He needed her to walk the dogs. To take them across the bridge. He would find his own way across, but he needed her to take them. Because he couldn't. Not just across the bridge – *to* the bridge. He was too shattered to get the leash-belt on. Physically, just for a start.

He needed her.

But she didn't need him. And not a handful of blocks away was Vatche's place. Safe haven with an open door. Esther had no reason to keep going. And Jairzinho had no right to ask that of her.

But he couldn't go back. Especially not now. That would mean all of this had been for nothing. Which was a stupid thing to think. It would all be for nothing if he got himself and the dogs killed, too.

There was no good reason to keep going. What else was new.

Esther was trembling. It was subtle. Jairzinho wouldn't have noticed it if he weren't leaning his shoulder against hers. She hid it well.

"No one is," Jairzinho finally replied. "I understand."

Esther didn't wipe her eyes; she clawed the tears out. Like she resented them. Which she probably did. "It's just real for me now. I know what that sounds like. But I can't think of other fuckin' words."

"I think I know what you mean."

"She just blew her own fuckin' head off. But she settled in first. When she sat down." Esther scooted from side to side, clearing her sitbones. "She just quit screamin' all at once and settled in like she wanted to get comfy. Before she shot her own brains out. I seen some shit, I'll tell ya. But I never seen nothin' like that."

Jairzinho wanted to suggest they leave the women's room… but nowhere else was much better. There was blood in the lobby. Obviously the men's room was a no-go.

Thinking of safe places prompted a brusque segue: "Vatche said you can go back to his place. Wait it out there."

"Yeah," Esther sniffed. "He's a real nice guy."

"He is."

Esther's softness didn't quite collapse. It…got covered, like an old sofa under a spooky white sheet. "You gonna come with, or do I gotta walk back on my own?"

Compensation or not, it was reassuring to see the old, brassy Esther peeking through. Still. Jairzinho shook his head. "I have to keep going."

"No you don't."

"...I know."

Esther nodded from the base of the neck. "You're gonna keep goin'. With your fucked up arm."

"Yeah."

"Nah. That's fuckin' stupid. Let's go back to Vatche's." She clawed at her eyes again.

"How do I get to the Bridge from here?"

"Jairzinho. I'm usin' your full fuckin' too-long name here as an emphasizement. You go to the bridge, you're gonna fuckin' die."

"Maybe not, if I know where I'm going."

"How you gonna get across? You sure ain't walkin'."

"I'm sure I'll find some other clown-faced blowhard to walk the dogs over."

She cracked a smile. It repaired itself in an instant. "I'm askin' about *you*."

"I don't know. I'll figure something out. Climb under the bottom if I have to."

"You're talkin' about a mile and a half of fuckin' monkey bars."

"Good thing I'm so Chimpish, then."

Esther plastered her hands over her face. Took a deep breath. "You're not so far. Just about fifteen blocks out. Keep headin' east on 3rd. Some point you're gonna wanna cut south to Houston, head east on that. You can do that whenever it's some kinda safe."

"Houston goes to the bridge?"

"Yeah. Yeah. This is dumb. You got a dumb fuckin' plan."

"Not true," Jairzinho shot back with a smile. "I don't have any plan at all."

Esther wasn't smiling. "And you're gonna drag them poor dogs along while you're tryin' to prove you're only half as shitty a guy as everybody knows you are?"

Jairzinho sighed. "Not quite. I'm gonna let them choose."

"*Choose?*" Esther furrowed her brow and stuck out her lower lip. "Either you hit your head pretty hard, or you got no clue how dogs work."

"The second one," Jairzinho replied. Thinking of carnivorous Barmit. Of necrophiliac Ducky. "One hundred percent the second one."

Jairzinho wanted to spare Esther the carnage of the men's room. So he asked her to wait outside. She was happy to oblige.

To step away and return reinvested the scene with its sick-summoning horror. Astrid was still rocking the *Carrie*-at-prom look. Barmit, meanwhile, was going for freshly-born *Alien* chestburster chic.

Ducky was still humping Wheaties' remains. *Basic Instinct*.

Jairzinho used the water bowl to clean off the dogs as best he could. Flicked it dry and put it back in his…

He sighed at his backpack. That wasn't going to make the trip. But that was okay. It was just fifteen blocks. He wouldn't need the backpack. He hoped.

Just fifteen blocks, he repeated to himself. They could follow him for fifteen blocks, right?

He opened the door to the bathroom. Held it open. Knowing full well this might be the last time he saw any of these dogs.

They stared at the open door. Heads cocked to the side.

Ladybug grunted her way over to it. Stopped at the threshold. *hhhLUHKPT.*

Meatball broke into a half-trot. Slipped in blood on her way to the door. Recovered gracefully as she ran outside.

"Heya Meatball!" Jairzinho heard Esther shout from the atrium.

One by one, the dogs filed out, and Esther greeted them. Ladybug, Barmit, Kelso, Astrid.

Propping the door open with his backpack, Jairzinho stepped over to the final pup.

He crouched down in front of Ducky. Still humping. His expression was terrifying. Jairzinho couldn't put his finger on why. But it was…too…quiet. Too focused to fit with such frenzied motion.

Jairzinho reached out his left arm to pick him up.

Ducky lunged for his hand. *rrrAR!* Skittered out the door. (Esther's greeting for him was "oh boy, here comes trouble!")

Jairzinho sighed and headed for the door. Paused. Stepped back into the room and grabbed a few leashes from the carabiner belt. For Esther to take any dogs who opted out. To take them back with her to Vatche's.

He rose and…paused again.

Crouched down to the backpack.

Retrieved the cold pack. The one with the pack-lunch Tia had made for him.

It fit in one of the large pockets at the front of his cargo shorts. They might not have been slick or sexy, but boy were cargo shorts useful.

He took a deep breath. Time to force his Giants to make decisions they couldn't possibly understand.

It occurred to him that Tia must have felt this way. When she said she'd wanted to move to New York. Asked Jairzinho to come. After he'd talked such shit about the city. She'd known he'd hate it here. She'd known he didn't fully realize what he was committing to.

His being miserable wasn't just making her miserable. It was making her feel *guilty*.

What Jairzinho would not have done to have had this eureka in a goddamned bathtub.

He shook his head and stepped into the lobby.

Esther looked up from her crouch. She lifted a blood-stained palm from Astrid's belly. Considered it. Showed it to Jairzinho. "Ya missed a spot." She smiled. It seemed like a fragile smile. "The fuck are you laughin' about?"

Jairzinho shook his head. "This is better than therapy."

"Ain't so reassurin' when somebody says that right after they walk outta a room's got a dead body in it."

"I'll tell you what, maybe that's what I should do. Become a therapist." Jairzinho nodded. "I'd make a k…ah, I'd do really well in this city. Have a survivor's discount. For the first few sessions."

Esther straightened her posture. First time for everything. "I feel like I got a civic obligation to stop you doin' that."

"I'm kidding."

"I figured."

They looked at the ground. Delaying the inevitable. Jairzinho wanted to ask Esther to come with him. She almost certainly wanted to ask him to come with *her* again. But neither asked their questions, because they both knew the other's answer.

Jairzinho limped his way to Esther. Extended his left hand.

She looked at it and smirked. Rose to her feet. Ignored Sheriff playing her shin like a xylophone. "We're shakin' hands now?"

"I was thinking I might maintain consciousness for the whole rest of the day."

Esther made a show of flipping her right hand upside-down to shake Jairzinho's left. "Pleasure doin' business with ya."

"Thank you, Esther. I'm serious." Jairzinho gripped her hand as tight as he could. "I would never have made it this far without you."

She nodded. Wriggled a few wrinkles out of her upper lip. "Me neither. You gotta be careful. Oh!" She plunged her hand into her pocket. Pulled out a handful of sweat-drenched lint. Withdrew her right hand from Jairzinho and burrowed her fingers into the pocketfuzz. "Hang on a sec. I wanna give ya somethin'."

A piece of lint fell on the ground. It went *splat*.

Jairzinho looked down. Looked back up. "Uh...I think I'm good."

Esther nodded. "You will be. Here!" She pulled a little white pill out of the mess. Not a pillbox. A single pill. "Put your hand flat so's I can give this to ya."

Jairzinho studied the pale little nugget in her hand. "What is it?"

"It's for pain. Real strong stuff. Should get ya through."

"...that doesn't answer my question."

"I know it don't. Take it."

"Why do you have it?"

Esther laughed. "Hope you're scratchin' detective off your new career list. I'm old and I ain't so svelte. I got arthritis and the osteo-porous. Can't do this job if I can't keep the pain down. Take the fuckin' pill."

Jesus. So she was always in pain. Another thing he'd never noticed.

Somehow, accepting her help felt like the only sufficient apology for his obliviousness.

"Okay," he said. He took the pill in hand, then mouth. "Youhawaer?" he asked, his tongue seemingly weighed down by the hairy capsule.

"Huh?" Esther asked. Smiling.

Jairzinho frowned. "Gieewaer!"

"What'sat?"

Jairzinho spat the pill back into his palm. "I need water t-"

"Gross!" Esther hammed.

"Oh, fuck yourself," Jairzinho laughed as he yanked his backpack out from under the men's room door and retrieved a water bottle. He threw back the pill.

It felt fuzzy on the way down. He tried not to think about that.

His eyes naturally drifted to Barmit.

That *definitely* didn't help. So he pulled them back to Esther.

"I'll hold ya up if ya zonk," she told him. "But I gotta get one more."

"Wha-"

Esther lunged forward and wrapped Jairzinho in a bear hug. Soft on his right side, though. The world collapsed a bit. But he managed not to pass out.

"Alright!" Esther shouted as she pulled back. "Enough of this shit. I'll see you later. And not in the fuckin' obituaries."

Jairzinho nodded. Yeah. It was time. The moment of...
something. "Goodbye, Esther." He limped towards the door.
The one they'd taken to get off the street, a million years ago.

He was aware of his heart beating faster. Oh, what a luxury,
to be able to notice such a thing.

This was the moment. He would offer his dogs a choice.
Which they couldn't possibly understand. But a choice it would
be. And really, who ever understood the consequences of th-

Sophistry. Bullshit. Stalling.

Jairzinho turned around. Raised his left hand. It had never
felt so heavy.

He snapped his fingers.

"Come," he ordered his Giants.

Astrid ran straight over. Ladybug and Meatball chundered
close behind. Then Barmit, Kelso, and finally Ducky.

Sheriff thumped his paws on Esther's leg. She looked down
at him. Vaguely disappointed. "Well shit, guess it's just you and
me," she said to him.

As if he suddenly understood, Sheriff turned to look for his
friends. Saw them all at Jairzinho's feet.

He leapt down from Esther's leg and ran to rejoin the Giants.

Jairzinho couldn't believe it. They'd all come. They'd all
heeled right away. Without the leashes. They...were self-regula-
ting? He watched as Ducky tried for Ladybug. Astrid didn't
move. It was Meatball and, more amazingly, *Sheriff* who put
themselves between the two. Kelso glared at Meatball, but
didn't run at her.

Astrid looked at Jairzinho and wagged her tail.

What a weird fucking bunch of dogs.

"Well," Esther said, "that's Stockmeyer Syndrome for ya."

326

"Holm," Jairzinho laughed.

"Yeah, you got one to go to. Brag about it."

Jairzinho's smile melted away. Esther's grew. It was as though she were taking his for the road. She could have it.

"So long, pal," she grinned.

Jairzinho gestured to the door. "We're both going the same way."

She shook her head. Not grinning anymore. "I need a minute."

Jairzinho nodded. He understood.

So did the Giants. They followed Jairzinho out the door and back into the smoke-blotted sunshine.

Esther watched them go. She'd hoped at least one of the dogs would come with her, just for selfish reasons. She was a little anxious to be walking back by herself. A bit like sleeping without a blanket in the summer. She was a goddamned adult, obviously she wasn't scared of monsters getting her. Still…she always preferred to have a blanket, between her and the monsters.

But as long as she steered clear of those three little monsters on Sixth, she knew she'd be fine.

Still. Company would have been nice. Everything was better with company.

She hoped Jairzinho would be okay. That he would make it. If nothing else, she wanted to see if the *placeboid* effect had worked on him. Like that British guy who tricks people. He loved *placeboid.*

She hoped he lived at *least* long enough for her to see his little face. When she told him all he'd taken for his pain had been an old breathmint.

- 8 -

Jairzinho walked the first three blocks in a daze. Maybe it was that pill kicking in. Maybe it was the otherworldly pall cast by the smoke coming from the park. Maybe it was walking with his unleashed dogs through empty, war-ravaged streets.

Maybe it was being all alone. No one to talk to. At least, no one who could talk back.

A chilling thought: vocal chords and tongue shape were probably the only things keeping Astrid from human speech.

Or maybe she would start chatting to him any second now. The world had certainly become surreal enough. Anything was possible.

Jairzinho lifted his right hand. Studied it. He felt the pain. Far away.

Yep. So the pill was working.

Sheriff danced around his feet as they walked. Meatball weaved from sidewalk to sidewalk, curb to curb. She was going to tire herself out. That might be the best case.

Keeping a lid on Ducky had become something of a group effort. It was going pretty well up until he sped forward and bit Jairzinho hard on the ankle.

The pain was far away. So was the frustration.

Ducky looked up at him. His devious little gremlin smile melted and pooled at his feet.

Jairzinho laughed. His own amusement was pretty far away too, but that was okay.

Then they got to Thompson. The corner of 3rd and Thompson. Jairzinho glanced north. Stole a peek at the main plaza of Washington Square Park. Visible through the gap between blocks.

The peek snatched the ground out from under him. Stole that feeling of distance. Of surreal indifference. Jairzinho scrambled to snatch it back.

Because he needed it. Needed that distance to look at the bodies smoldering in the volcano's mouth of what had once upon a time been the fountain. Or the ones strung up from the impossible height of the tank-ravaged arch. Or the piles of naked flesh, stacked like bulwarks against chainlink fencing…

Sweet surreality. Welcome back.

Jairzinho looked at the dogs. They looked at him. Seated patiently at his ankles. They looked *to* him.

And in a merciless and unsentimental way, he looked to them. To their slobbering, knuckleheaded dignity.

They weren't *his* Giants anymore. If they had ever been.

They were simply…*the* Curbside Giants.

And Jairzinho was one of them.

"Twelve blocks out from the bridge now," Jairzinho smiled. He blinked hard. Resteadied himself on his feet. "Are we ready?"

Ladybug shook herself out.

Meatball shimmied on her butt.

Sheriff did a downward dog stretch.

Kelso sneezed.

Ducky gurgled right at Jairzinho.

Barmit…continued to Barmit.

329

Astrid sat, chest shining forward. Nothing knuckleheaded about her dignity.

Jairzinho took a deep, slow breath. "Alright everybody. *Come.*"

TWELVE

BLOCKS OUT

- 12 -

Are those who run against the wind not justly served by that which hies 'pon crest and trough, to hearts which beat themselves out true in flight from what the wind does bring them? Yea, upon the wind! Tis death's calcareous paw cajoling, pleading, poised to strike those foolish souls for whom the skel'tal limn warns not of how this specter honors fealty! O, bend not thine knee, make not an oath 'gainst thine own life!

Yet hope, you fearless vanguard 'gainst the terror, rage, the *absence*, must ye birth thyself from suff'ring boundless such as slices through the fiery wake of hours dismal? Burning bodies piled, buried 'neath the buildings blasted unto bits. And bit by bit do many deaths consign to dust their secrets, slowly are these whispers born aloft by wind that pours them into waiting ears.

Begone ye locks and chains, and shut thyself no longer 'gainst the Giants! Welcome one and all, to Ladybug's high tower, lonely 'mongst the clouds!

No longer must so great a secret be one pug's alone – but ah! Forget not Meatball, 'pon whose shoulders portions of this burden have impressions made.

So look to Kelso, how he gazes 'pon thee, eyes a-boggle, teeth a-snaggle!

Look to Sheriff's tail, that truest vane of winds unseen, behold it wag and halt and spin and stop. Egads, such furious circles, slicing now in wild strokes!

Alas, from Barmit little more belied a broadened mind than lifted head, revealing eyes as dull as toenails. Eyes, it should be said, that turnéd towards her fellow trav'lers. Taciturn as Barmit was, a signal such as this was near hysterical!

No hope was held by Ladybug, that Ducky might be struck by mortal revelations. Gazéd though he had that wisdom carvéd into Ladybug's visage, the Frenchie heeds no lessons. This was his decision. Ladybug had glimpsed a further plain, had cracked an older riddle. She had died and lived and died and lived to gasp about it. Twas the choice of every dog, to heel or not.

O'er yonder, Astrid plodded, lost in thought. Twas clear she knew, as all her friends so clearly knew. What hounded them was nothing less than Death itself. And so they ran, as one, behind the Ferryman.

He reeked of resolution. *Death will claim you not, and if it makes its overtures, then I shall meet the Beast in kind.* How bold his scent! How clear his purpose!

Yark, what heat was this that bloomed inside her belly? Stems to which dead petals *rose?* A wind which neither sliced nor scoured, surely not for want of power?

Come, and give the warmth a word! A word that might be worthy!

hhhblllAAACCCCHHHH. And thus it was decreed! The newest word which carriéd its meaning, warmth, and worth! O hope, twas hope, and all the dogs must know its name!

hhhblllAAACCCCHHHH. Though heedless were her friends of either clarion call, she would not cease her labors, leavened as despair must be by *hhhblllAAACCCCHHHH.*

She pivoted to gauge her friends' responses. Blast! The ground gave way beneath her feet. A curb! Upon her face was Ladybug thus plonkéd.

Yet defeat this did not mark! For teaching friends the fear of death had taught her hope, ye greatest feeling borne of feeling known! At last!

hhhblllAAACCCCHHHH, and know it reaches for you even now, and as you know, ye shalt be known!

- 11 -

Sheriff didn't know *what* the heck was going on, but *gosh* it was all *brilliant* fun!

And the *absolute* best part was that he was running with all of his absolute best friends! He didn't know *why* they were running, but they were running! So Sheriff ran!

His friends were so much fun and they could play forever! The Babble Woman had given up! And so had the other guy back in the smelly room! He'd picked a game Sheriff had never played before called Bite The Large Person Until He Goes Into A Wet Sleep! It was hard to tell who won, but it really seemed like Astrid had!

Now they were playing a game called No More Leashes and *everybody* was winning!

The Babble Man fell over behind a honkbox! He said to them *COME* which wasn't babble because Sheriff knew that one!

He jumped right over The Babble Man and into his lap! The Babble Man said *AYCH!* And then he pet Sheriff on the head!

All of Sheriff's friends came to play with them! Except for Ducky! He just stood out in the open space and looked at The Babble Man and barked and barked and barked!

The Babble Man yelled at Ducky to *SHUP* and *CMERE!* But Ducky didn't Shup *or* Cmere. The Babble Man sounded very not happy about that.

Astrid ran out from behind the honkbox! Sheriff loved running! So he ran too! And so did Meatball!

The Babble Man shouted stuff but it was fine because Sheriff was running! Running with Astrid and...oh, Meatball had turned around, but anyway Sheriff was running with Astrid to go play with Ducky! And then Ducky was running away! Now they were playing Have A Chase and that was the *most* fun a pup could ever have!

"Come back!" Jairzinho hissed. The dogs didn't listen. Remarkably enough. He watched Ducky and Sheriff and, most harrowingly, Astrid go sprinting away. To who knew where.

He cursed quietly. As they vanished around a corner.

Jairzinho peered through the windshield of the car he was crouched against. The gunmen he'd spied had vanished around another corner. But they wouldn't be far. So he didn't want to call out for the three runaway pups again.

He punched the ground. Immediately regretted it. Oh well. What was one more regret among many?

Idiot. Sentimental idiot. Let the dogs make their own choice? *Fucking idiot.*

He looked at the Giants sitting obediently at his feet. Ladybug, Barmit, Kelso. Meatball came chundering back, tongue flapping in the breeze.

"Must be some kind of *Suicide Squad*," Jairzinho mumbled to himself. He laughed and shook his head. Oh yes, he'd gone over the edge.

He got suddenly self-conscious, being so flippant in front of the other dogs, when Ducky and Sheriff were very possibly in mortal danger. "They have Astrid," he defended himself to the Suicide Squad. "She'll get them back."

Jairzinho pressed himself up far enough to peer through the windshield again.

Coast was clear.

The Giants ran.

- 10 -

*...**barmit didn't feel*** so good...she hadn't since mr. whose-dogs had picked her up and punched her into meatball...and she didn't understand what was going on...but everyone was running, so barmit ran...but then ducky ran away...and then astrid and sheriff ran away...and barmit realized nobody was attached to mr. comeon anymore...so she didn't have to run anymore if she didn't want to...and why would she want to... she hated running...

...so she decided not to...

...she stood just where she was...and it was great...her feet were in charge...and they stayed where they were...and the

339

ground under them stayed too…and everything was still…and it was so nice…

…and then mr. comeon started running again…with the rest of the dogs that barmit hated…and they ran away…and left barmit alone…which was…

…

…not good…

…

…which meant…

…

…she…she didn't want to get left behind…she didn't like being alone…she hated it…she *hated* it…

…she lifted up her head and looked around…but she didn't see her friends…!!!

…she barked as loud as she could…even louder than she did at mr. whosedogs…but she couldn't see anybody…even underneath all of the cars…she couldn't see anybody…

…she was all alone…she should have run with them…she was so stupid…she barked again and then she gave up…looked at the spot on the ground…this was where she would shrivel up and die…all alone…

Kelso had no good reason to be running. He didn't even know why he was, did he? No he didn't. Everyone else had started running. So he ran too.

But then he got a good reason to stop. It was a sharp bark from half a block behind him.

Barmit. She had fallen behind. She was lost. Confused. Scared.

Alone.

Kelso rumbled quietly to himself. Why did he want to go back for her, that little homewrecker? Who had ended playtime forever?

Why had he been fretting over her this whole day?

He didn't know. That was another thing he didn't have a good reason for. Wanting to go back for her. Because he *did*, didn't he? He did, man. And he didn't have a good reason *not* to go back for her.

And so, he picked the more positive of the two unjustified impulses.

...the spot where barmit was going to shrivel up and die was dumb...it was a dumb spot where the street was boring and grey and there were flecks of garbage in it...garbage particles...

...and now there was a shadow on the ground...oh, *great*...

...barmit looked up and saw kelso...and she was so relieved...she was so...h...*ha*...she was so *happ*...

...she wagged her tail.

Barmit wagged her tail. Kelso couldn't believe it. It was like a big thunderstorm clearing in an instant. The tail wagged and everything made sense. There was the reason, man. The good reason to come back for her.

He'd needed to see her wag her tail.

He wagged *his* stub of a tail.

Barmit and Kelso wagged their tails at each other. Because sometimes you didn't know the reason to do a thing until you did the thing it was a reason for. Didn't you? No, sometimes you didn't. Until you did.

Kelso turned around. He couldn't see The Walker or any of his other friends. He craned his neck and *woofed* at Barmit. He ran.

She ran with him.

And they ran together.

Jairzinho crept through the intersection with his head down. He heard a notable paucity of paws hitting pavement.

He turned around.

Ladybug and Meatball panted back up at him. *Only* Ladybug and Meatball.

"Fuck's sake," he mumbled. Well, at least those two wouldn't be running off.

Frankly, Jairzinho wasn't sure they'd make it all the way to the Bridge.

Yet another thing they all had in common.

Esther's pill was working. But Jairzinho's head still throbbed. Like there was a little sculptor in there, trying to chisel his skull into a more pleasing shape. The migraine seemed immune to the medicine.

He could barely think straight. Which was his excuse for leaning back and shouting "ASTRID! KELSO! BARMIT! COME ON GUYS!"

His voice burst and bounced like fireworks.

As with every time Jairzinho had ever traveled to see fireworks, he regretted his decision instantly.

A mocking voice returned: "THOSE NAMES DON'T SOUND PROPER 'MERICAN TO ME!"

Impossible to tell what direction it had come from.

Shit.

- 9 -

LIFEHACK: when you're GOIN' up a CURB you can LET your fuckin' NADS scrape on the CURB when YOU'RE goin' UP and it HURTS in a WAY that feels DOPE.

Ducky STOPPED and looked AROUND since he HEARD bad MAN yelling. WOAH! WHERE did that JABRONI get TO? DUCKY had ALMOST FORGOTTEN about HIM. Since HE was RUNNIN' so MUCH. WHY was he RUNNIN'?

Bein' CHASED! ASTRID was ON his TAIL! When HE should BE on HERS, a-ROOOOOOOGAH! HUMMINA-HUMMINA a-ROOOOOO

GAH!

Astrid STEPPED to DUCKY. So HE spun AROUND and THUMPED his PAWS on the GROUND. She was ABOUT to CATCH these PAWS! Once DUCKY was DONE with bad MAN.

SHERIFF was HERE TOO. DUCKY didn't give a SHIT about SHERIFF.

HE knew JUST how HE was GONNA get BAD man GOT. Ducky HEARD some CHUMPS, and CHUMPS could be MIND controlled by a GENIUS like DUCKY!

So DUCKY hit the BRICKS back OVER to WHERE the BAD man's VOICE was SCREAMIN' from.

Meatball couldn't believe it. Freedom. This was freedom. The Liberator had broken his final chain. Meatball's friends ran every which way. Untethered. Unkept. *Free.*

And yet, all she wanted to do was keep running with The Liberator. She didn't know why. Maybe because she'd lost Sheriff? Or maybe because everyone else had started to run. And she didn't want to miss out. So she had joined them.

To be fair, it was mostly Ladybug she wanted to run with. The bond between scrunch-faced dogs remained as strong as ever. It was a powerful, edifying connection that had in fact only grown *stronger* since Meatball had learned what Ladybug had always known.

TCHTCHTCH! The Liberator clucked. He ducked down behind another car. He was suddenly all about ducking behind cars.

He made the noise again. *TCHTCH*

"SHUSH!" Jairzinho ordered Meatball and Ladybug.

Figures he would get stuck with the two flat-faced dogs. Couldn't they pant any quieter? It sounded like they were working a whipsaw into PVC piping.

They were trying, though. They were keeping up. They were with him.

He reached out. Stroked Meatball's chunk of a head. Scratched Ladybug behind the ears.

He lifted his gaze and scanned for the other dogs. Any of them. Nothing. No-

"SAY, WHADDA WE GOT HERE?"

Jairzinho's blood rushed to his feet. Then slingshotted back up into his head. Didn't improve the migraine situation.

He used his left hand to lever himself up and peer over the hood of the car. The hood sizzled the palm of his hand. "Ay!"

Jairzinho stumbled, but caught himself. He should have learned from Esther's example. Way back when. Maybe an hour ago.

Jairzinho watched from a wide squat.

Two blocks ahead, right in Jairzinho's path. Six gunmen stood in the intersection. Looking at the ground. Pointing. Laughing.

One of the pointers shouted "HE'S TRYNA FUCK YER LEG!"

Oh, Ducky.

Jairzinho dropped back to the ground. Looked to Meatball and Ladybug.

He couldn't sneak up on the soldiers with these two in tow. And what the fuck was he even thinking? *Sneak up* on six armed men? He was, functionally, a one-armed man right now!

The cross-street was tempting. He needed to cut south to get to Houston anyway. Now'd be a perfect time to do it. Sorry Ducky. Reap what ya sow.

No. He couldn't do that. Ducky was a little shit. Without a doubt. But he was a Giant. And Giants stuck together.

Jairzinho looked down at Meatball.

And only Meatball.

Ladybug was gone.

"FUCK'S SAKE!" Jairzinho hissed to himself.

Heedless of danger, he rose to standing.

Ladybug was trotting onto the next block. Towards the soldiers.

"LADYBUG!" Jairzinho whisper-shouted. "LADYBUG, HEEL! COME!"

Ladybug stopped. Folded around herself to look back at Jairzinho. *hhhhhBLECHTH!*

"LADYBUG! THE FUCK ARE YOU DOING?"

345

hhhhHHHHALCK!

"GET BACK HERE!"

hhRELTHK. Ladybug faced front. Continued her trot towards oblivion.

"LADYBUG! *LADYBUG!*" Jairzinho slapped his hand across his forehead. He needed to think fast. He needed to think *straight*.

He couldn't do either.

- 8 -

Astrid watched from her hiding spot beneath the car. Sheriff, apparently thinking this a game, cozied up next to her and bopped his paws on top of hers.

What was Ducky doing? Had he thought one of those six guys was Jairzinho? It didn't seem like it. He'd dashed right over to them just one block up there, begun to ply his trade on each of their legs in turn. It

hhhhhhPLECH!

Astrid looked the other way.

Ladybug was waddling down the block. Right for the soldiers. What was *she* doing?!

Astrid *woofed* quietly.

Ladybug turned in Astrid's general direction. Gurgled. Continued on her way.

Where was…ah. There. Jairzinho was galumphing along behind. Meatball at his heel.

Hoo boy. What a mess.

Sheriff rolled onto his back and worked Astrid's neckfolds like a speedbag.

Sigh. Speaking of *working* and *necks;* it appeared it would once again fall to Astrid to ensure her friends' safety. By way of tearing open throats.

She crawled out from beneath the car to intercept

the spot of ink depicting not the strokes of axes, heft in hands uncalloused, high o'er hooded heads. Begone, you executioner! Tis Ladybug who will, with magnanimity unparalleled, vouch-safe the life of her tormentor! Hope, ye conjure forth forgive-ness, kindness, diamonds of a heart from which the benthic pressure has abated; Rise! Now rise from dark of

hhbblllAAACCCCHHHH!

Jairzinho crept along behind Ladybug. They were within a few yards of the soldiers now. Just two or three cars between Jairzinho and them.

He couldn't quite believe they hadn't heard Ladybug's gurgling yet. But then he could: Ducky was *really* going for it. Making all sorts of squelching grunt noises. Yuck.

Jairzinho turned to see Astrid shimmying out from underneath a car. Her lips curled back over her teeth.

"PSST!" Jairzinho called, as softly as he could. "Astrid!"

She looked somewhat startled to see him. Sheriff dashed out from underneath the car. Headed straight for Jairzinho.

"No!" He pointed to his own throat. Shook his head. "No more! No more murder!"

If Jairzinho wasn't very much mistaken, Astrid *squinted* at him.

"Please. No more murder *please.*"

Non-plussed. That was how Astrid looked. She turned towards Ladybug. Jairzinho followed her gaze.

Ladybug toddered into the intersection.

Fuck.

Think fast.

Think straight.

Or else Astrid was going to kill those six assholes.

And maybe they deserved it. But Jairzinho had facilitated
Astrid's killing one person already. He could feel that traumatic
decision checking its watch in line behind all the rest of the
day's traumas. What a tremendous breakdown he was going to
have. If he got out of this.

He wondered if dogs felt guilty for killing people. Or for
anything.

One at a time.

Think fast.

Think straight.

"LOOKA THAT!" came a voice from the intersection.

- 7 -

The FUCK were these CHUMPOS LOOKIN' at when
THEY were SUPPOSED to be MIND controlled?

DUCKY humped HARDER and HARDER thinkin' KILL
em KILL em KILL em. But the LEGS were WALKIN'
AWAY!

WOAH! It was LADYBUG! SHE was CALLIN' for
DUCKY! She WANTED the D! DUCKY knew SHE'D come
AROUND. And SO he would TOO, HEYOOOOOOO!

348

But for SOME fuckin' REASON Ducky DIDN'T run STRAIGHT to LADYBUG. He galloped OVER to the LEGS and got BACK to HUMPIN'. Then his BRAIN couldn't stop THINKIN' about KILL EM KILL EM ALL KILL EVERY LAST ONE OF EM.

This was REALLY ANNOYIN' because DUCKY just WANTED to FUCK-*GUH* LADYBUG but his BODY was HUMPIN' these chumps' LEGS and his BRAIN was thinkin' YO kill em SMOKE these FUCKIN' JABRONIS.

THIS was all WRONG because IT was like INSTEAD of mind CONTROLLIN' the CHUMPS it was LIKE Ducky WAS so fuckin' SMART that he'd MIND-controlled HIM-SELF!!! And NOW he COULDN'T go FUCK-*GUH* LADY-BUG because HE couldn't STOP his MIND from MIND controllin' ITSELF because IT was so FUCKIN' SMART! So

"Chill," one of the gunmen said to Ducky. Just before he kicked him.

It wasn't a *hard* kick. But it was a kick. Not a nudge.

Astrid, now hunched down next to Jairzinho, put her paw on his knee. Glared at him.

He shook his head. "No. I'm thinking." He did a double-take at Astrid. Then peered around the car.

Ladybug held forth at the edge of the intersection. Stringing together gasps and wheezes. A soliloquy of suffocation. It was a serviceable stab at articulation. Probably.

It seemed like it meant something to Ladybug, at least. She stood as tall as she could, *hhhhLECH*ing and *hhhhBLACH*ing. Even as the gunmen ignored her, in favor of Ducky.

Astrid *woofed*.

"I'm thinking!" Jairzinho scratched at his forehead. Watched Ducky trying desperately to find a leg to hump. *Desperate* was right. He didn't look like he was enjoying it. "No more murders. N-"

One of the soldiers balled up a fist. Bent down. Punched Ducky hard on

the HEAD, who did THIS fuckin' GUY think he WAS, some FUCKIN' guy who GETS to thump DUCKY on the HEAD?

Nuh-UH, no FUCKIN' WAY!

DUCKY decided HE would HUMP the guy's LEG. *THAT* would show HIM who was BOSS! Ducky's BRAIN was BOSS. It was EVEN the BOSS of DUCKY. THAT was how MUCH of the BOSS Ducky's FUCKIN' brain WAS!

So DUCKY humped and NOW he BARKED too JUST to REALLY prove a POINT. And he WASN'T even THINKIN' about KILL EM KILL EM KILL EM or ANYTHIN' ANY-MORE he was JUST humpin' to PROVE a point. Because NOBODY thumps DUCKY except for DUCKY'S brain. DEFINITELY not some SACKLESS mutt with THUMBS. WHAT the FUCK were THUMBS even FOR?

Ducky BARKED and BARKED and he SAW the NEXT fist COMIN' so he JUMPED up and BIT the fist and the FUCKIN' guy SCREAMED so Ducky YODELED and THIS was even CRAZIER than BARKIN' it was AARRR-AARRR-AARRR-AARRR and this GUY didn't even KNOW how to HANDLE a SOUND this POWERFUL so he GAVE in and SHOWED Ducky a HOLE he could FUCK it was BLACK and it was the BEST hole in the WHOLE world and IT was so GOOD and IT was so IMPRESSED that DUCKY had WON

that the BEST hole in the WHOLE world FUCKED him FIR-
ST, RIGHT in the

Jairzinho didn't see the shot. Just the aftermath.

CRACK.

"NO!" He flinched and launched straight to his feet. Back
pain be damned.

Ducky's brains speckled the pavement. Blood poured from
the hollow bowl of his skull.

His legs were still flailing. His hips still humping and pumping.

Four of the soldiers fell about laughing. The tallest of them
just shook his head. "That's fucked up, dude. Don't shoot
dogs."

One of the soldiers spotted Jairzinho. Waved to him. Laughing. "Hey mister! You lookin' for a black Frenchie?"

Another one aimed his gun lazily at Jairzinho. "Hope you
brought some extra bags!"

"Why's he got bags?" A third asked.

"For pickin' up the shit."

"Ah, right."

Laughing. Laughing. They were *laughing.*

Ladybug shrieked at them.

One of those motherfuckers aimed his rifle at her.

Don't think fast. Don't think straight. Don't think.

"LADYBUG!" Jairzinho cried.

She turned to look at him.

Jairzinho pulled another fake ball out of his pocket. Threw it
down the cross street. To the south. "GOGITIT!"

Ladybug ran after it.

351

Sheriff took off as well.

Two more rifles rose. Followed Ladybug as she ran.

Jairzinho sprang to his feet. "HEY! HEY!" He waved his arms. "MY NAME'S JAIRZINHO NAVIAS! I'M BASICALLY THE LEAST AMERICAN PERSON YOU'VE EVER SEEN!" He limped into the intersection. Didn't realize he'd managed to hike his right arm up until it started hurting.

He fought for a glance over his shoulder. No dogs. He hoped Astrid and Meatball had followed Ladybug and Sheriff.

…at which point they would have no idea where to go.

Probably should have done at least a *little* thinking before launching into this.

"Astrid!" he hissed to the last place he'd seen her. "Nevermind! Murder! *Murder!"*

He hit the ground. That one felt like a rifle butt to the side of the head. Jairzinho was becoming something of a connoisseur of physical assaults.

The tallest soldier pulled a handgun out of a shoulder holster. Put it to Jairzinho's temple.

"WAIT!" Jairzinho screamed. "Wait-wait-wait!"

The tall soldier waited. "For what?"

"Uh…" Good question. Needed a good answer. So think. Fast. Straight. Keep it simple.

One step at a time.

Got it.

"Let me live," Jairzinho said as confidently as possible, "and I'll tell you where you can find a whole family of immigrants. Like, first generation. They don't even speak English very well. I'll take you to them."

The tall soldier turned to his five brothers in arms. "He says he can show us where there's more immigrants hidden."

"Yeah," another one of the other soldiers drawled, "we all heard him."

The tall soldier raised his non-gun-wielding hand. "I'm just repeating."

One of the soldiers with dip tucked into his lower lip spat. "Where they from?"

"Armenia," Jairzinho explained. "Armenia."

"Ain't that where Borat's from?"

"That's Ka...uh...sure. Yeah."

The other five men closed ranks around Jairzinho. "How many are we talkin' about?" one asked.

"Uh...there's a grandma, a dad, a mom, a son in his thirties and then two young kids. I was on my way back, I can take you to them. I can take you to them right now." He rose to his feet.

The tall soldier let him rise.

Jairzinho kept his hands up. His right side screamed. He ignored it.

Lip-Dip man sucked his tobacco. Sat back on a car hood and folded his arms. Smiled. "Tell you what, let's go say hi to em. You kill the granny yourself, we'll let ya live."

The other soldiers laughed.

Jairzinho gulped. "Okay."

Lip-Dip leaned back. "Damn, son. You're cold-BLOOD-ED!"

"I'm just looking out for number one," Jairzinho mumbled.

"You're not number one!" shouted a soldier who seemed younger than the others. "*AMERICA* is number one!"

"It's okay," another one of the soldiers cooed, "it's just a figure of speech."

"Well, I don't like it!"

Lip-Dip smiled at Jairzinho. "Alright. You answer me straight off, what's granny's name?"

Jairzinho didn't have to think. He was keeping it simple. "Hasmik."

"That a last name?"

"Hamasyan. Their last name is Hamasyan."

"The kid? What's the kid's name?"

"Which one?"

"All of 'em."

"Vatche is the oldest. The younger two are Eva and Bruce."

"Bruce?"

Jairzinho shrugged. "I've got no fucking clue, I didn't name him."

Lip-Dip made a De Niro grimace and nodded. He showed his friends his De Niro. They all De Niro'd back. "Okay, guy. How far we gotta go?"

Jairzinho nearly fainted. "They're close. Real close. Just about seven blocks out now." He led the way.

South. Towards Houston.

Towards the Bridge.

- 6 -

Astrid rehearsed the matter in her head. Six on one. She'd never have been able to manage them all. It was a good thing Jairzinho had checked her when her passions had run hottest. She'd have gotten herself as dead as Ducky.

She mourned for him. Ducky. After Jairzinho led his new walkers away, she sidled back in to investigate the body. Bastard though he was, the bastard had been one of them. So, Astrid should have been able to save him from himself.

There was no time to become overly maudlin, though. There was another Giant that needed saving.

Astrid looked back the way they had come. Still no sign of Kelso and Barmit. She hoped they would find their way.

Meatball lumbered out from behind a car. Followed Astrid's gaze. Then stared at Astrid herself and sat down. *Boofed* softly.

Astrid wagged.

Meatball *rumphed*.

Astrid licked her face.

The bulldog snapped playfully at the pitbull's affection.

Satisfied, Astrid turned the way Jairzinho had gone.

Ladybug, catching her breath on the pavement, pushed herself up to her feet. This did little to dissuade Sheriff from whatever game it was that involved jumping on Ladybug's head.

Hardly a surprise that Sheriff could keep up with Astrid — but the pitbull was pleasantly surprised by Ladybug's hustle.

A short snout was hardly ideal for sentry duty, but Meatball had given up ideals. Astrid would keep up with The Liberator far better, and in the event he rematerialized, Kelso would be able to follow her scent, and so lead Meatball back to Astrid and the others.

If Kelso *didn't* show up, of course, Meatball was in trouble. Because there was no hope of her ever finding Astrid's scent again, with such a scrunched-ass nose.

And yet…how was that a problem? Incredible, that she should think that way. Not finding the scent was trouble? That was freedom. She'd be *free!* Entirely *free!*

And, she discovered, it was hardly ideal.

Because there were good kinds of leashes. The ones with clips on both ends, and no handles. The ones that merely connected, rather than controlled.

To be entirely free, to be well and truly one's own master, was to divest oneself of these. To have none of those powerful bonds that connected friends, that tethered a dog to the pups and people she cared for. Friendship, love, these were responsibilities, and responsibilities were strictures of a sort.

But they offered their own kind of freedom, a greater freedom than could be found without them.

So Meatball sat, and she waited. Hoping Kelso and Barmit would come. Trusting that they would.

...the little speckly bits in the pavement were kind of interesting...if you looked at them in a certain way...they were really boring and hatable if you just thought they were speckly bits...that had been ground into the street by heavy honk-boxes...but they got kind of...not boring to think about if you tried to imagine what they'd used to be...maybe this one used to be the little plastic thing on the end of a shoelace...kelso started barking...and that one had been a chip of paint...or maybe this was just what the street looked like up close...bit-riddled gristle...somebody else barked back...maybe meatball...maybe none of these bits had ever been anything other than bits...

...oh...the show was over...a red curtain fell across the bits...

...once the bodywater slipped past barmit's front paws, she bent her head and drank.

the first lap was slightly sour.

the second stung.

the third made her wretch...

...she hated this bodywater.

hated it.

what the hell was wrong with it?

she lifted her head...the bodywater bubbled out of a ducky-shaped bowl...

...hm...if this was meant to be ducky-flavored, it didn't quite match that initial sip she'd gotten when she'd bitten him...she gave this street swill one last shot...caressing the leakage with her tongue...*yelch*...

...sickening...

...it was too...she swished the bodywater around her mouth...*desperate*...it activated all the wrong tastebuds, died too quickly on the middle palate...it lacked the metallic cast of finer vintages....

...she hacked out the bodywater...heaved once or twice after the evacuation was complete for good measure...

...oh, but what was this at the bottom of the barrel...?

Kelso couldn't believe the range of emotions he felt. Relief that he'd found Meatball. Confusion that he'd *only* found Meatball. Horror at Ducky's death.

And did he have a word for this last one, that feeling he felt as Barmit crawled into Ducky's open skull, curled up, and started munching on what was still inside?

No. No, he sure as shit did not.

Kelso stood snout-to-jowl with Meatball. The two of them watched Barmit take a bite of Ducky's brains. Chew it. Spit it out. Tear off another mouthful.

With each bite, Ducky's legs trembled and jolted.

Kelso and Meatball looked to each other. Back to Barmit.

Rrf, Kelso opined.

Barmit lifted her heavy-lidded gaze. Her jaw spun in little circles as she chewed.

Rrrrrr'FF! Kelso repeated.

Boof, Meatball added.

Barmit stared and chewed. The grey matter in her mouth sounded like Ladybug.

Slowly, Barmit lowered her head again. Took another bite.

Kelso wondered if he could keep being roommates with her. He'd have a hard time sleeping, knowing she was in the house.

But wasn't it interesting, that he should find himself thinking of ways he could make it work? Yeah, man. It was.

Kelso tilted forward to standing and totted over to Barmit. It took some cajoling, but he got her out of Ducky's coconut. See? She could be reasoned with.

Meatball waddled down a new street. Kelso hesitated. Then caught her meaning. Which was to say – Astrid's scent.

- 5 -

This game had a heck of a lot of rules! Which was really fun because most games Sheriff played didn't have *nearly* as many!

And the very best part was that the rules always changed! So the game was *always* interesting, because you always had to look at Astrid to see if you were playing it right! If you weren't, she'd *bop* ya!

This game was probably called Do What Astrid Does! Ladybug was just *brilliant* at it! Although after a curb or two it seemed like Ladybug was playing a different game called Have A Lie Down As Much As Possible! Sheriff had tried that one but Astrid had bopped him! So maybe there were different rules for everybody playing the game! *Wow!*

Astrid jumped up on a car! Sheriff tried to jump up too, but he only got his front paws on the ledge bit of the very end of the car! He tried really *really* hard to get up! He kicked his back paws and slapped his front ones on the ledge bit! He couldn't do it though! Heck! This was basically the hardest part of a game Sheriff had *ever* played in his whole *life!*

He fell off! Wheeeee! Back to the ground! He tried to jump back up again! Saw Astrid was just staring at something! Darting her head only just a *teeny* bit, like she saw an exciting bug and it was flying all *over* the shop!

Sheriff fell off again! Looked over at Ladybug! She was Having An Absolute Corker Of A Lie Down! Boy, Sheriff loved to see his friends do great at whatever they put their mind to!

Astrid looked in the other way than the way they'd just come from! Then she looked back the first way they'd *been* going! Then she flinched! And…seemed like she'd seen something she hadn't liked?

Uh oh!

Jairzinho picked himself up off the ground. It was that Lip-Dip son of a bitch who'd hit him.

"Dude," Tall soldier told Lip-Dip, "chill."

"He's fuckin' with us," Lip-Dip insisted. "He's usin' us like a goddamned escort right to the bridge." He grabbed a handful of Jairzinho's hair. Cranked his head back. *"Ain'tcha?!"*

Whatever magic Esther's pill had worked was wearing off. Jairzinho's vision was pure red. Having his neck at this angle caused his back to spasm.

He fell to his hands and knees again.

"Well lookathat!" Lip-Dip laughed, "he's gone and turned into his fuckin' dog!" He put the barrel of his gun to Jairzinho's head. "Bark!"

A few of the soldiers laughed. None of them rushed to Jairzinho's defense. They knew Lip-Dip was right. That Jairzinho was playing them. It was stupid of him, to assume they wouldn't see right through that.

"I've got an idea," one of the other soldiers said, "how bout he crawls!"

"I want him to *bark*," Lip-Dip cackled.

Jairzinho lifted his eyes. Met Lip-Dip's gaze. Held it.

"Bark," Lip-Dip ordered.

"Good dog," Jairzinho replied.

Lip-Dip just stared.

His friends stifled laughs. But Lip-Dip just stared.

Jairzinho stared back. He thought of the way Astrid held eye contact. Tried to channel that. Embody it. *Be* it.

Lip-Dip blinked.

"Let him crawl," one of them suggested warily.

"Yeah!" another agreed.

Lip-Dip forced himself to smile. Jairzinho dragged his face to the ground, but he knew Lip-Dip was smiling. The knot of tobacco squelched at his pleasure. "That sounds just fine to me." He kicked Jairzinho in the side. Hard. And again. "You *crawl* to the bridge, like a *dog*, I'll letcha cross."

Dark splotches consecrated the ground beneath Jairzinho. Oh, great. He was crying. Lip-Dip was gonna *love* that.

"Boy, you *cryin'?*"

More laughter.

Jairzinho couldn't believe he'd told Astrid not to murder these guys.

Another kick in the ribs. He had no choice.

Jairzinho crawled.

- 4 -

To frame it as positively as possible: they waited a whole block before they started throwing broken glass in his path.

"COME ON!" Jairzinho screamed. He couldn't help it. It was the way they laughed, as they scooped the shards from shattered windshields. The fucking laughing.

He'd hardly gotten the words out before Lip-Dip was pressing the barrel of his rifle down on the top of Jairzinho's right hand. "You crawl or you ain't never gonna jerk off again."

Jairzinho's entire body trembled. Not from indecision. The calculus was simple. Either he crawled across broken glass *now*, or he crawled across it in a minute, with ribbons for fingers.

Why oh why oh why the fuck *why* couldn't he have bumped into those three dipshit kids from Sixth again? Instead of this gaggle of psychopaths?

The joke of it was, except for Lip-Dip, Jairzinho imagined any of these guys *could* have been the kids on Sixth. There weren't many people who'd shoot a dog in the face or make a stranger crawl across broken glass. Or, rather, there weren't many *persons*.

You bunch persons up into *people*, and it was a whole different kettle of fish. Sadism was more often than not a team sport.

As if to prove Jairzinho's point:

"CRAWL!" Lip-Dip screamed.

"Bro," Tall soldier interceded. On whose behalf, Jairzinho couldn't tell.

Jairzinho led with his right hand. Not just to get it out from under the gun. His right arm was already fucked. He would just have to do his best to have that hand bear the brunt of this.

Slowly, he placed it onto the glass. Tried to spread his fingers as wide as he could. Based on some dimly remembered comments from high school physics. Pressure and surface area.

Even without applying weight, he was pretty sure he felt the skin break.

His entire face spasmed into a silent scream.

"I ain't gonna tell you again," Lip-Dip decreed.

Jairzinho wondered how many people were watching this happen. Peering out their windows. Shaking their heads at the rotten luck of that kid. There but for the grace of god crawl I, over broken glass.

Jairzinho leaned his weight onto his right hand.

The shards crunched. Then the entire palm of his hand seemed to cave in.

Glass carved its name into bone.

He screamed.

Kelso had been leading his friends at a healthy trot, but when he heard the scream, he booked it.

It wasn't until he'd gone a few yards that he remembered Barmit didn't run.

So wasn't he surprised, when he glanced behind him and found Barmit keeping pace? Yeah, man. Sure he was.

Astrid made no great show of the relief the other Giants' return brought her. She wagged at Kelso, Meatball, and Barmit, then returned her attention to Jairzinho.

He was trailing blood. A lot of it. It looked like his walkers had put something sharp down in his path.

But he was still crawling. That was good. She would need his help.

Astrid turned back to the other dogs.

Sheriff wagged. Ladybug flopped. Barmit dripped (oof, that smell, Astrid knew *precisely* where she'd been). Meatball melted. Kelso glowered.

Jairzinho crawled.

And Astrid? Astrid trusted. Counting Jairzinho, it was seven of them, six of the walkers. So what if they had the guns? Dogs had teeth.

There could be no plan. In as much as Astrid was able to formulate one, it would have been impossible to communicate. And even if she *could* have communicated it, she had no way of knowing whether or not her friends would understand what the plan was supposed to be.

So she simply licked each of them on the face, and ceremoniously sniffed their rear ends.

From each, she sensed an understanding.

- 3 -

There wasn't exactly a way to crawl through glass and "make it work". But Jairzinho had found a near neighbor to that. After he'd sliced his hands up the first few times, he'd discovered he could simply keep his hands in contact with the ground and drag them *through* the glass. They'd already leaked enough blood to satisfy his tormentors. And his knees crunching the shards made the ordeal sound genuine. He just kept hoping they'd get tired of it. That the glass-throwing would lose its novelty. Then he could just get back to the more bog standard humiliation of being made to crawl through the streets of Manhattan. Like, yes, a dog.

They didn't get tired of it. And now here they were, three blocks from the bridge. Jairzinho could see it through a rare gap in the cars. Just make out the throngs of people clamoring for passage in front of its makeshift barricades.

He wondered if any of them might turn around and see him. Might come to his rescue.

Of course not. Even if he hadn't been almost perfectly obscured by cars, he had six cackling soldiers around him. Nobody would dare. He was all alone. He w-

hhhhhBLAACH!

Jairzinho froze. Looked around. Listened to the echoes unraveling.

Lip-Dip kicked him. Not as hard as usual.

hhhhhLEEGCHT!

"You hear somethin'?" one of the soldiers asked.

"Hear what?" Tall soldier wondered.

"I dunno. Somethin'."

Lip-Dip scoffed. "Hell, there's plenty of somethin' 'round here." He raised his arms, as though gesturing to the sounds around them. The echoing cries of passageseekers. Helicopters booming over the Hudson. And still, errant gunshots from back within the city.

"No, it was more li-"

"WHAT THE FUCK IS THAT?!" Another of them screamed. He finished a full 180 back towards the West and raised his gun.

Jairzinho looked up. Watched them all start. About-face. Raise their weapons.

Doing his best to keep his hands on the ground, Jairzinho craned his neck to see what was spooking them.

He gasped.

Backlit by a sun eager to set, there loomed a pound of flesh upon the roof of a car. A misshapen mound of gore and sinew. Nothing more. And yet, it breathed. It lived.

It blinked.

It said *BARF!*

Oh. Good. His savior had arrived. Barmit was going to fix everything.

"I think it's that fuckin' dog you shot!" shouted the soldier who'd apparently just seen *Pet Sematary*.

"No it ain't!" Lip-Dip insisted. He sounded like he wanted to be convinced.

BARF! BARF! Barmit exclaimed.

Tall Soldier shook his head. "That ain't like any dog I ever seen before."

hhhhhBLUYCHT!

The soldiers did another 180. Facing towards the bridge.

Jairzinho looked.

Ladybug. Just standing. Watching.

"JESUS!" shouted the soldier with the deepest voice. "That one's been shot too!"

"Don't be fuckin' dumb," yelled *Pet Sematary*, "that's just its face! It ain't undead like that o-" he turned to point at Barmit.

Barmit was gone.

RRRRRRRRRR.

Growling from all sides. No dogs in sight. Just growling.

Jairzinho smiled. Tried to hide it.

Lip-Dip nudged Jairzinho's face with his shin. "The fuck is goin' on here, dogboy?"

Jairzinho quietly searched the ground with his hands. Searched for especially grippable chunks of glass. "itsoundsliketh-"

"Speak up, I can't here a fuckin' thing you're sayin'!"

"-edogsarehereto-"

Lip-Dip grabbed Jairzinho's hair again. Pulled him up.

Jairzinho clutched two thick glass shards as he rose to his knees.

"I can't…" he wheezed. "I don't…"

Lip-Dip shoved his face right down to Jairzinho's. Baring his teeth in a grimace.

Jairzinho bared his own teeth.

He swung his left hand up towards Lip-Dip's face.

Sliced a hole across his chin.

The knot of tobacco rolled out through the slice-hole. Plopped onto the ground.

Eyes a-boggle, throat clucking but forming no words, No-Lip-Dip just stared at the Barmit-looking blob of tobacco on the ground.

Jairzinho swung his left arm back around. Put everything he had into his right.

Drove both glass shards into Lip-Dip's neck from either side.

CRUNCH. They stuck like bolts on a flat-headed monster.

"HEY!" Tall Soldier screamed. He quit aiming at Ladybug. Aimed at Jairzinho's head instead.

Lip-Dip stumbled into Tall Soldier. Arms stretched out straight in front. Either grasping for help, or really committing to his new character.

Tall Soldier squeezed off a shot. It missed Jairzinho.

It didn't miss *Pet Sematary*, though. He grabbed his left knee and went down.

Barmit skittered out from beneath a car. Crawled onto *Pet Sematary's* face. He reached up to remove her.

Jairzinho grabbed another piece of glass. Lunged and stuck *Pet Sematary* in the gut. That took his mind off Barmit. Even as she chewed her way towards it.

Wiping tears from his eyes, Jairzinho watched as the very outside edge of his own thigh exploded. He stumbled and looked up.

Tall Soldier. Standing over Lip-Dip. Who was missing his entire head. Tall Soldier must have shot him. Friendly fire. Probably as near Lip-Dip had ever gotten to Friendly.

Focus. Tall Soldier reaimed at Jairzinho.

Kelso *leapt* from the roof of a car. Landed on Tall Soldier's gun. His weight tracked the barrel down down down. To the gunman's feet.

Tall Soldier had been committed to squeezing the trigger though. So he did.

His own right boot exploded. Shoe and foot alike, ground to confetti and launched. Like a surprise party for the left foot.

Tall Soldier went down. Kelso followed him.

Three gunmen down. Three to go.

And there they went. Running back into the city. Astrid and Meatball hot on their heels, thundering and chundering, respectively. Sheriff chased Astrid and Meatball. Didn't seem to fully grasp that they were playing a very different game than he was, though.

For a brief, glorious moment, Jairzinho pictured the gunmens' deaths. Wonderfully bloody, dog-based demises.

And then he was back on the cold tile of the NYU men's room, watching as the Giants snapped through taut, screaming flesh, clicked their cute little teeth against naked bone...

Letting the dogs rip more faces open would have been cathartic. Just like piling bodies into a burning fountain must have been cathartic. The only difference was the grievance.

Jairzinho cupped his hands to his mouth. "ASTRID! MEATBALL! LET THEM GO!"

Astrid stopped and spun around. Meatball wrestled a bit with inertia, but she did too. Sheriff jumped and splatted onto Meatball's face.

Jairzinho turned to Tall Soldier and *Pet Sematary*. The first was dead: Kelso had struck upon a rather important vein, it seemed.

Pet Sematary was alive. But fading fast, from being gutshanked.

By Jairzinho.

He wished he could be happy about that. But he couldn't. Nor could he be sad about it, or sick, or outraged. What was he? He was numb. He was nothing.

He was alive.

Jairzinho sat himself down next to *Pet Sematary*. Pulled Barmit off of his head. He wished he had something he could say to the guy. But he could only say what he was. Nothing. He would neither gloat nor commiserate. He simply sat and blinked tears out of his eyes, and would do until the guy stopped breathing. And if it stung *Pet Sematary* to be granted a strange dignity by someone from whom he'd gleefully stripped the same just moments ago...well, too bad.

Too bad.

And then *Pet Sematary* reached for Jairzinho. An open, upturned palm. Trembling. Seeking.

Jairzinho frowned at it. Blinked harder.

He pulled glass from his own palm. Reached out. Grasped that seeking, trembling hand.

Held it tight until gravity finally claimed it.

Jairzinho pulled himself to the sidewalk. Looked back at his trail of blood. Thin but unbroken. The opposite of him. Ha, ha. Ha.

He lay flat on his back. Closed his eyes. Stared into the dim, fleshy red of sun behind eyelids.

hhbbllllAAACCCCHHHH.

Jairzinho opened his eyes. Ladybug looked straight down at him. Her fat bunched up around her head. A chubby cowl punched into clear blue sky.

Something dripped on his forehead. Ah. Blood from Kelso's snout. As he panted down on Jairzinho. His breath smelled like death. But what else was new.

A tongue licked Jairzinho directly on his eyeball. He flinched. Smiled. Sheriff.

Barmit *harrumphed* her way into view.

Astrid and Meatball swung their heads over Jairzinho's.

Six Giants, staring down at him. So this was what it must look like to be them. Give or take. Ha, ha. Huh? Jairzinho didn't know. He didn't know anything.

No. He knew something.

He knew that the dogs weren't going to leave him behind.

So he had to get up.

Because they couldn't stay here.

And they were so, so close.

Good thing he was so numb. If he could have felt things, he wouldn't have been able to stand.

- 2 -

"Hi puppies!"

The crush of would-be emigrants started two blocks out. Few people looked like they'd had as rough a day as Jairzinho had. Not many looked like they'd had a particularly easy one.

Jairzinho paid them little mind. He just wanted to make sure everyone got to the bridge. Everyone being the Giants.

"Hi puppies!"

Even here, even now, people said it as he passed. He'd always hated it before. It was such a mindless refrain. He was sick of hearing it.

Now it was music. It was a symphony. It was the sweetest thing he'd ever heard. Because it gave him hope. That there was something kind and loving in people that this horrible day had failed to extinguish.

But, of course, the day wasn't over yet.

Jairzinho pushed his way forward, eyes to the ground. Making sure his Giants stayed with him.

They did. That was good. There was some jumping and ducking and weaving involved, but they made it. The big ones sheltered the little ones. Kelso kept Barmit covered, as Meatball did Ladybug, and Astrid did Sheriff.

Jairzinho did his best to keep them all from getting crushed. It got harder, the deeper in they went.

People shoved and shouted. They waved tickets in the air. There was some kind of lottery system the soldiers at the barricade had instituted. More casual cruelty. It was all so unnecessary.

He heard someone telling someone else about fifteen people who had been gunned down trying to rush the bridge.

He heard a different voice insisting that the blonde-haired and blue-eyed got across, no questions asked.

He heard a voice he vaguely recognized suggest they commandeer a tank and take the battle to "them." Jairzinho glanced over and saw the kid with the 'Sarcastic Comment Loading' T-shirt. The one from the Laundromat, six hundred years ago.

The kid saw Jairzinho. He smiled.

Jairzinho smiled back.

The kid's smile faltered. Came back a bit too strong.

Jairzinho frowned. Suddenly felt what the kid had seen. He reached a finger into his mouth.

He was missing two of his bottom teeth, on the left side. Huh. He wondered when that had happened.

At a certain point, the crowd became too thick to push through.

Astrid growled. Meatball and Kelso joined in. Sheriff looked at them, wagged his tail, and got on board. Even Ladybug and Barmit joined in.

The people in front of them jumped out of their way. Frightened by mysterious growling just behind them. Chimpish. But who could blame them?

They cleared a path. Jairzinho didn't know where they found the space.

He also didn't care. He just laughed.

And he growled.

The Giants jumped and glared at Jairzinho.

Wolfish.

"Just me," he laughed to them.

Only it wasn't just him. It was all seven of them, growling their way through the crush.

- 1 -

"WOMEN AND CHILDREN ONLY," cried a soldier with a megaphone. Given how many women and children Jairzinho saw in the crowd, that didn't seem to refer to letting people across. The guy was just shouting demographics. "WE'LL CONSIDER WOMEN AND CHILDREN. ABLE-BODIED MEN REMAIN." Click. He considered his words. Click. "THAT'S A SUBJECTIVE METRIC, BUT YOU KNOW WHAT? I STAND BY IT."

Over Megaphone's shoulder, Humvees served as the bricks of a mighty wall. Tetchy looking boys with great big assault rifles stood as mortar. And behind them stretched the Williamsburg Bridge.

Jairzinho growled to the front. He'd made it. He checked for the Giants. All there and accounted for.

"Excuse me," he croaked at a soldier with a clipboard.

Clipboard just shook his head. Sized Jairzinho up. "You fucking serious? No way."

"Please!" Jairzinho cried. "Look! I have dogs! I'm no-"

"Oh, you have *dogs?* Why didn't you say so?"

Jairzinho looked at the Bridge. Nearly two miles. Straight shot. No way he could just make a break for it. Even with all the cars abandoned in the road. Bang. He'd be dead.

But he was so. Fucking. Close.

"Please," he repeated in a softer tone. "I'm begging you. Man to man. *Person to person.* I just want to get these dogs off the island."

Clipboard seemed like he was listening. Then Megaphone tapped him on the shoulder. They spoke, then parlayed with a taller, older gentleman. He had no prop to serve as sobriquet.

Jairzinho watched an order trickle back down the chain of command to Clipboard. He checked his notes, then said something to Megaphone, who called something unintelligible into the crowd. He scanned it for a moment, then saw whoever he was looking for. Pointed. Waved them in.

Jairzinho watched a father with two children in his arms fight to the front. Toddlers. They were toddlers. They clung to their Daddy, but Daddy fought himself free of them. He pushed them towards Megaphone. Clipboard snagged them by their collars with a disarming tenderness. Directed them back beyond the barricades. Onto the Bridge. The toddlers bawled almost as hard as their father. He shouted something at them.

After a bit more shouting from all parties, the toddlers turned around. Began a long, lonely walk to safety.

Even now, Jairzinho found the intermittent kindnesses of the occupation far more disturbing than its cruelties. Perhaps because they were so often indistinguishable.

"Take the dogs," Jairzinho said to Clipboard. "Please, just let them cross. I'll stay. But let them cross."

Clipboard studied Jairzinho. Looked to the dogs. Shrugged. "Whatever."

Jairzinho gawped for a moment. "Thank you! Oh, thank you!"

Clipboard shrugged again.

Jairzinho blinked. "…so who's taking them?"

374

Sigh. Clipboard dropped his namesake to his hip. "What?"

"Who's taking them across?" Jairzinho asked.

"They can't walk on their own?"

"They…I don't think they will."

Clipboard gave the dogs another glance. "You got leashes for em?"

"…" was what Jairzinho said. He had grabbed leashes in the NYU bathroom. For Esther. Only she hadn't needed them.

Where were they? He must have dropped them. When? Who knew. So he committed to "…"

"You're wastin' my time," Clipboard growled. "Get the fuck outta here."

Jairzinho clenched his fists. Even though they were all cut up. Even though he felt his fingernails tickling tendons. He couldn't help it.

This could have been so simple. Esther could have shouldered her way up to the front. Probably wouldn't have even needed to growl. She'd have said "I got dogs," and boom. No, not that kind of boom. The *walking across* boom.

And what would Jairzinho have done, then? What had his plan been?

He seemed to recall saying something about doing whatever it would take to get across. Even climbing along the bottom of the Bridge.

And he would. He would do it because he needed to get these dogs off the island. Of course he still wanted off himself. But these dogs had fucking *earned* it. And they wouldn't leave him behind.

So he would do whatever it took, goddamnit.

He looked down at his fellow Giants. Knelt, so they were all on the same level. *Their* level. Which was how he needed to think. Not like a human, or a chimp, or an American or a Colombian or a man or a woman or a painter or an accountant or anything else that sprang from the simian. Not even like a dog. Because these six here had moved beyond that.

He needed to think like a Giant.

Jairzinho rose and peeled off his shirt. Clipboard said something, but Jairzinho wasn't listening. He ignored the people around him. Like he ignored his lack of embarrassment over the potato pouch of his naked stomach spilling over his belt. Like he ignored the pain of ripping scabs and blisters that had threaded themselves into the shirt. He balled up the bloody, sweaty rag that had once hung crisp on a rack at H&M. Raked it over the pool of moisture resting on his belly. Into the dank of his armpits.

He presented it to the Giants. As one, they stepped forward and sniffed it. Even Barmit.

Jairzinho pointed to the shirt. "Come," he said, making eye contact with each of them. "You follow me. Follow this." He sniffed at the shirt. Oh, *Jesus*. After he finished coughing, he repeated: "come."

Please, let that work.

Jairzinho slipped back into his shirt. Except *slip* was too graceful a word. *Slithered* might have hit nearer the mark. *Unmolted*.

He shivered. It was really remarkable that he'd thought nothing of the shirt's sorry state before. It was only with a bit of separation that he gained perspective. A bit of air-drying. And suddenly that same shirt was the most disgusting thing he'd ever felt.

Amazing how pain worked the same way. His right arm still felt weak. His back still killed him. But they had been killing him for so long that even death didn't mean what it used to.

Today in a nutshell.

He stood up and looked at the hastily assembled border. Back to his Giants.

Deep breath. To get the dogs on the bridge committed him to going under it. Nerves were okay. Nerves were good.

He reached into his pocket. Retrieved yet another invisible ball. "LOOK!" he cried to the dogs. They all perked up. Ears flopping. Heads cocking to the side.

Jairzinho threw his imaginary ball onto the bridge. "GO-GITIT!"

All of the dogs ran. Except Astrid and Ladybug. They lingered for a moment. Studied Jairzinho. Looking vaguely disappointed.

"Sorry," he told them.

Ladybug recovered first. She ran onto the bridge. Astrid followed slowly enough to keep an eye on her.

Jairzinho watched to make sure the dogs didn't try to turn around. Or that nobody *turned* them around.

"Right on," Clipboard admired.

"Fuck yourself," Jairzinho replied. He turned around. Had a much easier time getting *out* of the crowd.

He leapt over the guardrail on his right and followed the bridge's northern edge towards the river. Looking for his way out.

a HUNDReD FeeT UP

or

IN THE LaND OF THE GIaNTS

- 1 -

He found a way out almost immediately. But he kept looking for another, because *fuck that*.

Jairzinho swung onto Ridge Street. Slipped beneath the bridge. He looked up. Girders and gaps. Hard to gauge the width of those gaps from down here. He could imagine himself scrambling up...somehow. Bracing his ruined back against one beam, and his feet against the other. Shimmying all the way to Brooklyn like that. But there were a lot of other scenarios that were even easier to imagine. None of which involved getting to Brooklyn.

The bridge shook as *something* went boom up there. Uh oh. So he'd just barely missed *some* sort of excitement. Impossible to say whether that was good or not.

He wondered if the 'Sarcastic Comment Loading' kid had commandeered that tank after all. Wouldn't have been the wildest thing that happened today.

But the other Giants were still up th-

Dust streaked from the overhangs. Like Jairzinho was in an Egyptian tomb, and had just opened a box the ancient Pharoah would really have preferred to keep closed.

One pinch plopped directly into Jairzinho's eye.

"GAH," he shouted.

GAH GAH GAH, the bridge laughed.

Scratch the shimmy scheme, then.

Rubbing his eye, Jairzinho shambled back out from under the bridge. A few ex-petitioners from the gate breezed by, one knocking Jairzinho on his bad shoulder. Well, his *worse* shoulder.

"GAH," he shouted again.

The bridge had nothing to say about that. This was something to keep in mind: if he crossed from the *side*, at least he wouldn't have to get bullied by infrastructure.

"What happened?" he asked the people flooding past.

Nobody stopped to reply. The running seemed to rule out a successful overtaking of the border though.

He needed to hurry. The longer the dogs stayed on the bridge...

Jairzinho took a second look at the first route he'd spotted.

Fuck that was still the conclusion. This time with the post-script *fuck me*.

Finish the thought. The longer the dogs stayed on the bridge, the greater the chance of something bad happening. They were on his scent (he hoped). So he needed to get his scent across the bridge.

Maybe there was another way, but he didn't have time to find it.

"Fuck me," he mumbled.

ME ME ME

- 2 -

To be deceivéd thrice by but the single trick did send one's sense of self-possession soaring, as the sphere which flies but never falls. Begone, then, dignity and poise, let prose speak plain in pithy parenthetical what pain doth teach of play and purpose!

(The Ferryman throws a ball which does not exist. He cannot be blamed for this – for he is only human, and all humans possess such invisible orbs, if not the restraint to keep hold of them – but it is worth considering the intention with which the ball is thrown. Poor is the character of whomsoever tosses the gravity-defying orb in times of earnest play. But he who does so with grave purpose must be considered a separate animal. What must this animal want, then, but that the trusting dog doth make a lead of her trust, and let it lead?)

And thus, as Astrid strutted twixt the empty memories of human passage, snuf'ling air for purposes unknown, twas Ladybug divined the course their Ferryman had cast a star to chart!

Thus on and up she ran, and after her, her friends did follow!

- 3 -

He tried to over-complicate the climb with mechanics. But the first obstacle brooked no muddying: slick hands made for poor grip. And the fucked up arm, of course. Still, Jairzinho made it halfway up the pole before sliding back down. This was progress.

383

The objective was enragingly simple. There was a pole with a street crossing signal on it. One of those ones with the red hand and the white man. The ones that tell you when you can walk across the street. The sort of signal that didn't mean anything anymore. The pole stood right next to where the concrete base of the bridge gave way to the steel I-beam girders of the side. Not underneath the bridge. No luck down there.

The *side* of the bridge. Exposed to the elements. Nothing to grip, nothing to catch him if he fell. Just...

Sigh...

One at a time.

The objective would be accomplished by means of similarly enraging simplicity: climb the crossing signal pole, reach over to the miniscule nook where the concrete base of the bridge ramp met the girder, then pull himself across. One two three, bing bang boom.

He tried again. Reached his sweaty, bloody hands up the pole. Tried to pull the rest of himself up. Still no bing bang boom. Just plenty of Larry Curly Moe.

Whatever strange web of bonhomie had briefly snared the Curbside Giants could well be fraying. Jairzinho imagined the unit breaking down. All six of them going in different directions. Granted, they were on a bridge. Their options were pretty limited, directionally speaking. Still, this was a compelling enough fiction to get Jairzinho to the top of the pole in five slippery lunges.

Okay! Up the pole! He wouldn't be able to hold this for too long. He had his hands on the very top of the pole. Legs wrapped lower down. The red hand in the yellow box flashed right next to his head.

It suddenly seemed imperative to get off the pole before the little white man showed up again.

He'd managed to favor his left arm on the ascent. But reaching to the concrete ledge would require favoring the right. He'd need it to find purchase on that concrete shelf that had looked a *lot* deeper from nine feet down. Fucking Christ, there was hardly room for him to set four fingers up to the knuckle in there. *Anyway,* he'd have to make *that* work with the right hand, as he unknotted his legs from the pole and pistoned the rest of his body onto the bridge. That'd mean all of his weight would need to rest on his shredded right hand. Clinging to concrete. Connected to an equally savaged shoulder. It'd all be down to that damned right hand, with one knuckle of purchase, until he managed to scramble his feet up onto the ledge.

Which…Jairzinho studied the proposed ascent…would only work if he took his right hand off the ledge to make room for his feet.

He'd need to instantaneously swap his right hand for both feet. While curled into a ball.

And the ledge was just a few inches deep. And it was a dozen feet above the unflinching concrete sidewalk.

AND, his whole body was already at DEFCON 1.

If he fell, he'd break his neck. He saw it happen. Clear as day.

But his friends had been brave. The Giants. Esther. Vatche. They'd all risked their lives for him.

Some of the Giants had lain theirs down.

"Don't fuck this up," Jairzinho told himself. He frowned at the bridge. Waited for it to crack wise. Wisely enough, it kept schtum.

Jairzinho tightened his legs around the pole. Hugged it to the bottom of his torso as tightly as his left arm would allow. Reached for the bridge with his right.

His fingers met solid concrete, inches short of the shelf. Inches. *Two of them.*

He took a deep breath and tried again. Maybe a fraction of an inch closer. The nail of his ring finger caught on a divot in the concrete. Tore. Jairzinho hardly noticed.

If his reaching hand had been even half a foot off the mark, he might have given this up. Tried a different approach.

But two inches? *Two inches* separating bing from bang? That was a rotten joke. Jairzinho'd be damned if the bridge got the last laugh.

Fuck the mechanics. His hands knew what to do. Jairzinho gave them the reins. Height. Trajectory. Microadjustments.

Jairzinho put his feet on the pole. Launched himself as hard as he could at the bridge.

- 4 -

Astrid knew what Jairzinho wanted: for the Giants to follow his scent. It had been a good idea that the elements saw fit to undermine. The wind picked up, and swept the trail away.

The good news for the Giants was that they really only had two ways to go: forward and back. And thus far the trail had only moved in the former direction (save a quick double-back near the beginning). Then Ladybug had gotten into the spirit of things, leading them onwards over the bridge.

No way could Ladybug smell Jairzinho, not if even *Astrid* had lost the scent. But Jairzinho probably couldn't mark his own stink either. Humans were even worse sniffers than scrunch-faced pugs. So if Jairzinho couldn't mark the scent himself, yet knew the dogs *could*…it could only be because he understood that the Giants, well, uh, *could*.

So Jairzinho was trying to think like a dog. Smart human.

And maybe Ladybug was thinking like a human, because humans had a tendency to keep chugging straight ahead no matter what. Smart dog.

But Astrid needed to think like Astrid. She needed to protect her friends. She knew there was a chance she might never see Jairzinho again. Whatever he was doing was dangerous. She didn't understand what it was, but fear had been the unmistakable *soupçon* in his stink.

Yes, he had sent them across the bridge…but his track record for keeping them safe was spotty at best.

Whereas, while the city behind them was in bad shape, they had a safe haven there. Astrid could get them back to the crate place that Boo was still at, if she needed to.

The question was, how would she know if that need arose? If Jairzinho was well and truly gone? Losing Jairzinho's scent didn't necessarily mean losing Jairzinho. But losing Jairzinho meant that turning back was probably the best course of action. And his scent was nowhere to be found. So…when was *he* lost?

Astrid trotted after Ladybug with the rest of her friends. For now. But at some point…she would need to make a decision. There could well be a point of no return, after all.

And given the unexpected reserves of speed Ladybug was tapping, both of those points were likely to come sooner rather than later.

- 5 -

"GHHH!" said the oxygen leaving Jairzinho's lungs all at once. He couldn't breathe. Gulping air wasn't getting him anywhere. It was like trying to breathe concrete. If only, huh?

Tiny sips. He took tiny sips. And with it, stock of his situation.

So much for two inches short. He'd come in fast and low. Cracked into the concrete shelf with his breastbone. Fortunately, there was no pinballing off. Bad news for his legs, which scraped down the concrete. Bye-bye, knee flesh. You died that Jairzinho might live.

Because he did. He made it. Got both hands on the concrete shelf.

Bing bang and boom, all at once.

There was a new fourth step, though. Call it boink. Why the fuck not.

Jairzinho gave himself time to take a deep, full breath. Just one. All he could afford. He was dangling from eight *very* tired fingers, after all.

Then he kicked his legs against the concrete and scrambled. Scrambled enough to put Sheriff to shame. He bent back his toes. Pedaled himself up far enough to swing his left elbow onto the shelf.

He stopped pulling and started pushing. Elbow down into shelf. Right knee onto shelf. Left knee. Right foot.

Both feet. Boink!

Okay, so that was kind of a technicality. Only his right foot was *on* the shelf. His left rested directly atop the right. Not enough room for both. But he was up.

He was on the side of the Williamsburg Bridge.

He splayed his arms out to either side to balance himself. Chest flush against the off-green steel. Like he was trying to give the troubled-water-crosser a hug. The bridge flushed with appreciation. And then boiled.

Jairzinho groaned. The steel had been soaking up the sun all day. It was *scorching*. Hadn't thought about that. Really should have.

But here he was. Clinging to the side of the Williamsburg Bridge. And there, just above his feet, was his way across.

The I-Beam girder. Jairzinho pegged it at about five feet tall. Maybe a little taller. Not quite as tall as him though. That was going to be a problem.

Anyway. The I-shaped beams had been set in a serif font, with little skirts protruding along the bottom. He didn't think these nubs served any practical purpose. Just an artifact of mass-production.

And Jairzinho's escape route. A little nub just a few inches deep. For almost two miles.

His mouth groaned a scratchy little groan. The rest of him paid it no mind.

He lifted his left foot and planted it on the base of the I. Toes pointing towards Brooklyn. Almost two miles until he was (one thing at a time). The serif was maybe, *maybe* three inches deep. There wasn't even room for a full half of his foot to (one thing at a time).

Fuck. This.

So said his every natural impulse. The very same ones that had ensured him an unbroken line of ancestry from the dawn of life on Earth until this very moment.

Jairzinho, heir to a dynasty of survivors, lifted his right foot off of the concrete shelf. Onto the steel of the I. Placed it heel-to-heel with his left.

As his body rose, his head tapped the concrete overhang.

The I itself was five feet and change. But atop was another four or five feet of concrete, jutting out further than the girder.

Since Jairzinho was taller than five feet and change, this meant the concrete was filling the exact space that his head would have liked to.

Ducking his noggin down wasn't an option. He wouldn't have been able to drop it low enough. Maybe if his neck weren't so shredded. Alas.

His only other option was to lean *backwards* slightly. As in, *dangle his head over the drop.* Slightly. But really, there weren't degrees with this sort of thing. Either you were flat against a steel beam, or you weren't. Jairzinho wasn't.

But time was ticking. Where were the dogs now? Still on the bridge? Who fucking knew? He could second guess himself when he'd made it across.

Something up top exploded. The whole bridge jived. All Jairzinho could do was say *hnngggg.* He couldn't even hold on. There was nothing to hold on *to.*

With his head tilted backwards, an ill-advised glance downward would be almost perfectly unobstructed.

He tested this hypothe*fuck bad idea.*

Where he was now couldn't have been much higher than fifteen feet off the ground. Already his head was spinning. Granted, that could have been the heat radiating off of the

390

steel. But the height, too. The heat and the height. That was okay though. If he could only shimmy himself all the way out over the water, he would plummet to his death into the refreshing frigidity of New York river water.

That was the *good* news.

Jairzinho scooted his left foot out, towards the river. He scooted his right foot along, bringing the heels back together.

Thus began the escape.

Scoot scoot. Scoot scoot. Scoot scoot. Scoot scoot. Scoot scoot.

Scoot scoot. Scoot scoot.

Scoot scoot.

- 6 -

*...ladybug was in front...*which was definitely weird...but barmit was also running...and that was weird too...so actually the whole world was weird...but it was alright because they were together...

...everybody was slowing down...ladybug was getting tired probably...she wasn't very good at running...so barmit did something she didn't usually do...she looked around...

...she noticed astrid had stopped...she was standing way in the back where they'd come from...just sort of looking at the rest of them...like she wanted to go back to where stuff was still loud and hot...

...barmit stopped and looked at astrid...and astrid looked at barmit...seemed like she had expected everybody was just gonna stop with her...

...barmit turned back the other way...where they were going...kelso had stopped and was looking at barmit...but ladybug and meatball and sheriff were still going...and they were going to get separated...because of astrid...when usually she was the one keeping them together...that was the weirdest thing of all...

...so barmit said *barf* at astrid...

...and astrid said *arooooof*...

...and barmit said *barf barf*...

...astrid just tilted her head...

...there was nothing left to *barf*...so barmit turned around and walked to astrid...walked around behind her...and bit her on the leg...

...astrid hated that...she said *BARAR!!* and leapt away from barmit...which was the way they were supposed to be going anyway...so barmit chomped her teeth and followed astrid... but she didn't have to bite her a second time...

- 7 -

Scoot scoot. Scoot scoot. Scoot scoot.

Jairzinho blinked sweat out of his eyes. Dehydration. Imagine if *that* was what did him in.

He didn't dare peel a hand from the beam to wipe his forehead. He did, however, dare to check his progress. He'd certainly been at this long enough.

A quick glance down, over his right shoulder.

The pole he'd climbed to get up here was about five feet away now.

Only two-odd miles minus five feet to go.

Jairzinho set his jaw.

Scoot scoot. Scoot scoot. Scoot scoot.

After scores more scoots, Jairzinho succumbed to that invulnerable feeling of having done something risky and gotten away with it.

Thus: scoot scoot, scoot scoot became scootscootscootscootscootscoot. And before long Delancey Street fell away from him like he'd hurt its feelings. The cars slotted into parking spaces and scattered along the road served as merciless references of scale. Ten, twenty, thirty feet over concrete, Jairzinho braved the wind and the sun and the lemniscate of pain.

Sweet relief! He reached a little grate-metal walkway that encircled a concrete pillar. For maintenance or something. He didn't know. He didn't care.

He flopped over the guardrail. Clanged onto the grate platform with about as much square footage as an elevator. Fought the urge to lay on his back and go to sleep. He could dream of this elevator taking him all the way to the top. No. The bottom. He wanted to go *down*.

God almighty, but scootscootscooting was hard work. His legs had gone rubbery. His, ha, his *abs* were quite upset about all the leaning. The space between his eyes was a breakdance competition.

And after all that: the river was still yards and yards away.

Yet a smile pinched Jairzinho's cheeks.

Because smack in the center of this catwalk was a ladder leading to the top of the bridge. Next best thing to an elevator.

He pushed himself to his feet and gripped the rung nearest chest-level. It was cool to the touch. Which was magical. It was

just as sun-baked as the rest of the bridge. Yet the rung was cool. Like the knob to NYU's law school. More echoes. Even on the side of the bridge. Cool. Neat. Nice. Ha. Ha.

Chuckling, Jairzinho hefted himself upwards. One impossibly pleasant rung at a time.

He lifted his head over the edge of the bridge. Peered down the cattle chute of the walkway.

Came face-to-boot with a gunman.

A gasp caught in his throat.

He slipped back down as quietly as he could.

So they had sentries posted *on* the bridge, too. Or maybe this guy was just trying to steer clear of the rough stuff happening at the barricade. Like the kids on Sixth had the carnage of Washington Square Park.

It didn't matter though. It all came out to the same thing for Jairzinho:

Scootscootscootscootscootscoot.

- 8 -

Ladybug had been in front for a bit but then she got tired so Sheriff went in front! He ran *really* fast and he was getting chased by his friends which was *terrifimendous!* But since some of his friends were really really good at playing Chase Sheriff, he'd have to run way *extra* fast to make sure the game lasted longer!

Only no *way* could he run faster than Astrid! She was just about the fastest dog who ever *lived!*

So Sheriff would change the game to being instead of just Chase Sheriff, it was Chase Sheriff And But Only After First You Have To Find Him Because He's Hiding!

So he ran around a car so nobody could see him! Then he crawled *under* the car! And Astrid *definitely* couldn't see him because she was *way* in the back!

Sheriff watched Meatball come around the car and have a really good look-about for Sheriff! But she couldn't find him! He'd done a really good job at hiding! His tail wagged and said *krr krr krr* when it hit the bottom of the car! That might give him away but that was okay because getting found was basically the whole fun, except for the hiding part!

Now Ladybug was having a look-about too! And then Kelso and Barmit and Astrid! They were all having a lookie-lookie-look-about but *nobody* could find Sheriff!

Krr krr krr krr.

Kelso's ears flopped to the top of his head. He cocked his noggin to the side. Placing the sound. Recognizing the rhythm. He knew it.

Sheriff wagging. Where?

Kelso ducked his head.

Under the car.

Arumf, he announced.

The rest of his friends ducked their heads to look under the car.

Sheriff *launched* out. Took off running.

Ladybug and Meatball followed.

Kelso watched them run. Turned to look the other way. They were just about at the center of the bridge, weren't they? One direction looked kind of like the other, didn't it? And they'd all gotten a bit turned around looking for Sheriff, hadn't they?

They were. It did. They had.

So Kelso didn't know for a fact that Sheriff was currently leading them back the way they'd just come from. But he suspected.

He looked at Astrid. Tilted his head.

She returned his gaze.

Barmit bit Astrid's leg. That got her moving. Got them *all* moving, after Sheriff.

Back the way they'd just come from.

- 9 -

Thirty, forty, fifty feet up. Or more? Jairzinho was scooting himself past reference. At a certain point the cars lost their essential car-ness. They were nothing but patches of color. That was probably for the best.

Jairzinho scooted past a second, third, fourth, fifth, sixth ladder-and-grate combo platter. For every odd numbered sighting, he gave himself permission to climb the ladder. Every time his hopes were dashed. At least one soldier. Usually more.

During one ascent, a stooped old woman caught a glimpse of Jairzinho, from the far side of a man (who looked old enough to know better) with a firearm half his size. Jairzinho made a sad face at her. She made an even sadder face at him. Back down he went. Scootscootscoot.

He didn't even get a chance to check how the Giants were doing. They were on the Manhattan-bound lanes. The car lanes. Duh. These ladders led to the pedestrian walkways.

The people lanes. Ha, ha.

Then came the first great girder hurdle. Discovered at ladder number umpteen. It was…quite a hurdle.

More of a concrete wall. Not a metaphorical one, either.

The girder Jairzinho had been scooting along terminated at the side of a big fucking concrete keep. Like the boxy bit of a castle where you park the drawbridge. There was no way to slink around from the side. This was obvious, but another regrettable glance to the ground provided evidence. Three human-shaped pimples on the concrete, far below.

So he had not been the first person to have this bright idea.

He wondered how many people had done this and *succeeded.* Would have been interesting to know. Either interesting or crushing. Depending.

Neither here nor there. If nobody had gone all the way yet, he would be the first. And that meant going up this ladder here. To the bridge. With the soldiers on it.

It was the only option.

He paused with his hands on the rungs. Wiped his forehead on his sleeve.

If he got *this* far, and then got fucking *shot*…he'd be *so pissed.*

He lugged his aching body up the ladder. Stole a peek topside.

Nobody *right* in front of the ladder. Okay. That was good.

Nobody to his right, back towards Manhattan.

Nor to his left, towards Williamsburg. The way that he needed to be going.

Ok! He flung himself the rest of the way up the ladder. Reached for the gate of the red human crate that was the bridge's pedestrian fencing.

And only *then* realized the obvious.

Of *course* the gate would be chained and padlocked. Why had he expected otherwise? Not even in terms of infrastructure security. Just based on how his luck had been breaking thus far.

Fuck it. He was already a hundred-some feet up. What was another, what, ten or twelve?

Jairzinho threaded his fingers through the square links of the fence. Dug the toes of his shoes in as far in as he could. Got to climbing.

The shift in perspective and approach brought the terror of this whole adventure back from wherever he'd forcefully retired it. He was *really fucking high*. Not in the fun way. Knowing no other means to smother the terror, Jairzinho decided to hum a song to himself. For reasons he would never, ever understand, the first song his brain nominated for the situation was "Step In Time". From *Mary Poppins*. So maybe he *was* high.

Alright. Schtep in toime, Schtep in toime, come on mateys, schtep in toime! He hummed and bobbed his head. It kept him smiling. Which kept him from screaming.

He was sort of hoping he'd climb over the top of the fencing at the "up on the railing" part, or maybe the "over the rooftops" part. It ended up being at "link your elbows". Which wasn't as good. But he didn't fucking care.

He tumbled over the side. *Cracked* onto the sweet, sweet pavement of the walkway.

So much wonderful pain shook his bones. The pain of steadfast footing. Of solid Earth. Uh. Well, it was a *bridge*. But it was the part people were supposed to be on.

It was…beyond words.

And fleeting.

He pushed himself to his feet. Looked out beyond the Keep. Over the water. He still had a hell of a long way to scoot.

Assuming he decided to climb back over the fence on the far side of the Keep.

Which...

If he didn't *have* to...

There were no soldiers in sight.

He looked to the first ladder beyond the concrete Keep. The one that lead him back to the side of the bridge

He looked straight down the steady, reliable walkway. The empty one that led to Brooklyn. Nice and easy.

Ladder. Walkway. Ladder. Walkway.

Not much of a question.

He stuffed his hands in his pockets. Ducked his head. Limped towards Brooklyn.

- 10 -

Astrid and Kelso both seemed to catch The Liberator's scent at the same time. The only problem was, it sent them in two different directions.

The six of them couldn't make sense of which way was which. Meatball was fairly certain they should have been going *this way*. But, really, that was only because she thought *this* was the way they had *been* going. Were they supposed to keep going the way they'd been going?

[Be pretty frickin' screwy if that guy sent us up on this goddamned ramp figurin' we'd just turn right around and frick right back down.]

Well put. But The Liberator was nothing if not "screwy."

[Ya got a point.]

Meatball decided to go with her gut. She hoped her friends would follow.

Just as she rose and started walking *this way*, Astrid set off *that way*. They both stopped. Turned to stare at each other.

[We shouldn'ta looked for Sheriff.]

Of course we should have.. We couldn't have left him behind.

[But now we got a frickin' impasse.]

We've had worse.

[Look at us, makin' all these frickin' points!]

Meatball and Astrid both returned to the other four. They *boofed* and *woofed* and *barfed* at each other.

Ladybug laid down. She was either counseling patience...or she was tired from all the running.

[Why not both? *We're* frickin' both of somethin'.]

Yet another well-observed point. Most times it was both. But sometimes...it could only be one or the other. It could only be *this way*...or *that way*.

Of course...they didn't all have to go the same way.

- 11 -

The road part of the bridge being below him meant there was zero chance of connecting with the other Giants until the very end. Unless there happened to be a stairwell leading down from the walkway. Jairzinho wasn't holding his breath.

Not for *that*, anyway. But he did have to remind himself to breathe.

Because he saw two gunmen up ahead of him.

They were too far away to recognize Jairzinho as a *persona non grata*. He hoped. But they were close enough that he couldn't just climb back over the side of the bridge to resume scootscootscooting without catching their attention. And it was certainly too late to turn around. That would be too obvious.

What the hell were they doing up here? They should have been down on the road!

Ah, of course: they were up here to shuffle the people down on the road along. From above. Like cattle.

Jairzinho took a glance over the side. The East River had reclaimed the western bank. Winking its deep baby blue.

Jairzinho was *so. God. Damned. Close.* Failure was emphatically not an option.

He just had to remain inconspicuous. Hope for the best.

He wished he had a trench coat collar to flip up. Instead he did what he could: he plopped his chin to his chest. Staring at the ground. The Full Barmit.

He walked as casually as he could. Covered in blood. Closer and closer to the two men. Pulling his shoulders back. *Head-down confidence.* His stench could have been deliberated at the Hauge. He stepped closer. To the men. And their assault rifles.

- 12 -

Jairzinho was gone. There was no point pretending otherwise. Either he was back where they'd come from, or he was gone. Like Misha, like Ducky.

Astrid had made the decision. She was going to take them all back where they'd come from.

She just…didn't quite know which way that was.

Tilting her head back, she sniffed at the air. Nothing. The wind whipping across the river was snatching up every scent before it could touch Astrid's nostrils.

She looked at her friends. Smelled dissolution. That was one stink the wind couldn't quite whisk away.

They wanted to split up. Some wanted to follow Jairzinho's path. Others craved the safety of certainty, of the crate-place.

Astrid saw sense only in the latter path. And yet…dissolution of the Giants was inconceivable.

Even though she didn't know which way her heart was leading her. Literally. The bridge had only two directions…and Astrid was clueless as to which was which. Oh, damn this scent-snatching wind!

She knew Ladybug would go with her. Meatball and Kelso wanted to go the other way. Sheriff and Barmit would probably go with them.

But which way was which?

The Giants couldn't stand here forever. Choices had to be made.

And she had to respect them. For she was but one Giant among many. And Astrid wasn't about to bite someone into going somewhere they didn't want to. *Barmit.*

Astrid gave the wind a final sniff. Symbolic, really.

Nothing.

So she stepped forward and nuzzled Meatball, and Kelso, and Sheriff, and Barmit. The Giants who would go their own way. One at a time. A farewell.

- 13 -

The two guys were leaning on opposite guardrails. Jairzinho would have to pass directly between them.

Trudging within earshot, Jairzinho picked up their conversation. Cocking his head like Kelso, he listened for clues as to what was happening back on Manhattan.

Oh, how nice it felt, to say *back* on Manhattan.

"...thought it was pretty dumb," an older-sounding guy was saying.

"Mhm," a younger-voiced guy replied.

"And you didn't?"

Young guy shook his head. "You know I didn't." He sounded exasperated. Like they'd had this conversation before.

Jairzinho was within twenty feet of them. He didn't like that they were so keyed up. Might make them jumpy.

"How?!" Old guy exclaimed. "You're a smart kid. They're doing a body swap subplot and you're not even like, 'since when was this an option?'"

"It's in his power set!"

"Since when?"

"They set it up in the scene wh-"

"I'm talking about the original comics!"

"Oh, here we go."

"Have you even *read* the original comics?"

"Heeereeee we go."

"Don't say 'here we go' like I'm just, like...I'm saying if you don't know the *source* material, th-"

Young guy threw his hands out to the sides. "It's an *adaptation*. You have to take it on its own merits."

An…oddly disappointed Jairzinho closed to within five feet of the fearsome gunmen. Only *one* of whom had read the original comics.

"So it's alright to just shit all over the original comics, huh?" Old guy demanded. "Why don't we just burn *all* original comics *everywhere*, and then *shit* on them, is that it?"

"Nobody reads the fucking comics anymore, dude!"

"A-*ha!*"

It disturbed Jairzinho, that even now he felt himself helpless but to take sides in the argument. It was the sort of inane 'debate' he'd have had with his own friends in college. Probably the same sort of debates the kids at NYU had been having. Before the murder club these two were both a part of piled those kids into the park fountain and burned them. That w-

Old guy stomped his foot and turned towards Jairzinho. Just when Jairzinho was threading himself directly between the two men. And their guns. "YOU!"

Jairzinho froze. "Er?"

"What do y-"

"No," Young guy snapped. He gave Jairzinho three soft *get outta here* pats on the back.

Jairzinho winced. Stumbled forward. Had to remind himself how to walk.

"You always do this," Young Guy continued as Jairzinho plodded onwards, teeth chattering in the sweltering late afternoon sun. "You always try to take a…straw poll, like if you can just get all your buddies to side with you then you're automatically right."

"You just don't wanna hear how everybody knows you're wrong!"

"Strength in numbers, is that the best you got? In terms of a defense f-"

"A *body swap subplot!*" Jairzinho could *hear* Old Guy waving his arms. "Since *when?* Since *when* did they establish he had that power?"

"In episode two!"

"I'm talking about in the original c-"

"WE'RE TALKING ABOUT THE SHOW!"

"BASED ON THE ORIG…" And then Jairzinho passed beyond the furthest reaches of their argument. He fought mightily to keep his pace steady. To unwind his fists from the handfuls of pocket lining they'd snatched up. He felt the skin of his left palm peeling back. He'd been squeezing the keys to his apartment without realizing it.

He kept his hand in his pocket, so he wouldn't have to see how bad it was. The peeling. It was nice to imagine it balanced out the glass-shredded right, though.

Jairzinho thumped across the bridge, his apprehension growing as his gait deteriorated. How would he face a more robust obstacle than two heavily armed nerds mid-bicker? Did he have enough left in him to flip back over the fence? To scootscootscoot the rest of the way? If that was what it came to?

These questions remained unanswered for going unposed. Jairzinho saw not one other person, living or dead, all the rest of the way across the bridge.

A mile and a half of easy, unmolested perambulation.

It made him angry. Depressed. Confused. It made him *feel* again.

The numbness was gone. He felt. He felt everything. And here was the final cruelty of the day: there was no grand catharsis to draw a firm line under the whole nightmare. Just a long walk to Brooklyn. Plenty of time to think about what he'd been through. What he'd done. Plenty of time to wonder what the rest of his life looked like. The *one at a time* mantra revealed its deep, agonizing hollowness.

The day closed in on Jairzinho like fingers, wrapping gently around his neck.

Even as he stepped off of the Williamsburg Bridge and into its namesake neighborhood. Even as Emergency Personnel pounced, wrapping him in blankets and questions. Even as the entire borough seemed to collapse on him with no concern save his well-being. Still, Jairzinho felt those fingers snake around his neck. Squeezing. Ever so softly.

This wasn't the end. He wasn't free. He wasn't safe. There *was* no end. This was all just the beginning of a life in which this had happened. Would always have happened.

Peace was not a matter of traveling twelve blocks. Or getting his dogs in the right crates. Or…

"Hey," Jairzinho said to one of the nurses currently trying to hook him up to a juice bag. Or vice versa.

The nurse gently stayed Jairzinho's hand from wandering skywards. "Don't worry, sir, w-"

"Tell me 'one at a time'."

The nurse paused. Shook his head. "You're in shock, sir, but you're s-"

"One at a time," Jairzinho told himself. He reached down and ripped the juice bag stickey-straw from his arm.

"SIR!"

Jairzinho swung out of the cot he hadn't remembered sitting on. Cot? They called them something else when it was doctor stuff. Gurney!

And the juice bag was just letters. ET? IV. An IV.

Oh! And the nurse wasn't a nurse. Nurses were inside. Outside was...more letters. EMT. He was an EMT.

Cots were gurneys, juice bags were IVs, nurses were EMTs. Nothing was what it seemed.

"Sir, can you hear me?" The EMT asked as Jairzinho stomped back towards the bridge. "I need you to come this way. You've lost a lot of blood."

Jairzinho shook the hand off his shoulder. "Blood isn't blood," he insisted. He didn't know what it was. But he sure knew what it *wasn't!* Blood!

He could hardly remember how he'd gotten here. He'd scooted here? Scootscootscoot?

Scooting wasn't scooting. It was living. It was how you lived. Scoot scoot. Scoot scoot. One scoot at a scoot!

"I need my dogs," he mumbled.

The EMT gripped him more firmly. "Your dogs need *you* to get better, so you can go get them." He tried tugging Jairzinho towards one of the many waiting firetr...amulances.

Jairzinho shoved the EMT away. He was the tugger in this world. Not the tuggee. Unless those fingers on his neck were a collar.

The EMT sharpened his tone. "If they're on the island, th-"

"They're not on the island." Jairzinho took off his shirt, his left hand splashing blood from his pocket. "They're on the bridge."

He waved the shirt over his head. Spun it like he was at a Steelers game.

The EMT shut up and watched. A few other people glanced at Jairzinho. He could hear their eyes. Hear their thoughts. Just another poor guy in shock. Hardly the strangest thing they'd seen today.

Well, he'd just see about *that.*

Jairzinho threw his head back and howled.

"AAAAARRRRROOOOOOOOOOOOOOOO!!!!!!!!"

He stopped spinning the shirt. Waited. Watched.

Nothing.

"Sir," the EMT snapped, "I'm sorry, but if you don't come with me right now, I'm afr-"

AAAAAAAARRRRRRRRRROOOOOOOOOOOOOO!!!!!

The bridge howled back. Not an echo this time.

- 14 -

Astrid smelled him before she heard him. She threw her head back and howled along with him. Not just for Jairzinho's sake.

Because Meatball and Kelso and Barmit, they thought they were going across the bridge. But they were going back to the island.

Meanwhile, Astrid and Ladybug and Sheriff had thought they were going back to the island. They weren't.

Figured. Soon as they separated, they got all turned around.

Astrid stopped howling and listened. Waited. She would go and get them if she had to.

All three of their howls traveled back to Astrid.

And then she heard them coming.

Beside her, Sheriff barked and ran in circles.

Wonder of wonders: Ladybug wagged her little curlicue tail.

Kelso, Meatball, and Barmit weaved between cars. Galloping as fast as they could. Tongues flapping in the breeze.

Astrid barked once. And then they were running. Together. And ne'er before had [this dog] or [that dog] felt …like they were all…the same! Like they were playing …a new game… and [those dogs] each calléd it by sobriquets which [ain't frickin' different] from what the others did, wasn't it? Wasn't it like that? Yeah, man. It was.

If it wasn't true that their paws struck the ground in synchrony, that their hearts beat in unison, that their tongues flapped as one…it was still *true*.

They ran and ran and ran, Astrid leaping over parked cars, Barmit sliding under them, Kelso struggling to squeeze in behind her, Sheriff slaloming between legs and tires, Ladybug and Meatball in the rear, just trying not to die.

They ran past soldiers.

They ran past refugees.

They ran past their limits.

They ran past pain.

They ran until the bridge dropped off, they ran down the slope, they ran under a gate and around a loud van and through reaching arms. They ran past everything and everyone, except for one. The one who was taking a knee, with his arms stretched wide.

The Curbside Giants plowed into Jairzinho at speed, hard enough to knock him to the glorious firmament of Williamsburg.

MADE WITH LOVE

- 1 -

The new EMT who popped out of the ambulance hadn't wanted to let Jairzinho bring the dogs in with him. It was a violation of this health code and that traffic code. That sort of thing. Jairzinho calmly went about explaining the sort of day he'd been having.

The EMT stopped him pretty quickly. Told him to get in. *With* the dogs.

He lay back on the gurney. A bag of something cool dribbled into his veins. Astrid lay across his lap, despite Barbara the new EMT's protests. Ladybug perched atop his chest. Meatball melted on the bed between his knees. Barmit settled on his head like an awful Harpo Marx wig. Kelso had tried and failed to strike the same pose, instead finding his happy place on Jairzinho's thigh, nose-to-nose with Meatball. Sheriff, as always, ran laps around them all.

Barbara stabilized Jairzinho for the ride to the hospital, and then set about filling him in on what was known about the so-called "Siege of Manhattan".

He quite literally could not have cared less.

He reached for the bulgiest, bulkiest pocket on his cargo shorts. Couldn't reach.

"Hey," he interrupted her. "Sorry."

"Huh?" she asked, which was the first part of her explanation Jairzinho had understood.

He pointed to said bulgey, bulky pocket. "There's a little black pouch in there. Could I have it?"

"Oh, yeah." Barbara rather boldly plunged her hands into the pocket. Not bold. Professional.

"I'd get it myself," Jairzinho chuckled dreamily, nodding to the IV bag, "but this stuff is... *preeeee-mo.*"

Barbara smiled. Retrieved the freezer pouch from the pocket. Handed it to Jairzinho.

"Thank you," he whispered. He unzipped the pouch. Savored the salve that was the gel-padded interior. Lovely. Still cold. After all that. Just lovely.

He removed the sandwich Tia had made for him this morning. Exactly 13.4 billion years ago. He unpeeled the cling wrap. Admired the craftsmanship of the pack-lunch. Took a giant bite.

Finally realized why it was more than just meat and cheese and bread. Why it had nothing to do with taste.

Barbara resumed her story. The story of today. But Jairzinho couldn't focus on it. All he could think about was how relieved he was. How alive.

The fingers tightened around his neck.

He laughed quietly. Hard to do with those chilly little digits squeezing his windpipe. But laughing knocked them loose. The fingers. For just a moment. One beautiful moment at a time.

So Jairzinho laughed. Peeled off a bit of his sandwich and gave it to Astrid. She took it with gentle jaws.

There was so much rage inside of him. *Hatred* for the people who had done this.

He hoped Esther had made it back to the Hamasyans'. He hoped they were all okay. Their day wasn't over, he realized. They hadn't even the *illusion* of an ending.

He wished there was something he could do for them.

He passed two handfuls of sandwich to Kelso and Barmit. Neither was graceful — both were grateful. Tears speckled Jairzinho's vision.

The people who'd attacked Manhattan were a lot like him. They'd probably have denied that, race purists that they were. But Jairzinho knew they were. It terrified him, how much that was true.

Meatball inhaled her chunk with the usual vacuum-cleaner cacophony. That startled Barbara from her tale. For a moment, anyway.

Jairzinho wondered if it made him a terrible person, to feel good right now. To feel relieved. To be alive.

It made him feel guilty. That was a thing, he knew. Survivor's guilt. He'd never truly grasped how that could work. But it did. It worked like a power drill applied to the breastbone.

He tossed a piece of sandwich to Sheriff. Who caught it in midair. Sprightly little guy.

Jairzinho offered the last piece to Barbara. She declined it. Jairzinho insisted. Barbara shrugged and took it.

He wanted to add Ducky to the bathroom report. The time of death. Jairzinho did. Want to add it. But he didn't know what time to put. He couldn't remember where…it had happened.

But worth completing the document. As best he could. He checked his watch. Put the current time at the very bott…the very top.

4:33 PM. The Curbside Giants were safe…more or less. With the worst shit behind them. More or less.

He grinned and wept.

The fingers around his neck drew tighter.

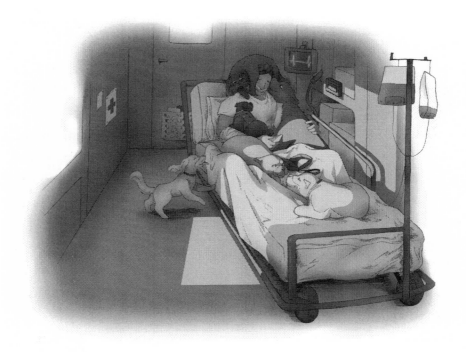

- 2 -

The hospital didn't want to let the dogs in either. Violation of this health policy and that safety policy. Jairzinho wanted to throw down the gauntlet. Say either they let the dogs in or leave him on the curb.

Barbara to the rescue. "They're registered service animals," she matter-of-factly explained.

The intake goon raised his eyebrow. "All of them?"

"Yep."

Intake peered around the nurses futzing over Jairzinho. "You got documentation for 'em?"

"Yeah," Jairzinho chuckled. "I'll fax it right on over tomorrow."

"I think I saw a news crew or two outside," Barbara suggested. "I could get them in for a shot of you denying ser-"

Intake shook his head. "Whatever. He's in the bed anyway. I don't care."

Jairzinho smiled at Barbara. She nodded back.

A kindly nurse also broke protocol by patching up the dogs. To say thank you, Jairzinho alerted her to some quarters in his pocket. Insisted she take them and buy some Oreos from the vending machine. That made her laugh, which was nice. It hadn't been the intention. But it was nice.

Turned out Jairzinho needed surgery. Something needed to be repaired? Okay. Whatever. Bring on the forms. He was feeling downright loopy. He'd have volunteered for the *RoboCop* program if that'd been an option. He wished it were.

"Call Tia," he insisted through the haze.

"That your girlfriend?" one of the doctors asked.

"She's the love of my *love*. The life."

The doc smiled. Even though she was wearing a mask, you could tell. "She's on her way."

"Whaaaaat?" Jairzinho looked at his fellow Giants. "Did *you* call her?" Nope. They couldn't believe it either! He looked to the doc. "Howzzat?"

"She called *us*. You were on the news. You and your dogs."

"They're Giants! They're…" Jairzinho's head bobbed. He looked to the juice b…the IV bag. "Woooaaahh! Can I wait for…woaaah?"

"Afraid not. She'll wait for you, though."

Jairzinho lunged upright. Grabbed the doc's arm. A final burst of coherence. "The other Giants?"

The doc's eyes remained steady, calm. Like getting lunged at by patients was a standard part of scrub-in. She nodded to, well, the other Giants. "Your dogs here?"

Jairzinho couldn't turn his head to take them in. But he listened to their panting, wheezing, gasping. He nodded. "Giants."

"They'll be fine. I hear they're service animals." She winked.

"Serbissssss," Jairzinho confirmed. Coherence was an exhaustible resource, after all. And Jairzinho was *exhauuuusssss…..*

- 3 -

Sound returned before sight. Dogs panting, grunting. Little canine nails ticking across linoleum. Someone laughing.

Jairzinho lolled his head from side to side.

The laughter stopped.

He felt pressure on the bed.

Sight returned.

Tia smiled.

Jairzinho lunged at her, too. Less nimble than his pre-surgery acrobatics. But far more enthusiastic.

He hugged her tight. She hugged him back. Soft, at first. Worried about breaking him. Then harder.

Jairzinho cried enough for both of them. But that didn't stop her from joining in.

Once he got his words back, he told Tia what he should have said the night before. What he wished he'd said that morning. When he'd failed to understand her.

Naturally,
revisited

(six years later)

It would have been a dumb fight, naturally. Which was why they decided not to have it.

"How about this then," Jairzinho suggested to his fiancée, currently resting her head on his chest, "instead of a gender reveal party, we have a *genital* reveal party."

Tia laughed. "That's not better!" She pushed herself up to rest on her elbow. "You wanna invite our friends over to look at our child's genitals?"

Jairzinho shrugged. "I just feel like if we don't do it right away, we'll have to wait at *least* eighteen years before it's socially acceptable ag-"

"Nooo," Tia laughed, shaking her head. "You're wrong for that one."

There ended the matter. Tia had been right. A gender reveal party was stupid. Jairzinho hadn't even wanted the party; he'd just wanted the excuse to know his child's gender. The party had seemed like a convenient way to backdoor that, since Tia *loved* parties. But she'd been adamant. Which was fine, because really, what did it matter what the kid's gender was? The kid would be who the kid would be, and Jairzinho would love them for that.

Tia, for her part, would have been willing to do a party of some sort. Absolutely not the kind of binary-reinforcing party decorated in all-blue or all-pink, but something. She loved parties, after all. She also happened to know that Jairzinho *hated* them — he still struggled in large groups of people. He'd certainly improved somewhat since the immediate aftermath of *that day*, but...he struggled. So the only reason he'd be suggesting a party was because he knew *she* loved parties. So she demurred.

Boof!

"Your turn," Tia chirruped brightly.

Jairzinho kissed her on the forehead and wriggled out from under her. Stretching his limbs, he rocked on his back until his legs swung over the side and touched the hardwood.

He sighed and reached his right arm across his body. Winter always played havoc with that old grievance, i.e. his entire back. It was manageable, though. He just had to limber it up.

As he did, he smiled at their wall. At the array of framed photos and artwork. Most of the former were personal shots — Jairzinho and Tia at one of those gorgeous hidden lakes in the Black Hills, a crummy iPhone selfie of their sweaty-ass faces they'd taken after a night of dancing themselves back to sober (funny enough, Jairzinho could handle noise and crowds, as long as he could *dance*), and, of course, Jairzinho down on one knee, presenting Tia with a ring.

Well, it hadn't technically been *him* doing the presenting.

Boof!

"Coming," Jairzinho announced. He took one last look, smiling at the Boy Bison print in its ancient frame. He smiled at the hole from the thumbtack. Perfection was overrated. Nothing taught you that quite like a patchwork of scars all over your own body.

Boof!

Jairzinho slapped his knees and pushed himself upright. "You gonna want breakfast now, or should I hold off?" he asked over his shoulder.

"Mmmm," Tia grinned as she melted into her pillow.

Jairzinho smiled. Hold off it was.

He shuffled towards the door to see to his ringbearer. Boy, *that* had been a harrowing few weeks of training. She'd gotten the concept quickly enough, but not the application. And discretion? Forget about it. Jairzinho had worried the jig would be up after the *eighth* small square pillow she had presented to Tia for no apparent reason.

Boof! Meatball announced to the doggydoor.

"What's up?" Jairzinho asked.

Meatball turned to look at him, precisely as she had when Jairzinho had finally told her to go give Tia the ring: with deep confusion.

RooooOOF, she editorialized.

Jairzinho smiled, precisely as he *hadn't* when Meatball had decided to sit stationary and drool onto the ring-bearing throw pillow. "Is it stuck?"

In answer to his question, Sheriff and Mishka, a young goldendoodle puppy Jairzinho and Tia had adopted (and renamed), scrambled in from outside. They took a quick lap of the living room, leaving melted-snow pawprints as they passed, and dashed back outside.

Jairzinho crouched down to Meatball. "What's up?"

Meatball whimpered quietly, then rose and trundled towards the doggydoor. She made a respectable attempt to squeeze herself through. No joy, though.

She'd gotten too dang fat.

Jairzinho laughed. "I know the feeling," he reassured her as he stood and opened the door.

Meatball dashed outside as best her creaky old joints would allow. Leapt straight into the amorphous, frolic-based game Sheriff, Mishka, Kelso, and Barmit were playing in the yard.

Jairzinho went back inside, set a coffee pot to gurgling, got his winterwear, then poured a cup of fresh-brewed dark roast. Blowing the steam, he stepped outside, brushed fresh snow off the top step of the porch, and settled in to watch the dogs play.

He hugged his arms against himself and smiled. He loved the peace here. On their land.

That was a weird thought, wasn't it? But this *was* their land, a brambly little hill in the unincorporated New Jersey township of Dearhook. It was quiet here, and you could see the stars at night. Plus, it was just under an hour's drive into the city.

Not that Jairzinho had ever gone back. For a whole host of reasons. It was impossible to say which was the main one. Was it those cold fingers that, even now, drew tight around his neck when he thought about New York? Six straight years of therapy had made a lot of difference in a number of ways, but it'd done (excuse the psychiatric jargon) *fuck all* to ease the grip of those icy claws.

Was it that he was, in some abstract way, a public figure now? He'd made it *LIVE* on the news as he'd scooted along the side of the Williamsburg Bridge, and his reunion with the dogs had apparently gone viral. From there, people started sending cell phone footage they'd shot of Jairzinho from their windows to news networks, hoping for a quick buck. Because why *wouldn't* you film the guy wandering around with all of those dogs? Sure, he wasn't the only dogwalker on Manhattan that day — but he was the only one who'd barnacled his way across the last extant bridge, and brought said dogs along to boot. Which was, in this day and age, heroism by default. So naturally it had only been a few months before Netflix stitched the best angles into chronological order, peppered in some security footage from the NYU law school lobby, along with forensic speculation about what had happened in the restroom, and released it as a documentary called *American Dogwalker.*

(Jairzinho Navias was reached for comment, requested privacy, and so on. Naturally. He also remained eternally grateful that the current owner and operator of the Curbside Giants, Esther Tubcut, had categorically refused all media interviews pertaining to Jairzinho himself. Coverage of *her* was emphatically welcomed. Also naturally.)

Was it that he despaired of seeing how much his old route had changed? It had taken a full two years for Manhattan to reopen to the public after the pacification of the so-called "Vanguard of the Nation of Magamerica". The relevant authorities wanted to ensure that no unexploded ordinances remained, or that there weren't any deep-deep-dipshit sleeper operatives who either didn't know or didn't accept that the battle was over, that they'd lost. In those two years during which the population of the island was displaced, a mad burst of construction had (according to Tia) given the entirety of Manhattan a pretty remarkable facelift. Obviously Jairzinho hadn't expected that (for example) The Edbrooke would be rebuilt precisely as it had been. But somehow the idea that a hyper-modern temple of glass and steel and hard angles should be standing in its place…it tightened the noose of winter.

No. He liked it here in Dearhook. The way they'd come to afford it was…slightly embarrassing. Maybe another reason to avoid venturing back into the city.

After Jairzinho started to become something like the face of the human cost of the tragedy (a shot of him crying over Misha's body, taken by some shutterbug vulture prowling about for Pulitzer-worthy shots…well, it won the goddamned Pulitzer), someone had started a Gofundme for Jairzinho. It raised over *a million goddamned dollars,* exactly none of which made its way to the alleged recipient. Jairzinho was pissed about that, but unwilling to press the issue. Tia, however, lawyered up and came home (her parents' place upstate, at that time) with a favorable verdict from a jury, and nearly half a million dollars to boot. With it, they bought their land, had a modest little cabin built, and worked parttime. Even though he hadn't ever been directly involved in the suit, that constituted Jairzinho's first real foray into public since the…the day of the Siege.

He wasn't looking forward to the second.

But, of course, there was no getting around it. That day had arrived.

Today was the day he would return to Manhattan.

Tia nudged her way through the door, steaming mug in hand.

Jairzinho smiled and purred. "Changed your mind?" He brushed more snow from the stoop.

She sat on the freshly-cleared concrete. "I heard them playing."

He shimmied to his side and tilted his head onto Tia' shoulder. His neck kinked up a bit. It got better when he reminded himself to relax.

"Are you…thinking of changing *your* mind?" she asked him.

"Sure am!" He laughed through a cough. Cleared his throat. "I'm not *going* to. But I'm definitely thinking about it."

Tia kissed the top of Jairzinho's head. "We'll all be right there with you."

"Mhm." They watched the dogs play. Jairzinho wondered if *they* would remember. Not Mishka, of course. But the rest of them. If they did, maybe being old would make it easier. Sheriff was the only one who couldn't be comfortably called *geriatric*, but even he was starting to go a little grey around the whiskers.

Jairzinho settled more heavily on Tia's shoulder.

The pups had definitely missed their old owners. Sheriff's and Meatball's had all died. Of the couple that owned Kelso and Barmit, only Sam had survived, and she'd insisted she couldn't care for the dogs anymore. So Jairzinho and Tia had adopted them. And the first year had been tough. For all of them.

Now, though, they were doing well. The dogs.

Jairzinho hated to admit it, but he envied them the brevity of their bereavement.

His first therapist had laughed when Jairzinho said that. Which was why he'd switched to his second (and current) one.

Jairzinho had a feeling he was going to have a *lot* to talk to her about, after today.

Tia drove. Jairzinho didn't trust himself to stay on the road. He was having a hell of a time keeping it together as the passenger. Drumming on his thighs, turning on happy music, turning on sad music, turning on a podcast, turning it all off and closing his eyes. His dear fiancée was the picture of patience.

It was, like most noteworthy pictures, not one achieved on the first attempt.

The skyline hatched from the horizon. Jairzinho only recognized about half of the buildings. He'd have been perfectly happy to have never seen any of them again.

He felt Tia's hand on his thigh. It was only as she squeezed reassuringly that he heard the thin whimper escaping him.

And the sympathetic whimpers coming from the back.

Jairzinho took Tia's hand and threaded his fingers through hers. The thick scarring on his palms seemed to ache more and more, the nearer they got to the city.

He saw it again. Crawling across broken glass. Saw it with the clarity of a nightmare — because it so often featured as one. A nightmare in which the path stretched for miles, in which he could see his face reflected in every shard, every sliver.

He drew a cutting breath through his bottom teeth. Turned around to smile weakly at Meatball, Kelso, Barmit, Sheriff, and Mishka. Crated for their own protection, which they seemed to understand. "Sorry guys," he told them.

They seemed to understand that too. Which could certainly have been projection…but Jairzinho didn't think so.

Which, for whatever it was worth…seemed to be worth something.

He spun frontwards again and leg-pressed himself into his seatback. Did his best to slow his breathing. "Ooooooh Jesus."

Tia squeezed his hand. "You can do this."

"Depends on how you define *this*."

"I mean shit your pants."

Jairzinho gave a short, choked laugh. "That I can do. For sure."

His stigmata throbbed. Stig-paw-ta. Haw, haw.

The lower lid of his left eye twitched.

Both of them knew — and Tia had articulated — that taking a bridge into town would be (ugh) a bridge too far. Maybe if Jairzinho did well going in, Tia hoped, they could push their luck crossing a bridge on the way back.

Tia's own therapist, who had been necessary to help her cope with her own traumas from the day (Tia had been off the island, but psychological distress certainly wasn't delimited by waterways) had assured Tia that it was far from selfish to find oneself drowning in another person's misery, even if you loved them. And Tia, yes, *loved* Jairzinho. Which just went to show how illogical the Chimpish heart could be.

Tia's therapist, furthermore, encouraged her to push her fiancée *juuuust* a bit further than he might go himself. Not over the edge. But right up to it.

A bridge right now would be over the edge, though. So they took the Lincoln Tunnel.

Jairzinho kept his eyes closed. His breathing hovered around a reasonable pace. It clearly took effort. But he was making it.

Tia smiled. "You're doing g-"

"I'm really sorry baby but I can't talk right now."

"Okay." Tia sighed and drove. She understood. It could be difficult to understand sometimes. But this time, it was easy.

They parked on West 11th. Jairzinho only found out when Tia told him; he'd kept his eyes clamped shut the entire way.

They leashed up the dogs, and helped them out of the car. Jairzinho kept Sheriff in his arms, holding him tight. "He doesn't like getting the rock salt in his paws," was the excuse.

Sheriff was all too happy to be carried. *Being carried* seemed to be tied with *not being carried* as his favorite.

Jairzinho kept silent as he walked, except for a few explosive exhalations. *PSHOOOOO.* He kept his head down, ostensibly looking between Sheriff in the crook of his left arm and Meatball, Kelso, and Barmit, whose leashes he held in his right hand. Tripling up leashes in that weaker hand was okay, since they were more for show than anything. These dogs could walk without leads. Oh yes they could.

"Thank you," he mumbled to Tia, at his side with Mishka on leash.

Tia reached out and placed her hand between his shoulder blades. Even through the thick down coat, she felt him relax.

Over Jairzinho's shoulder, she saw a guy double take, then nudge his friend and point. They recognized Jairzinho. And they were coming over to tell him as much.

Tia stared death at them.

The two guys slowed, then stopped.

As soon as the Hudson broke into view from between the buildings, Sheriff started whimpering. At Jairzinho's feet, the other three actually began to strain against their collars.

"It's okay," Jairzinho reassured them with an unsteady voice. "I know." They were nearing where Jairzinho had lain on the hill with Esther and Vatche, to see the fucked-up bridge. The first time he'd ever unclipped himself from the dogs out in the world. Why oh why did they need to meet *here?!* "I'm nervous t-"

Barmit said *BARF!*

Kelso and Meatball seconded her.

"Guys," Jairzinho ventured, with a nervy glance to Tia, "what's the b-"

He heard paws thundering against pavement. The rattling of chains.

Astrid came galloping into view from behind the corner. A bit chunkier than Jairzinho had remembered her, but certainly no slower.

Her rope leash whipped freely behind her. Jairzinho laughed. He expected to see Lina in hot pursuit any second now.

Jairzinho released his leashes and let Sheriff down. The little guy scrambled his way to Astrid, trailing his three friends. They all but collided, sniffing each other with aplomb.

Tia gestured to Mishka. "Should I let her go," she asked, "or give 'em a minute?"

"I think give 'em a minute," Jairzinho replied.

He smiled as he heard Lina, Astrid's owner, frantically calling "come, girl!"

"She's okay!" Jairzinho called back.

At the sound of his voice, Astrid pushed through her friends and resumed her dash, heading straight for Jairzinho. He crouched to embrace her. She jumped. They accidentally headbutted each other.

"Ah!" Jairzinho laughed. Astrid *woofed,* then jumped again and licked Jairzinho's face. She pounded his chest with her paws.

"Oh, wow," Lina panted as she caught up. "Jairzinho! It's so good to see you!" Astrid's owner Lina had survived the day of the Siege, and in fact now lived with Astrid in the building that had replaced the Edbrooke. That struck Jairzinho as ghoulish. But then, they were different people, she and him. And besides, that sense of continuity had made Lina one of the first of Jairzinho's old clients to heed his referral to Esther.

"Thanks," Jairzinho offered. "You too." Which was true... but not as true as it was of Astrid. He hadn't seen her for about four years, the last time Esther had brought her out to Dearhook on a 'field trip'.

He scratched Astrid behind the ears, in the spot that got her leg pumping. By now the other four Giants had converged to crash the love-fest, Meatball going so far as to crawl into Jairzinho's lap. "How've you been?" He asked Astrid. "You been good? You been a Good Girl?"

Astrid did that ferocious wag that shook her entire rear.

"Bit of hip dysplasia," Lina answered on Astrid's behalf. "Not uncommon at her age."

Jairzinho nodded. *At her age.* He could have done without that reminder. Six years was a long time.

But then, that was why they were here.

"Am I holding things up?" Jairzinho asked.

Lina squeezed an eye shut and bobbled her head. "No way! Oh, absolutely n-"

"It's okay," Jairzinho laughed, creaking back up to his feet, his hand full of leashes. He passed Astrid's to Lina. "Oh! Shit! Sorry," he added, "this is my fiancée. Tia. Tia, this i-"

"I think we've met," Lina said.

"We did," Tia confirmed. "Way back. Good to see you again."

"Likewise."

Tia rubbed Jairzinho's back, *very* softly. "You ready?"

He thought so. He hadn't imagined this would be the hardest part. Seeing Astrid again, though, seeing how she'd changed…

He nodded and said nothing.

They walked towards the river. As they did, Jairzinho heard a familiar foghorn bellowing: *HA HA HA HA HA.*

Jairzinho laughed. Cackling at a goddamned funeral. Esther hadn't changed a bit.

Once they'd crossed the street, Jairzinho dropped the leashes again and let the four old Giants run to Esther.

She saw them coming. "Heeerrreeeeeee cooooommeeeees trroooouuuubbbbbllllleeee!" she screamed. Then she lowered the box in her hands so all of the dogs could sniff it. "Guess what Auntie Esther's got?"

Tia laughed out loud. "Jesus Christ."

Jairzinho laughed too. It was an empty laugh, but it felt good.

"Jairzinho!" Esther called. "How do you like bein' back in the city? You got some post-dramatic stress or what?"

"She has prepared this joke," Vatche explained as he stepped into hugging distance. He and Jairzinho embraced. When they separated, Vatche stepped to Tia. "How are you?" he asked her as he kissed both cheeks.

Jairzinho couldn't help but laugh. Vatche had been adamant that you shook hands when first meeting someone, and had conducted himself accordingly with Tia — but after that first meeting, apparently, all bets were off. He'd proven himself both a hugger *and* a kisser.

He'd also proven himself a dutiful husband and a capable father. Not with Tia; when Hasmik died, Vatche's parents gave him the apartments above the sports bar – all of which, astonishingly, survived the entirety of the Siege. The condition for the bequest, of course, was that Vatche start a family with his longtime girlfriend Lonnie, who on that fateful day six years ago had been visiting her family in Idaho. The condition was met, and then some.

To wit: "I will have child number four, do you believe this?"

"*You* will," Tia asked wrly, "huh?" She glanced over to Lonnie, who was introducing her three little Hamasyans to the Giants.

Vatche laughed and shrugged. "This is your language. I but speak it!"

"Yo!" Esther called to Jairzinho. "Catch!"

Jairzinho turned in time to see Esther's box flying towards his head. "Gah!" To his own astonishment, he caught the box. "The fuck?! Ah," he added to Vatche, "sorry."

Vatche looked at him blankly. "Why do you apologize?"

"For, um, swearing in front of your kids."

Vatche shook his head. "They are so young, they do not know these words. See this?" He turned to his family. "Children! Look to your father!"

They did.

"Vatche," Lonnie warned.

"Fuck!" Vatche enthused. "Fuck and shit!"

"FUCK!" His oldest kid repeated.

"Fuck and shit," the middle kid parroted.

Lonnie glared at Vatche.

Vatche turned back to Jairzinho, his mouth a perfectly flat line. "I will be very much in the doghouse for this."

440

Jairzinho nodded and looked at the box in his hands. It was quite small, about the size of a smartphone, and maybe three inches deep.

The gold plate on the top said "LADYBUG".

"Kinda crazy they can stuff her in there," Esther said from over Jairzinho's shoulder, "ain't it? Only I got no way of knowin' is that her ashes, or do they just burn up a bunch of dogs at once, and mix em up and scoop outta the pile. Or fuck, might be sawdust. It ain't like I took it to the lab."

Jairzinho looked from the box to Esther. "I really hope you're not planning on delivering a eulogy."

"What'm I gonna say? 'Here's a spot Ladybug liked peein' and poopin' in, here she goes out the box, plop, sayonara'?"

Tia inhaled sharply through her nose. "I thought you were scattering her ashes in the river?"

Esther looked at Tia like she had just suggested trying to bring Ladybug back to life, by baking her ashes into a loaf of bread and putting googly eyes on it. Then she smiled. "I'm real glad you two came." She wrapped an arm around Jairzinho. "I know it ain't easy. But I think this is where she'd wanna be at."

"I couldn't stay away forever." Jairzinho looked at Tia and smiled. "She wouldn't have let me."

"*And,*" Tia added, "avoidance isn't a coping mechanism."

"*And,*" Esther added, "you gotta see my new fuckin' digs!"

"Please do not swear around my children," Vatche requested, with a nervous glance towards Lonnie.

Esther waved him away. "Alright, we doin' this?"

Jairzinho looked around. "Where's Boo?"

"Oh!" Vatche smacked himself on the side of the head. "I have forgotten to say to you, the adopters came for him! He is on a farm upstate!"

"A real farm," Esther was quick to clarify. "Not like the upstate farm Ladybug's at."

Jairzinho couldn't help but wince at the off-handed way Esther referred to the late Ladybug, at the cavalier manner in which she handled the box of the pug's ashes. He could keep these thoughts to himself, though, because he knew she was grieving. Ladybug's owners had both died on the day of the Siege, and so Esther had volunteered to care for the pug. Jairzinho and Tia would have, but by that point, Ladybug's failing health necessitated full-time attention.

Which Esther more than supplied. So much so that Ladybug had lived to...

"How old was she again?" Jairzinho asked.

"Eighteen," Esther replied immediately. Her smile was a crack in the façade. For just a moment, he saw through to the real Esther. The one who had called Jairzinho, immediately after finding Ladybug lying lifeless across her shoes at an impossible angle. The one who couldn't form a coherent word for the first two minutes of the call. "Eighteen fuckin' years young."

"Fuck!" Vatche's oldest repeated.

"You said it, kid." Esther caught Lonnie's glare. "Sorry."

They gathered around what Esther assured Jairzinho was *the* tree-pit. She'd already cleared the snow off to reveal a few tufts of dead grass. Now Esther crouched down and tousled them with her bare hand. She'd told Jairzinho, when she had first asked him if he would be willing to come into the city for this, that Ladybug had loved these little patches of life amidst the dirt, even when they were dead and frozen. She would march around the treepit for a minute or more, nuzzling her face in the grass ("motorboating" was how Esther had described it, even in the deep well of her grief), until some mysterious criteria had been met. At which point, she would do her business.

The only time Ladybug ever ran, Esther insisted, was once she caught sight of this treepit. Even on the day before she'd passed, she'd wagged her little piggy tail and booked it to the patches of grass.

Esther didn't say anything now, though. She simply opened the box and turned it over.

A small plastic baggie full of ashes flumped quietly onto the dirt.

"Ha," Esther practically whispered, "forgot to open the baggie." She reached down and dug her fingers into the plastic until it tore. Scattered the contents into the pit.

She rose with tears in her eyes. Sniffed.

Practically collapsed onto Jairzinho.

"She was the best fuckin' girl!" Esther sobbed. "She was so sweet and funny and I loved her so much!"

Jairzinho hugged Esther tight.

"Psst," Jairzinho heard Tia hiss, *"woah! No!"*

Jairzinho looked over Esther's shoulder.

Meatball had squatted in the treepit. She was peeing.

Jairzinho stepped forward.

The bulldog's face was one hundred percent focus. She turned it on Jairzinho. It halted him. It had heartbreak in its fatflaps.

Esther, caught in the emotive spillover, turned and stared.

"I'm so sorry," Tia mumbled, shaking her head. She rushed forward to grab Meatball's leash.

"No," Jairzinho and Esther said at the same time.

Tia curled her nose. "But…she's…um…she's *literally* pissing on Ladybug's grave."

"No," Jairzinho said, pre-laughing at his own dipshit joke, "she's just peeing her respects."

Esther didn't give the booming laugh Jairzinho had expected. She just fell on him with another tearful embrace.

One by one, the remaining Curbside Giants poured some out for Ladybug. It was definitely odd, to watch this and find it acceptable, let alone view it through a lens of reverence...but Esther had been right. All those years ago, not a mile or two from here, she had been exactly right: Jairzinho had no clue how dogs worked. He didn't know how people worked. He didn't know how his own goddamned brain worked.

But as Jairzinho Navias stood at the final resting place of Ladybug the Little Pug, here by the Hudson River, with this motley gaggle of loved ones, he did know two things for certain: none of them worked for long, and all of them worked best together.

They crossed the Williamsburg Bridge to get to Esther's new place. The fingers closed back around Jairzinho's throat the moment he saw the bridge. But as they did, he laughed and kissed Tia. Because they were closing *back around*.

Which meant, on Manhattan of all places, they had briefly let go.

That Spring, one of the treepits running along West Street was inexplicably verdant. They didn't usually have quite that much grass in them, but it was beautiful. Which meant *somebody* must have planted it. So everybody left it alone.

Besides, all the neighborhood dogs seemed to love it.

ABOUT THE ILLUSTRATOR

REBECCA COULSTON is a student living in Wellington, New Zealand with a schnoodle named Ruby. She loves to make art, and since you're probably wondering, a schnoodle is a Schnauzer/Poodle mix.

Instagram: @pepper_tree_

ABOUT THE ILLUSTRATIONS

IF YOU WANT to see Rebecca's illustrations for this story at maximum resolution, head on over to http://www.judwiding.com/curbside

Also by Jud Widing

Novels
Go Figure
The Little King of Crooked Things
A Middling Sort
Westmore and More!
The Year of Uh

Stories
Identical Pigs

Made in the
USA
Middletown, DE

76731110R00267